The Knight of Her Dreams

Dragons and Dreamphasers Book One

Jen Robyn

This is a work of fiction. All names, characters, places, events and incidents either are the product of the author's imagination or are used fictitiously. Any similarities or resemblance to actual persons, living or dead, events, situations, or locales is entirely coincidental.

Published by Jen Robin Kaltman

First paperback edition June 2013

Cover designed by Melody Simmons of eBookindiecovers.com
Cover model Jimmy Thomas, image licensed under Romancenovelcenter.com
Castle image by Ellerslie licensed under Fotolia.com

ISBN-10: 0989449203
ISBN-13: 978-0-9894492-0-5

This book is dedicated to

Mom and Dad

Thank you for your love and support

Acknowledgments

A special thank you to my Mom for her help with the editing, suggestions, and great patience through many read-throughs.
Your help was invaluable.

And a special thank you to my good friend who encouraged me to self-publish this novel.
You are a great inspiration to me.

Prologue

There's someone else here.

Suddenly feeling goose bumps on her arm, the young woman turned in her saddle, her brown eyes cautiously scanning the beach. The secluded area looked serene, the sky as blue as the shimmering satin gown she wore beneath her dark cloak. Not a soul in view.

Just my imagination, that's all. The goose bumps remained.

Pulling her cloak closer, Julianna accidentally tugged the reins as well.

Her ivory mare's surprised whinny sparked her full attention. Reining her away from the ocean's edge, Julianna patted the horse apologetically. "Easy, Duchess," she soothed. "Your friend's just daydreaming again." Duchess snorted her agreement.

Shutting her eyes, Julianna deeply inhaled the crisp sea air, allowing the worry to drain out of her. *There is nothing at all like the ocean*, she thought blissfully. *It has a way of calming the soul.* Feeling the sweetness of freedom, Julianna smiled playfully, urging the mare faster.

Enjoying this change of pace, Duchess whinnied again in agreement, echoed by her rider's laughter. Shaking her head, the hood of Julianna's cloak fell to loose her streaming auburn hair. Reaching well past her shoulders, the spicy curls danced in the wind as the travelers flew across the sand.

Suddenly, a pair of strong hands gripped her waist. She screamed as she was pulled from her mare.

Duchess noticed her absence instantly, abruptly turning

to face the reason for her friend's screams.

"Let me go, rogue!" Julianna shouted, struggling against her captor. Her steed gave an angry whinny, raising her forelegs in warning.

"***Hold*** there, Duchess!" a deep masculine voice called out, calming the mare almost instantly.

Julianna gasped in surprise, just before turning to the man who held her. He too wore a hooded cloak, his face hidden except for a smile. A man of strength, she decided, noting how the cloak molded itself to his muscular body. And quite tall, especially against her average height.

"Duchess rarely listens to the commands of anyone," she commented, finding her voice. "How is it that you know her name?"

"I know many things," the stranger replied. "I've seen you ride your steed along these banks before, sweet lady, and since I live at the castle yonder beside this ocean, I felt an introduction was due." At her pout, he gave a short laugh. "Fear not, my beauty. I mean you no ill. I merely seek a moment of your time."

Despite his smooth words, she remained suspicious. "I think it's been a moment too long," she whispered, tilting her head to one side. "What is your name?"

"Ah, 'tis a secret, which I will reveal when I choose."

Put off from solving that mystery, Julianna became more curious to see the face of the stranger, reaching towards his cloak. He gently stopped her hand, lifting the hood on his own and allowing it to fall back.

Julianna blinked her eyes several times in amazement. Having assumed the worst, she wasn't expecting the handsome face of the man before her.

His eyes were the most intriguing shade of deep blue she'd ever seen. Running a hand loosely through his wavy midnight black hair, those captivating eyes now glittered. "I hope that your silence denotes approval," he told her with a slight chuckle.

Realizing she was staring, Julianna blushed but stood her ground. "Of your looks, yes. Of your barbaric kidnapping, no. And might I ask how you managed to do that without the aid of a horse of your own?"

He thought for a moment to consider this, and then his expression turned cheerful. "Magic?"

"Ah, magic... the ever-popular excuse," Julianna said with a laugh, not masking her inner skepticism. "And I suppose this same magic brought you here to find me."

"Possibly." He folded his arms with a smirk. "Disappointed?"

"No, I don't think so," she decided. "If Duchess takes to you, then I suppose there must be something within you worthy of her favor."

"And is there something within me worthy of ***your*** favor?"

At his not-so-subtle request for flattery, Julianna gave him her brightest smile and shook her head. "No, I'm quite positive you're just as I dubbed you before... a rogue." His smile faded slightly, but he said nothing. "So then, o' Mystery Man, now that you've had your requested moment of time, Duchess and I will bid you a good day, and good riddance."

Nodding in mock politeness, she strode purposefully back to her waiting mare. But just as she was about to pull herself up on the saddle again, once more she was pulled free. This time anger, not fear, brought a scream to her lips as she turned to strike the man.

Before she could, he spun her around and pulled her close, his face mere inches from hers. "Do you truly hate me so much for merely startling you earlier?" he asked softly, his voice underlying a shade of hurt.

She struggled against him. "A true gentleman wouldn't

displace a lady from her horse as you did. Twice!"

"Ah, but then you labeled me a rogue, did you not?"

"Well, aren't you?"

He was silent for a moment, his expression serious. "I thought not earlier... but I believe you could turn me into one." Not giving her a chance to reply, his arms tightened around her as he leaned forward to kiss her. Unable to say anything, Julianna beat her fists against his chest. For a few moments he let her, and then broke away from her to speak. "I'm sorry about that," he whispered with a smile. "I'm afraid I seemed a bit unable to help myself."

Julianna wanted to protest, but instead merely glared at him. "Who ***are*** you?"

His confident look returned as he raised one brow. "I'll tell you what, my sweet lady. Grant me one kiss freely, and I'll tell you my name."

"You have a rather high price for information."

"The high price being a mere kiss?"

She sighed heavily, but her curiosity remained. Not that his last kiss had been unpleasant. She'd never been kissed with such passion before. "All right," she replied, if only to silence her last thought. "One kiss for your name. But that's it!"

"That's it." He brushed her hair back to cradle her face in his hands. Julianna stared into his eyes curiously.

"What are you doing?"

"If I've only the luxury of one kiss, I intend to make the most of it," he replied, his fingers lightly caressing her cheeks. "By all the heavens, with the sun casting light to the flames of your hair and the fire in your eyes, you are indeed a beauty, my lady."

She blushed beneath his gaze, shutting her eyes as he lowered his head to kiss her again. This kiss was different from the first, gentle yet seeking. Oddly enough, despite his behavior earlier, Julianna found the sensation of his kiss most pleasant and began to respond in kind. As soon as he sensed this, he smiled, his hands threading through her thick reddish-brown curls, as he'd wanted to from the start.

Shifting slightly to kiss her cheek, he murmured against it, "Do you still wish to know my name?"

"Yes," she whispered.

"You can call me Dominick."

"Dominick…" she repeated, allowing another moment to pass before reality returned. Eyes narrowing, she pressed her hands against his chest. "You said just one kiss."

"And I gave you my name," he agreed.

Julianna's eyes narrowed. If this rogue thought she was going to ***extend*** their bargain, he was sorely mistaken. Glancing down, she raised the heel from her boot and brought it down sharply on the man's foot. Cursing in fury, he was unable to recover immediately, giving her a chance to leap astride Duchess again.

Reining her steed around as Dominick looked up from his injured foot with an angry grimace, Julianna glanced down at him smugly. "I'm sorry about that. I'm afraid I seemed a bit unable to help myself."

Recognizing his own words, Dominick's expression gradually faded into a knowing grin.

"As you were unable to help yourself from reacting to our shared kiss?"

At first she blushed, but then smiled as well.

"You ***are*** a rogue," she laughed.

He moved to stand closer to her, resting a hand gently upon Duchess's head to keep her calm. "You didn't seem to mind just now. Am I wrong?"

Slowly, she shook her head. "No," she replied softly. For a moment their gazes remained locked, but before he could speak again, Julianna gave Dominick a casual wave and rode off.

She smiled as she heard his footsteps following close

behind, yet was startled to see him keeping pace with her swift mare.

"I never had the chance to inquire, my lady. You know my name now, but what is your own?"

Julianna flashed him a grin. "Ah, 'tis a secret, Dominick!" she called out through hearty laughter, urging Duchess to a faster pace and leaving him behind.

*****

As she disappeared towards the horizon, Dominick ceased following her, breathing heavily as he watched her vanish.

"'Tis a secret!'" he echoed, shaking his head. Turning the other way, he whistled to a steed of his own, which seemed to magically appear out of nowhere. As he mounted up, preparing to ride off, Dominick shook his head again with a smirk. "Saucy wench!" he murmured through a chuckle, clicking his heels against the stallion to send it riding in the opposite direction.

A moment before he literally ***vanished***, steed and all.

Chapter One

It was all a strangely unusual memory to her now.

Although he remained ever elusive, the mysterious Dominick remained in Julianna Sherborne's thoughts. Even though she believed herself far too ordinary for a man like him, she secretly hoped that her dashing knight would return, chasing away her sorrows.

She certainly felt in need of comforting now.

As if her life was a sailing ship, she felt it was one step from being a wreck on the beach. Somewhere along the last several months, she felt as though she'd lost control of it.

Part of her wished Dominick would miraculously appear and rescue her from what had happened, taking her away from the unrelenting whirlpool of her troubled thoughts.

There were only two problems.

The first being that her only meeting with Dominick had been two months ago, and she hadn't heard from him since.

Yet she knew she only had to close her eyes, and he would appear in her mind as she remembered him. His raven-black hair, dark and wavy as it framed his strong-featured yet smiling face. His expressive blue eyes that seemed capable of melting her heart, and the warmth of his kiss that she couldn't forget…

Just before she stomped on his foot and rushed off to leave shortly afterwards.

Something she regretted now.

Yes, that was something she would never forget. For despite her words and actions at the time, she found that she'd grown to miss him in his absence.

Which was quite ridiculous, considering the second problem.

For in reality... Dominick was a man who existed only in her dreams.

*****

Surely such thoughts about a dream would be ridiculous to most, but with Julianna, lately her dreams were kinder to her than reality. Not that she didn't have a 'good life.' She had a loving family, a nice place to live, good health, and material comforts.

But she also had loneliness and heartbreak.

Julianna had tried dating, but none of the men she'd gone out with had made her happy.

So far, only one man had brought her happiness. A happiness that fell apart.

Roger Collins.

She'd known him since they were teenagers, when he'd moved into her neighborhood and then wound up in the same high school. Right from the start, they'd become close friends. On one occasion, a bit ***too*** close for her father's liking, she thought with a smile.

*****

"You're crazy!" declared Julianna.

"And you wouldn't want me any other way!" replied Roger, earning laughter from her with a nod. "How many guys do you know who would risk climbing up the railing to greet you at your bedroom window?"

"None," she decided. Though surprised by his visit, part of her was flattered, being a fifteen-year-old sophomore with an admirer who was both a senior of nearly eighteen and her best friend. "Most people I know use a more conventional method of communication... the phone."

"What unimaginative people."

He shook his head, and they both laughed, as he moved

to sit beside her on the bed.

"So why did you come out to see me tonight?" she asked.

"Oh, don't ask me that."

"No really, why?"

He sighed, turning to her with a smile. "I missed you."

"We see each other at school practically every day."

"Yeah, but that's different." He reached out to clasp her hand and she shyly reciprocated. "I can't do this in a classroom."

"No," she agreed softly.

His eyes holding hers, he leaned closer, his mouth inches from hers. "And of course it would be really nice, if I could..."

A pillow abruptly halted him.

Glancing up in confusion, Julianna was grinning at him. "Gotcha!"

Catching onto her mischievous nature, he grinned back. "We'll see who's got who," he replied, picking up her other pillow to retaliate, while she fairly squeaked with laughter and did the same.

Their pillow fight turned into a veritable war, both ignoring the stream of white feathers that began to fly out, soon covering the bed and filling the air. After several minutes, they stopped to catch their breaths, each one holding a pillow in warning, but still laughing.

"You never told me you were a pillow ninja," Roger informed her.

"You're a bit of a featherhead yourself," she decided with a smirk.

"Oh, so now I'm a featherhead!" Catching her off-guard, he leaned forward to embrace her, resting his body lightly over her own. She squirmed helplessly as his touch accidentally tickled her. Her laughter only spurred him to tickle her in earnest.

"Roger, please stop!" she fairly shouted, giggling. "You'll tickle me to death!"

"Hmmm… no, I wouldn't want to do that," he replied, brushing a few feathers from her nose. As her laughter faded, she smiled back at him. "You're not like anyone I've ever known, Julie," he whispered.

"Is that a compliment?"

He paused for a moment, and then his expression became serious. "Meant to be one," he agreed softly, lowering his mouth to kiss her. At first, she merely stared at him. In the past six months she'd known him, he'd never done ***that*** before! But gradually, she relaxed beneath him, kissing him back and feeling a surge of happiness.

Almost from day one, Julianna felt that she'd loved him, and now it seemed he felt the same. *Roger loves me!* she thought, her arms reaching around his neck to hug him. Perhaps a bit too tightly, as he gently reached up to loosen her grasp.

"Easy there, Julie," he laughed, moving his hand to caress her cheek. "The last thing I want is for you to strangle me now."

"Then allow ***me*** the honor instead!" snarled an angry voice.

Julianna glanced up with a gasp, Roger following suit. "Dad," she blurted out. "I can explain."

"Explain what this boy's doing in your room at all hours of the night, like ***this***?" her father growled. Before either could say anything, he pulled Roger away from Julianna. Being stronger, her father gave him a rough shake. "You're lucky I have the self-control not to beat the living daylights out of you," he hissed. "My daughter is only fifteen, damn you, and not some cheap tramp for you to ruin, you little bastard!"

"I'd never think of Julie that way!" protested Roger.

"If that were true, you wouldn't be here at this hour in her room, let alone in her bed! Now you can either exit by the front door, or I can throw you out the window. Which is it?"

Steeling his expression, Roger strode past him without a look to Julianna. "Roger, wait!" she yelled after him. Tearfully, she tried to follow, but her father pulled her away as Roger's departing footsteps stomped down the stairs, followed by a door slam. Turning to her father, she shook her head. "He didn't do anything, Dad," she said witheringly. "Roger would never hurt me."

Sighing once, her father's temper faded. "I'd like to believe that, pumpkin," he replied gently. "And despite the fact that I've worried that boy is too aggressive, I've never stood in the way of your friendship before. But Julie, he ***is*** several years older than you are. If your mother was still alive, I'm sure she would have explained all this to you, so you'd understand my concern." She blinked once, but said nothing.

"Pumpkin, I love you very much. You're young and naïve, and I just don't want you getting hurt." Lowering her head, Julianna blushed. Her father was never one to mince words. "Do you understand, sweetheart?" She gave a quick nod and he hugged her, patting her back.

"Does this mean I can't see Roger anymore?" she asked.

"No," he sighed. "I suppose you can see him. Just make sure it's during daylight hours, and no more creeping into your bedroom. Otherwise I ***will*** throw him out the window next time. Fair enough?" She smiled slightly with another nod. "All right then," he replied, kissing her forehead. "Now why don't you get some sleep? We'll talk more about this tomorrow." As he was leaving, he turned once. "And before you go to bed… please pick up all those feathers."

Julianna glanced at the mess strewn across her bed and groaned, just before proceeding. It was only when she heard a low whistle that she dropped the feathers she held and raced to the window. Roger peered in from the ledge, glancing once around the room.

"Your father's gone, right?" he murmured.

"Yes," she whispered, "but you can't stay here. When he gives a warning, he means it, and I don't want to be responsible for your being tossed from a second story window."

"I'll go, but only so I don't get you in trouble, Julie. And to be on the safe side, I'll keep away for a few weeks to avoid your father's wrath. That should settle things down somewhat."

"Well, if you feel it's best."

"I do." He gave her a knowing smile. "Trust me?"

"Always," she said solemnly.

He leaned forward to give her a quick kiss. "See you in a few weeks," he replied, grinning before heading back to the ground.

As he waved and ran off towards his house, Julianna waved after him with starry eyes. *He loves me!* her young mind echoed happily. *And I'll love him forever*, she vowed, slowly shutting her window with a blissful smile.

*****

Julianna smiled at the memory.

That was many years ago.

After that evening, Roger didn't cross the line of friendship again, as if it had never happened. While this saddened her at first, their bond of friendship still seemed strong, so she assumed time would restore the rest eventually. She even shrugged off the occasional jibes from her friends regarding her 'older boyfriend.'

But as often happens with childhood friendships, time steered them down different paths, leaving her feeling lost when he went off to college. They corresponded for a while, but as their lives grew busier, the letters grew fewer. And when Roger's family moved to a different neighborhood, ultimately they lost touch with each other completely.

Which was why Julianna was so surprised at what happened four months ago.

*****

Why do I let her drag me to these things?

True, her close friend Marybeth meant well. But every time Julianna came to these silly gatherings, she could count on having to force at least one plastic smile for an unknown guy who would be interested when she wasn't.

At twenty-five, all shades of her teenage years had vanished, replaced by a very attractive woman. Although she was happy with her looks and wouldn't change them, sometimes the unwanted attention she got left her wanting to become a hermit.

While the music blared in the main room, Julianna sneaked over to a quieter one, resting her head against the armrest of a sofa. And silently counting the minutes until she could leave.

Staring at the floor absently, she heard an unexpected voice.

"Doesn't look like the floor's moving tonight, no matter how hard you stare at it, Julie."

With wide eyes, Julianna bolted upright and would have fallen over if she hadn't already been sitting. "Roger?" she gasped. "What are ***you*** doing here?"

"Same as you I imagine. Heard there was a party, and got dragged here, right?" At a loss for words, she simply nodded as he sat beside her. "Been a long time, hasn't it?"

"A lifetime," she agreed. "Are you with someone?"

"Not anymore. How about you?" She shook her head but retained a look of curiosity. "I just got out of a relationship a month ago, so I figured I'd start socializing again. Never thought I'd find you here."

"Small town," she laughed.

He smiled, reaching out for her hand and she took his, their eyes speaking volumes, erasing the years of separation.

"It's good to see you again, Julie," he said quietly.

*****

After that evening, everything seemed to fall into place for them. Their conversation from the gathering led to their dating, and for a few months, Julianna starting enjoying herself again.

But then a rift developed, when it became apparent that each had a very different view on what they wanted from their relationship.

One evening at Roger's place, Julianna was surprised to find he'd set up dinner, complete with candles and soft music. The evening had gone well, until she got ready to leave.

As had become the norm, Roger tried to persuade her otherwise.

Julianna smiled against him, gently trying to keep him at arm's length. "Roger, you know how I feel about this."

"And you know how I feel about you," he murmured against her mouth, silencing her protests while threading both hands through her hair. "Stay with me tonight, Julie. I promise it will be wonderful for the both of us."

His kisses temporarily swayed her, only reminding her of how persuasive he always was. Part of her yearned to give him what he wanted, yet there was still another part that was hesitant. Although waiting for marriage seemed strange to some these days, Julianna felt strongly about wanting at least an engagement before giving herself completely to anyone. Or at the ***very*** least, to know the person she was with loved her. He'd never spoken the words.

"Roger, not tonight," she broke in, pushing against his chest this time. Beneath his impassioned gaze, there was no mistaking the look of hurt. "I know you want me, and I'm not saying a part of me doesn't want you too, but..."

"But you've been saying that for two months," he sighed. "Julie, for the thousandth time, it's not like we just met. We've known each other for years. Since we were teenagers, in fact. What is it you want?"

To know you love me, her heart answered, though she couldn't tell him this. Either he loved her or he didn't. And at this point, she wasn't sure. Asking for the words wouldn't necessarily bring an honest response.

"I need more time before jumping into something serious," she replied finally.

"Fine," he said heavily. "Whatever you want. Maybe we should just call it a night."

She didn't want to simply leave it at that and tried to make him understand how she felt, but the negative tension in the air only got worse, ending up in a loud argument, ruining what was left of the evening. They parted without even saying good night.

They didn't speak for a week afterwards.

*****

While apart, Julianna had time to think about the situation and regretted what had happened. She decided to try and make it up to him, although her older sister Crystal tried to convince her otherwise. Being more objective, she'd never trusted Roger herself. But since Julianna had known him for so many years, that time worked against her cautions, and Crystal knew she couldn't stand in her sister's way.

Julianna went over to Roger's apartment unannounced. Knocking on the door, she was surprised when he didn't answer right away, since his car was outside. She knocked again and finally the door opened.

Roger was there, bare-chested and in his sleepwear, emphasizing his muscular figure. His brown hair was slightly askew, while his slate blue eyes seemed to light up with surprise. Out of instinct, her heart skipped a beat, but she calmed it quickly.

"Julie," he replied, rubbing his eyes once. "What are you doing here?"

"Oh, did I wake you? I'm sorry. It's only nine, and since you're always up past midnight, I didn't think it was that late."

"No, no, it's fine. What's up?"

"Well, I really hated the way we left things. I suppose you're right that a relationship can't remain at a standstill forever, and…"

"I know what I said," he interrupted, reaching out to take her hand. "But I probably shouldn't have pushed so hard either. I didn't mean to put you down for your beliefs."

Now he sounded more like the Roger she'd fallen in love with. Crystal would certainly be surprised at his words! Her heart buoyed, she continued, "In that case, maybe we could just forget the other evening, and try again?"

"I'd like that very much," he whispered, leaning forward to kiss her.

She put her arms around his neck, gazing into his eyes happily.

"Roger?" an agitated voice called out. "Are you going to keep me waiting here all night? How long does it take to answer a door?"

Julianna felt her blood turn cold, eyeing Roger with confusion. "Who's that?"

He shook his head, growling against his hand. "Nobody," he murmured, moving towards the hallway while trying to pull the door shut behind him.

She wouldn't let him, pushing past him to catch sight of a pretty brunette emerging from his bedroom, wrapping his robe around her.

"Who are you?" the woman asked.

Glaring at her briefly, Julianna tried to force a smile. "I'm his ***girlfriend***, unless there's something he neglected to tell me last week."

"Must be, if you're the 'ex' he mentioned."

Feeling her cheeks burn, she turned to Roger with a mixture of hurt and anger, and shook her head. "It certainly didn't take you long to find someone else more compliant. It would have been nice if you'd let me know we were through first."

"Julie..."

Not wanting to hear anymore, she strode back to the hallway, but he followed her outside, this time successfully shutting the door.

"Julie, wait a minute," he insisted, grabbing hold of her arm. "Let me explain."

"Oh, come on, Roger. I may be naïve, but I'm not stupid. She was wearing less than ***you*** were when I walked in."

"Okay, so I'm human. After the last time I saw you, I assumed we were broken up. Marilyn's an old friend, and she just came over to comfort me."

"W-e-ll…" she replied, forcing a bitter laugh. "How could she fail with that ***particular*** method?"

His eyes narrowed in anger. "Hey, it's not my fault if you decided to suddenly drop by unexpectedly. And I'll thank you to leave Marilyn out of this. She's not to blame for what happened between us."

"Oh, and I suppose here's where you blame it all on me, right?"

"Well, if you hadn't put up that wall of ice for the past month, maybe the other night wouldn't have happened and we'd still be together."

"I see, so just because I wouldn't sleep with you, that's reason enough for you to dismiss our relationship like it never meant anything."

"You're the one who brought that about, sweetheart, not me."

Before she could reply, he turned his back on her, heading inside and slamming the door.

Julianna was a wreck when she got home, although Crystal wasn't surprised. A week later, her friend Marybeth found out that Roger was now living with Marilyn. So much for her being ***just*** a friend!

Her family and friends worried about her reaction, but Julianna merely shrugged off their concern, busying herself with work.

It was only when she was alone that she let the tears surface. She wrote in a small journal to comfort herself, transferring her inner pain to it.

She'd initially written of happier times between them, but now there was only sadness. After a brief time, she stopping writing in it completely, locking the journal and hiding it in the bottom of her jewelry box. As if she could lock away her pain in the process.

Now almost two months later, she wondered if she'd ever get used to the emptiness she felt.

So far, the answer remained 'no'.

*****

No one in the hallway.

A clear path to the water fountain.

Breathing a sigh of relief, Julianna strode towards a few moments of peace and refreshment.

Until someone suddenly bumped into her from the nearby conference room.

"Julie!" the person said amiably. "Well, isn't this a coincidence?"

No more than the other three times this month, Julianna thought with a sigh.

The water would have to wait… again.

"Marybeth," she acknowledged.

"It's been awhile since we've chatted."

"Yes, all of a week. Now if you'll excuse me, breaks aren't that long." Before she could leave, Marybeth stepped in front of her.

"Come on, Julie. We've been friends too long for you not to satisfy my curiosity. When are you going to kick that seductress out of Roger's life for good?"

Julianna fought back a glare. "Never. Roger and I are history. That's it. End of story."

Her friend's smile became catlike. "For now," she chimed.

"I'm heading back to my desk."

"Oh, Julie," Marybeth crooned after her. "There's something I've been meaning to tell you for days. It concerns Roger." Julianna stopped walking, wondering at the odd tone in her voice.

"What's happened?"

"At the last few gatherings, he showed up alone. It would seem things aren't going as well with Marilyn as he wanted everyone to think. She walked out on him over a week ago."

Her long-buried emotions stirred at that, but Julianna wouldn't let them get control this time. "That's his problem. Now if you'll excuse me."

"Julie, he misses you. There isn't one of us who can't see it. Don't you realize there isn't a single woman we know who hasn't wanted to go out with him? But all he ever does is ask about you."

Wanting to protest, Marybeth wouldn't let her interrupt. "Ever since you had that fallout last July, he hasn't been himself at all. When he did show up with Marilyn, they'd usually find excuses to be in separate rooms, unlike when he used to spend every moment with you."

Momentarily forgetting her anger regarding Marilyn, Julianna nearly smiled. "I never could understand what he saw in her. I've heard them say she acts like an absolute Medusa, like Almira."

At the mention of their boss, Marybeth's eyes narrowed. "Almira ***is*** Medusa. Stone face, stone heart."

"Was there a point here?"

"You're underestimating yourself, Julie," Marybeth continued, "but take it from me, you've got him hooked, even though he hasn't said anything yet." Folding her arms conspiratorially, she whispered, "Besides, having a boyfriend helps to keep the other jerks away."

Her friend certainly spoke from experience, dauntlessly persisting in her quest for the ideal man. Julianna knew how difficult that particular challenge could be, though admittedly, Roger had always been highly attractive.

Shrugging off the thought, she shook her head. "I wouldn't need Roger for that fortunately. If I did have a problem with an unwanted suitor, I'd just chain the door and threaten him with my ferocious hellhound guard dog." Upon Marybeth's glance of skepticism regarding her playful dog, she shrugged once. "Okay, so Shadow's too cute for that, but she does ***sound*** like a hellhound sometimes."

"You could always borrow the kids next door, and claim them to be yours and your husband's," she suggested. "Might give a hint to Roger at the same time."

Julianna smiled. She'd wanted that once.

She shook her head immediately against the thought.

"No, I'd just as soon hire bodyguards, and have them toss him into the neighbor's pool."

"Or better yet, simply record and amplify Shadow's barking to scare him into the neighbor's pool."

Breaking into laughter, they never noticed their boss' approach until hearing the tapping of her heeled shoe. Marybeth caught on first, tugging on Julianna's sleeve to gain her attention. The domineering nature of their boss didn't make it any easier to face her with completely serious expressions.

"Miss Thompson," whispered Julianna, struggling to

cover her mirth with a cough. "We were just about to return to our desks."

"Were you now?" drawled the older woman.

In her early forties, Almira Thompson was the epitome of business, business, and more business. From her straight prim haircut, her overdone makeup, and her assortment of never-ending gray 'executive' business suits, the woman was a human business machine in high-heels. If she even ***suspected*** a lax attitude, she'd use a practiced cold stare to wear down any employee. One could always tell she was angry when her eyes squinted and her bright red lipsticked mouth was drawn into a tight line.

She was all that now with an equally red angry face.

"Yes, we were just discussing the merits of the company pool," added Marybeth, causing Julianna to smile again.

Almira's eyebrows shot up. She took a step towards the culprit with an intimidating smile. "Something ***funny*** you'd care to share with us, Miss Sherborne?"

Julianna shook her head quickly, coughing again to regain her composure. "Not really, Miss Thompson."

"Then why don't you and your sidekick return to your desks before you're sent home instead. Now!" Glaring for emphasis, she spun on her heel and strutted down the hallway. Marybeth made a face and imitated her movements. From around the corner, Almira's stern voice called out, "I'd take that as a warning if I were you, Miss O'Neill!"

"Great," sighed Marybeth. "Now the she-beast can see through walls. How does she ***do*** that?"

Julianna shrugged with a smile, finally escaping to the water fountain.

*****

Wheeling the shopping cart forward, Julianna rubbed her eyes tiredly. Why was it that the workdays seemed to keep getting longer? Stopping to lean against the cart, she wondered how long her back would take to feel normal again, after eight hours of sitting at the computer all day.

As if complying with her thoughts, a pair of strong hands began to skillfully massage her shoulders, startling her, even as she recognized their familiarity.

Roger's deep masculine voice murmured against her cheek, "Give me half a minute, and I'll take care of that pain for you." Nodding tiredly, she allowed him to help. "You really should get away from that desk now and then. The human body isn't meant to be a machine."

"Don't have much choice with my boss."

"I understand. Feel up to moving now?" he asked.

"Keep that up, and I won't feel like moving for a week."

"A tempting idea, if we weren't in grocery central." Kissing her neck in spite of this, Julianna arched towards him instinctively, earning a pleased smile from him. "We could continue this back at my place."

Rational thought returned slowly, delayed by those kisses. She turned, sighing heavily since nothing had been settled in her mind. "Roger…" she began, distracted again as he slid his arms around her waist. The latent passion in his eyes and languorous smile mesmerized her. As he brushed his hand against her cheek, her words nearly came out as a whisper, "Roger, I heard what happened."

"Then you know Marilyn's not living with me anymore." When she pulled away slightly, at first he looked about to protest, but the conflicted look in her eyes stopped him. "I'm sorry, Julie," he said quietly, stroking her hair with one hand. "There's no rush."

Feeling her apprehension melt at his unexpected reassurance, Julianna felt like kicking herself, since part of her wanted to go with him now and simply forget the past few months ever happened.

"If you have time tonight, could we talk later?" he asked,

reaching forward to take her hand.

Her fingers slowly returned the gesture, as she stared upon their clasped hands. "I don't know. I suppose it'd be..."

"Okay, Roger, I've got everything," a voice called out behind them. "Should I just meet you at the car?"

"Dammit, Marilyn, will you hold on for five minutes?"

Just seeing the other woman, Julianna's eyes shut with anger. "I am such a damn fool," she hissed, pulling away from Roger, and leaving her cart to storm away from the pair.

"Julie, wait. It's not what you think."

She evaded his grasping hand and fairly ran to the exit, jumping in her car and speeding home without looking back.

*****

How much pain can one heart stand?

Alone in her room that night, Julianna's thoughts went back to the evening where everything had turned upside-down with Roger.

Much as she hated to admit it, deep down she began to wonder what was wrong with her. There was no questioning the attraction she'd felt for Roger, and he'd made it quite clear he wanted her. So why then had she been so hesitant about their relationship?

If she hadn't been, then Marilyn wouldn't have had the opportunity to steal his attention.

Even after their separation, he still held sway over her. Unfortunately, she'd been having trouble sleeping lately because of the situation, allowing her no peace even at night.

Which was why her mind played back her dream of Dominick.

Having dreamed of him after the breakup, it was the only comfort she had, so she hoped she could somehow trick her mind into dreaming of him again.

Folly, of course, to think this way, yet she did.

Julianna walked to the window of her room and drew

back the curtains, sitting beside the sill. Somehow seeing the stars always made her feel better.

She glanced upward into endless darkness, but as her eyes adjusted, the stars winked into her vision one by one, twinkling and bright as their silent welcome shone upon her. They always seemed like friends that understood her when no one else did, and they always gave her comfort. She smiled up at them fondly.

Just before one suddenly shot straight down from the sky.

She gasped slightly, even as she realized it must be a falling star.

Wish for something! her thoughts reminded her. As the plummeting dot of light continued to drop, Julianna clasped her hands and spoke the quickest wish she could think of, watching as the star disappeared completely from view.

"Please help me find the Dominick of my dreams." Moments after she finished her plea, feelings of foolishness washed over her. *I can't believe I'm wishing for a person I've only dreamed of!* her mind mocked her. *As if a star can really create someone out of thin air.*

A bright flash of light illuminated the window, startling her. *Lightning!* she thought instinctively, hurriedly drawing the curtains closed. Soon afterwards, she did a double take. *That can't be lightning*, she mused. No thunder followed, nor had any storm been mentioned in the evening's weather forecast. Obviously, her imagination had simply hallucinated.

Yet even so, she felt oddly disturbed, cautiously moving the curtain aside to glance once more at the now quiet and serene stars above—all present and normal as ever—and wondered if someone up there was playing tricks on her.

A lot of people seemed to down here, so why not from heaven above too!

Her fear receding, Julianna saw an unfamiliar star, which

seemed like it was right outside her window. The ever-twinkling star soon intrigued her to the point that she couldn't take her eyes from it, pressing her hand against the window. And since she'd made it a habit of naming bright stars that stood out, she smiled, with a whispered name to remember it by...

"Dominick."

As if hearing her, the star seemed to twinkle brighter with acknowledgment, but Julianna was too tired to take notice. Half-shutting the curtain, she climbed into bed, picking up her latest romance novel.

After reading about ten pages, the novel began to remind her of what she was missing in her life. Something always made worse during cold nights like this one. Finally, she dropped the book and turned over on her side, tears of loneliness filling her eyes.

"I suppose the only Dominick I'll ever find is one I dream of," she said with a sigh. Brushing a hand against her eyes to clear them, Julianna slowly felt sleep tugging at her. Sniffing one last time as her breathing became more even, she whispered semiconsciously, "Oh, Dominick, if only you were real and you could take this pain away."

One hand slid down the pillow as her features relaxed completely in slumber.

For a few minutes, all was quiet in the darkness. Then abruptly, a bright light shone as the newly named star appeared beside Julianna's sleeping form.

While asleep, she had absolutely no awareness of its presence, as it now blinked chaotically beside her. Nor had she noticed when it dimmed its light earlier to float through the glass window of her room.

Dimming its light again, as if not to wake her, the star now hovered over where the book had fallen—cover side up—and then slowly floated back to Julianna.

Blinking brightly again, she still remained lost in slumber.

As if satisfied, the star blinked thrice more in rapid succession. Just before it abruptly winked out of view.

Chapter Two

Where the hell am I? wondered Julianna.

It appeared to be a ballroom.

An odd ballroom with walls of mirrors.

All the people surrounding her were attired in clothes and gowns out of the early nineteenth century. Glancing down at her own attire, she found herself similarly dressed in a long gown of creamy white with lace frills, which complemented her reddish-brown hair that fell loosely about her shoulders. It almost looked like something out of a romance novel, leaving her perplexed at how she'd gotten here.

Not wanting to appear unsociable, she nodded to several unfamiliar people, wishing that she wasn't quite so alone and friendless in this strange place. Out of the corner of her eye, she saw someone laughing while casting his eye in her direction. The man in question was laughing with two gentlemen beside him.

Turning to a well-dressed gentleman beside her, she tapped his shoulder and asked, "Who is that?"

The man gave her a casual glance, and then looked ahead to where she pointed. "Are you referring to the man in black, my dear?"

She was about to nod, but before she could get a closer look, the stranger suddenly darted away, whisking around a corner.

Not that it should matter, of course, unless... an unsettling thought crossed her mind abruptly. *Could it be?* she wondered. As the forgotten bewildered man looked after her, she began running in the same direction the so-called 'man in black' had disappeared. Instinctively, she called after the stranger.

"Dominick, wait!"

A bit miffed at the long gown that threatened to trip her up with every step, she picked up handfuls of the heavy dress, shocking several ladies who gasped as she ran on. "Dominick!" she yelled louder. When she rounded the corner, running alongside more mirrored walls, and after weaving through countless people, she realized she was completely lost in the bizarre mirror maze.

Gasping for breath, she finally gave up the chase. Whoever the stranger was had probably left, if there was a way out of here. Besides, she'd made enough of a fool of herself, running after someone she didn't know, who probably wondered just who the devil 'Dominick' was.

Several of the well-bred people who had glanced her way now resumed their interrupted conversations, even as Julianna realized she'd become the subject of them. *How embarrassing!*

"Are you quite all right, my lady?" a deep voice asked behind her.

"Not really," she sighed. "However, I should be so in a moment. Thank you for your concern, sir." As her breathing became less labored, the person handed her a glass of dark purple liquid. She took it gratefully, sipping it slowly.

"Now then, my lady. I believe I heard you calling after me. Pray tell what for?"

Julianna nearly choked as she turned.

It was ***him***!

And he looked ***exactly*** as she remembered the charming rogue she'd met before.

Not quite six feet, the man provided a contrast to her shorter height. His ebony hair was thick and wavy, framing his strong features perfectly. But most bewitching were his eyes...

that similar deep shade of blue, perfectly complementing his warm smile which could seem serious or boyish at whim.

In fact, the only real difference between them was that Dominick had been mostly hidden by the cloak he'd worn. This man wasn't similarly hindered. He wore a velvet black jacket in the style worn by other men here. Added to this, he wore a white shirt, and black pants, which emphasized his well-muscled body quite nicely.

Down to his hair, he was indeed the man in black.

There was little doubt in her mind that this was the ***same*** Dominick, yet of course that was ridiculous. What would ***he*** be doing here now?

For that matter, what was ***she*** doing here?

If this had been Dominick, she mused, in his new well-fitting attire, she would have sworn he looked even more handsome than the last time she'd seen him; even more than Roger, as a matter of fact. Still, it looked as if this man didn't know her, so she considered it best to be careful.

"Forgive me, sir," she said nonchalantly. "It's just that for a moment you reminded me of a former acquaintance of mine, and I've been having difficulty finding anyone else that I know here."

The blue of his eyes seemed to deepen even more with amusement. "And who might this acquaintance be that I remind you of?"

Julianna laughed, trying to convey some manner of etiquette. "Sir, I am quite certain you wouldn't know him."

He smiled warmly. "Perhaps I do. His name?"

"Dominick."

"Ah, then my ears did ***not*** deceive me. You have found me out, my lady," he replied, proffering a bow. "Dominick Westbrooke, at your service."

Dear heaven above, it ***couldn't*** be true!

Julianna's face blanched, and now she really wished she

could find an immediate exit before she died of embarrassment.

"You must excuse me, sir," she faltered, her eyes glancing about furtively. "I didn't mean to mislead you. Forgive me for bothering you, Mr. Westbrooke." Now where was that elusive exit?

Before she could make a hasty retreat, he reached out to take her hand, gently pulling her back. "Please don't rush off, my lady. I must admit to finding these affairs a bit tedious myself, especially when I can't find my companions so easily."

"You seemed to know a few whom you were speaking with earlier."

He warded this off with a hand wave. "Merely an appearance, my lady. They're total strangers. And in truth, if not for your timely intervention, their conversation was about to put to the test whether a person can fall asleep while standing up."

"Really, sir, such ***subtlety***!" she said, with a smirk. "Even though after seeing the stuffy, strait-laced atmosphere here, I think I can heartily agree with you." They both laughed, not totally oblivious to the added stares this earned from the onlookers. "But seriously, Mr. Westbrooke," Julianna added, "if you ever have need of further rescuing from such people, I'll be happy to oblige you if I'm in the vicinity."

Dominick flashed her a warm smile, just before leaning closer to whisper, "Don't look now, my lady, but I do believe the tongue-waggers are about to sharpen their knives on us."

Glancing around, Julianna could agree. Several of the well-dressed people were gossiping quietly while giving less-than-discreet stares to the chatting pair. While this might have once made her uncomfortable, for some reason, right now she was simply amused.

"They do look a bit like vultures ready to pounce, don't they?" she laughed.

"Ready to destroy is more like it," he murmured through

a grin, glancing up as the sound of lilting ballroom music filled the air. "However, if I may offer an easy solution and a means to repay your kindness, would you care to dance?"

"I'd love to, but I don't know these dances." Just walking in this attire alone was proving difficult.

"Believe me, my lady, 'twill be far more embarrassing if the town decides to print our names in tomorrow's gossip columns. Besides, I'm afraid I have my own selfish reasons for wanting to dance with you."

Several indeed, he thought, silently remembering how she'd mocked him at their last meeting.

He gave a slight bow, taking her hand to bestow a gentle kiss. Only the briefest contact, yet Julianna felt her heart leap, wondering if she was blushing as his eyes met hers again. Tightening his grip on her hand, he began to lead her onto the dance floor. Sensing more than one pair of eyes upon them, Julianna shook her head quickly.

"Mr. Westbrooke," she faltered, "I really don't think this is such a good idea."

Smiling reassuringly, he remained silent as he led them amidst the other dancing pairs. Several of whom gave knowing smiles to the new couple. Now she ***knew*** she was blushing! Amused, Dominick said nothing, merely squeezing her hand once as he led her through the steps of a waltz.

"Not so difficult, is it?" he asked, earning a smile from his companion.

"No, it's quite pleasant really," she agreed brightly, a moment before curiosity surfaced. "Now then, sir, just what did you mean earlier when you said you had selfish motives for this dance?"

It was a good thing she couldn't read his mind at the moment, Dominick thought privately. For right now, it kept playing back their last meeting, and how she'd quite cleverly wounded his pride. *Especially over that damned kiss.* He still remembered how she'd slammed her heel on his foot when he hadn't expected it. After that incident, he'd been adamant in not wanting to see this particular female again in this lifetime.

Yet in spite of his best intentions, he had not been able to forget her. When he'd come here tonight, he hadn't expected her to remember his name, much less chase after him.

It was only when he caught her staring that he remembered her earlier question. So she wanted his motives for this dance, did she? What would she say if he simply kissed her again? he wondered. He doubted she'd stomp on his foot this time, as that surely wouldn't be the proper etiquette here in the middle of a dance floor! No, not likely. But then again, maybe she ***would*** toss etiquette out the window and repeat the incident. In any case, he doubted she'd be so smug with him after tonight. If it was motive she wanted, best not keep her waiting.

"Well, my lady, for one thing, I happen to find you pleasant company to talk to," he replied casually, spinning her about. "For another, I don't wish to relinquish you to someone else." He smiled at her look of surprise, a bit surprised himself at the truth in his words. Pulling her closer against his chest with a quick tug, ignoring her gasp and what any onlookers might think, he leaned his mouth closer to hers, adding softly, "And third of all..."

"Excuse me, sir!" came a voice from behind.

"What the devil?" hissed Dominick, ignoring the confusion on Julianna's face as he turned his head quickly to confront the interruption. Another gentleman stood there, several years younger than him and somewhat shorter.

"Despite your ignorance when I patted your back, may I cut in?"

Dominick gave him a brief look of contemplation, not masking his annoyance. "No, you may not," he said curtly, turning away from him.

"Sir! I do believe that this concerns the lady more than

you."

"The lady, you say? All right then, Lord Whoever-you-are, hold onto your dinner jacket for just a moment." Turning to Julianna, he began, "This ***gentleman*** here..."

"Lord Daffordshire," the man supplied.

Dominick turned at that. "You're not serious," he replied, barely concealing a smile. The man nodded. "My lady," he continued quietly, facing her again, "it would appear you have another admirer by the name of Lord Daffy-something. Would you rather end our dance now, to no doubt ***literally*** trip over the lights fantastic with Lord Daffy here... or do you wish to remain with me to continue our dance and our conversation?"

Julianna's smile faded into a downcast look. "And will this conversation include another public display of you trying to kiss me?" she asked softly.

For the first time since the awkward ending of their last meeting, Dominick felt a wave of compassion for her. True, he hadn't been thrilled over what she'd done back then, but since he ***had*** been a total stranger to her, maybe it wasn't so difficult to understand. And certainly not something he cared to dwell on, since she still sparked his interest.

"No, my lady," he replied gently. "I promise I won't attempt to kiss you here on the dance floor again."

She nearly laughed. Still, the sincerity in his eyes looked real, and after giving a swift glance to Lord Daffordshire, she made her decision.

Turning to the awaiting younger man, she said sweetly, "Your offer is most kind, sir, but I'm afraid I must decline, since I'm already having a most enjoyable time with Mr. Westbrooke here. Perhaps another time, sir."

Dominick flashed him a triumphant smile, attempting to resume the dance.

"This is scandalous, sir!" protested Daffordshire. "I hope, madam, that you realize just what ill-breeding this man must come from."

"Ill-breeding?" interrupted Dominick, facing him again with a scowl. "Look, Sir Daffy!" he began, earning a barely concealed grin from Julianna. "If you want to dance so much, go find yourself a more suitable simpering miss. ***My*** lady has already made it quite clear that she isn't interested in changing partners with a foul-mouthed youngster, and you can stuff ***that*** in your local society column for all I care!"

"I'd put it on page one," Julianna suggested over her shoulder as Dominick whirled her away from the gaping man. As if cued to match their break away from him, the music changed to a faster tune, brightening the smiles of the other couples on the floor who ignored the flustered young man still standing there. "He was foul-mouthed, wasn't he?" she commented after a brief silence.

"And ill-mannered," he agreed. "I'll be careful to make sure that my future sons have a more respectful attitude towards ladies." A furtive smile replaced his somber look as he added, "And especially towards their mother." Julianna found herself blushing at his words, even though he was obviously speaking in the general sense. At least she assumed he was!

They resumed dancing silently until the music stopped to change again. Seeing Lord Daffordshire and a few of his friends approaching from the sideline, Dominick quickly gestured towards a group of people on the other side. Nodding once, Julianna followed him to where they could converse without being bothered, nor bumped into on the dance floor.

"You're not a bad dancer, Mr. Westbrooke," she told him. "I guess your ill-breeding isn't as bad as all that."

"Watch your tongue, fair minx," he chuckled, "or I won't be responsible for what consequences my so-called ill-breeding might bring forth." Seeing several people turn to them again, Dominick shook his head. "My lady, I have a better suggestion. Why don't we break away to continue our conversation where there are less people, out in the cool night air of the garden, beneath the moonlight?"

Julianna knew from the moment she looked into the warm gaze of his fathomless blue eyes that she was lost. It was as if they could make her forget who she was, and she doubted she'd care if she did.

Yet after his attempt to kiss her on the dance floor, she wasn't anxious to go anywhere out of public view with him. Drawing herself up, she tried again to speak with some modicum of etiquette, partially for the benefit of those around her who would almost assuredly be listening in.

"Mr. Westbrooke, you must have mistaken me for someone else entirely. I assure you I didn't mean to give you the impression that I was a lightskirt." Dominick gave a deep laugh at her words.

"I didn't believe that for a moment," he told her, with a grin. "And may I reassure you in return, my lady, that I am not some rake who is planning to ravish you." She blushed at his words, but remained silent. "I merely thought it would be more pleasant to go outside and avoid the local gossips. We should then be able to elude their loose tongues which will no doubt be wagging about us otherwise."

Despite any attempt to remain serious, Julianna felt a bubble of amusement well up within her, which finally escaped as a soft laugh. As he extended his arm to her with a smile, she took it gratefully and followed where he led. Part of her wondered if there was in fact any exit at all. Yet it soon became clear that Dominick was familiar with this place, since after leading her around one mirrored corner, they found an open doorway leading to the aforementioned garden.

Julianna was relieved to see several other couples outside watching the stars, comforted that at least they wouldn't be all alone. Releasing her arm, Dominick leaned nonchalantly against the waist-high stone wall where the flowers curled over it, and turned to face his quiet companion.

He wondered for a moment whether or not she was aware that he knew exactly who she was from before. After all, while she'd remembered his name, he hadn't heard any mention of their last meeting together. For that matter, she didn't seem entirely convinced that he was the same Dominick she'd met before.

Perhaps, he considered, it might be interesting to see how she'd react as if ***this*** was their first meeting. As such, it would have the advantage that she hadn't stomped on his foot... at least not yet anyway!

And this time, he would find out who she was.

"Now then, my lady," he said smiling, choosing his words carefully, "although you seem to have the psychic gift of knowing the names of new people, I find myself a bit more hard pressed to do the same. Would your name be Rose perhaps?"

"No," she laughed, "though I shall take that as a compliment. My name is Julianna Sherborne."

"Julianna," he whispered, the tones echoing lightly. *Ah*, he thought triumphantly. *At last I finally have your name, o' fiery one who has haunted my thoughts relentlessly for the past few months!* But almost immediately, his soft expression that hid these thoughts soon reached deeper within to become something more. *Julianna.* He'd never met a woman by that name before, and it seemed in a way like her… unique. "So tell me, Miss Sherborne, do you make it a habit to race after your suitors, or do I have the rare privilege of such an honor?"

She blushed slightly through a smile. "If you please, I'd prefer it if we could simply get past that awkward introduction."

"Not awkward at all," said Dominick, grinning. "As a matter of fact, I feel some thanks are due for your giving me a reason to escape that endless hall of mirrors. Not that you would have any such difficulty I'm certain, Miss Sherborne, since any man with half a brain would gladly chase after you to partake of your company for an evening." Leaning against one elbow on the wall, he caught her gaze and saw her blush again. "I couldn't help noticing that you were alone earlier when I first saw you. So tell me, did some clumsy oaf foolishly leave you to mingle about on your own, or did he simply disappear to drink several glasses of port in the back room with the local tavern barmaid?"

Having merely spoken the last in jest, he was totally unprepared for her reaction. Julianna's face grew pale, and moments later, she burst into uncontrollable tears. At this sudden change, Dominick's leisurely expression turned serious with concern.

"Dear heaven, Julianna, I'm sorry," he whispered honestly. For all that had happened during their first meeting, the last thing he'd wanted was to make her cry! Quickly reaching for his handkerchief, he stepped forward to gently dab the tears from her eyes. As her sobs continued, he muttered an oath to himself. "It would seem we share the trait of awkward actions."

"I-It's not you," she sniffed, wiping her eyes with her hand. "I did come here all alone." *Although I'm not sure quite how*, she thought, giving him a forced rueful smile. "I'm sorry that this fact seems to have reduced me to nothing less than a blubbering fool."

"You most certainly are not that," he insisted, holding her shoulders firmly for a moment before releasing her. "But I can see that something must have triggered this sudden unhappiness, so tell me not otherwise." She nodded, trying unsuccessfully to stifle her tears. "Come with me," he said gently, taking her hand in his and leading her down the nearby garden steps.

She barely noticed any of this, as he led her to a vacant bench and she sat down beside him. Reaching forward to clasp her hand tightly in his, he turned compassionate eyes upon her. She was staring at the ground, the tears still apparent on her face. *What in the universe has made you so unhappy?* he wondered. *Or more accurately,* ***who*** *is the culprit?*

Obviously a fool.

While Julianna ***was*** being unusually quiet for a change—which nearly made him smile—he took the time to appraise his silent companion, not having had much chance to do so openly while amidst the crowd.

She was beautiful.

Even with her warm brown eyes sorely reddened by tears, she was still breathtaking. Her auburn hair was long and curly, despite the more popular trend of short hair that many other women here sported. Privately, he decided this style suited her better anyway.

While Dominick was fairly tall, Julianna was only about five-foot-five, giving him the impression she was like a sprite, especially when they were standing face-to-face. Even her large animated eyes contributed to this sprite-like appearance. But then, he reflected, he'd never had anything against pretty sprites!

She was reasonably slim, but not emaciated like some women he'd seen who weren't to his taste at all. Julianna had a healthier quality about her, and the gown she wore certainly complimented her rather pleasant curves. When her eyes lit up with amusement and her face glowed, as he'd seen earlier, she was even more beautiful.

How he wished he could kiss away the crystal tears in those eyes now, so that she was once again smiling and happy as she'd been before.

Dominick resisted the urge though, forcing himself to remember that he was still a relative stranger to her, and the last thing he wanted to do was to anger or frighten her. However, finding out the cause of her unhappiness was something he intended to do right now.

"Tell me all," he said softly.

He could sense it wasn't easy for Julianna, but slowly the

words came. At first, she started with only the briefest account of the betrayal she'd felt by Roger. But whenever he caught her pausing, Dominick would gently ask her more questions, thereby helping her to relay what had happened. He didn't force anything from her, and soon she appeared to be warming to him, allowing him to put his arm about her comfortingly during the conversation.

At some point during her story, she leaned her head upon his shoulder, relaxing completely against him while she spoke, her trust warming his heart as he listened. Likely, some of what she was telling him, she'd been keeping to herself until now.

She went on to tell him that thanks to Roger, and several other mishaps with men beforehand, it left her feeling resigned to either marry the wrong type or remain alone forever.

After hearing this, Dominick hugged her closer, whispering against the top of her head that surely neither would happen. It was only after she began crying again that he realized the true reason for her unhappiness.

Julianna was lonely. She clearly couldn't bring herself to believe that all men weren't like the wrong ones she'd known, especially after what had happened with Roger, whom she'd trusted since she was very young.

For all her twenty-five years, she'd never known anyone different.

She was little more than an innocent.

Julianna knew nothing of this line his thoughts had taken towards her. She only knew that for a few moments, she felt safe and cared for, and it was a feeling she was reluctant to let go of. Since she'd been staring blankly ahead most of the time during her explanation, she completely missed seeing the changing expressions that flashed across her attentive companion's face.

Especially his dark looks at any mention of Roger.

Although having never met the man, Dominick felt a surge of anger and dislike towards this Roger Collins. He'd preyed on her trust to get what he wanted, and when that hadn't worked, he immediately turned to another. And then when his latest amour hadn't worked out, he saw nothing wrong with pursuing Julianna again, even though he wasn't fully detached from the other woman.

If only he had the opportunity to do something about the ungrateful bastard. Thankfully, Roger hadn't called her after his betrayal earlier this day, which could only have caused her more grief. If he were to show up again for whatever reason now, Dominick would certainly like to grab the insensitive blackguard by his collar, and…

Sighing once, he refocused on Julianna.

"I know I was a fool to believe him," she murmured, "but he always sounded so enthusiastic with his promises that I kept giving him more chances. And to think, for years I kept hoping he'd come back, like some lovesick child. I was a fool even then."

She gave a short strained laugh, oblivious to the way Dominick's jaw tightened at her words, and her tone changed to sharper bitterness. "I guess there's no mistaking his insensitivity now. In one breath he said he wanted to meet with me again, but the whole time he was still with Marilyn. Seems like I never learn not to trust him."

Dominick suddenly turned her to face him, resting his hands gently against her cheeks.

"Listen to me," he replied, gazing into her eyes. "Stop tearing yourself down. This man was nothing but a user, and you certainly weren't in any way responsible for his callous behavior. If anyone's a fool around here, it's not you, but him. You're a beautiful, intelligent woman with a good heart and a soul that shines. And when the right man comes along, if he has any brains, he'll realize how fortunate he is to have such a loyal, loving treasure for a companion. Don't ever let anyone tell you otherwise, Julianna, because if they do, they're not worthy of your favor."

She found herself speechless, and all too conscious of his eyes upon her and the gentle touch of his hands upon her face. *Was he serious about there being cool air out here?* she wondered, feeling as if it was warm and summery instead.

"I wouldn't worry on that count," she said finally. "Even before Roger, most of the men in my life have left me strictly alone, and those that might not have weren't ones I'd care to associate with."

He smiled at that. "And what kind of man ***would*** interest you, Julianna?" he asked softly. She turned away for a moment, considering this. His expression became knowing. "Ah… a knight in shining armor to sweep you off your feet. Not a bad idea, but wouldn't that be a bit awkward if taken too literally?"

Julianna whipped back to stare at him with surprise. It was as if he'd just read her mind! Were her thoughts that obvious on her face?

She was about to inquire further, but as she opened her mouth to speak, he leaned forward to capture hers with his own. Her surprise becoming shock, Julianna pushed both hands against his chest to force him back, but his hold on her was stronger. *So much for his claim of not being a rake!*

Despite her protests though, she found that Dominick wasn't hurting her at all. His arms were securely around her, but he wasn't kissing her so as to bruise her mouth. In fact, she was finding it increasingly pleasant the way his lips lingered on hers with each kiss. So similar to the other Dominick of a few months back. And even though this couldn't be the same one she'd met before, she was obviously attracted to him all the same.

Even if this Dominick was a rake, he seemed a gentle

one of his breed.

When he sensed her calming down, his one hand loosed its hold slightly to stroke her back, sending tingling sensations throughout her spine.

Slowly, her hands reached up to rest on his shoulders, this time successfully breaking the connection between them. His eyes stared deeply into hers, as if he could read her soul, and the look nearly frightened her, but she willed herself not to give in to that.

"You're trembling, my lady," he whispered, his mouth mere inches from her own.

"I am?" Her heart was beating too fast for her to realize it.

"Yes, you are." He smoothed back a few loose auburn strands from her face. She shut her eyes and smiled as his hand brushed against her cheek, the soft touch of his fingertips causing her breath to still... just before a gentle wind caused her eyes to snap open again. Dominick was standing now, one hand extended towards her. "My lady, may I escort you back to the affair above?"

A peculiar choice of words, Julianna mused. Now that her rational thoughts were returning again, she blushed, furious at herself. In another few minutes, there might have been an affair here all right! She turned away from his offered hand, wishing the ground might swallow her up before he noticed how red her face was.

"No, thank you, my lord," she replied softly. "But I would prefer it if you would leave now to rejoin the others on your own."

He shook his head with a smile. "I wouldn't advise it, my lady. There are always rakes aplenty at these gatherings, and I wouldn't want you to be subjected to them."

Her eyes flashed angrily as she abruptly stood to face him. "You mock me, sir?" she demanded. "Just who are you to warn me against rakes, when you may well be the master of them! I've dealt with your type before, Mr. Westbrooke, and I don't take kindly to being taken advantage of. False pity, combined with kisses, are not a winning combination with me."

He was silent, his expression unreadable.

"If you will excuse me, ***sir***!" she added coldly with finality, pushing past him to walk towards the steps.

As she took a preemptory glance towards the garden terrace, she was surprised to see it empty. Apparently the other guests were all inside the building now. Despite their highbred nature, for once, Julianna found that she couldn't wait to join the safety of them again.

But as her foot barely touched the first step, she found herself spun about to face Dominick again, his hands gripping her arms. There was hurt in his eyes, almost akin to anger, that left her shivering in his grasp, but she was too startled to speak.

"You're wrong on all counts, my lady," he said firmly. "I didn't kiss you to take advantage of you, Julianna, and it certainly has nothing to do with pity. I kissed you because I find you to be a fascinating, attractive, and desirable woman. One who just needs the right man to prove how true this is."

"I don't need anyone!" she countered, glaring at him. "Especially not..."

Dominick kissed her to silence, leaning her head back against his hand as he did.

I should have known better than to trust him even for a moment! she thought, just before she felt a gentle voice—***his*** voice—touch her mind.

I would never do anything to hurt you, Julianna. You need to know that.

Confusion filled her eyes, even as his kisses became tender, once again stirring up odd fluttery sensations within her. *How are you reading my thoughts?*

Magic.

When she realized that he wasn't about to release her, Julianna felt a renewed wave of panic. She was trapped all alone, held captive in the arms of a stranger who had fairly clear motives.

She felt his soft laughter in her mind. *You know it is possible for a man to kiss a woman merely to share that pleasure alone.*

Trying to escape his words, Julianna knew she should yell for assistance from the guests in the building, since surely one would hear her. Or maybe she should kick him while he was distracted to break free… after all, it had worked with the other Dominick.

His voice persisted undaunted. *Do you have any idea how wonderful it is just to kiss you? Tempting though it is to want more, a true man listens to his lady's heart.*

Her inner arguments faltering, she knew that she should be freezing in this gown, so then why did she feel so warm?

What you feel is a feeling we share. You don't need to run from it this time.

She trembled against him, but this time because she realized the truth of his words.

"Dominick…" she whispered against his mouth, her arms encircling his neck to pull him closer. It was nearly amusing the way he all but jumped with surprise, upon realizing she wasn't backing away. A surprise that didn't faze him for long as he lifted her off the ground.

I'm here, my sweet sprite.

Deepening his kiss, Dominick gently parted Julianna's lips to touch her more intimately. She felt a shiver run through her again, stronger than before, an odd sound escaping her as she felt his arms surround her more completely to lower her against the steps.

Feeling the edge of the stairs against her back brought a slight gasp from her, but Dominick was instantly beside her, his arms cradling her close against him, making her feel like she was floating. His caresses were so warm and soothing against the fabric of the gown that seemed to just lightly cover her skin. And his kisses set her whole being afire.

When he finally pulled back to gaze at her, his eyes were tender.

"Julianna… how could any man be unmoved by you?" he murmured.

She smiled, a slight laugh bubbling up which earned his curiosity. "Not so yourself, sir," she told him lightly.

He echoed the smile back into her eyes, amusement lighting his features, despite the raggedness of his breathing. "Even with the fires of passion kindled between us, am I to be reduced to remaining forevermore 'Sir' to you?" She laughed again, before a more serious smile stole through.

"Dominick," she amended. "Or would Sir Dominick suit you better?"

"Ah, back to playing the knight in shining armor, am I?"

"Perhaps. Although armor is cold, whereas you certainly are not," she said teasingly. "I think you should stick to the title of knight and forget the rest."

"And are you to be the damsel in distress?"

"Hmmm, I'd rather be just a damsel in this dress. But you seem warm enough to play the part of the dragon."

"What an interesting idea," he replied, growling in a deep voice as he kissed her neck.

She gave a quick squeak of laughter, just before he returned more serious attention to kissing her mouth again. Julianna barely managed to stifle the urge to laugh again upon thinking of how silly it would seem for the dragon to be kissing the damsel.

He quickly saw to replacing her amusement with desire, his arms' hold on her waist tightening while his other hand edged the gown off one shoulder. Her breathing quickened as he kissed her bare skin there, the feeling sending her pulse racing.

"Julianna... my dear sweet Julianna," he murmured, his voice little more than a whisper against her cheek as he kissed her again.

She smiled against him, even as she suddenly felt an odd cottony sensation pulling her senses away. Her eyes expressed apprehension as her vision of Dominick became strangely blurred, growing steadily worse.

"Dominick, what...?" she gasped suddenly, clutching him fiercely, her eyes questioning him. If his expression held an answer, it was lost to her due to a sudden brightness obscuring her vision.

The last thing she felt was his grip tightening on her, while his voice shouted out her name, nearly in desperation, "*Julianna!*"

*****

Her eyes popped open, and she found herself alone again in the darkness of her room, where the sun's rays were now burning it away. Rays that had been resting on her eyelids long enough to wake her.

"*What?*" she gasped, bolting upright.

The sound of birds chirping outside was her only reply.

"It was all a dream?" she whispered in disbelief, not disregarding her strangely racing heart. After blinking a few times at the sunlight, she brushed a hand against her mouth tentatively. She could almost ***feel*** the memory of Dominick's kisses, and that alone seemed very strange, since it was all an illusion. One that certainly seemed real moments ago, yet...

It was just a dream.

Of course this was just as well, she supposed, since she could now remember quite vividly the last part of her dream where she'd wantonly given herself up freely to Dominick's warm embrace. If she hadn't woke up when she did, they might have...

Yes, they ***'might have'*** indeed!
"Damn," she murmured regretfully.

Chapter Three

"Damn!" echoed the frustrated Dominick, upon returning to his own realm. After an ensuing set of angry curses, he wasn't too surprised to hear the familiar mocking laughter of his annoying elder brother. Glancing over to the far wall of his room, his eyes narrowed. "I'll thank you to keep your amusement to a minimum, Riff!"

Sitting opposite him casually, his brother coolly ignored the warning, as he would with anyone else. But to be fair, in the name of blood relations, he treated Dominick with some respect... using his most irritating pranks on him instead.

As far as Dominick was concerned, the only similarity between them was their appearance. Even though Riff was three years older than Dominick's twenty-seven years, he and his brother shared nearly the same face. Unlike Dominick's wavy hair though, Riff's own was fairly straight, and unlike his brother's deep blue eyes, Riff's were an emerald green.

Those eyes combined with Riff's expression were often mirthful, especially at times like this. Due to his capability for endless troublesome shenanigans, some had dubbed him Riff-Raff. Only his enemies spitefully used this other name, which always earned them a dose of fistfights in return for their ***understanding***. His friends and family knew better, and would only refer to him as Riff.

At the moment, he appraised his brother with curiosity. "No can do, Bro," he said cheerfully. "At least, not until you tell me ***all*** the details. Was this one pretty, Phase?"

Phase?

Dominick started for a moment, before shaking his head

to clear it. Remembrance came swiftly towards his middle name Phaser, which his brother and father frequently used. As an occasional after-effect of using his special powers to travel into the mind of an extremely distant person, once again, he'd experienced memory lag upon returning. It didn't always happen, and some might consider the side effect laughable; but in truth, it wasn't pleasant for the person experiencing it. Still, since it was infrequent, he wasn't about to let it ***faze*** him now.

While an unusual name in many outer regions, Phaser was an accepted name for a supernatural living on the mist-concealed island of Barokka. The island was comprised mainly of supernaturals, a race of people who were gifted with inborn magic abilities. Whether bearing one magic ability or two, sometimes a supernatural would have a separate name based on an ability or a personality trait, in addition to having a second more ordinary name. Some of the supernaturals preferred the added distinction.

Although Riff didn't have an alternate name, his own was actually a nickname. He'd once sworn he'd never reveal his true name to anyone outside of his immediate family. Though they disagreed, even Dominick would never break that trust.

Dominick's names emerged from a parental disagreement, where his father wanted to name him Phaser after his supernatural ability known as dreamphasing, while his mother preferred the name Dominick. Hence, he was born Dominick Phaser Westbrooke. His father was only mollified by this decision when his mother said that she'd chosen to give their son the same initial as his own name.

He preferred his true name, especially when meeting females in the dream-state who resided on the other planet he frequented via astral travel, since he knew it to be more accepted there. A name that curiously enough had been remembered by the attractive woman Julianna whom he'd met with again last night on that self-same planet… Earth.

Earth being the foreign world on the other side of the sun.

At least it was foreign to most on their world of Chavernos, with the exception of dreamphasers like him.

Rubbing his eyes tiredly, Dominick then leaned back against the comfort of his bed, resting his head against his hands on the pillows.

"Phase?" Riff prompted.

Ignoring the impatient look on his brother's face, he merely stared at the ceiling lost in thought.

This was often quite literally the case of a dreamphaser.

Despite the unknown explanation of whatever forces of nature had granted the supernaturals of Chavernos their varied inborn magical abilities, the fact stood that their powers ***did*** exist. Dreamphasing was only one ability, and very often a dreamphaser had a second inborn ability as well.

A supernatural's powers were usually genetic, yet often differed even amongst direct family members. Dreamphasing was the one exception that was shared by many of the supernaturals, but a second inborn ability would generally be more distinctive. Oddly enough, some supernaturals—and especially dreamphasers—could go the majority of their lives unaware of having a second inborn ability unless actively sought out or accidentally triggered.

Such was the case of Dominick and Riff. Both were dreamphasers, but to this point, neither had any knowledge of a second inborn ability, although they did have friends who were both dreamphasers in addition to having secondary powers.

Dreamphasing was an ability that was normally considered both useful and pleasant. However, in the rare case that a dark soul abused the ability, it could be devastating.

The basic principle of dreamphasing was two-fold. First, it allowed a person to effortlessly transmit his or her astral spirit from one location to another; and secondly, it would allow that person to safely travel in astral form into another's dreams. Whether to become a part of a nightly fantasy, or even if only to control one's own dreams, it could provide confidence to the recipient.

Most dreamphasers limited their astral traveling to visit other dreamers on Chavernos. These supernaturals made it a rule to stay away from the minds of beings of other worlds.

Dominick had never been the type to listen to rules.

Instead, he'd made use of his ability to travel across the vast distance to Earth. In his astral form, he often satisfied his curiosity by secretly visiting the people of this world. He gained a fascination of the differences between the two worlds, seeing the various buildings and structures the Earth humans had created, and seeing some of the forms of entertainment they enjoyed, although the technical devices remained a mystery. And of course, finding pleasant company in dreams was always welcome.

Yes, that planet in the solar system certainly had some good things to recommend it!

Despite rare occasions of a brief memory lapse upon returning, or sometimes in the dreams themselves, dreamphasing was fairly safe to the astral voyagers. There was no known limit to how long a dreamphaser could remain in another's dream, until of course the other person woke up, a fact which could send the dreamphaser back home instantly. Not always though, since a dreamphaser did travel in astral form, and might choose to linger in the astral plane if desired. Dominick himself usually only lingered before entering a person's dreams, rather than afterwards.

His dreamphasing ability, which had been identified as a child by the experienced physicians of Barokka who were most familiar with it, had been honed with help from his grandfather Chaos who was also gifted with it.

When he was fifteen, Dominick had first traveled to

Earth with him, and after a few visits, the young man's curiosity grew towards the distant planet. By sixteen, he was traveling there on his own. Shortly afterwards, he began to notice and appreciate the ability to meet fair damsels in their dreams.

One of the only things he had in common with his elder brother.

Now, just over a decade later, Dominick still traveled occasionally to Earth, but he'd tapered down on his visits with female dreamers lately. For of all these women he'd encountered, no matter how pleasant their brief company was, the fact remained that dream affairs had become unsatisfying over the years. Contrary to his carefree bachelor attitude, Dominick sometimes found himself wishing that he had one special woman in reality, rather than those who were only of brief dreams.

Perhaps... a woman like Julianna? he wondered.

"Chavernos to Phaser!" Riff shouted in his brother's ear, jolting Dominick to turn to him. Narrowing his eyes at his grinning elder brother, he was tempted to send Riff a nightmare later! "By Chaos, you're impossible when you're off daydreaming. I asked you, was this one pretty?"

Dominick paused before answering, for some reason ill at ease with his brother's typically glib remark.

"Pretty enough," he commented dryly.

"Well, don't just sit there close-mouthed!" chuckled Riff. "Cut to the chase, and tell me what happened. What was she like?"

Dominick grimaced at this particular question, knowing what he referred to not so subtly. He knew it shouldn't bother him, as he and Riff had often discussed their dalliances with females in the dream realm. If their father knew, he'd likely have skinned the pair alive, but as the brothers were discreet, this never happened. As it was, their grandfather who ***did*** know, was less than pleased at this idle use of a supernatural gift, and never made secret his disapproval.

Not that this stopped the brothers from pursuing their nightly encounters. They only kept this information to themselves.

Information they'd sometimes shared in the past.

Yet now, oddly enough, Dominick wished his brother hadn't shown up with his usual line of questioning.

"I'd imagine she's the same as any other Earth girl." He tried to sound convincingly disinterested, hoping it would discourage Riff.

Naturally it didn't.

"Come on, Phase. You're acting like someone who got kicked out of someone's dream." He paused, a catlike smile spreading across his face. "Oh... so she woke up first."

Anger shot across Dominick's face. "Look, I didn't invite you here, and I sure as hell don't need an inquisition from you right now! If you can't keep your amusement to a minimum, why don't you bother the other guys instead?"

"Thanks loads, Dom," laughed a voice from the hallway, as the bearer and one other person entered the room. The speaker continued, arms folded. "So you're the one who sends this joker after us with his pranks. I never would have guessed it."

Dominick gave the dark-haired man a weak smile. "There's a lot you couldn't guess regarding me, Buddy," he replied, turning to the blond-haired man beside him. "Inferno, do me a favor. If my brother won't leave my room willingly, would you kindly heat things up to make him more amenable?"

Inferno nodded once, rubbing his hands together. "It is chilly in here."

Riff patted his shoulder meaningfully. "One flame out of you, my friend, and you'll be drinking coffee by the barrel to stay awake from what I send after you at night."

"Thanks for the invitation, but I actually value my sleep,"

Inferno replied smiling, gesturing his hand meaningfully towards a nearly plant on a table, which thrived under the sudden warmth. Truthfully, he wouldn't be eager to use his fire powers to irritate Riff. Even though being a dreamphaser too, he could probably counter anything Riff came up with, it could still make for some very disturbing nightmares.

Buddy was a different matter, since he was a guardian angel. Not the conventional type with the halo and wings—he had the former, but not the latter—since his father had been a guardian devil himself, explaining Buddy's forked tail that no guardian angel should possess.

All guardians were less susceptible to the powers of dreamphasers, since they normally went to another realm altogether to retire. And fellow guardians usually protected their own. So outside of a physical fight, Buddy deemed he could argue with Riff at leisure without likely retribution.

"As we were traveling down the hall, we heard you mention an Earth girl," Inferno remarked. "What happened, Dominick? Did you travel into someone's nightmare again?"

"The last one from Earth was certainly a beaut," Buddy chimed in with a laugh. "Being chased by an army wielding swords in an otherwise tranquil surrounding of green fields could make anyone want to steer clear of dreams."

Dominick said nothing, but betrayed a grimace. No, he certainly hadn't forgotten that particular trip. What really amazed him was how imaginative the people of Earth could be as far as creating ideas for such movies and books. Imagination, of course, was most revered by the dreamphasers, since without it, dreams would be humdrum.

Of course, there was nothing humdrum about being chased by a nightmare of an army. That was a little ***too*** much imagination for comfort in the dream-state, best kept to a movie screen.

"No, no," said Riff, shaking his head. "This doesn't

sound like it was from a nightmare. It sounds more like he got shot down in his latest attempt to win a female." The others turned to Dominick with curiosity.

He groaned in irritation. There was nothing—absolutely ***nothing***—more annoying in the universe than his smart-mouthed elder brother.

"It's no big deal," he told them, glaring at Riff. "I met a distressed female who was dreaming of a ball scenario dated back a century or so on her world. She was overwrought regarding someone who jilted her, so she turned to me for comfort." Riff gave a low whistle. "Not ***that*** kind, you idiot!" he snarled.

"If that's true, then why were you swearing like a hurricane just a few minutes ago? Were you interrupted from something ***important***?"

Dominick shut his eyes and sighed, his irritation dissipating somewhat as his memory faded back to his last moments with Julianna. Her sweet kisses, her laughter, the touch of her gentle hands... At least before those hands suddenly gripped him in fear of their impending separation. He could still hear her calling out his name.

His meeting Julianna somehow seemed like a device of Fate, he decided, thinking back to the first time he'd seen her a few months ago. He remembered how she'd been dreaming of a beach scene, galloping along on horseback, when he'd drifted into her dream that night. He'd been searching for a pretty dream companion to spend a pleasant evening with, astral traveling through multiple towns before he found her. Not so much travel compared to his coming from the other side of the sun!

When he'd first met her on the beach, his intentions were the same as always. A quick courting, followed by a few stolen kisses, and then... well, what many times followed. During their kiss, he'd been thinking that perhaps he'd enjoy this encounter more than others he'd known.

Just before she'd nearly crushed his foot beneath her heel.

This was one incident he certainly hadn't mentioned to Riff, but despite his surface irritation at the time, the dream had lingered in his mind ever since. Hence, he began searching for her again as of a week ago. Much as he'd thought at the time, who ***was*** this spirited woman to get away with wounding his pride?

A woman who'd succeeded in erasing his irritation last night, when he finally found her again.

Was it her tears that drew out another side to him? Or was it her personality, which never lacked for being unique in her own way? Whichever, there was no denying the sparks between them were mutual by the way they'd clung to each other in their most powerful embrace.

Just before they were suddenly interrupted by the annoying disturbance of morning on her world.

Earth! he thought, glowering.

If only she'd been here on Chavernos with him in reality, ***then*** their sparks wouldn't have been forcibly extinguished so soon.

"I don't know what might have happened," he lied, feeling justified in this case since it really was none of Riff's business. "She woke up too soon for me to tell."

Having a more sensitive nature, Inferno picked up on his friend's hidden disappointment, voicing a suggestion. "If that's all it is, why don't you go back to find her?" Dominick's gaze snapped up to face him with uncertainty.

"Go back?"

In all these years, that was the first time one of his friends ever suggested the notion.

"Sure," continued Inferno. "You told us that you've contacted dreamers more than once before."

Not often, but yes he had, he admitted privately, obviously including last night although the others didn't know that. He'd only done that regarding a few of his favorite paramours, but he'd said good-bye to the last of them years ago. Finding Julianna again hadn't been easy in itself, although determination was one of his more prominent qualities.

Having been to her house twice now, and thankfully having an excellent memory, he knew he could locate Julianna easily should he wish to be with her again, but a part of him was hesitant. If all she'd spoken of was true, then Roger and the others she'd known had hurt her badly emotionally. Given this fact, Dominick wasn't eager to return to perhaps accidentally hurt her in her sleep as well. She'd dealt with enough.

Yet at the same time, he couldn't deny that a part of him yearned to continue where they'd left off. He wanted to kiss her again, to hold her, and to feel their hearts beat as one. To brush away her tears, and see her come to life again in his arms. Just remembering last night rekindled the warm desire of deepening blue in his eyes.

Eyes that blinked rapidly to erase the sensation, as he heard Riff's mocking laughter.

"It would seem my little brother's suddenly lost his touch. Or is it the girl herself who displeased you?"

Dominick's jaw tightened, setting his strong determination once more, with a forced smile. "Neither, I assure you. And for your information, I fully intend to see Julianna Sherborne again. Tonight, if possible. After that, we'll see who's laughing, brother."

Riff took undisguised amusement from his words as he finally left, followed by Buddy, but Inferno remained behind, his expression concerned.

"I didn't suggest it as a challenge, Dom. I meant it genuinely, since you do seem to care."

His friend nodded. "At times like this, you're more of a

brother to me than he is. But rest assured, my wanting to see her again really doesn't have anything to do with Riff. I do care about her."

More than I initially thought, he mused privately.

*****

The woman glancing in the full-length mirror turned this way and that, making sure every fold of her new gown was correctly draped over her slim figure. The dress was a pale blue, drawing out the similar color of her eyes. Every strand of her flowing golden hair was firmly in place. She was proud that she'd never needed to use her illusion magic to enhance her beauty, but sometimes it made it necessary to use her force-field ability against persistent suitors.

"You look like an absolute angel," her mother confirmed.

Turning with a smile, Sionne looked past her ever-doting parent to find someone else appraising her similarly. "I'm quite sure my grandson will think so as well," said the man beside her, kissing the younger woman's hand.

"Maybe," she sighed, "but I doubt he'll be as agreeable with the prospect of marriage."

"He'll accept," assured her mother, her eyebrows knitting together. "After all, with his status, he can't very well expect to remain a bachelor forever. And who better than a beauty like you to stay by his side always?"

Sionne blushed becomingly, more out of her breeding than an innocent gesture. Most men, even worldly ones like Chaos, often mistook this as genuine.

"I heartily agree," he said, just before hearing a voice call out from downstairs. "Ah, that sounds like the prospective groom himself. If you'll excuse me, ladies." Both nodded as Chaos strode down the hall, just before Sionne's mother eyed her daughter speculatively.

"I'm afraid he'll take a bit more charming than his

grandfather," she murmured. "You'd best use all your charms to advantage, my girl."

Sionne fluttered her lashes once. "Why, Mother, I think you underestimate my intelligence. Why else would I choose such a low-cut gown?" Nodding once in approval, the older woman departed.

"Surface beauty only goes so far, sister," said another voice, highly similar to her own. Not surprising, since it came from Sionne's twin Sireni. "But a man like Dominick Westbrooke will want far more than a pretty face. He'll desire a willing woman to warm his nights, which you my dear sister, are not."

Her words struck an expected minor chord from Sionne, for unlike her sister, she had a strong dislike for physical closeness, repulsed even by kisses, and had no intention of giving up her virtue lightly. Fortunately, intimacy was required but once to consummate a marriage. After that, she had every intention of keeping things in name only with her future husband.

"Dominick doesn't need to know that," Sionne retorted. "And ***you*** aren't going to tell him, unless you want me to let it drop that you're having an affair with his worst enemy."

Sireni's cheek twitched, but she maintained her usual catlike smile. "Touché, Sionne," she murmured, folding her arms. "And may I ask how you intend to keep your husband at bay with forced celibacy?"

Sionne's smile rivaled her own. "Very simple, dear sister. I shall suddenly contract a migraine every night." Laughing at her own cleverness, she waltzed out, ignoring Sireni's skeptical expression.

"Sir, I'm sure he'll be down presently," said the palace butler, trying desperately to maintain decorum.

A pointless battle with the Westbrooke brothers.

"Grandfather!" Dominick shouted again.

"Blazes, boy, you don't have to crumble the castle walls

with your bellowing!" Chaos barked back from the staircase.

"***Yes, you rival our kind when you do that,***" chuckled a deeper voice, as a silver dragon emerged from another room, earning the attention of both. Fortunately, the wise Chaolyn had altered his size to fit more comfortably in the palace without bumping into furniture, although he knew Chaos wished he'd revert to his human form altogether when indoors.

Calming slightly, Dominick faced him apologetically. "I'm sorry for that, Chaolyn, but I received an urgent message to come, and I didn't want to waste any unnecessary time."

"***Humans can't help that with their limited lifespans, but I understand, my young friend,***" the dragon replied. When the elder man came downstairs, eyeing him questioningly, he gestured a taloned claw forward. "***After our talk earlier, I'd hope you wouldn't mind my merely listening in, my friend.***"

"As you will," sighed Chaos.

Dominick's expression became grim as he strode towards his grandfather. "I got here as soon as I could. Don't tell me. The pyromasters are at it again, right?"

Chaos's green eyes widened, before he gave a short laugh. "Not quite. If that was the case, Chaolyn and I could have handled it." Ignoring his grandson's bemused look, he shook his head. "No, Dominick, this involves a more personal issue, regarding these foolish dream-state affairs of yours."

Thinking of Julianna, Dominick frowned. "Riff certainly doesn't waste time in spreading lies about me," he said icily. "Look, Grandfather, contrary to what he may have told you, I've been steering clear of female dreamers for the past several months. But as to the one Riff may have mentioned..."

"I might have known," sighed Chaos. "Dominick, it's time you stop chasing dream women, and settle down with one woman of our world. In other words, it's high time you married."

Chaolyn's ears perked up at that, while Dominick began

to laugh. "You've been saying that for years now. You hardly needed to drag me here for that."

"***Chaos,***" Chaolyn interjected softly, sensing his friend's thoughts. "***This might not be the best way to...***"

"I've received your counsel earlier, and you agreed to listen only. Now let me finish," Chaos replied, shooting him a sharp look before returning his gaze to Dominick. "There's more," he continued solemnly. "I've decided that if I wait for you to find someone, you'll end up like your excuse-ridden brother, and I'll never see any great-grandchildren. Thus, I've taken the liberty of making the decision for you."

Dominick's eyes narrowed suspiciously. "And what's that supposed to mean?"

Footsteps on the stairs answered him as Sionne appeared, resplendent in her new gown. "Dominick," she said lightly. "It's so good to see you." Turning to Chaos, she flashed him a dazzling smile. "Am I interrupting anything?"

"Your timing is impeccable, my dear," he replied, taking her hand as she reached the bottom step, before turning to his bemused grandson. "Sionne's been with us for many years, and has become quite a beauty, has she not?" At the younger man's reluctance to answer, he frowned, nudging his arm.

"Yes, she is that," Dominick said finally.

"Now you're being reasonable," murmured Chaos, beaming moments later. "Which brings me to the point. You're no strangers, and have gotten along well over the years."

***Tolerated** each other is more accurate*, Dominick thought.

"Thus, I've decided your betrothal will be announced today, and your wedding will take place in a few weeks."

Chaolyn gave a low funereal whistle, to Chaos's chagrin.

Dominick's mouth dropped open, anger filling his eyes. "You've ***decided*** this?" he hissed, erasing the pleased looks from the human pair. "Grandfather, if you want to find Sionne a husband, then I'm all for it. But as far as I'm concerned, I have no intention of being the shackled groom. Now if you'll excuse me, I have a life to resume."

As he strode towards the door, Chaos began shouting after him. "Damn it all, Dominick, I won't have you ignore me this time! I'm announcing your betrothal, and that's final!"

Turning at the last minute, while resting his hand on the door handle, Dominick shook his head. "You can announce what you like, but the humiliation will be on your head later when your words are proven false. And as for this obsession with great-grandchildren of yours, let me assure you that a forced marriage won't bring them any sooner."

Slamming the door behind him as he exited, his grandfather's face turned purple with rage. "Blasted impertinent boy!" he growled.

"***You gave him little choice in the matter, old friend,***" Chaolyn said quietly.

Not replying, Chaos abruptly remembered Sionne. "I apologize for my grandson's rudeness," he told her. "Take heart, child. He'll come around in time."

"I know," she replied softly, a few tears forming in her eyes. "I just wish it was sooner than later."

"***More likely when the netherworld freezes,***" murmured Chaolyn, earning a glare from Chaos before exiting the room.

Eyes narrowing with determination, the elder man squeezed Sionne's hand comfortingly. "Never fear. I may not be able to do anything about his brother, but one way or another, I intend to see Dominick married as soon as possible. And once I've set my mind to something, it's as good as done."

She smiled knowingly through her craftily conjured tears. Chaos prided himself on keeping his word.

Soon, Dominick would be hers.

*****

Dominick had passed the well-tended castle gardens and

approached the outer gate, still seething at his grandfather's bullheadedness. Not the first time he'd tried to marry him off, but the elder man was becoming more adamant, bringing Sionne into the matter. Knowing her scheming nature all too well, demonstrated over the years with her other suitors although she thought him ignorant—let alone her narcissistic manner—he'd sooner disappear amongst the dragons and live peacefully as a hermit than be forced to marry her.

Approaching the gate guardians who'd been talking, they saw him and immediately saluted. Smiling, he waved his hand. "At ease, guys, he's still in the castle." The pair relaxed, knowing Dominick was less interested in formalities than the others. "Right now, I just want to get as far from here as possible."

"***Allow me to assist,***" a voice called out, as he glided to a halt beside him.

"Chaolyn, you don't want to get in the middle of this."

"***Exactly. So let's get out of here.***"

Smiling at the knowing look of mischief in the dragon's eyes, Dominick climbed up, and the pair took to the skies.

As the clouds soared by, the wind cooling Dominick's brow, he did start to feel his anger ease. Chaolyn was as wise at reading him as he was with his grandfather.

"***Feel better?***" the dragon inquired.

"You know I do. But I doubt Chaos will. After all, he is your *keizha benirrai.*"

The dragon smiled at the ancient Chavernian term for 'soul's friend,' long used by dragons regarding their oaths of friendship with specific humans or elves. Chaos had been his *keizha benirrai* for many years, able to communicate privately telepathically when needed, and to sense when the other needed help. Typically to represent a one-to-one friendship, but occasionally regarding a small group, it was a term long respected by all races and revered by the recipients.

"***Soul friends are not obligated to agree, and Chaos would never expect it of me.***"

"You're lucky then. At least he respects your opinion."

The rumbling laugh that shook the dragon nearly caused Dominick to lose his grip. Realizing this, Chaolyn quickly composed himself, but there was still mirth in his voice when he spoke. "***I've been needing a good laugh today. Thank you. But believe me, Chaos is as stubborn with me as with you, as has been proven by as many of your years. It's just his way.***"

"I'm not marrying someone just because he has visions of great-grandchildren in his head. The only way he's getting those from me is if I find a woman to love."

"***Might this Julianna be a possibility?***"

Dominick's eyes narrowed. "Where did you hear ***that***, as if I didn't know?"

"***Actually, I was lounging in the main hall, when I overheard Riff and Buddy speaking of it as they passed through to the kitchen earlier. I didn't have a chance to ask you about it before Chaos went off on his tirade. But from what little I did hear, Riff sounded frustrated you kept much to yourself.***"

"My brother doesn't need to know every detail of my personal life. The time I spend with Julianna is none of his business."

"***May I inquire if you're planning on meeting with the lady again?***"

Dominick's irritated expression softened. "Inferno asked the same thing, suggesting it. Even if he hadn't though, I already knew I wanted to see her again."

"***Then what's stopping you?***" At his ensuing silence, Chaolyn smiled. "***There's a difference in your tone of voice. You really like this one.***"

Knowing without asking that Chaolyn would keep a confidence between them, Dominick nodded. "Yes, I do.

Which is why I don't want my family interfering. Chaos would have a fit if he knew she was from Earth, and Chavernos knows I trust Riff even less."

"***Ah… so she's an Earth maiden. Now the rest makes sense. Well, don't worry. I'll say nothing to any of them, though I agree you should be mindful of your brother and say no more to him especially.***" The dragon smiled again. "***Is she very pretty?***"

"That and more. She has a beautiful spirit to match. Someone had made her unhappy on her world, but after we spent some time together, she seemed much happier. As a matter of fact, she seemed happy to be with me even before we got into that."

"***Then your friend is right. You should visit her again, and see if she feels the same.***" His tone abruptly became fatherly, almost rivaling Chaos's. "***Now remember, keep your intentions honorable.***"

"Chaolyn, you know me better than to have to tell me…" Sensing a small, teasing laugh from the dragon, he hugged him. Of course he did.

"***She's a more fortunate lady than she believes.***"

*****

Lost Limbo. A meeting place that catered to all walks of life on Barokka. Once a tiny pub, it had flourished by the constant patronage of dreamphasers, shifters, pyromasters, guardians, and other empowered beings, and thus had not only been remodeled to a much larger establishment, but it also had won its share of acclaim. Here, a group of friends met frequently, consisting of the guys—Riff, Buddy, Inferno, and Dominick, and the gals—Kiri, Jarissa, and Psych.

Buddy and Inferno were mulling over the earlier scene between the two brothers, hoping the women wouldn't suddenly show up to interrupt them.

"Did you overhear anything else?" asked Inferno.

Buddy shook his head. "Only what you did. She's from Earth, and Dom's mad as blazes over Riff's jibes."

Earth, he mused. So far away from Chavernos—although not as far as a dreamphaser was concerned—it was elsewhere in the solar system, on the other side of the sun from them. No short distance there! Buddy couldn't help but be impressed at how often Dominick traveled there, even though he and Inferno didn't always agree with the purpose of said visits.

But then again, Dominick had never known a steady girlfriend for any length of time, either in the dream-state or the reality of Chavernos. In fact, Buddy sometimes wondered if he was as content with his single status as he claimed, or if he secretly envied the relationships of his friends. Even Riff and Kiri saw each other from time to time, depending on where their moods were at.

Inferno and Psych were the only pair who were an official couple, and they often mediated the interactions of the others. Especially with Riff and Kiri, who at times would bait each other into arguments, although they certainly displayed jealousy when one or the other seemed to be looking elsewhere. And as for Buddy himself, he more than had his hands full with the unpredictable Jarissa. A situation that might never see a solution, considering he was a guardian angel, and she was a guardian devil.

And considering the fact that half the time they were at each other's throats.

Conjuring her image in his mind, Buddy couldn't help smiling. Every guardian devil of Barokka, and a great many guardian angels, sought the curly-haired Jarissa as well. Her long-lashed brown eyes teased her suitors mercilessly, as any female guardian devil would, and she'd stated hundreds of times that she'd had boyfriends aplenty over the past several years.

However, Buddy knew it to be more an act than anything else. Proven once, when he demanded the truth from a so-called 'lover' of hers. The hapless guardian confessed that there'd been nothing romantic between them, despite the surface gossip. Buddy then swore him to secrecy, and allowed Jarissa to continue believing him fooled until she tired of it.

Only one of many games between them over the years.

Granted, she was a beauty, clever, and mischievous as any guardian devil of her breed, her curly hair sometimes obscuring her horns. But she couldn't deny being part angel as well, thanks to her wings, a gift from her mother's parentage. Perhaps that accounted for her inner vulnerability that she tried to hide, unlike the more wanton females of her type. It was Buddy's knowledge of her hidden innocence that brought on the protective angel side to him, and he was determined to keep the local devils away from her.

Of course, she'd provoked ***his*** devil side often enough with her flirtations.

***Too** often!* he decided, knowing that there were complete guardian angels that'd wanted to cast aside their halos forever for Jarissa's attentions. He was no different, except he was close friends with her, which was better than the rest could say.

Theirs was a relationship of literal heaven and hell, but to a half-and-half guardian like Buddy—and the similar situation of Jarissa—they truly seemed meant for one another.

Or at least meant for Bedlam.

His dreamlike stare was enhanced when he saw the three familiar females enter Lost Limbo. Kiri pointed towards their table instantly, but Buddy didn't notice. He was too busy staring at the brown-haired guardian devil who was heading straight for him, an odd expression in her eyes. Her warm smile caused him to discount her gaze... moments before she smacked him stingingly in the face.

Good-bye, dreams!

"What the hell was that for?" he demanded as he stood.

Jarissa stared up at him with undisguised fury that bore no hint of fear. A common trait of female guardian devils.

"You men are all alike!" she exclaimed, pounding him on the chest once with her fist. "Kiri just visited Riff, and her mind reading ability tapped into your conversation with Dominick earlier. You men seem to think that we women are here solely as the targets of your conquests. Well, think again, buster!"

Right now, he could only think that Kiri's powers helped her to eavesdrop way too much.

"It wasn't ***my*** idea!" he protested. "Why don't you vent your anger on Riff and Dominick where it belongs?"

"And you call yourself a guardian angel!" she hissed mockingly. "Yet you'll stand by while a poor girl in a fragile emotional state is seduced by the petty whims of your ***friend!***"

"Guardians aren't dreamphasers, Jarissa. Even if you told me to interfere, I couldn't. Dammit, you know that!"

Yes, she knew that, but it still didn't sit very well with her. "You could talk him out of it," she suggested, her quiet tone barely concealing her anger. "A guardian's power of suggestion can be of some use with dreamphasers."

"Maybe with some, but Dom's will's too strong, and I really don't want to get involved." He turned away to walk over to the window, hoping that would end this discussion, but the persistent Jarissa followed him.

"I see," she said, spreading her hands defeatedly. "You know, Buddy, maybe you're right. After all, it is just a dream to the girl, and that certainly excuses all else. And I know you'd be just as morally upstanding if I told you that a dreamphaser had shown up in ***my*** dreams recently."

Things went from quiet to chaos in less than five seconds.

"***What?***" he shouted, whipping about to face her, while earning the attention of everyone else in Lost Limbo as well.

Jarissa casually ran a finger against the edge of a table,

nodding with a serious expression. "Given your most ***understanding*** nature, I suppose you'd have absolutely no qualms over my telling you that I was pursued by a dreamphaser more than once, and that he finally succeeded in ravishing me. After all, it was ***just*** a dream, and we all know how you feel about... Ouch!"

Having grabbed her shoulders with a steel grip, Buddy shook her hard. "Who did this?" he demanded loudly. At her silence, he prompted her with a shake. "***Who?***"

"Buddy, you're hurting me!" she protested.

"Much less than the pain I'll inflict on whoever the bastard is that's responsible for this!" he swore. Jarissa felt a rare wave of fear sweep through her as she stared into her angry companion's eyes. No longer the friendly blue, they seemed darkened beyond recognition now, more characteristic to a guardian devil. "If you don't know his name, give me a description to go by. Just tell me what you know, Jarissa!"

"Nothing, nothing!" she blurted out, shaking her head. "Buddy, I was just trying to prove a point, that's all."

"Really now?" he sneered. "Judging by your character, I tend to doubt that. Now for the last time, who are you protecting?"

"No one, I swear! I..."

"***BUDDY, LET HER GO, OR ELSE!***" a loud voice shrieked, nearly causing him to release Jarissa if only to cover his ears. Several other patrons did reach for their ears, causing several mugs to drop and shatter.

While he merely gritted his teeth against the pain from the ear-piercing shout, many others in Lost Limbo loudly protested the usage of Psych's deafening ability. When she got angry, there was no one with a louder voice, and since she and Jarissa were so close-knit, Buddy knew better than to push the issue.

"Mind your own business!" Psych called out in a more

normal shout, "or I'll shatter the rest of your beer mugs for you!" The grumbling continued, but more quietly. "Sorry, Zantarl," she told the barkeep. He waved a hand in dismissal, using his own ability to raise the shattered glasses and restore them whole again. The patrons affected then brought their repaired mugs over for refills, including several newcomers who were surprised by Zantarl's ability.

"She's telling the truth, you dummy," supplied Kiri, folding her arms. "She only said what she did to make you understand the Earth girl's plight. You won't lend a hand in her case, but you don't seem to like the idea of a dreamphaser chasing after Jarissa, do you?"

Glaring at her once before turning back to his silent companion, Buddy squeezed her arms tighter, his anger still close to the surface. In a low voice, he said warningly, "If you ever, ***ever***, throw a lie like that at me again, I'll send you gift-wrapped to an appropriate dreamphaser myself!"

"Don't bother," she murmured coldly, exiting in a literal flash as she vanished.

A singeing flash which left burn marks on Buddy's hands.

Gasping once at the sharp pain, while waving his hands quickly to cool them, Buddy angrily heard murmuring and laughter from the attentive crowd around him. *Leave it to Jarissa to exit with a bang!* his thoughts mocked him. Striding back to his table, he rubbed his sore hands, without giving the slightest glance to the two remaining females.

"If that crazy she-devil thinks I'm going to interfere with a friend's affairs, then she's got less of a brain beneath those curls than any of her would-be suitors know," he told Inferno. "I also have more faith in Dom than to believe he'd take advantage of a woman, dream-state or no."

"A typically male response," hissed Kiri. "But it's the women who pay the consequences for your actions, angel-boy."

"Now just a second," Inferno broke in. "Aren't you forgetting that we're talking about Dominick? I don't argue that some dreamphasers might be as you say, but I agree with Buddy that Dominick is ***not*** the type to force his attention on this woman or any other."

For a few moments, Kiri's expression softened. Of the two brothers, she knew Dominick did seem to have a deeper sense of caring when it came to another's feelings. Something she wished would rub off on Riff now and then, although privately she was certain he wouldn't force his attention on women either. Even knowing this though, the situation didn't seem right.

"Maybe there's a mutual attraction there that we don't know about," he continued.

"Sure, if someone spilled glue over them," murmured Kiri, tossing her reddish-gold curls angrily.

Buddy turned to her with a forced smile. Moments afterwards, Kiri gave a loud gasp of outrage. Slapping him in the face, she stormed out.

Psych stood in confusion, glancing after her departed friend. Admittedly, Kiri had a chip on her shoulder regarding men, no doubt built with assistance from Riff over the years, but she had a good heart. She just didn't want to see someone hurt, emotionally or otherwise.

Given Kiri's ability to read people's minds, Psych grasped the obvious, turning to Buddy accusingly. "All right, angel-boy, just what were you thinking that caused that?" she demanded.

"Merely an added thought to her glue comment," he replied nonchalantly.

"Which was?"

He shrugged. "Simply that glue's the only way she'd ever attract anyone willingly, much less the attentions of the most desperate dreamphaser."

Psych slapped him too.

"Beast!" she hissed, following in her friend's footsteps.

Maintaining somber expressions, it was only when the door slammed that Buddy and Inferno released their laughter. Picking up their glasses, they held them aloft cheerfully.

"A toast to the wiles of unpredictable women," said Inferno.

"And a toast for bravery to good ol' Dominick. If this Earth maiden of his is anything like Barokka's females, then he may be in more danger than she is!"

Laughing boisterously, they clinked glasses.

*****

The Earth maiden in question might not be in danger right now, but she was certainly agitated.

Julianna paced the floor nervously as she struggled to keep awake. Glancing at the clock, she saw that it was past two in the morning, yet the last intention on her mind was of sleeping. Last night's dream had haunted her endlessly with its disturbing vividness, as if it had really happened. And as it had been on her mind all day, she was worried she'd wind up back with Dominick again.

Not that the dream last night had been unpleasant. Far from it.

But it had been all too ***real***.

Why, if she hadn't woken up when she did... well, even if it ***was*** just a dream, she found it disturbing!

Her feet soon tired from her pacing though, and rather than wear out the floor, Julianna reluctantly sat down on her bed to read a book instead. Maybe she could erase thoughts of Dominick with a good science-fiction novel, she thought hopefully, picking up the first one to catch her eye, 'Warp Zone of Doom'.

Quite an appropriate title lately.

The idea seemed to work, because after reading several

pages, all she could think of was futuristic people on space ships, instead of the nineteenth century characters of a romance novel. No more thoughts of hall-of-mirrors ballrooms, no more fancy ball gowns, and no more Dominick. She yawned once as she flipped through a few more pages, just before sleep began to overtake her. Realizing this, she reached out to grope for the light switch. With a quick flip, the room was blanketed in darkness, and she leaned back with a contented sigh.

Moments later, a curiosity broke into her tired state.

Her eyes drifted half-open upon sensing light upon their closed lids, and she struggled to see ahead. Her eyes weren't adjusted to the dark yet, but she could see the streetlights from outside through the edges of her window curtains. *Nothing unusual there*, she thought. *No doubt my imagination working overtime again.*

Relaxed as Julianna was, she soon gave it no further thought, turning to her side while her eyes fluttered shut again.

She was totally oblivious when a string of countless, tiny star-like lights filled the room moments later. Lights which circled the room, just before forming the silvery outline of a certain dreamphaser.

Feeling for a moment as if he was in fact truly part of her world, Dominick's ghostly astral form cast a shimmering glow on the peaceful expression on Julianna's face, only enhancing her beauty. He couldn't help smiling, as she looked so innocent while quietly lost in slumber. Despite the knowledge that there weren't many hours left in which he could be with her again, Dominick found himself reluctant to abandon this moment where he could gaze upon her freely without retribution.

The silvery light framed her face, much like moonlight, as he moved to stand beside her. Glancing down at her with longing, he found himself wishing that he had the ability to become tangible here, if only for a moment, so he might touch her cheek just once in reality.

He sighed heavily, knowing his powers could never allow him to do that.

Funny how a search two months ago had brought him to this.

Back then, he'd been traveling about this town in his astral form, floating through each house's walls as if they were made of mist. He'd nearly brushed through Julianna's room without a second thought too, but even on that first night, he'd found her crying herself to sleep.

Oddly moved by her tears, he floated closer. She was pretty, he'd decided instantly, looking all of a child for how small and fragile she'd seemed. Yet there was no mistaking that the pleasant curves outlined by the blankets surrounding her were those of an attractive woman, not a child. Her sadness touched a chord in him, setting his determination to try and bring a smile to this dreaming child-woman of sorts.

Thus he'd met her that night in a dream he'd engineered to comfort her.

He hadn't counted on the most strong-willed young woman behind those tears.

Upon returning months later, he was surprised to find her much as he'd left her before, still unhappy, and crying herself to sleep again.

Appearing in one of the only visible forms he could while the other dreamer was awake, he'd remained close by her window, no doubt seeming like a star to the unaware woman, despite his much closer proximity. He'd been startled when she gasped, and even more when she wished aloud to see the Dominick she'd dreamed of before.

She still thinks of me? he'd mused, oddly pleased.

And then she seemed to stare directly at him, mentioning his name again. As if she'd known that he wasn't a star at all, although that was surely impossible.

When she'd returned to her bed, he dimmed his light so

she couldn't see him, and followed her to glance at the book she was reading. The people on the cover dressed differently than what he'd seen of her world lately, but if the history lessons he'd overheard on Earth were of any consequence, this story took place in another era. Unseen, he moved in back of her to read what she did, grinning at the rather interesting segment she was fascinated by. So she liked romance, did she? Well, perhaps he should oblige her then.

Hence followed their meeting in her dream.

He'd been interested to find more than just beauty or passion in her. She was also intelligent and amusing when she'd overcome her initial hesitancy towards a stranger. And then when she told him of Roger, he'd found yet another side to her. One that seemed to crave comforting as he'd once noticed before.

Far be it from Dominick to resist lending his own assistance there!

Tonight, he noticed her science fiction novel with its spaceship on the cover, wondering briefly if Earth might one day use one to find Chavernos. Highly unlikely, due to its mist obscured appearance and its parallel position on the other side of the sun. Yet if it ***could*** be made possible... perhaps he might one day receive the chance of meeting Julianna while they were both awake.

But for the time being, a dream rendezvous would have to suffice. *Science fiction scenes*, his mind thought quickly. Perhaps Julianna would prefer that background instead this time, nodding once to the idea.

In the next moment, his astral form vanished and his dreamphasing ability took over.

Chapter Four

Julianna's boots echoed as she walked across the spaceship floor to the nearby viewing deck. As before, she had no knowledge of how she'd gotten here, but it felt real enough. This time she was garbed in a skintight suit made of a shiny white material, with green and blue stripes across the shoulders. The outfit was also adorned with a gold belt. Her feet were encased in black boots, which reached halfway to her knees and fit against her like a second skin.

Hearing laughter, she backed closer to the observation port. A small group approached, a few women and a few men, wearing similar outfits. All of them passed by her obliviously, with the exception of one man who turned to smile at her. His eyes were a familiar striking blue. Slowly remembering the evening before, confusion surfaced.

Before she could react, he'd turned the corner with the others.

Deciding to follow, she'd only gotten a few steps when her hand brushed against something cold, startling her. Looking down, she saw it was a silver gun attached to her belt.

Removing the weapon swiftly to examine it, she ran shaky fingers over its metal surface. Several blinking red lights upon it only unnerved her further. She'd never seen anything like ***this*** before on Earth. And for that matter, if she was in space, just where ***was*** Earth? Was this ship hovering above it, or was it halfway across the galaxy?

With her luck, probably the second.

She gasped sharply as warm hands eased the gun from her shaking grasp.

"Careful, my lady," came a familiar gentle voice. "You don't want to accidentally blast a hole in the wall and send us hurtling into the vacuum of space, do you?"

Julianna looked up in shock. "You!" she exclaimed.

The man grinned back at her. He was dressed similarly, except that his outfit catered to his male form instead. And while she was certainly surprised to find him here, she couldn't help but notice how well the suit fit him.

Still, she was unnerved by this strange coincidence. Could this be the same Dominick that she'd met the day before?

Sensing her confusion, the man spread his hands. "Aren't you glad to see me, Julianna?" he asked, his voice expressing a touch of sadness.

"You know me?" she inquired cautiously.

He could only laugh. By Chaos, how long would it take her to catch on to the repeated coincidences of their meetings, and realize that he was the same person returning each night?

Still, he was a dreamphaser and used to such things.

His fair companion was not.

"Of course I know you," he replied patiently. "I'm Dominick Westbrooke, remember? We met at a fancy ball yesterday, wherein some mirrored rooms you pursued me most successfully."

"I thought we agreed not to mention that again!" she snapped, even as she put her hand to her mouth in renewed surprise. The realization was clear. This was the same Dominick.

"Ah, I must have forgotten," he said quietly, strangely subdued. "I'm sorry, my lady. I won't trouble you again."

Julianna stared after him in disbelief.

He was just ***leaving*** without another word?

For a moment, she remained where she stood as he continued down the unfamiliar corridor, disappearing from view. *Surely he'll change his mind and come back*, she thought. But he didn't. And here she was, stuck on a strange spaceship, heaven only knew where in space, all alone.

She couldn't run fast enough to catch up with her departed companion, although she assured herself she was only doing so because there was safety in numbers. As she rounded the corner, she kept going until a voice suddenly halted her from behind.

"Looking for me?"

Gasping for breath, she turned to see Dominick staring at her knowingly with a grin, arms folded. Oh, the nerve of him! Expecting her to come running after him, as he undoubtedly knew she would. If she weren't stuck in the middle of nowhere, she'd certainly burst that bubble of his and continue running as far away from him as she could get!

"Only because I was curious as to why we're here," she assured him. "Care to enlighten me?"

"Why we're here in space?" he asked. "Or why we're together again?"

"Both."

Dominick smiled, unwilling to give away the tricks of his trade so easily. "As to the space issue, it must have to do with the local alien threats to the galaxy. As to why we're both here, I can only assume Fate conspired to bring us together."

"Hmmm, remind me to have a long talk with Fate when I get back home to Earth," she murmured. "Or should I say a long ***argument*** over messing around with a person's life?"

"Don't look at me," he laughed, gesturing innocence. "I'm sure I know as much as you do as to why we're here. Too many sci-fi novels I suppose."

Julianna quirked one eyebrow at that. Sci-fi novels... for some reason that triggered a chord. But what would they have to do with why she was suddenly on a spaceship now, let alone stuck with this most infuriating man?

"Cheer up," he said brightly. "At least you're not alone

anymore."

"Except for you," she retorted. "I'm not so sure that's much safer. I'd probably be better off captured by aliens." Her words trailed off as she walked to sit beside the observation port to gaze at the stars.

An apt choice of words, thought Dominick, *considering that we **are** both aliens from different worlds.* Although of course she didn't know of his real identity on Chavernos. As to the capturing part, he might not mind doing so with this particular auburn-haired alien!

With her attention distracted, he was free to appraise her new attire, and it was a change he certainly approved of. If the gown she'd worn yesterday enhanced her surface beauty, this new spacesuit she wore emphasized what the gown had hidden. Presenting a problem all its own, since the damned outfit left relatively nothing to the imagination as far as her shapely body was concerned. One he'd like to be holding right now, and kissing, and caressing, and…

Shaking his head as he remembered Chaolyn's words, Dominick moved to sit beside her. "Julianna, I didn't follow you here to upset you. I merely wanted the opportunity to get to know you better."

Her warm brown eyes looked up at that. "Why?"

"Why?" he exclaimed. "Why not? You're a beautiful, intriguing woman who haunts my waking hours. I couldn't stop thinking about you all day today."

Her brow wrinkled, and she was about to ask where he'd been earlier.

"You there!" boomed an unfamiliar voice, earning the attention of both instantly.

A man walked up, followed by a few others, all dressed in similar attire to their own, albeit with different colored stripes, no doubt to signify rank or job assignments. The one who'd spoken was tall, apparently in charge, and wore an outfit with unique symbols along with corresponding black and silver stripes.

"What are you doing just sitting there?" he demanded. "You should be at your posts. We need all hands to help speed our departure to get as far away from the Warp Zone as possible."

For some strange reason, the words sounded familiar, yet Julianna couldn't place them. "What's the Warp Zone?"

The man sighed. "A place our scientists should never have felt the need to study, since now we're being pulled towards it."

"As in a black hole?" inquired Dominick.

"Seemingly yes, but our scientists don't believe that's what it is. ***They*** feel the Warp Zone is a safe conduit to another location, akin to bypassing light years in a quick jump. But their information is all theoretical, and they didn't count on it having a similar gravitational pull to a black hole or a planet. They were going to ***study*** it first." The last he sneered.

"Scientific leaps cannot be made without such attempts," said a small voice, capturing the attention of all. He was a man slighter of build, holding a foreign device.

"No offense, Landers, but this from someone who's convinced himself he's found a way to deal with the Rengar. Last I checked, those weapon prototypes of yours still shoot sparks more than doing anything useful."

"Scoff if you must, Kyron, but one day you'll see just how useful these weapons are."

The leader clearly wasn't impressed, returning his attention to Dominick and Julianna. "As I was saying, if that wasn't enough, we've been pulled into a territory that's under the control of the Rengar."

"And who are the Rengar?" asked Julianna.

Kyron shook his head with a forced laugh. "A group of space renegades whose only goal is to capture space crafts, enslave crewmen, and destroy anything they don't deem useful to their cause. How have you gotten this far into the fleet without at least being briefed on them?"

"She was transferred from a different system," Dominick supplied, which surprisingly enough mollified the man.

"In any case, our monitors have just located one of their ships in our vicinity. You'd best get to your posts, and Landers, you have other duties to attend to."

The other man nodded reluctantly, walking away, while the leader continued down the hall with his group.

Julianna was about to follow, but Dominick's hand on her arm stopped her. "What are you doing?" she asked.

"The question is, what are ***you*** doing? You're no more familiar with the workings of this ship than I am." She couldn't argue that, having no knowledge of how she got here to begin with. "So what are we waiting for? Let's explore this place."

Gesturing towards another branch of the hallway, he led the way and she followed beside him. This corridor was better lit and surprisingly devoid of other people. The quietude renewed Julianna's former curiosity.

"Dominick, you never really answered my question earlier. How is it that we're on a spaceship, and I have no knowledge of arriving here?"

"Space travel can be disorienting." At the dubious glare she shot him, he shrugged. "All right, maybe there is a more logical explanation." Waving his hand, a door slid open up ahead to their right, and he turned to her with a smile. "Something which is best demonstrated. Come with me."

"I really don't think…"

"Please. Trust me, Julianna."

Without further protest, he took her hand gently and led her inside.

The room was moderately lit and large, but oddly vacant. For long moments, they walked about, their footsteps echoing from the emptiness.

Julianna turned to Dominick with a smile. "Mm-hmm," she said finally. "Let me guess. You emptied this room by magic."

"No," he laughed. "This room never existed before now."

"I beg your pardon?"

"It's very true. We're the only ones who know about it. Even that door wasn't there until I conjured it. Its sudden appearance was only obscured because we weren't standing directly beside it. And before you question this, I ask you to suspend your disbelief, and simply watch."

Waving his free hand in a slow arc, flowers literally bloomed in the empty room. Not just one type, but an infinite variety with a rainbow assortment of colors. Julianna was too stunned to speak, left gaping at additions to the scene. Acorns appeared, sprouting into small trees that in seconds grew to be full and lush.

As the garden continued to expand, in the center of the room a small disk of water grew into a very large circular pool, with stone around the edges to encapsulate it.

After Dominick completed his sweep of the room, he turned to his wide-eyed companion. "Julianna, are you all right?"

"Yes," she replied finally. "I'm just a bit overwhelmed."

He breathed a sigh of relief.

"Good. By the look on your face, I was afraid you were about to tell me you're allergic to flowers."

A laugh burst from her before she thought, and he joined in.

The sound of birds chirping captured their attention. Several were flying around the room, including robins, bluebirds, and white doves. Not missing the possible romantic symbolism of the last type, confirmed by Dominick's knowing smile,

Julianna found herself blushing.

"What do you think?" he asked.

"It's beyond amazing." She took a step closer towards the pool, but he prevented this gently.

"Wait half a moment longer, my lady. I have one more surprise for you."

Raising his hand forward, a fountain of water sprang up, extending out to fill the large pool. As the water cascaded, it sparkled and shimmered with brilliant colors, unlike anything Julianna had seen before. It even began emitting a lulling, musical hum. At her questioning look, Dominick nodded, and she took a step closer, reaching a hand towards it herself. The flowing water felt completely normal, in spite of its magical appearance.

"It's beautiful."

"Much like you," he replied.

Feeling her cheeks flush, she turned to her companion, shaking her head. "That's flattering, but how did you do all this?"

"Magic."

She sighed heavily. "Dominick, we're both adults, and magic doesn't exist. So seriously, how did you ***really*** do this?"

He reached forward to take her hands in his, his mesmerizing blue eyes locking with hers. "There's something you need to accept first before all else. I wouldn't lie to you, Julianna."

"But magic doesn't exist on Earth."

"Ah, but we're not on ***Earth***, are we?"

"No," she agreed, though her mind remained confused.

Squeezing her hands, he smiled warmly. "The truth is, magic helped me to find you here. It was the only way I could see you again."

"But you barely know me."

"Something I'd like to remedy, if you'll allow me, my

lady." Brushing one of her auburn curls from her forehead, his touch sent a shiver through her.

Feeling her heart race at his closeness, she knew she should back away, but something within wouldn't let her. Tentatively, she reached up to touch his hand, feeling only gentleness and warmth. Slowly, their fingers intertwined, chaste and yet intimate at the same time.

"I barely know you either," she whispered.

"I can remedy that too," he replied with a smile. "And what better place than a secluded paradise that's ours?"

Hands still clasped, they leaned closer, seeming to melt against each other as they kissed. Each seemed to be seeking what the other felt, and like the fountain, their kisses expanded, becoming warmer and deeper. All the while, the magic of the room surrounded them with its bower of music and serenity, enhancing every moment they shared.

Slowly, an eternity later, Dominick pulled back, his forehead still resting against hers with closed eyes as he smiled.

"My dear Julianna," he murmured, "it's true I know more about you than you of me. And there is so much I want to tell you."

She echoed his smile. "I'd like to know."

"Where to begin? I…"

A loud ***bang*** interrupted the reverie, causing both to turn towards the door.

"Where the hell did this door come from?" a familiar voice yelled from the other side. "This isn't even on the system's directory!" A swift pounding ensued. "Get this open immediately!"

At the muffled sound of others approaching swiftly, Julianna turned to Dominick worriedly.

"Relax, my lady," he whispered, smiling confidently as he made a casual gesture towards the room.

Taking far less time than its earlier transformation, the

paradise vanished, instantly replaced by the original empty ship room.

Abruptly, the door was pried open by two officers. Kyron stood in the middle, his expression shocked and angry.

"What are ***you*** two doing here?" he demanded. "I told you to get to your posts!"

Dominick squeezed Julianna's hand. "My apologies. As I mentioned earlier, my companion is newly transferred to this ship and unfamiliar with the protocols. I was merely showing her around the ship."

"Under ordinary circumstances maybe, but with the Rengar threat looming nearby, this is no time for a scenic tour! Now get back to your posts before…"

Alarms interrupted, jarring everyone, while flashing lights filled the corridor.

"Too late," one of the other officers finished.

Inhaling deeply to control his anger, Kyron eyed Dominick and Julianna meaningfully. "We'll discuss this in my quarters later. For now, get to your posts, ***both*** of you!" In moments, he'd rushed from the room, along with the other officers.

"Should we follow them?" she asked.

"Considering we never signed on for this operation, I think it's time we found our way out of this nightmare instead," Dominick replied.

"For once, I agree with you."

"There has to be an escape hangar on this ship somewhere." Spying a small wall directory in the hallway, he strode over to identify the location. Turning to see a look of worry on Julianna's face, Dominick clasped her hand. "Come on. We're getting out of here, together." She squeezed his hand gratefully in return.

The corridor seemed to go on forever. Fortunately, the people they passed were too busy racing about to ask further questions. There were distant sounds of explosions and gunfire, occasionally shaking the ship, but the pair maintained their focus on their destination.

As the hangar doors appeared, both breathed a sigh of relief. It was short-lived though, for the sound of lasers on the other side indicated some unwanted company would soon arrive.

"Back the other way," Dominick said quickly, just as the doors started to give beneath the laser fire. They hadn't gotten far when the sound of footsteps filled the corridor behind them.

"We'll never outrun them," Julianna protested. She felt his grip on her hand tighten, looking back as they ran.

Abruptly, everything shifted.

Feeling her stomach lurch, Julianna could only gasp as she saw the ground pull away. But more than that; suddenly, she found her head pressed against the ceiling. Breathing heavily, both from confusion and the height, she opened her mouth but no sound came out. As if prepared for her startled reaction, a warm hand was there to silence her.

"Hush, sweet angel, until our pursuers are out of hearing."

Due to the high ceiling, the Rengar passed beneath them obliviously. In moments, the sound of their heavy boots faded.

She managed to turn her head to face a smiling Dominick, her eyes questioning. For a moment, he looked like an angel himself.

How? she questioned with her mind, since she couldn't speak.

Another magic ability, he replied silently, removing his hand, while still holding her closely with his other arm. "I'm sorry to have startled you, but we had to move quickly."

"I understand that," she got out, shaking her head. "But we're flying."

"Levitating to be precise. Flying implies movement. However, that's not a bad idea to get us back to our original destination. Hold on, and I'll take us there."

Shifting her arms about his neck, she allowed Dominick to carry them along the ceiling of the corridor, silently but swiftly. Julianna had never experienced anything like it, feeling weightless as they traveled, both nervous but also enchanted at this use of magic. Shutting her eyes at the pleasant sensation, all too soon she felt a shift as Dominick brought them back to the floor. The hangar doors were destroyed, leaving a gap wide enough for them to step through.

They'd barely crossed the rubble when the unwelcome sound of lasers filled the air.

"Get down!" Dominick yelled, pulling Julianna behind a pile of storage crates. Huddled together until the blasts ceased, he looked her over. "Are you all right?"

"A bit shaken, but…" She stopped, noticing a reddening spot on his arm. "Dominick, you're hurt!"

"Just a scratch, and it can wait," he demurred. "Right now, we have to focus on getting out of here." Scanning the area carefully, he pointed ahead.

"Escape ships?" she asked hopefully.

"Just what the dreamers ordered," he agreed, ignoring her puzzled look as he tried to edge around the crates. Another volley of laser fire forced him to retreat back again. "They're definitely going to be a problem."

"Have you tried flying over them?" a voice whispered.

Both jumped as they turned to find several men, including the science officer Landers, crouched behind them.

Dominick shook his head. "Where did ***you*** come from, and what are you talking about?"

"Now, now, don't play innocent. You were too busy dodging the Rengar to notice us watching through the doorway to our laboratory. A pretty impressive trick, by the way. Could you show us again how it's done?"

He sighed. "It wouldn't be of much use here, since

they're already aware of our presence this time."

Landers grinned. "In that case, maybe this calls for our prototypes." As he lifted the gun he'd carried earlier, Dominick gently pushed it to the side.

"Whoa. From what Kyron said, that might not be a good idea."

"Yes, but we don't have time to continue tinkering with them until they're more effective. At this rate, the Rengar will capture the ship, allowing the Warp Zone to pull us in while things are in chaos."

Dominick thought quickly. "Then we'd better get these prototypes working immediately. Landers, let me try something." As he reached out, the other man somewhat reluctantly handed the gun to him. Scanning it quickly, the gun abruptly sparked, and a blue glow surrounded the weapon.

"It's never done ***that*** before!"

Without replying, Dominick continued to focus on the weapon, and it seemed to alter slightly in his hands. "Let's see if this does anything." As he stepped away from the crates, Julianna reached out an arm towards him.

"Dominick, wait!"

As the laser fire resumed, he pulled the trigger on the weapon, emitting a loud blast that knocked him back a few paces, while sending what looked to be an invisible barrage of energy at their attackers. Three Rengar went down, while several others scattered. Instantly, he re-aimed and took care of them as well.

As the room was blanketed with silence following the blasts, those behind him stared open-mouthed.

"Yeah, that should work," he decided. Tossing the gun to Landers, he reached out to modify the other weapons that the stunned crewmen held. It took the same short amount of time to complete the task. "Take these to the bridge and stop the Rengar, so you can save the ship and its crew. If you play your cards right, Kyron will not only think kinder of your science projects, but you might even get promoted for services rendered."

Landers smiled broadly. "We'll do that. But what of you and the lady? Won't you be coming with us?"

"Actually, the lady and I are in need of an immediate transfer. I got the feeling Kyron would like nothing better than to throw us in a brig."

"Understood." Landers gestured to the right. "That ship was newly fueled before the boarding party arrived. It should get you away, although you'll still have the Warp Zone to contend with."

"We'll have to take our chances, though we appreciate the advice."

Shaking his hand briefly, Landers nodded and turned to leave with the others. "Fare well, flying strangers."

As Dominick turned, Julianna reached out to hug him, but he winced, holding her back gently. "Easy there," he told her.

"Oh, your arm."

Smiling, he reached out to embrace her with his good arm. "It's all right. There'll be plenty of time for that after this heals." Casting a side-glance at the wound he'd sustained on his left arm, he wasn't concerned. It was a bit painful, but at least it was minor and not his shooting arm. Something he could remedy shortly. "Now, let's get out of here."

Heading to the recommended ship, he helped Julianna climb its nearby ladder and followed after her, moments before a regular ship crewman came running into the room. The man noticed the bodies of the Rengar, but his curiosity soon focused on the fleeing pair.

"Hey, do you have security clearance for that?" he yelled.

"Seeing as we're the repair crew, I would think so!"

Dominick replied in kind. "Unless of course you want this thing to continue leaking fuel."

"Leaking fuel? We just checked that this morn…" The man's brief confusion didn't last long as the pair disappeared within the ship, and rational logic took over. "Hey, I'll need to see some I.D. numbers!"

"He can I.D. ***this***," chuckled Dominick, punching a few lighted buttons. The entry hatch snapped shut and the ship lifted slowly, just before lurching forward into space, leaving the crewman behind.

As soon as they were safely away from the larger ship, Julianna turned to her companion with amazement. "I didn't know you could fly one of these things."

"Who says I can?" he mumbled, just as a wave of laser fire from the greater ship jolted them. "Great. That guy can do more than just complain. That's the thanks you get for trying to help." As he attempted to turn the craft, another blast hit them, earning a frustrated grimace. "Just what I've always wanted. To be stuck a million miles away in outer space and about to be barbecued by Mr. Trigger-Happy." He gave a withering look to Julianna. "Couldn't you read something a little less dangerous the next time?"

Before she could question him, a loud growl was heard behind them. Julianna looked back and her eyes widened.

"Dominick, there's something..."

He brushed aside her grasping hand, shaking his head. "Whatever it is will have to wait. I'm still trying to figure out how to fly this thing." Another louder growl caused Julianna to scream as the 'something' in question attached itself to the back of their seats, one talon extended menacingly, forcing Dominick's attention this time. "What the blazes is that?" he exclaimed.

"An unwelcome stowaway?" she gasped, as another blast of laser fire hit their ship, shaking the alien free. It gurgled in fury as it landed on its scaled back, its multiple taloned arms flailing to right itself.

"Would you still rather be captured by aliens?" he laughed.

"Well, not ***that*** type!" Suddenly a beeping noise, accompanied by flashing red lights, filled the ship. "What's that?" she nearly yelled.

"Try our fuel tank's been shot," he murmured, hitting various switches. "Come on, come on... Doesn't this thing have a spare gas tank?" The lights on the control board flashed brilliantly for long moments, just before they all went dark. "Okay, guess not."

"Garunkk!" spouted the alien.

"Would you mind thinking of your stomach later?" snapped Dominick. "We've got a crisis here!"

The alien's several golden orbs rolled about as if considering this, moments before its taloned arms shot out to cling to the sides of the ship. Humming a strange haunting melody, its skin took on an equally eerie glow, growing brighter by the second, until the creature abruptly vanished.

"What the...?" sputtered Julianna. "Where did it go?"

"Another universe hopefully. Now if we can just... oh, great."

Julianna didn't have to voice a question this time to ask what was wrong. The ship's engines were dying down, slowing the ship until it merely drifted along. The larger ship was now farther out of range, and no longer firing. At first surprised, a different kind of jolt shook the ship.

"What's happening?" she asked.

Dominick sighed matter-of-factly. "It looks like the Warp Zone's gotten hold of us, which would explain the other ship not pursuing us."

Completely unexpectedly, he began to laugh, which prompted her to stare at him with even more curiosity.

"We're about to pulled into a black hole wannabe, and you're laughing like we're watching a space comedy from a comfortable couch in the living room. Am I missing something?"

"No, but this might put a damper on continuing our evening tonight," he replied with a smile. "So before we might become part of the atomized universe, any last requests?"

"To be safely back home again comes to mind," she whispered, rubbing her forehead worriedly.

"Hmmm, I might be able to manage that request." Her gaze flashed back to his, searching for a jest that wasn't there. "I am a man of many talents, Julianna. Surely you realize that by now." Before she could answer, he put his arm around her shoulders comfortingly. "This hasn't exactly been a pleasant evening, and certainly not what I'd counted on," he said knowingly, as she found herself leaning against him. "Despite the most pleasant company, of course. Hopefully the next time won't be fraught with such difficulties."

"Difficulties?" she laughed. "You're always talking in riddles, Dominick. Can't you just state the clear-cut truth for once?"

"You wouldn't believe me if I told you."

"Why? Because you've led us onto a path to destruction? No, surely that's not reason enough to doubt your methods."

His laughter rumbled through her as he kissed her cheek. "All right, my dear lady, if you want truth, you'll have it. This is a dream. A dream you'll wake up from at any moment."

"What?" she gasped. "I don't believe you." At his 'I told you so' stare, she found herself blushing. "Not to say I don't trust you," she amended, "but how can something this real be a dream?"

"Ah, Julianna... never underestimate the power of your dreams, especially when they're combined with your very strong imagination."

That can't be! she thought inwardly. And yet, she did have no memory of how she'd gotten here to begin with. She also couldn't account for Dominick's sudden reappearance from... a ***dream*** she'd had the night before? No, that was impossible. *It couldn't be that simple!*

"It is."

Anger filled her eyes as she pushed his arm away. "Will you please stop reading my mind?" she exclaimed, even as she continued to wonder how he could.

"It's a part of my special powers actually," he told her. At the glare she shot him, he added, "While in this realm, they allow me to pick up on some of your surface thoughts. Just in case you were wondering."

"Hmph! Just in case. As if you didn't already ***tune*** in."

"It comes in handy sometimes," Dominick agreed with mock nonchalance. "Especially in the case of dealing with dream animals like your old friend Duchess."

Dream animals! she thought, nearly laughing. This whole thing was totally unbelievable.

Abruptly, she froze. *Duchess?*

Her expression lost all amusement instantly.

"***Duchess?***" she fairly shouted, her eyes narrowing. At the infuriating look of innocence he shot her, she felt sorely tempted to strangle him. "Why, you conniving scoundrel. You ***are*** the same Dominick I met a few months ago!" she accused, her hands clenching angrily.

"Oh, didn't I already tell you?" he asked lightly, snapping his fingers before she could reply. "Damn, I knew I'd forgotten something."

Seeing his amused reaction only angered Julianna more. "You liar!" she snapped. "Why didn't you tell me about this last night, instead of leading me to believe I was seeing double?"

Dominick folded his arms with a knowing look.

"Because I knew you'd lose your temper like you are right now." Realizing that any retort would prove his point, she merely glared at him again and sat back in a huff.

"All right, I'll tell you the whole reason why I didn't mention it," he continued seriously, slowly earning her attention. "I admit that my motives may not have seemed the most honorable the first night we met, but I'm not the type to persist with an unwilling woman. You, however, seemed more than responsive when I kissed you." His smile curled into a sneer. "Until of course you ***had*** to pull your little stunt of crushing my foot and mocking me afterwards!"

"Maybe you deserved it," she retorted.

"And maybe ***you*** deserve an acting award for being able to change from fire to ice in less than thirty seconds."

"Who's calling ***who*** an actor around here, ***Mr. Westbrooke?***" she challenged.

"Before you say another word, let me assure you that ***is*** my name, just as much as Dominick is," he replied. "But to continue, after seeing that most unpredictable attitude of yours, you've occupied the better part of my thoughts since then. I finally decided to exact a suitable payback for your actions, and thus sought you out again."

"Hence the dream at the dance last night."

"Exactly."

"Which also explains why you tried to embarrass me on the dance floor in front of everyone else."

"At first... admittedly, yes."

Julianna nodded once before giving him a cold smile. "I don't believe any of this. People can't just insinuate themselves into other people's dreams!"

"They can if they were born with that magic ability," he replied quietly.

For a moment, she was silent, and then broke out laughing. "There you go talking of magic again. Dominick, even if this ***was*** a dream, there is no magic in reality. Now why don't you give me the real truth behind your constantly visiting me each night?"

"In the name of Chaos…" he murmured in frustration, "I just ***told*** you the real truth!"

"Right, and all this is just a ***dream***, as you say!" she retorted in disbelief, turning away from him. "Excuse me if I don't want to hear more stories."

The anger in his eyes seemed to flare like a stormy ocean for a moment, but then it faded as he shook his head. "Very well, Julianna," he sighed. "Since you seem so inclined to believe I'm lying, feel free to sit there and sulk quietly if it'll make our imminent disintegration any easier." Folding his arms, he leaned back lazily, without the least look of worry.

Not so in the case of Julianna, who quickly took in the impact of his last casually spoken words.

Disintegration? her thoughts echoed. The full danger came back to her as she sighted the ominous gas cloud, now much closer than before. *This had* ***better*** *be a dream*, she decided. Dominick's peaceful expression seemed to believe this wholeheartedly, which made up her mind about one thing. If he wasn't going to panic, then she certainly wasn't.

Copying his manner, she leaned back parallel to him as before. He glanced her way with a smile, admiring her sudden bravado, although inwardly he wasn't too thrilled that they only had a short time left together. Yet after the fiasco this evening, he'd decided long before that he wasn't going to continue with any romantic overtures this night. Julianna had been duly frightened, and he wasn't about to take undue advantage of the situation.

Surprisingly enough, he didn't mind so much that their meeting had been mostly platonic this night, even with their recent dispute still left in the air between them. He was rapidly coming to notice that she had a great deal more than just physical appeal, with a most intriguing spirited nature. A fact that he'd have to be sure to keep from Riff, lest his brother become curious enough to seek her out for himself. At the mere thought, his expression darkened. After all, it wouldn't be the first time Riff had interfered with women he'd known, sparking no end of fights in the past.

However, as far as Julianna was concerned, Dominick knew that he'd annihilate Riff if he so much as appeared to her, let alone touched her, or…

He glanced up sharply upon accidentally tuning into his silent companion's troubled thoughts. It was a good thing his dreamphasing powers extended to this. Her earlier expressions of anger and bravery were completely gone, and she was now staring wide-eyed at the outer space, her hands white as they clenched the armrests of her seat.

She's truly convinced this is real! he mused in wonder.

Not that she'd dealt with dreams as frequently and thoroughly in the ways he had, to nearly ***always*** know the difference from reality, his mind supplied. Their earlier argument faded from his mind instantly, replaced by a need to reassure her.

"Julianna, I meant what I said before," he said seriously, prying one of her hands free to clasp it tightly. "This is a dream. There's no need to be afraid of that swirling pile of interstellar gases or that distant garbage scow."

Despite the many negative aspects of the situation, a slight laugh escaped her. "Isn't garbage scow a bit too regal a title for that thing?"

"You're right. A dumpster is more like it."

He could sense her fear ease slightly as he pulled her close, and to his surprise, she didn't back away or protest. "Julianna," he whispered, "whether or not you believe what I told you about where we are, I just want you to know that I am sorry I led you to believe we were strangers again yesterday. And truthfully, I didn't return merely out of wounded pride from our first meeting. I came back, because as I've said, you haven't left my thoughts since we met."

Julianna gave him a skeptical look. "You didn't tell me our ship was running low on oxygen too. Obviously your mind isn't getting enough to think rationally."

He gave a low chuckle, hugging her tighter. "You impossible minx! I try and compliment you, yet you turn my words into just the opposite."

"Maybe because I find them hard to believe."

"The only thing hard to believe around here is how a woman as beautiful as you can come to think so little of herself. A fact I intend to work on remedying, despite your constant attempts to thwart me." At first she emitted a sound of challenging disbelief, but then simply smiled faintly. Even if he hadn't seen this, Dominick could sense that despite her silence, she was softening towards him. "Will you forgive me, my lady?" he murmured against her ear.

She shrugged once with a smile. "Well, I suppose I'll have to. If not, you're liable to pester me about it for countless other nights."

"Countless nights, eh? Hmmm… sounds interesting."

"***Now*** who's impossible?" she laughed, rapping him lightly on the shoulder. A moment later, Julianna gasped as the rest of the ship's cabin lighting unexpectedly went out around them, except for a dim red glow. Apparently, their ship's remaining power was rapidly draining away. Clutching her companion against the near-total darkness, she glanced up at him with fear-rimmed eyes. "Dominick, you seemed so certain that this is a dream. Is it really true?" He nodded against the top of her head, and she relaxed slightly. "I trust you," she whispered.

In spite of her words, Dominick could sense her lingering doubts, but was still gladdened. Just to hear her speak of trust was a step in the right direction, given her past history with the men she'd known.

"Don't worry, Julianna," he murmured soothingly. "When this dream ends, you'll be safe right back where you started."

"With you?" she asked.

A sad smile crossed his face. "Unfortunately, no. Your waking world isn't mine to join you in, sweetheart. I'm afraid you'll have to wait until tomorrow night if you want us to meet again. Would this be all right with you?"

"Yes. I'd like that," she replied, holding him tightly. She missed seeing his pleased expression over her quick response, but she did remember something from earlier, immediately releasing him. "You were hurt. I shouldn't..." Her words trailed off as she noticed that the bloodstain on his arm was gone, as well as any signs of his shirt being torn. Glancing up at him in amazement, she fairly gasped, "It ***is*** a dream, isn't it?"

Smiling gently, Dominick nodded, nearly laughing at his oversight that could certainly have convinced her sooner. Once he'd had a moment to do so, he'd taken care of quickly healing his arm, since it wasn't difficult to do in dreams.

Gladdened that he wasn't hurt, Julianna hugged him again, brightened by Dominick's honesty but saddened by the truth that she'd soon be returned home without him. Even if he'd just read her thoughts now, she didn't mind this time.

"Until tomorrow then," he whispered, kissing her softly. "Now… close your eyes and relax. I won't let anything hurt you."

She nodded against him, following his instructions. A smile crossed her face as she felt his hand lightly brush against her cheek, while at the same time, she heard him humming a pleasant and unfamiliar melody, no doubt to soothe her further. It worked.

But as the sound of the ship being pulled into the unknown vortex drowned out the gentle music, Julianna's eyes shut tighter and her hold on Dominick strengthened. She knew she trusted him now, understood that this was a dream, and felt confident that he wouldn't lie to her about their predicament.

Unless... Was there another explanation regarding his healed arm after all? Had he just said those things before to dissuade her mind from the probability of this being the end? In spite of her best intentions, the fear crept back.

There was a thundering sound as the ship was being crushed, and Julianna screamed.

Chapter Five

She kept on screaming as she sat up in bed.

Even when it sank in that she'd been dreaming, Julianna was still shaking. She didn't need to feel her pulse to know her heartbeat was racing, nor to ask why her curls were now plastered damply against her forehead. That dream had been a nightmare in nearly every perspective.

Except for one thing... Dominick had reappeared to join her again.

Glancing down, she saw her book lying on the floor. Well, that certainly explained the science fiction scenario of her nightmare. And her situation had been similar to what she'd read, where a pair had fled from a squad of renegade spacemen. Luckily, they'd been as fortunate as the characters in escaping, although flying into the Warp Zone itself hadn't been pleasant.

As for Dominick's reappearance, surely it was due to her constant thoughts of him the day before. And as this dream was as vivid as the last, she remembered with dismay some of her last words spoken.

She'd agreed to meet him again the following night.

Her mind returned to their other meeting at the ball, and she worried that it was only their unforeseen state of conflict last night that had kept him from making advances towards her again. What if tomorrow presented a quiet scene? Would she be reduced to having to fend off the charming rogue instead?

His kisses ***did*** have a way of bewitching her, but still…

"Julianna!" a pair of voices called out discordantly, causing her to gasp. She looked up with relief as her two older sisters ran into the room. She'd nearly forgotten Crystal and

Vicki lately since her own thoughts were so preoccupied.

"We heard you scream," said Crystal, resting a hand on her shoulder. "Are you all right?"

"Yes," she whispered. "I-I guess I had a nightmare."

Both of her sisters exchanged knowing looks, as Julianna's overactive imagination often led to them over the years, and this was by no means the first time they'd come running to her, though more often it happened in the middle of the night.

Vicki gave a short laugh, emphasizing the dimples in her chin. The middle sister at nearly twenty-eight, she acted much younger than her years. Her formerly straight, dark hair—once reminiscent of their father—was now a golden blonde permed with short curls. Unlike the others though, she had the same blue eyes as their father, although like Crystal, both were fairly tall.

Basically, Vicki was the bubbly spirit in the family who managed to find humor in everything. Her fiancé Luke certainly appreciated this aspect, and for the second time, Julianna was soon to be a bridesmaid.

The eldest sister Crystal was thirty-two, having been married for nearly ten of those years. Similar to their mother, she had long, brown hair that fell past her shoulders and brown eyes, maintaining her composure with a parental smile. She was the career-oriented dynamo of the family, managing a top notch position in a business while managing her five-year-old son Sam, affectionately called Sammy by all. Proud pop Jerry—now thirty-six—who'd come from a large family himself, instantly took to Vicki and Julianna as a loving older brother.

After the sisters' parents both passed away—eleven years ago their mother, and nine years ago their father—Jerry and Crystal left their apartment to move in with the girls. Vicki only stayed at the house over the summers, as she was in college at the time. But as Julianna was just sixteen, she'd almost come to regard Crystal as a second mother. Fortunately, Jerry had a successful business career of his own, which gave them a fairly comfortable living.

Having started school very young, Julianna was seventeen when she'd gone to the local college, but as she was less independent than her sisters were, she'd decided to commute instead of living in a dormitory. Crystal didn't mind at all, and Julianna certainly proved her worth. Not only scholastically, but also in helping Crystal both before and after Sammy was born.

Since Julianna always loved children, she and her young nephew took to each other right away. And to her delight, one of Sammy's first words was her name. She'd always felt a bit funny about having the name Julianna, since Crystal and Vicki were much more common, but before her mother died, she told Julianna that she'd always thought the name was pretty from one of her ancestors, and so had bestowed it on her youngest daughter. For the most part; however, the people she knew—including her family and little Sammy—generally called her Julie.

Only with Dominick had she failed to mention this.

She rather liked the way he said it in his own way, when he'd look in her eyes and…

Abruptly rubbing her eyes to brush the last remnants of sleep from them, while dodging the morning rays of the sun, Julianna turned to her clock. "Eleven-thirty?" she murmured, privately angry with herself for having overslept again. It was an annoying habit she'd never been able to kick, even sleeping late as a baby. Thank heavens it was the weekend, so responsibility wasn't about to bust down her door with reprimands. As her sleepy thoughts faded, she turned to her sisters with alarm. "You're back from your trip a day early. Is something wrong?"

Crystal smiled as she sat beside her sister. "Ever worrisome, Julie," she replied, "but no, we just decided we'd had enough of the shore for the week."

"That and the weather kept raining most of the time,"

Vicki supplied with a cheerful laugh. "Not to mention, we couldn't seem to convince Sammy that we weren't leaving his Aunt Julie for good. He's still asleep from the car trip, but he should be awake soon."

Julianna smiled warmly. She'd be equally glad to see her reddish-haired little nephew, not quite remembering when a week took so long to pass. True, it had been by her own choosing that she'd wanted some time alone, instead of going with the others, but now that they were back, she was more appreciative of having the family with her again.

Especially since she'd now have other things to replace her thoughts with, leaving no room for thinking of further encounters with Dominick, either when awake or asleep.

*****

It had turned into one hell of a night!

Or more accurately, a night of... well, never mind.

While busying himself with work around the island earlier, nothing he did seemed to distract his thoughts from meeting Julianna again tonight. Not even meeting his friends at Lost Limbo managed that.

The sun was finally setting, drawing his attention to the sky and its everchanging myriad of colors playfully fading.

"Sounds like that girl's dreams are dangerous," commented Inferno, as if sensing where his thoughts were. "I'm sorry I suggested you follow up on your association with her."

Dominick smiled, keeping his voice quiet as if guarding a secret. "Despite it all, I'm not. Twice now, nothing's happened, yet I'm twice as interested in her."

"No doubt simply because she ***has*** eluded you twice," Buddy added with a sneer. "And I'd appreciate it if you'd tell Jarissa so, because she hasn't said a word to me since yesterday over your latest dreamphasing affair."

Upon seeing the curiosity on his friend's face, Inferno related events quickly, earning a surprised laugh from Dominick.

"I'll be sure and steer clear of her then," he chuckled. "Can't have a guardian devil breathing fire down my neck." *No, that wouldn't be advisable!* "But if ***dear*** Jarissa shows up again, kindly inform her that Julianna's agreed to see me again this night... by choice."

Buddy whistled at that, earning a warning look from Inferno. The guardian angel had assumed this Julianna to be different from the rest, but if she'd agreed to another rendezvous with Dominick, it was all too obvious that it could only be for one reason.

Hopefully afterwards, he'd have the decency to leave the girl alone in the future. After all, it could otherwise make his own life miserable in regard to his relationship with Jarissa, who was still fully opposed to Dominick pursuing the supposedly innocent Julianna.

A fact that was now more in question.

Buddy's expression darkened slightly. "In all fairness, Dom—not to say that I agree with Jarissa's railing at me over this, of course—you aren't intending on forcing the girl into anything, are you?"

For the most part, Dominick's anger was well hidden when it existed at all. This wasn't one such time.

"What are you implying?" he asked in a deadly voice.

Buddy continued with little heed. "Look, it's just that you're so used to charming women, you probably don't consider one might say no."

"Take care what you say, Buddy," Dominick warned slowly, a gleam of anger sparking in his eyes, just waiting to be kindled into a blaze. "For your information, there ***have*** been those who declined, and I've always respected their wishes."

"Maybe," Buddy agreed in a low voice. "But you've been acting different towards this one, as if she's become your sole objective. If she refuses your advances, will her voiced protests be enough to stop you, or will you let your momentary desire blind you to the right and wrong of it?"

Dominick's fist slammed into Buddy's jaw faster than he could breathe another word. As he went flailing into another table, shattering it beneath his weight, several women screamed in shock while the men got to their feet. Buddy shook his head painfully, rubbing his sore mouth, as he stared up in disbelief at his angry friend who now stood before him.

"If you ***ever*** hint again that I would take a woman by force, either in the waking realm or the dream-state, you'll regret the day you joined this universe, ***guardian***," hissed Dominick.

As he strode by the downed Buddy to leave, he bumped into several stunned females, one of whom drew his angry gaze instantly. "You'd do best to remember that too, Jarissa," he warned her. "For while I've made it a policy never to strike a woman, if you start spouting similar lies about me like your companion, you'll earn the right to be the first I break that rule for."

Jarissa merely gaped at his words as he swept past, both Psych and Kiri moving to stand on either side of her, just in case Dominick returned to carry out his threat.

*****

What do you do when your own friends turn on you? Dominick wondered, angrily stalking back to his home. Once in his room, he continued to wrestle with his thoughts. The aggravating part was that the entire day he'd looked forward to seeing Julianna again, but now the voices of reason and chaos started playing back-and-forth in his mind, leaving him unsettled.

If Riff hadn't been so annoying recently, he might have considered asking his opinion. However, he knew how his 'dear brother' would likely respond, since once long ago, they'd had a similar discussion. When he was younger, Dominick had asked what Riff did when the women in dreams refused his advances, and he'd simply replied that he became even more persistent.

An approach that Dominick had never followed himself.

To his way of thinking, he'd never believed it to be a desirable tactic, considering the best liaisons were those of a mutual nature. When Dominick had encountered reluctant women, he'd simply let them go as they wished. Yet Buddy did strike a minor point. Knowing his code of honor at it stood, why then was he finding it difficult to sever his attachment to Julianna?

The answer seemed simple enough, stemming from their first few meetings together.

It had been a responsive woman that kissed him back those nights. Not someone who despised his company, or wished him to leave her forever. For hadn't she agreed to meet him this night as he'd asked? Yes, the answer was clear enough.

If only some of his friends hadn't suddenly turned condescending.

Leaning his head tiredly against the windowsill of his room with closed eyes, Dominick sighed heavily. "What ***does*** one do in a situation like this?" he whispered.

"***By Chavernos, you depend on your trusty dragon, of course,***" came a deep voice in answer. "***Must I teach that lesson to you a hundred times more?***"

Unable to suppress a smile, Dominick raised his head knowingly, facing the familiar forest green eyes and bright blue scales of his faithful dragon ally. "Roderlin," he murmured. "I might have known you wouldn't hide for long."

"***Hide!***" sneered the dragon, raising his head in disdain. "***Loyal dragon allies are never far when you need them, as well you tend to forget.***"

True enough, mused Dominick, gladdened anew at being gifted many years ago by their meeting. As a child, he'd been awed by the strong bond of friendship between his grandfather Chaos and the wise silver dragon Chaolyn. So much so, that at the age of twelve, the dragon had granted him the rare honor of being present with Chaos at a hatching of baby dragons.

An even greater honor was bestowed upon him that day, as one of the hatchlings took to him instantly, sparking the beginning of a time-honored kindred friendship that would last a lifetime. A rare and treasured gift indeed.

As pureblood dragons matured quicker than those of mixed breeding, and twice as fast as humans, in human form Roderlin looked the same age as Dominick when his human friend turned twenty-five. Around this time, Roderlin had surprised Dominick by returning from a journey with a female dragon, Alysadaria, who'd become his mate. Though a bit jealous at first, she'd quickly become good friends with Dominick as well, so despite their constant travels, the dragon pair often visited.

"***I just found out what happened regarding that tiff with your friends at Lost Limbo, and also this betrothal plan of your grandfather's,***" Roderlin added quietly. "***Chaolyn filled me in on the last.***"

Dominick smiled weakly. "And what's your verdict?"

"***As to the betrothal, I applaud your actions. Chaos means well, but a forced marriage isn't the best way to continue a family line.***"

"Nor will I ever accept it," agreed Dominick. "If I ever marry in this lifetime, it will only be for love." His thoughts turned briefly to Julianna, smiling at the memory, before shaking his head to clear it. "***Only*** for love," he whispered.

"***A wise decision,***" said Roderlin. "***As to your friends, may I inquire what the argument was about?***"

Sighing heavily, Dominick explained the situation, relaying his meetings with Julianna, both now and from their initial meeting months ago. He also mentioned how she'd agreed to meet him again tonight. Roderlin listened patiently, only interrupting occasionally with a question or two. By the end of the explanation, the dragon nodded in understanding.

"***Don't take what they said too harshly. They meant***

no harm either. And regardless of their words, Alysadaria and I will always stand by you, since we know you to be more honorable than they've implied."

Smiling wholeheartedly this time, Dominick patted his nose. "Thank you, dear friend," he replied softly. "Now, where is 'Lysa? I'm surprised she's not with you."

"***Who says I'm not?***" a light, mirthful voice called out from above. Leaning out the window to glance upward, Dominick grinned at the amused white dragon staring down at him, waving her talons.

"It's a good thing we made the roof stronger," he chuckled. "Otherwise, you might end up in Riff's room again."

"***A pesky human, if ever I've seen one,***" she sighed, moving swiftly to hover in the air beside Roderlin. "***The way he'd complained that day, one would think* he'd *never made a mistake in his life!***"

All laughed at the impossibility of ***that***!

Looking out towards the distant stars now winking into view against evening's canvas, Dominick's laughter faded. Earth was one of them in reality, even though he might not be able to see it from here. If only he knew just what to do about Julianna.

Maybe she didn't realize the response she was capable of invoking in someone else. That Roger she mentioned certainly hadn't given her any feelings of self-worth or esteem, so it might have left her feeling inferior to other women.

As if that were true! his thoughts retorted.

From just three days together, he'd seen so many sides to her: happiness, sadness, anger, fear, strength, passion, and a touch of mischief. Each one endeared him in its own way, although his body seemed all too certain sometimes which one it approved of best.

Such feelings aside, he decided he preferred the side of her that laughed and made comical quips to hold her own. It was quite a change over some of the women he'd known. Most were either reluctant to talk, or laughed to cover their lack of intelligence, and while these might be fine as temporary paramours, they weren't the type he wanted to keep seeing.

Julianna was different. There was something intriguing about her, although part of him wondered if it was more due to the chase. Once he'd quenched his desire for her, would he then think of her as the rest, as merely a fond memory? For some reason, the mere thought left a bitter taste in his mind.

"***You're thinking of that girl again, aren't you?***" Roderlin asked knowingly.

Dominick nodded once, briefly explaining the situation to a curious Alysadaria this time. "I don't want to hurt her," he said softly. "Even though we're supposed to meet tonight, maybe it would be best for her if I don't return in her dreams anymore."

Alysadaria's ears perked up. "***After all you've told us and Chaolyn of her, you're giving up so soon?***"

"Why not?" he sighed. "She'll forget me quickly enough if I end our association now, and it'll avoid hurting her later. For whatever reason, she'll believe that she's cleared her mind of me, and go back to her normal dreams." Staring at the stars, he continued, "It'll also get Buddy and Jarissa off my case." *Although I'd sooner sever ties with them than lose Julianna*, his thoughts added silently. "It's the perfect solution, worthy of a guardian angel."

"***Maybe so,***" agreed Roderlin, with a chuckle, as he joined his companion in the air. "***But remember, you're a full human, and by no means one of their kind. Even Buddy is no saint, in case you've forgotten.***" Dominick couldn't help smiling slightly at that. That all was certainly true, especially with he himself being a descendant of Chaos.

"***If your preoccupation with that girl over your two month separation is anything to judge by, Dominick,***" the dragon continued, "***I'd say you'd best think twice before***

leaving her for good. After all, there is something to be said for finding the right companion."

"***Aye,***" agreed Alysadaria, with a mischievous grin. "***It's too bad I'm still searching for mine.***" As she flew off with a laugh, Roderlin bid Dominick a quick farewell before following her with an irritated reply. Dominick smiled after them, mulling over what they'd said.

It was a good thing Chaos hadn't overheard it.

Not that the elder man couldn't be reasonable about some things, such as in his attempts to expand one of his multiple abilities—the rare ability to fully maintain the age of his choosing. He was currently working on a magical device to harness this power to grant a similar ability of longevity to his loved ones, so as not to lose them as swiftly to time. He theorized it might even be possible to extend the range to encompass the entire island, but he'd cross that bridge later.

This was what Chaos would consider a reasonable endeavor.

However, there was one most undeniable fact regarding Chaos in Dominick's mind as to what both he ***and*** his father Discord would say over his continual meetings with Julianna.

For true to reality, Chaos would never see reason here, and Discord always followed suit.

His mother Warp might see things differently though. Sometimes hard to contact, since she was a teleporter who adored visiting the outer regions of Chavernos whenever possible, Dominick couldn't help wishing she was here now. Although she didn't approve of his meeting women in the dream-state either, and especially the very long distant category, there were times when she'd inquired if he'd met anyone he was truly interested in. Time and again, he'd denied this.

Dreams were one thing, but reality was another.

Some gaps just couldn't be bridged.

She might like Julianna though, he found himself

musing. His mother could hold her own in a verbal dispute when angry, much like Dominick's long-distance Earth companion, and never hesitated to stand up to her husband or sons when called for. Yet Warp would more likely be fond of Julianna simply because she was an intelligent and amiable woman. The kind that could charm the sternest guardian devils to rest... or unrest!

And unrest would remain within him unless he went back to find his dream companion again. Maybe it was desire solely from the chase, but right now, it wasn't something he had the will to fight.

His dragon friends were right.

Come what may, he had to keep his promise to see Julianna again this night, and although he most certainly wouldn't force her into anything as Buddy and Jarissa seemed to think, neither was he about to give up easily.

Shutting his eyes at the thought, a smile crossed his face as he wondered what strange dream they'd end up in this time. And then, he considered lending a hand in selecting a suitable one for their nightly rendezvous. This time, one without spaceships or squads of officers to bother them.

*****

"Ooof!" gasped Julianna as her enthusiastic nephew pounced onto her bed, narrowly missing her. Dropping her book, she gave him an amused smile. "And just what are ***you*** doing here at this hour?" she asked mischievously, tickling Sammy once.

"I want a story, Aunt Julie," he laughed, looking up at her with his brown eyes shining.

Julianna glanced quickly at her clock. *It's after nine-thirty, and way past this little guy's bedtime*, she thought, amazed he was still up. But as always, she could no more refuse her nephew than if he'd been her own child. A fact she doubted greatly ever to see, hence she was determined to make the most of things with Sammy.

"All right," she agreed. "But then, off to sleep."

"Okee dokey," he said, jumping into her lap.

Laughing a bit at the phrase he'd picked up from her over the years, Julianna proceeded to tell him a story about a knight who sought to vanquish a terrible creature that dwelled just outside his kingdom. Naturally, no one could defeat this creature, until the knight received a gift from a beautiful sorceress that saved the day, enabling him to slay the creature. She went on to say that the knight married the sorceress and they surely lived happily ever after.

Sammy's quiet snoring ended the tale!

Carrying the sleeping child back to his bed, Julianna was unaware that she was being followed by an invisible—yet familiar—presence.

Dominick gaped upon first arriving at Julianna's house, seeing the child she held as she told him her story. *Is this child hers?* he wondered in partial irritation. She'd certainly never mentioned having a ***son*** before, let alone the boy's father she'd been involved with, if not Roger.

He was also bothered due to her falsely having him believe her innocent, when she apparently couldn't be as much so as he'd thought. She'd told him repeatedly of her lack of association with men, yet if this was true, then where did the child come from?

Despite his surprise over this news, he couldn't help but notice the affection she lavished on the boy, between cuddling him as she told him her story and kissing his forehead now as she gently covered him with a blanket.

Even after she left the room, Dominick lingered to gaze upon the boy, finally deciding that it didn't matter. If the child was hers, then he was fortunate indeed, even if his father had been too blind to realize it. And admittedly, the boy was a cute little one, he thought with a fond smile.

Just before an unfamiliar male voice rang out from the hallway, soon joined by Julianna's, draining Dominick's pleasant thoughts to nothing instantly.

Eyes narrowing, he left the child to float towards the direction of their voices, halted by a sight that chilled his blood. Although he missed the first part of what was said, Julianna was talking to an older man. ***Much** too old for her!* he decided, catching the tail end of their conversation.

"...fortunate to have such a loving husband," he heard Julianna say with a smile. "I'm sure your son in there will take after you in that respect someday."

"Not for many years yet I hope," laughed the man. "Considering how restless he was during our vacation, I'm just glad we're home again, since your imaginative stories always seem effective in putting that energetic tyke to bed."

"Well, thank you," she replied, with a blush.

Smiling back, the man leaned forward to hug her, bestowing a quick kiss upon her cheek. "Julie, you must be tired yourself. Why don't you head off to bed while I make sure Sammy isn't sneaking in some prehistoric wars in the dark with those toy dinosaurs of his?"

Julianna nodded once, afterwards returning to her room. Her brother-in-law Jerry certainly doted on his only child, although perhaps that last fact might change if he could convince her sister otherwise as he hoped. A discussion which would have to wait until his wife and Vicki got back from the late night movie they'd gone to see an hour ago.

As she shut the light and got into bed, she had no idea that a certain man was scowling at her in the darkness.

A man who now gazed upon her with the pain of betrayal, shaking his head against the apparent duplicity of her nature. He'd seen others betrayed by women of her type before, but never thought he'd succumb to one himself. Growing increasingly angrier at the thought, he vanished with an unmistakably wry look filled with silent intent.

*****

Darkness encompassed Julianna as she walked through a foggy atmosphere beneath the full moon. According to her friends, that type of moon always signified that people would be acting strange on nights like this. Perhaps not to the point of becoming werewolves—although maybe there were a few—but strange people lurking about nonetheless.

Wonderful thoughts to carry in one's mind late at night!

Well, it didn't matter, since she wasn't far from her castle. Maybe it wasn't the most elaborate one in the world for a sorceress of her caliber, but then again, she was only one person and saw no need for a monstrous museum of a home.

Her shimmering lavender satin gown swished about her feet, hugging each and every curve like it was part of her, covered by several gossamer veils of blue, green, and violet which deemed her a sorceress. Drawing her fur-lined, midnight black cloak closer, she shivered slightly. The night air was crisp, even if it wasn't altogether freezing.

Fortunately, her castle shouldn't be far now, since she'd walked this path countless times during the day. Yet for some reason, perhaps due to the darkness, her castle was still hidden from view. She could only hope the lunatics in the kingdom, influenced by the full moon, weren't prowling about just yet. Not when she knew she was so close to home.

As she picked up her pace, a sudden ice-filled voice froze her.

"What's your hurry, lady? Afraid of night creatures?"

Julianna whipped about to see who dared address her so, even as she knew instantly without seeing his face. What she wasn't expecting was the cold unfathomable look in his eyes as the silver rays of the moon shone upon him.

Yet it ***was*** him, as she now remembered hearing him say before that he'd meet her here. "It depends on the type, I suppose," she answered. "Are you referring to evening night creatures, or chivalrous ***knight*** creatures?" At his continued silence, she took it to assume that he hadn't caught her pun, yet at the same time, she felt the uneasy need for caution.

Something was wrong.

Has the full moon gotten to him too? she wondered.

After an uncomfortable pause, he replied, "Why should that bother a sorceress, when she can weave ***spells***?" *And lies!* his angry thoughts added, barely containing the words.

"You know, I nearly forgot that. Thanks for reminding me." Her attempt to break the ice only met with more silence. "So," she continued lightly, "since I'm the local sorceress around here, have you decided to play my resident knight in truth?" Hoping to rekindle his former easygoing manner from their earlier meetings, she flashed him a smile.

She was surprised when he didn't return the gesture.

"Truth?" he exclaimed, striding forward with folded arms and a forced smile. "Ah, yes, let's speak of that for a moment. I find it a most peculiar word to be coming from you, since deception seems more fitting." She wanted to protest, but his eyes stopped her with their cold amusement. Yet beneath this... was that a look of pain in them?

"You seem to understand deception as well, since you're not acting like yourself at all," she replied, resting one hand against his arm. He flinched from her touch as if singed by fire. "What's wrong, Dominick?" she pressed, more quietly. "I thought you wanted us to meet again, or weren't you the one who asked me?"

He considered her words for a moment before laughing without humor. "You're right. It was my idea, wasn't it? Well, no matter, after this evening you'll never have to worry about that again, since tonight is good-bye."

"Good-bye?" she whispered in confusion. "But why? I don't understand. I thought..."

"You thought I'd never notice your web of lies that you've tried to ensnare my sympathy with, ***lady***," he sneered, hissing the last. "But those self-same lies have managed to tangle you up in them as well."

"Lies?" she protested, a touch of irritation in her own voice now. "Since when have I ever lied to you? Or have you forgotten it was ***you*** who played the mystery stranger lately?"

"No!" he interrupted. "You'll not continue to cuckold me with your false innocence." A weak smile creased his expression. "I thought I understood you once, Julianna. I believed your words of unhappiness and loneliness, and I wasn't going to rush things with you. I even considered leaving you forever, since I thought you deserved better. But now..." He gave a forced laugh. "To think that you were so easily lying to me, and I've just been wasting my time with you. Well, no more, lady. No more. Tonight the charade ends once and for all."

Julianna had never been one to stand for accusations without reason, and now glared at him with undisguised anger of her own. "Now see here, Dominick, everything I told you before was true, whether you believe it or not. And if there's something else that I don't know about, then you'd better damn well tell me what it is!"

He shot her a crooked smile, his eyes narrowing. "Why don't you ask your husband for the answer to that?" he hissed.

"My ***what***?" she yelled, leaving the anger in his expression undiminished.

"I said your ***husband***!"

Before she could even think where he'd developed this conclusion, both had their attention diverted by an ear-shattering roar nearby. So loud that the ground started to quake, shaking Julianna backwards. Without a second thought, Dominick reached out to catch her.

Even when the ground rumbling stopped, he still held

her.

"Are you all right?" he asked.

"A bit shaken up, but yes," she whispered. "What ***was*** that?"

"I'm not sure," he replied, "but seeing how your dreams have a tendency to turn into nightmares, I have a feeling we're soon to find out." Abruptly, he faced her with renewed anger. "What happened this time? Were you watching a monster movie before telling bedtime stories to your son?"

"Oh, so now I have a son too?" she snapped, pushing away from him just before her eyes opened wide. A husband... and a son? The realization hit her instantly. He must have seen and thus assumed... Well, he was certainly in for a surprise!

But before she could tell him the truth, another one dawned. The story she'd told Sammy before was happening here. She was dressed as a sorceress, Dominick was obviously the knight, so that must mean...

"Uh-oh," she murmured.

Dominick's eyes narrowed. "And what's that supposed to mean? Coming from a guilty conscience perhaps?"

She glared at him. "No, you idiot! It means..."

Another roar and a ground quaking.

"What in blazes have you gone and conjured up now?" he demanded, shaking her once.

"Would you believe the monster from that bedtime story?" she replied, just before said monster in question pushed aside several trees to reveal itself.

It appeared to be a two-story tall green-scaled dragon, although a bit warped with pointed spikes protruding from its sides. Stretching out its claws, they looked like steel butcher knives, and no doubt could make mincemeat out of whatever they chose. Its teeth weren't any more comforting.

"Your story's monster was a ***dragon***?" Dominick asked with a forced laugh, just before shaking his head. "Not to disillusion you, but I know a few dragons who'd be rather insulted at being referred to as evil monsters."

"All right, so it's of no relation to your scaly friends," she retorted. "Can we argue this later, and deal with this gruesome green lizard first?"

"We certainly ***will*** continue this later," he swore, turning his attention back to the dragon that roared again. The creature took several steps towards its newly sighted prey, blasting a spray of fire towards the sky, and causing them to edge backwards. "So tell me, how did your story characters defeat this thing, my dear sorceress?" Dominick asked with a sarcastic look. "A fire extinguisher perhaps?"

"Try some on that temper of yours, and we might get somewhere," she replied tartly, even as she tried desperately to remember what gift the sorceress had granted the knight to defeat the monster. "I've got it," she said finally, snapping her fingers. "It was a palm-sized crystal. One that wouldn't be melted by the dragon's fire, but would absorb it instead."

"***That's*** the grand plan?" he laughed. "Considering how minuscule that crystal sounds, just how badly did your sorceress and her knight get burned to a crisp?"

"Not at all!" Julianna protested, reaching within her cloak to withdraw the crystal she'd spoken of. It glowed brighter than the moon itself, temporarily blinding the monster and causing it to turn away with a growl. After a few moments, the glow subsided. "Here," she continued, pressing it into his palm. "According to the story, the knight's supposed to use it to defeat that creature."

"You've got to be kidding. And how pray tell do I do that?"

"I'm not sure," she replied honestly. "I never went into the exact details."

Dominick sighed heavily. "That does present a bit of a problem for us now, doesn't it?"

"Look, how was I supposed to know we'd become part of that stupid story? Just figure that thing out before we get shish kebabbed!"

Rolling the crystal about in his hand, there didn't seem to be any deviance from its smooth surface. Certainly nothing that might activate a hidden power. Just a slight indentation on one side that wasn't readily visible to the human eye. Hmmm, but if that was the case, then maybe...

Holding it up carefully in direct line with the monster, Dominick pressed his thumb sharply against the indentation and kept it there. At first, there was merely a low hum, but it gradually grew in intensity.

"Sounds promising," he murmured. "If nothing else, maybe it'll lull the creature to sleep." Moments later, the crystal's glow returned and expanded to form a disk-like aura around him, causing him to step backwards slightly. Seeing the chance of losing its prey, the creature sent an immediate barrage of flame cascading towards Dominick, but as Julianna had mentioned, the flames were completely consumed by the crystal, vanishing into thin air. "The blasted thing works!" he laughed. "Maybe you are a true sorceress after all."

"Don't be silly," she replied, although not masking a smile.

Neither expected the creature to retaliate by bounding towards them. While Dominick was protected by the crystal's glow, Julianna was not. As she tried to flee, the creature reached out its clawed hand to grasp her waist. The sharp talons pierced her skin as it lifted her off the ground, causing her to scream in pain.

"No!" yelled Dominick, raising his free hand just as a silver sword materialized within it. Glancing briefly at the crystal he still held, he shouted to his companion, "Julianna, can you catch this?"

Struggling against the creature's hold, while biting her lip against the pain, she nodded weakly, stretching forth her shaking hands. He tossed it to her carefully, just before shifting to a more defensive stance against the monster. "What now?" she yelled.

"Shine it in the creature's eyes to distract it!" he instructed, rewarded by another bloodcurdling roar from the dragon as Julianna accomplished her task.

Racing around the creature to attack it from behind, as was his intention all along, he was abruptly frozen upon seeing the creature drop his screaming companion to the ground, silencing her instantly.

"Julianna!" he yelled, as the crystal's light faded around her. New-found rage filling his eyes against the monster as it turned to face him, Dominick pulled back his sword and flung it like a spear directly between the creature's own eyes.

The ground shook again as the creature grabbed hopelessly at the sword embedded in its forehead. Black smoke arose from its wound, gradually encompassing it until the dragon was no longer visible. During this time, Dominick had rushed to Julianna's side, picking up her limp form as gently as he could. The motion stirred her. Dropping the dormant crystal from her hand, she clutched her injured waist, feeling herself hugged tighter.

"Dominick?" she whispered against closed eyes.

"Right here, honey," he assured her, cradling her close. He was surprised when the crystal abruptly renewed its glow, humming again on its own, but crackling as the black smoke fell upon it. Instinctively, Dominick carried Julianna away from the site as quickly as he could.

Long moments later, he turned upon hearing the creature give another loud roar, just before the crystal exploded with an ear-shattering bang. Shielding Julianna from the blast, Dominick continued away with her, while the smoke slowly began to dissipate behind them.

Sighting a small stream up ahead, Dominick brought her over to it, resting her carefully against the bank as he dipped a cloth in the water and gently touched it to her forehead. Her eyes fluttered open.

"Welcome back to dreamland," he said smiling.

Dreamland? Her eyebrows puckered slightly. "Why didn't I just wake up?" she asked.

"Because fortunately, you weren't fatally wounded," he explained, soaking the cloth again as he glanced at her wounds from the dragon's claws. They weren't as bad as they might have been, but still more than mere scratches. Frowning, he warned, "This might sting a bit." Touching one wound with the cloth, he wasn't surprised when she flinched.

"Ouch!" she yelped. "Is that really necessary?"

"Hmmm." Rubbing his chin in consideration, he shook his head. "No. I have a better idea." Resting his hands along her waist, she couldn't help flinching again, although perhaps for a different reason this time. "Relax, sweetheart, this won't hurt you."

Focusing his gaze, a white glow began to surround his hands. As he moved them slowly over the still bleeding wounds, Julianna nearly swooned at his touch. Not because he was hurting her, since the pain was certainly receding, but instead due to the unfamiliar sensations he was evoking.

Ignoring the way he'd stirred her, Dominick continued his ministrations, closing the wounds and erasing their marks as if they'd never existed. When the last one was healed, the glow faded from his hands and he turned to face her.

Flushing a bit at his stare, Julianna grasped at the first distraction she could. "This is amazing," she gasped, seeing not even the slightest blemish remaining on her skin. "The only thing still slightly torn is my dress, and that's minor." Smiling up at him, she clasped his hand. "Thank you, Dominick."

"Your well-being is thanks enough," he replied,

returning her smile. Just before the reasons for their earlier argument returned to plague him. Steeling his expression, he moved to stand, gazing absently towards the horizon. "I'm surprised the monster hurt you though, since your story characters were unharmed."

"Maybe," she agreed. "But the sorceress wasn't present during the knight's battle with the monster. Obviously, I created an alternative to the plot by being there."

"Yes, well, I'm sure your son would have accepted it either way," he replied softly.

"Ah, yes... my son," sighed Julianna, standing as well. "Dominick, there's something I think you should know about him, and this so-called husband you mentioned. You see..."

"Please," he interrupted, raising one hand. "I don't need the complete details thrown in my face again. It's bad enough I saw you playing with your child, moments before you were engaged in pleasant conversation with his father, not to mention your ***husband***." He fairly bit out the last. "I just wish you'd told me that a few nights ago."

Julianna walked about to face him, despite the fact he seemed determined to look past her. "Dominick, I've only known you for a few nights. Yet sometimes I feel like I've known you for much longer, even a whole lifetime. For that reason, I guess I took it for granted that I never mentioned the circumstances of my family to you before, since they were on vacation at the time, and I'd like to change that."

"What are you proposing?" he asked, sneering slightly, although without much force. "That I meet your husband and son?"

"That would be a good trick, if they existed. But the child you've spoken of is my ***nephew*** Sammy, and that man whom you labeled his father is indeed that, but my ***sister's*** husband Jerry." Her smile brightened. "Let me assure you, there is absolutely ***nothing*** going on between us."

For a brief moment, Dominick felt a surge of relief, just before a certain memory nagged at him, rendering his face impassive again. "You'd like me to believe that, wouldn't you?" he asked. He expected her to back down, but she wouldn't, prompting him to fold his arms with unmasked disbelief. "All right then, if this is true, answer one simple question. Why were you declaring that man to be such a loving husband to you?"

Julianna gaped for a moment, about to shout that she never said anything of the kind. Why, just the fact that he'd somehow been eavesdropping annoyed her! But... her brief annoyance faded when she caught on to what he referred to, only bringing a calm smile to her lips.

"Obviously you only heard ***half*** of what I said," she told him plainly. "My words as I recall them were that my ***sister*** was fortunate to have such a loving husband. Not ***me***!" At his sudden silence, she continued quickly, "Search my thoughts if you don't believe me, Dominick! You've already proven that you're good at that. But let me assure you right now, you'll find nothing less than the truth of what I've told you."

It was a matter of seconds before her words were driven home and confirmed. Moments afterwards, his expression took on a slight smile of amusement, before he started to laugh. Gradually, she found herself joining in.

"I thought he looked a bit too old for you," admitted Dominick.

"I'll say," she replied. "For all that I love him like a brother, the man's nearly old enough to be my father." Seeing the slightly chagrined look on his face, Julianna placed her hand on his shoulder, catching his gaze before continuing. "Hey, you've rescued me from pesky late century admirers, men from space, and even a dragon. I think you're entitled to one minor misunderstanding."

Clasping her hand tightly, he nodded once. "I'm just grateful it was a misunderstanding. The thought of you being married to someone else... Well, I'll admit I wasn't too pleased with the notion."

"Oh?" she teased. "I can't see why."

His expression took on a mischievous smirk. "In that case, I'd certainly better correct what I'm doing wrong with my approach to sorceresses." Her knowing laughter warmed him as his arms encircled her waist, pulling her into a fiery kiss that stole every drop of her laughter away.

It was long moments before either spoke.

"By the heavens… I should leave," Dominick murmured finally against Julianna's cheek.

She blinked in confusion. "Why?" she asked quickly. "It can't be morning yet, since I'm still here."

He shook his head with a brief laugh. "I know you've had your share of bad luck with men, but if you want me to remain a knight about you, my dear Julianna, I think you'd understand why I'd best be on my way."

No longer an immature teenager with a lovestruck crush, but instead a more intelligent woman of twenty-five, she knew exactly what he meant.

She also knew that while this might be a dream come morning, the memories would be real now and likely remain so later as well. If she gave in to her current thoughts, would the rational side of her mind condemn her when she woke up? she wondered. And yet by the same token, would it condemn her if she didn't? For once, Dominick didn't seem to be reading her mind, or else he surely would have been surprised at what she'd been debating.

A debate that ended swiftly.

"I understand why," she replied, gently moving her hand to touch his cheek again lightly. "But I still don't want you to leave." She could feel as well as hear his sharp intake of breath. His apparent shock was no more than her own, as she wasn't typically the wanton type, but it only took one glance in his eyes to strengthen her resolve again. "Please, Dominick," she implored, "don't leave me now."

He hesitated for a moment, kissing her hand fiercely afterwards.

"By heaven, Julianna," he murmured, "I'll fight the rays of morning itself to stay with you."

Dominick's oath trailed off as he pulled her close, kissing her stormily with unleashed passion. Sharing the same desire, Julianna's feelings soared. She was as eager as he to cherish this brief time they had, no matter what happened later.

It was only when he broke away abruptly that any sense of reality returned to her.

"This is all wrong," Dominick said quietly, his own breathing unsteady as he gestured towards the area around them. "Any two-bit moron could stumble upon us here when we don't need disturbing, and that's the last thing I want, let alone to remain in a dark place like this. Besides, I wish to make amends for our earlier disagreement."

Julianna gave a short laugh, stroking his cheek. "You can't change the world to accommodate us at will," she told him. "I understand."

"I don't believe you do," he replied mysteriously, giving her a quick kiss, before stepping back a few feet with a knowing smile. "Once more you underestimate my talents, my lady, thus let me prove otherwise. Close your eyes."

"What?" she laughed.

"Trust me, Julianna. You'll see what I mean in a few moments." As she followed his instructions with an amused smile, he echoed her expression. "Keep them closed, and it'll soon seem as if that time before never happened."

She remained skeptical, even as she felt the wind pick up around her. "Dominick?" she whispered uncertainly. He gave no reply as she felt the ground disappear beneath her.

Chapter Six

Gasping as the ground abruptly returned, Julianna was almost afraid to open her eyes, until curiosity overwhelmed her. The familiar sound of ballroom music hit her ears before she realized she was standing outside a large building, where a small staircase nearby led to the entryway. A formally dressed, older gray-haired man stood there, gazing her way with a nod.

She was surprised to find her earlier torn attire gone, replaced by a brand new formal gown, similar to the one she'd worn a few days ago when she'd met Dominick again. But this one was an ivory white instead, combining lace with satin. She was even wearing a matching set of soft white slippers, rather like a fairy-tale. If that was the case though, where was the prince?

As if in answer, there was a slight rustle behind her.

"Fair maiden, thou art a beauty to take away the breath of any man, in dreams or otherwise," came a deep voice. "Any man who doesn't notice is indeed a fool."

Turning with a smile, she gazed silently at the man who'd recently become the prince of her dreams. Dashing as always in black, the warmth of his blue eyes now filled with appreciation and tenderness as they met her own.

Before she could speak, Dominick stepped closer to take her hand, kissing it gently, his eyes warming her with their gaze. "Now do you see just how versatile my powers can be?"

"Yes," she replied. "I'm amazed by it all."

"There's still much more I could show you," he said softly, not relinquishing her hand. "If you'll let me."

She blushed, through a smile. "I'd like that," she

whispered. "I want to experience everything with you."

Dominick's expression changed only slightly, becoming more tender if possible. "Then we shall, beginning tonight, my lady," he assured her, pulling her into his embrace. Glad to feel the strength of his arms about her once more, Julianna nestled her head against his chest comfortably. So much that she nearly fell forward when he abruptly pulled away. "Now, come, my lady. The gathering awaits."

Her eyes narrowed in confusion. "Gathering?"

"Oh, didn't I mention my unpredictable nature?" he asked innocently, snapping his fingers. "Knew I forgot something. Well, there's nothing to be done about it now, nor I suspect in the future either. You'll just have to trust me." Extending his hand towards her, Julianna took it warily, allowing him to tuck it under his arm.

"I thought you didn't like tongue-waggers."

"I don't," he agreed, "but since this is a mere dream, I find it highly unlikely we'll find ourselves in a newspaper tomorrow. Therefore, we can do anything we want to, and let their tongues wag until they fall out."

Julianna laughed at the imagery as he led her up the stairway to the open door of the ballroom. The man nodded once to Dominick before announcing their names, moving aside for them to enter. Glancing about, Julianna could see that this room was different from the mirrored one they'd visited previously, with a large dance floor in the center, surrounded by smaller tables. However, once again, people wore clothing dated back a century, conversing as before.

Patting her hand as he caught her staring at the many couples whirling about the floor as they danced, Dominick led her towards them without a word. As before, she initially protested, but he countered this easily, leading her into the appropriate steps.

In no time at all, she was enjoying herself, smiling up at

her companion as he squeezed her hand in admiration. After that, the lights became as stars to them, and the other people seemed to disappear. Neither noticed the sudden attentiveness they'd drawn from the crowd.

When the dance finally ended, Julianna's face was flushed a soft pink and she looked quite breathless.

And altogether beautiful, Dominick thought.

He wasn't the only one to notice, as several pairs of male eyes lingered upon her.

Sighting a table where others were drawing punch from a bowl, she gestured towards it. "I know you've got unending stamina on the dance floor, but some of us rookies get thirsty," she told Dominick. "Would you mind?"

"Not a bit," he replied. "This night, your every wish is granted, my lady." He kissed her hand lingeringly before departing, earning a very dreamy look indeed from her. If this was any indication of what the rest of the evening would be like with him, she was looking forward to whatever else lay in store.

"Angels do roam this world, and need not have wings," said a slightly familiar voice behind her. Turning, her eyes widened as they fell on three elegantly dressed men, led in front by the one who'd spoken.

"Daffordshire?" she mouthed in disbelief.

The other man nodded, amusement on his face. "Ah, you remember me then, Miss Sherborne," he told her. "I heard your name announced, along with your partner ***Westbrooke***." He fairly hissed the last.

"You're quite correct, sir," she replied, with a nod. "Now if you'll excuse me, I'll be getting back to him." The other men instantly came around to block her way.

One of whom, a darker-haired man who seemed a few years her senior, cast her an appraising glance before smiling. "There would seem to be no rush, since the ladies here must choose several dance partners, before rejoining their original ones. Perhaps we can make your decision easier."

Ill at ease with their smothering attitude, Julianna tried unsuccessfully to look past the men to find Dominick.

"If it's Westbrooke you're looking for, you'll not find him easily," Daffordshire drawled casually. "You see, he has a habit of partnering as many women as he can, both on the dance floor and off."

Blushing furiously, Julianna whirled to face him. "Look, Mr. Daft-in-the-Head, if you say one more word against my companion, I'll crack that empty skull of yours."

Daffordshire merely laughed, nodding towards the dance floor. The other men 'gently escorted' Julianna, pushing her towards the grinning man who caught her easily. "Why, Miss Sherborne, I'm so happy to see you've had a change of heart." Clasping her hand tightly so she couldn't flee, he slithered closer. "Perhaps I won't be as foolish as your earlier partner to relinquish you for the evening."

"You labeled yourself a fool as soon as you opened your mouth, let alone started tormenting innocent women," hissed a voice full of barely controlled anger.

The younger man shot Dominick a look of disgust. "Out of the way, Westbrooke. This one's not yours anymore."

"Don't think I'm ***yours***," hissed Julianna, ceasing her struggles just before kicking his unguarded leg.

Dominick nearly laughed upon witnessing her familiar mode of attack, but his anger at Daffordshire was too strong. Even before the pained man recovered, he'd pulled Julianna behind him, clasping her hand upon his shoulder.

"It would appear the lady has other plans," he said with a smirk.

"We'll see about that!" snapped the younger man. "If you value this wench so much, prove your mettle with a duel!"

"Wench?" gasped Julianna.

Before she did the predictable thing of striking out at

him, Dominick blocked her intentions gently.

Glaring at Daffordshire, he folded his arms. "You know, it takes a complete chowderhead not to know when to take 'no' for an answer from a woman. Do other women know of your clams for brains?" Growling viciously, Daffordshire eyed the sword on his ally's waist, unsheathing it while drawing the crowd's shocked surprise. Dominick merely chuckled. "I do believe the clams are a bit feisty today and need taming." Gesturing to the side, someone tossed a sword into his hand, which he caught easily. "Now then, Lord Daffy, shall we commence?"

The other man needed no more coaxing, lunging forward to instigate Dominick's defense. He parried the attack easily, never losing his look of amusement as the bout grew more heated. Seeing that the older man seemed to be toying with him, and that all the others knew it, Daffordshire nervously loosened his collar.

"What's the wench to you anyway that you can't share her, Westbrooke?" he demanded.

Dominick's eyes twinkled dangerously. "I'm not a man open to such things. And especially regarding the ***lady*** I assume you're referring to, let's just say I'm too fond of her to share her with the likes of you or any other man."

Daffordshire sneered. "After you lose this bout, you'll have no choice but to relinquish her to me this night."

All amusement left Dominick instantly. His stance became aggressive, forcing the younger man backwards. "Win or lose, the lady has a mind of her own," he hissed, "but right now, I wish to see you lose, if only to pay back your ill remarks towards her."

He jabbed at Daffordshire where he was vulnerable, not striking the man, but causing him to drop his sword and leap backwards sharply. The irritated younger man never noticed his close proximity to the fireplace.

Eyes widening as he felt the flames lick up behind him, burning his unprotected posterior, Daffordshire leaped away with a bellowing cry.

"Touché," Dominick replied smugly.

Still afire, Daffordshire shouted to his bemused allies for assistance, cursing their inattentive nature as they scrambled for the punch bowl. Picking it up, they sped back to their friend, tossing the contents all over him, fairly drowning him in punch while dousing the flames.

Unfortunately for the soaked man, the slick bowl slid from their grip, smacking Daffordshire firmly on the jaw as it knocked him to the floor.

When it became evident that the downed fencer was conscious enough to swear with a frenzy, several of the onlookers burst out laughing, while Dominick gave the man an exaggerated bow.

"I believe I've proven the lady is mine, Lord Daffy. Now you'll have to excuse us, but do enjoy the punch." Taking Julianna's hand, he led her away, earning a grateful hug from her.

As they passed the man who'd loaned Dominick the sword, he returned it with an appreciative nod, while the other man looked as impressed as the rest of the crowd.

His companion smiled when they were on their own again.

"I'm glad you weren't hurt," she whispered.

He laughed softly. "Julianna, the only way he could hurt anyone would be if someone tripped on the punch he's carelessly wasted. Speaking of which, I seem to remember your requesting some."

"I think I'd rather skip it now."

Grinning, he snapped his fingers to materialize a sparkling glass. "You were saying, my lady?" he asked, handing it to her.

"Would a thank you be enough?" she asked.

He didn't reply, but kissed her hand, apparently satisfied.

*****

The triumphant duelist took great pride in leading his lady to the floor among the other couples again, earning several smiles of admiration, rather than mere stares. Even so, when the music changed to a slower dance, he escaped with his companion to a secluded corner hidden by a velvet curtain, just beside a window where they could see the stars as they danced.

"Poor Daffordshire," laughed Julianna. "I doubt the other ladies will easily forget his unexpected singeing by the fireplace, nor his unflattering attitude as he stormed out with his friends."

Dominick shook his head nonchalantly. "***Poor*** Daffy created his own trouble when he sought to claim you again. And if any of his other friends decide to pull the same thing, I'll deal with them similarly."

"You seem to be a fairly capable fencer."

"I was an attentive learner with a good teacher," he replied. "It is a talent which comes in handy sometimes where I'm from."

Julianna caught onto the obvious. "And where is that?"

Sighing once with a smile, he shook his head. "I'll tell you later, at a more appropriate time."

Nodding once in resignation, her eyes brightened moments later. "Could you teach me how to fence like that?"

Dominick's eyes twinkled with amused admiration. "Eager to rout Sir Daffy on your own, are you?" She shrugged, but smiled at the inspired notion. "All right, I'll teach you," he agreed. "But even so, allow me to deal with your unwanted suitors. It takes awhile to master a sword."

Gazing up at him with a smile, she shook her head curiously. "Is there anything you can't do?"

He thought for a moment and then smiled. "I can't seem to get you out of my mind," he replied softly. Not expecting his reply, she blushed becomingly, while his arm at her waist hugged her closer. "You look absolutely beautiful tonight." Before she could blush again, Julianna leaned her head against his shoulder, hugging him too.

All the while, she was conscious of how comfortable she felt in Dominick's arms, even when his hand loosely began to stroke her back. With closed eyes she smiled, as he pressed several kisses against her cheek, just before brushing her long hair back to kiss her neck.

"Dominick..." she whispered. "You shouldn't."

"You labeled me part rogue, remember?" he murmured, moving his hand towards her rapidly beating heart.

"Yes, but..." She broke off as he lightly caressed her sensitive breast, unable to prevent her body's warm response to his gentle touch. Fortunately, they were in complete solitude from the rest, but even so...

Chuckling softly at her sudden silence, he moved his hand to her waist instead, adding just as quietly, "You're right, my lady. This isn't exactly an appropriate place for the type of slow dancing I'd like to teach you."

"There's another kind?" she breathed.

Smiling lazily, Dominick's eyes darkened with passion. "Yes," he replied, kissing her cheek again, while he slowly pulled her tighter against him. "It's similar to this, but a bit closer... and without the hindrance of our current attire." Feeling the evidence of his desire, while blushing at the implication, Julianna was unable to turn away as he cupped her face with his free hand. "Surely you're not surprised that I want you. I have ever since I first set eyes on you."

Clasping his hand, she nodded. "I'm flattered," she replied. "And in truth, I can't deny I've been attracted to you from the start as well." She gave the hint of a smirk. "But I suppose that's not news to you either."

He shook his head with a smile. "Especially not after our

time in the garden, finding we shared similar feelings. If morning hadn't intervened when it did, there's no doubt in my mind what would have followed."

Julianna blushed again, but only for a moment. "And if it had?" she began softly. "Would I have ever seen you again?"

"You really need to ask me that?" he nearly laughed. At the serious look she gave him, Dominick's own expression sobered with a long pause. "Well, it's true I didn't know you as well then as I do now, but…"

"I think I understand," she whispered regretfully.

"Really?" he murmured. "I don't believe you do. I was about to say, I had every intention to see you again, regardless. Julianna, do you know how many days I thought of you during the time I spent away from you initially?" She could only shake her head. "I'd estimate it comes to about two months."

"Oh, don't be silly. No one remembers a dream companion that long."

His expression became thoughtful. "You did," he reminded her. "Or do you often chase after strangers by the name of Dominick?"

Sensing amusement rather than ridicule in his words, Julianna smiled. "I suppose you have a point."

"It's much more than that now," he continued. "In the past, I've never involved myself with any married woman, since even as a rogue, I have my limits. But with you, even when I was angry over your supposed husband, I found I still wanted to continue seeing you. You have no idea how grateful I was to find you're not married after all." His arms swept her against him gently. "Julianna, at first, I returned in order to clear you from my thoughts, but instead my own logic trapped me with the reverse. My feelings for you have only grown stronger."

"That much, I ***do*** understand," she replied, stroking his cheek before she thought. Dominick raised one surprised eyebrow. "Surely ***you*** don't think I freely kiss just ***any*** dream men I come across?" Her eyes twinkled mischievously. "And you being a ***chivalrous*** knight."

"You labeled me a rogue first," laughed Dominick, "and rogues have more fun." Leaning closer to prove this, his mouth claimed hers with a fiery kiss that could have set the curtains ablaze. Julianna nearly melted in his arms, murmuring softly as he pulled back to meet her gaze. "Do you mind this knight of yours being a rogue on occasion?"

She smiled up at him tenderly, saying in a whisper, "I've become very fond of that rogue. Especially since he insists on protecting me from every disaster one can dream up."

"My lady, I'd always protect you, at any cost."

"Then does this mean you won't leave me forever as you said earlier, my dream knight?"

Dominick gave a low chuckle at her words. "Dream knight?"

She shrugged with a slight pout. "Well, you once said that a knight in shining armor was a bit too unusual these days, and I suppose that's true, since you might feel stifled by clanky armor."

"Mmmm, true enough," he murmured against her cheek. "You might not like it either though, since it's probably rather uncomfortable for fragile soft-skinned damsels to be hugged by iron-clad knights."

Julianna sneered once at his appraisal of damsels, before she caught the teasing glint in his eyes. "Since you often act like a knight in my dreams, that title seems appropriate."

"Fair enough, my sweet lady. And as to your earlier question, I have no intention of leaving you. Not forever, and not this night."

The desire in his eyes kindled similarly in Julianna's heart, prompting her to encircle her arms about his neck. "I'm glad, Dominick," she whispered. "After all, you haven't yet shown me that other version of slow dancing."

He smiled slowly. "I know of a quieter place where I could, if you'd care to leave this most fascinating gathering a bit early."

"I'll make the sacrifice," she agreed before she thought.

What was this between them that affected her beyond reason? she wondered afterwards. Would she be the same way if she didn't know this to be a dream? Dominick didn't give her long to ponder, sweeping her up in his arms as if she weighed no more than a child.

"Just close your eyes then, sweetheart," he told her softly. "I'll take us there immediately. As long as you're sure it's what you want."

Shutting her eyes with a smile of consent, she leaned against him. "Teleport away."

*****

"Honey, we're home," Dominick said cheerfully, hugging his arm about Julianna's waist. As she opened her eyes, they widened considerably upon seeing the stately white castle before her, easily several stories high, and gleaming in the moonlight. "A bit speechless now, love?"

Speechless indeed! she thought, glancing about in wonder with an absent nod, barely noticing when he set her on her feet again. She was even more surprised at the title he'd called her, although nonetheless pleased.

"I thought you might be interested to see the exterior before I brought you inside," he explained, gesturing towards the archway of the open door.

Taking his hand, Julianna was newly amazed at the modern way the castle was organized inside. Her eyes lit up at the winding stone staircase reaching towards the upstairs rooms, the steps covered by white velvet carpet.

"Where does that lead?"

"A few miscellaneous rooms, and… Julianna, wait!"

Laughing, she'd already broken free to race towards the

staircase, doing fairly well considering the heavy train of the dress she carried as she ran up the steps. Just as highspiritedly, Dominick chased after his swift companion, taking the steps two at a time to catch her easily.

She squealed as she felt his arms encompass her at the very top, lifting her from the floor to carry her easily.

"What are you doing?" she asked.

"No doubt keeping you from finding trouble as usual," he chuckled, walking down a hallway to nod towards one of the many doors. "Since you've interrupted my plans for a tour of this place, I suppose we'll have to postpone them, and start with the last room I meant to show you."

The door swung open of its own accord. Julianna glanced within and gasped. The room was filled with beautiful furniture and items.

Setting her on her feet, he gestured about the room. "A few comfortable chairs for us by the window, so we might gaze out over the beach and ocean while we talk. And over there, a doorway to a hidden library, where you can find all the romance and science fiction novels your heart desires."

Julianna remained speechless as he went on to mention a chest of jewels in the corner, a wardrobe filled with beautiful gowns—as well as casual attire for when she wished it—and minor descriptions of the other rooms in the castle that he'd show her later. Even if this dream could only be for the moment, it was wonderful to feel so cared for by someone she felt similarly about, and she intended to etch it in her memory forever.

Not that her memories towards dreams hadn't improved lately anyway!

"And of course, a comfortable place to rest," he added, kissing her quickly as he nodded towards the nearby four poster bed.

As she ran her hand along the velvety blanket, Julianna

smiled with pleasure, glancing up at the elaborate canopy overhead. A thin veil surrounded the bed on all sides, making it seem as if the beautifully carved wooden structure was separated from the world.

In a way, thanks to the dream-state, this was true for them too.

Finally, she turned to her silent companion.

"But why did you do all this?" she asked. "Surely it won't always be here when I dream every night."

"Ah, but it shall, my dear lady," Dominick said reassuringly. "Though you might be elsewhere in the dream-state, you can usually return here at your request. Merely concentrate, and you should be teleported hence. As to why I created this for you, consider it a gift for becoming a most special part of my life. I hope it meets with your approval."

"Oh, yes," she replied enthusiastically, reaching forward to hug him. "It's the most beautiful place I've ever seen, and I'll return here often."

"I had hoped you would," he replied knowingly.

Kissing the top of her head as he embraced her, Dominick felt immensely pleased by her reaction, especially since he'd never conjured up something like this for anyone else. Sometimes he'd changed the backgrounds, but he'd never felt the desire to set the illusions in their minds, although his special powers could help make this possible. Hopefully the brief forgetfulness of his powers wouldn't keep occurring—no doubt brought on by the pleasant distraction of his enjoyable companion—so he could more easily keep them from the nightmare scenes they'd experienced.

After all, they ***were*** meeting in dreams.

Yet even dreams had their own reality, and right now, there was no denying the very real desire that was building once more within him, just holding her like this. How much time had they left? he wondered. After all, time was ever difficult to determine here, sometimes seeming far longer than the reality, other times much less.

Ah, no matter. They were together now.

He kissed her again, not wanting to rush things with her. Tonight... he desired this evening to be perfect for her, and he'd make sure it was, feeling a warming tenderness towards her.

She slowly raised her head to face him, surprising him with the intensity in her eyes. His feelings of desire were reflected in them.

A desire neither could fight anymore.

Moving to the comfort of the bed, Dominick kissed her gently, his lips ever so lightly brushing against hers, while his hand caressed her cheek. *Chavernos, she's sweet*, he thought. As if having heard him, Julianna's own hands reached up to pull him closer, coming to rest about his neck. Her slightest touch was an enchantment, spurring him to clasp her tightly to him, deepening their kisses until they were left nearly breathless.

So much for fighting the inevitable.

Pressing heated kisses along her cheek, he murmured, "My dear sweet temptress..."

Through the gown, Julianna could feel the urgency in his hands as they tightened about her waist, one breaking free to stroke her back lovingly. Inwardly, she felt it wasn't enough, silently wishing the fabric was no longer between her and his touch. All the while, he whispered sweet endearments which left her trembling with anticipation.

Despite her lack of experience, Dominick exuded an air of confidence and tenderness that was too intoxicating to resist. Deep down, she knew he wouldn't hurt her, and the thought comforted her more than any other.

When his kisses traveled past her neck, a fluttered sigh escaped Julianna, certain that this time there would be no interruptions. Nor did she want there to be anymore.

Dominick's hands raised slightly as he reached behind

her to unfasten the dress, parting the material easily, and drawing it from her, leaving her garbed only in a thin slip. The dress fell to the floor as he tossed it lightly aside, resuming his kisses even as he tugged off his jacket and shirt.

Seeing her trepidation, he gently lifted her hands to place them against his bared chest, holding one more tightly there. "Don't be afraid, love," he said softly. "Feel how strongly my heart beats for you. I swear by it, and by my life, I'll not hurt you this night."

She nodded once without speaking as he kissed her again, resting his hands against the softness of her shoulders, and stealing a gasp from her as he edged the slip from her as easily as the dress.

"Dominick..." she protested, when he drew back to gaze at her openly. Suddenly realizing how bright the room was, and feeling most vulnerable, Julianna found herself wishing they were in concealing darkness instead. Blushing, she tried to turn away, but his hand on her cheek gently prevented this, his tender smile like the warming sun.

"Don't feel the need to hide from me, love," he whispered, caressing her lightly. "You're beautiful, Julianna. If I have to tell you a million more times tonight to convince you, I shall."

She tried to return his smile, but felt awkward. "I'm just not used to being seen like this," she said quietly. "I'm sorry I seem..."

"No," Dominick interrupted, silencing her with a soft kiss. "You have absolutely nothing to be sorry about, Julianna. Nor any need to be afraid. I swore I wouldn't hurt you, and I meant every word." Waving a hand towards the lights above, they dimmed to a softer glow.

At his swift understanding, her smile became more relaxed. "I know you won't," she whispered.

"Good," he replied, kissing her once before reaching

forward to pull back the covers. As she quickly slid beneath them, Julianna smiled at the hidden satiny coverlet and sheets within. "Comfortable?"

"Yes," she fairly purred, shutting her eyes as she snuggled against the feather pillows.

Dominick smiled at her warmly as he removed his remaining clothing. She was such an odd combination of child and woman all wrapped up in one, he thought. Yet for all the desire he felt, he resolved to be extra attentive to her innocence, even if this would be merely a dream to her in the morning.

When he joined her beneath the covers, she stared at him with mixed trepidation and curiosity. Dominick shifted closer, caressing her cheek and gazing into the brown depths of her wide, ever blinking eyes.

"What's that look for?" he asked softly in amusement. "You act as though I've become a frightening ogre."

"Oh, no, nothing like that," Julianna said quickly. "Although I must admit I prefer being with you when you're like this, rather than distant and angry."

Dominick kissed her temples as he spoke. "Even if we have our arguments, as couples often do, you never have to worry beyond a verbal tiff. I swear I'd never harm you physically, in any way."

"Then I'll grant you the same courtesy," she decided, earning a chuckle from him.

"I'm certainly glad to hear ***that***, since you're so good with that kicking maneuver," he replied honestly, slipping his hands beneath the covers to caress her back and pull her closer. "Now come here, my sweet tigress, and let's speak no more of fighting this night."

As his mouth recaptured her own, Julianna surrendered to his embrace willingly. His warmth encompassed her totally as their bare skin touched, and she reveled at the contact. Different, yet comforting, feeling his heart beat against hers.

Dominick felt a rare wave of protectiveness flood through him as he realized how much trust she was granting him. Kissing her endlessly, while he expertly enflamed every inch of her trembling body, he silently vowed she wouldn't regret the endowment of that trust.

As his kisses moved to her neck, her response was greater this time, only heightening his desire for her as well. Against the comfort of darkness, his mouth covered her breast, and her surprised gasp swiftly changed to sounds of pleasure as he kissed and worshipped her there, slowly, thoroughly. She clasped him against her, kissing him even as he did the same with the other, until finally he captured her mouth with his again.

She responded passionately, even as she felt his hands travel lower. Arching against his exploring touch, his increasingly intimate kisses swallowed a moan from her, while he slowly continued to set her every sense aflame.

So much so, that Julianna was becoming increasingly stirred up by the restless newness of passion, running her hands along his back and over his shoulders, her kisses as demanding as his own, sending the already burning heat between them up several more degrees. Her questing hands stroked across his chest and then tentatively reached lower.

She felt his sharp responding shudder, as he groaned against her mouth and quickly but gently pulled her hands away. Staring into his eyes, Julianna felt her face flush crimson. "I'm sorry, Dominick," she whispered uneasily. "I've never done this before, so I'm not sure what to do. I guess you might have thought otherwise."

He stifled her words with a gentle shush, holding one finger against her lips. "I thought exactly what you've just told me, that this is your first time," he replied. "You have no need to apologize for anything tonight, the least of which for having a lack of experience. I'm grateful to be your first." He smiled knowingly, kissing her quickly. "And the one to show you what to do."

"But before..."

"It wasn't wrong," he chuckled. "I'm afraid you just caught me by surprise, and even dream knights only have so much self-control."

Understanding now, Julianna smiled. "I don't mind if you lose some of that control, Dominick."

"I'm glad," he replied softly, the temporarily banked flames of desire rekindling in his eyes. "Because in another moment, I'll no doubt lose whatever remains of it."

The urgency in his kisses emphasized this as he reached his arm beneath her waist to pull her still closer, allowing his other hand to stroke upward to caress her breast again warmly, evoking a magic all its own. Emitting a soft sigh of pleasure, Julianna shut her eyes in dreamy abandon.

At last, she understood what she'd been missing. With the right person, romance could indeed be a beautiful thing. Roger's attempts paled in comparison. Dominick's kisses and caresses were taking her to a realm of wonderful sensations she'd only imagined before, which she had no desire to return from.

When he finally moved over her, Julianna's breathing quickened, her eyes opening to stare back into his own glazed expression.

"Julianna, love," he breathed. "Tell me... are you certain of this?"

Simple words, but tenderly meaningful. In answer, she smiled with consent. "I'm certain, my dream knight."

Dominick's features softened into a thankful expression as he kissed her again, encouraged by her response, and inwardly relieved that at least in the dream-state, there wouldn't be any pain for her in their loving.

In the midst of his next kiss, Julianna sensed his own breathing quicken, but despite her prior words of acceptance, she was hesitant. "Trust me, love. I'll always keep you safe," he whispered, gazing into her eyes as he smiled upon her reassuringly. "Remember that always." She nodded assent, clinging to him as her eyes fluttered shut.

Cradling her close, Dominick continued to whisper soft endearments to her, enticing her acceptance as he covered her mouth with his own. Enraptured further by his ensuing sweet caresses, she gave a low moan, tugging against his shoulders, pleading with him not to wait any longer. Slowly, he brought them together, feeling her sweet warmth all around him, just before she gasped softly.

Pausing to kiss her cheek comfortingly, he smoothed her hair back. "Easy, love. Remember my promise. There's nothing to be afraid of."

Warmed by the compassion in his voice as he kissed her again, she nodded slightly while he drew them closer still. What she'd heard of this act couldn't describe ***everything***, she realized, a small cry escaping her from the unexpected feelings of his complete possession.

Feelings that might as well have been new to him too, he decided, experiencing an unexpected deeper sense of soul-filled pleasure at finally being one with her.

Expressing this through his kisses as he held her, he waited until she'd adjusted to their newfound intimacy. It didn't take long for her to reciprocate, kissing him back. Upon sensing Julianna's grip tighten, her soft murmuring beckoning him, Dominick gratefully acquiesced, withdrawing only to gently thrust deeper, sending ripples of pleasure through them both, and building into a slow and easy rhythm.

Julianna's last fears dissolved, replaced in her mind by brightly colored lights dancing before her, the sweet strains of beautiful music humming in her ears.

There was no imagining the man responsible for this.

With heartfelt happiness, she smiled against his kisses.

"Dominick, it's like magic," she whispered blissfully.

"It is that, love. The sweetest magic," he agreed, smiling back. "And it gets even better." She was about to question this, but as soon as he began to move again, their thoughts became equally lost to their desire.

Before long, she caught onto the rhythm they shared, as he guided her with a quickening pace towards quenching the desire they both felt. The sounds of passion that escaped Julianna were foreign to her, yet she seemed no more able to control them than Dominick could stifle his own.

Her heart was soaring with sheer euphoria, climbing ever higher, until she suddenly felt a wave of pleasure that left her breathless. Dominick echoed this, breathing her name against her cheek, as he followed her into the timeless ecstasy of lovers.

When their racing hearts gradually slowed, Dominick finally looked down to gaze into his companion's eyes, seeing the same tired bliss in them as she stared back. Smoothing a hand against her forehead, he smiled upon her with a wave of adoration so strong, she found herself blushing.

"Are you all right?" he whispered.

"When I can breathe again, I'll let you know," she replied softly. He started to move from her, but her hands clasped him tighter, her smile unmistakable. "That's not what I meant," she assured him. "I don't mind."

"Maybe not," he chuckled, "but the rest of me will voice itself again if I don't back off slightly, while your own sweet body deserves a respite from its initiation to love."

Julianna blushed, but made no further protest as Dominick leaned back and pulled her close against his side. Shutting her eyes, she nestled closer with one arm resting across his chest, while his own grasp on her tightened possessively, tugging the covers higher over them.

"Seriously," he murmured against her cheek, "I didn't hurt you, did I?"

"I was a bit surprised at first," she replied. "But there wasn't any of the pain I expected, and after that, all I felt were rainbows and the most beautiful music singing through me."

"Ah, that sounds about right for a dream," he laughed. Even as she echoed his laughter, he could feel her begin to stiffen in his arms. "What's wrong?"

Julianna sighed once, before speaking. "I just realized that we probably don't have much longer together," she murmured regretfully. "Soon I'll be awake, and this will all be just a wonderful memory." As she glanced up at him, he saw sadness in her eyes. "Oh, Dominick, I wish we could be together in the waking world. Not just for a few hours each night. It's so damned unfair."

Gently resting her head against his shoulder, he kissed her forehead. "I know, love," he whispered, squeezing her meaningfully. "But take heart. Maybe one day we can find a way around the rules that govern our being together. In the meantime, we still have our stolen moments until the dawn."

"Yes," she agreed. "Better that than being without you altogether." Even as Julianna spoke the words, a new concern entered her mind. She shut her eyes against it, but Dominick wasn't fooled.

"There's something else bothering you," he said softly. She bit her lip, not wanting to cast a damper on this perfect night they'd shared. As if hearing her thoughts, he raised up on one elbow. "Tell me what's troubling you, love."

She nearly had to force the words free.

"Us, Dominick," she replied finally, earning a look of confusion from him. "From day one, you've made it quite clear what you wanted from me, and now... now that you've gotten it, I'm afraid I'll never see you again."

Surprised, Dominick nearly laughed, but his conscience stopped him. For in the past, there were times that had happened between him and his nightly paramours. However, his mind added quickly, those women weren't Julianna. Even now, his desire for her was already returning.

But even with this knowledge, he knew it was more than a physical attraction that kept him coming back to her. He genuinely liked being with her. He appreciated her smile, her laughter, her fun and teasing manner, her air of intelligence, her very pleasing and responsive nature—definitely that! he decided—her shifts from being playful to serious, her strength even when vulnerable, and most importantly, her loving and loyal heart.

Ah, surely loving, as Julianna had proven time and again, be it with affection for her nephew, or to the feelings and passion they'd shared tonight. Oddly enough, Dominick felt similarly loving towards her now, although since he'd never known real love before, he wasn't sure if that was accurate. He supposed it could be, but didn't want to tell her so unless he believed it completely.

Yet now, she'd spoken as if afraid he'd tired of her already. *Definitely not!* his mind exclaimed, only then realizing that he'd remained silent for some time, leaving her staring at him now with what seemed like mixed emotions.

"You shouldn't think so little of yourself, love," he said seriously. "It may be true that I desired this from you at the start, but as I've gotten to know you, I ended up desiring much more. I have no wish to break off our relationship, unless you tell me you wish it so yourself. Instead, I'd like to spend more time with you, so we can learn more of each other."

"In the bedroom?" Julianna asked suspiciously.

"No, not just for that," laughed Dominick, not loosing the expression from her face. "Well now, if that look bears any truth, it would seem I've changed from knight to ogre yet again, unless you think ogre is too complimentary."

At her attempt to hide a smile, he continued, "I'll tell you what I'd like to do, my fair Julianna. I want to hear about your life and family in the reality of your world. I want us to go to new and pleasant dream scenarios to enjoy our time together, and to show you all that can be." At her curious smile, he cuddled her closer to add, "And perhaps to show you more games lovers play."

To emphasize his words, he kissed her lingeringly. Afterwards, the look of doubt faded from her eyes.

"All right, I trust you," she said finally. "I just hope you're not going to disappear on me to find another like my former boyfriend Roger."

Dominick shushed her gently. "I'm not leaving you. And let's not talk about him tonight," he suggested, earning a nod of agreement from her. Pulling her closer, he murmured against her cheek, "Dearest, promise me you'll try and forget about him altogether."

Liking his endearments more and more, she smiled. "Roger who?" she murmured back, earning a chuckle from him.

"Ah, that's my Julianna," he whispered, even as things began to fade around them. "It would seem we'd best say our good-byes quickly, love," Dominick added knowingly, his grip tightening on her shoulder. "Though by heaven, I wish it didn't have to be like this."

"You'll come back for me tomorrow then?"

"I promise, love."

Their embrace strengthened still more, stealing a few more kisses before they were separated once again. Julianna tried hard to memorize Dominick's face, just in case there would be no next time for them, and she tried to take comfort in his strength, even as his hold on her became lighter and she felt herself drifting away.

Not yet! her mind demanded. *We need more time!*

She knew such time was not to be granted however, and in desperation, her troubled thoughts gave rise to the truth of a new emotion. One she wanted deeply to express.

"Farewell until the morrow, love," she heard him whisper faintly.

Wait, Dominick, I love you! she tried to shout in response, but the words were as lost to him as he was to her.

As she started to wake up in her own room, Julianna heard herself whisper her last thought again, just before full reality set in. Sitting up sharply, she glanced down at her attire. She half expected to find her nightgown lying on the floor, but of course, everything she and Dominick had done was only in a dream.

Despite the fact that it ***was*** just a dream, Julianna couldn't help but feel that she'd lost a part of herself, along with losing Dominick. The vividness and beauty of her dreams made waking all the more painful, and the gap between these two worlds began to weigh heavily upon her.

For it was the dream world that was becoming her favorite world. And what kind of crazy girl would fall in love with an illusion?

Chapter Seven

"Are you drunk?" Vicki asked suspiciously.

Julianna shook her head with a laugh. "What a nice way to greet someone in the morning. Most people just say, 'How are you doing?'"

Vicki had no reply, merely watching as Julianna moved airily about her room. Something strange was going on, she decided. It ***was*** only 10:00 AM. Normally, her younger sister wouldn't be up this early on the weekend, usually trying to catch up on sleep after a busy workweek. When Julianna did get up early, she was often listless at best, irritable at worst. But instead, Vicki awoke to hear her humming in her bedroom.

Humming! her mind repeated.

Upon knocking, if she hadn't heard Julianna respond in her familiar voice, Vicki would have sworn her sister had been kidnapped and replaced by an alien duplicate. When she emerged from her room immediately after, the smile on her face looked bright enough to renew Vicki's suspicions that this couldn't possibly be ***her*** sister.

Even Crystal was surprised to see Julianna in such good spirits, but she merely laughed at Vicki's concern. "Better she be unusually happy than depressed," she stated.

Their sister was totally oblivious to their opinions, caught in her own euphoric state of cloud nine. True, Julianna couldn't understand what kept bringing Dominick back into her dreams, now three nights in a row. Nor was she sure how long this seeming 'coincidence' would persist with its surprising vividness, both when she was asleep and awake. But for all its strangeness, she didn't question it anymore. She was happy now, for the first time in months.

Her dream knight had given her an inner strength, the feeling of love given and returned—even without the words themselves being spoken—and he was truly a positive influence on her life. He'd even helped ease the pain over Roger's betrayal. And now, she was beginning to believe the saying that time healed all wounds.

Giving due credit, of course, to Dominick!

"Aunt Julie, can I pul-ease have a cookie?" asked a familiar voice behind her, just before Sammy's arms wrapped around her legs.

Laughing as she disentangled herself from his grasp, Julianna knelt down to his level, rubbing her chin thoughtfully. "Isn't it a bit early for cookies?" A sad-eyed pout replaced his former brightness, but he said nothing as he shifted feet. "Oh, good heavens. This looks to be an emergency, isn't it? Well then, I suppose one cookie can't hurt. Come on."

Sammy grinned, taking her hand and pulling her towards the kitchen. Julianna laughed heartily at how such a little thing could inspire delight in a child. As she watched her nephew contentedly munching away at the cookie she'd retrieved from the jar up above, she found herself wondering what her own children might be like someday.

Maybe... like Dominick?

The doorbell rang, and moments later Vicki shouted, "Julie!"

"I'll get it!" she called back, still a bit dreamy-eyed as she walked to the door. Absently, she wondered where she'd meet Dominick tonight. Another romantic setting? A space scenario? Or perhaps back at the castle again.

Smiling warmly in remembrance of how they'd spent the evening there last night, she opened the door...

And abruptly froze.

"Julie," the quiet yet familiar voice said, as if from far

away. "You're looking better than ever."

"No," she whispered, shaking her head and feeling her skin suddenly turn cold. *Roger!* What on Earth was ***he*** doing here, now of all times, when she was finally moving past what happened? "I'm sorry," she stammered finally. "You must have the wrong house."

"Please," he protested, holding the door ajar with his foot. "I need to speak with you. What you saw in the store wasn't how it looked. Things have changed in your absence. Can't you spare me a few minutes, so I can explain?"

Anger replaced her shock. "Explain what?" she bit out. "Explain that you're in love with another woman? Explain that I'm just someone to pass the time with when it's convenient? No thanks, Roger. I neither need nor want your explanations. Just get out."

"I don't love Marilyn, and she's out of my life for good."

So the rumors were true, Julianna thought. Still, true or not, it didn't erase the scene at the store, and she concluded it didn't matter, hardening her expression.

"I'm very happy for her," she said coldly.

"And I realize what an idiot I've been in regard to you," Roger continued. "Julie, look I know you must be angry, but I'm really sorry for what happened between us. I was trying to tell you in the supermarket that I was helping Marilyn out simply because her car broke down. But I would have done that for anyone."

"How convenient that you were able to be there for her, but not for me when I needed it."

"I see. So this isn't about Marilyn so much as what happened between us during our last evening together." The somber look in her eyes confirmed his words. "Julie, if I could do it over, don't you think I would?"

"I don't know. Would you?"

"Of course I would."

Having heard lines like this from him before, she shook her head. "You know, that's all fine and good for you, Roger. But you're wasting your time telling me this," she replied, her voice shaking slightly. "What's done is done, and there's no going back. Just because I wanted to take things slow, you couldn't wait to jump into bed with someone else. All those years I thought you were different, but obviously I was wrong. Now please, just leave." Before she could shut the door, Roger deftly stepped inside, placing his hands on her shoulders. She flinched against him, but her back was to the door. "Roger, let me go, or I swear I'll scream," she nearly yelled.

"Julie, listen to me!" he said firmly, his grip tightening. "The last thing I want is to have you screaming for your family, but I'm not leaving until you hear me out." Sighing once as she fell silent, he began more quietly, "I understand your anger, Julie, and I don't blame you for it. Heaven knows I haven't done much to earn otherwise from you lately. But ever since that evening you came to my apartment to find me, all I've wanted to do was run over here to set things right between us."

Keeping her expression neutral, she asked quietly, "So why didn't you then?"

"I didn't think there could be any going back, so I chose the simplest route by trying to forget you instead," he replied. His eyes became almost pleading. "But I couldn't do that, which is why I'm here now. Our relationship means something to me." Seeing the uncertain disbelief in her expression, he released her shoulders, continuing even more gently, "Julie, please... can't you give us another chance? I swear things will never be like before again."

Julianna turned away quickly, as if she feared being burned from having conversed with the devil himself.

Not too far from the truth actually, she considered.

His words were just what she'd wanted to hear before, and yet... how could she go against every fiber of her being to forgive him? He'd done nothing but hurt her before, and undoubtedly would again if she gave him his so-called chance. Her mixed feelings voiced a different response.

"I don't know," she said brokenly. "You're like a stranger to me now, Roger. How can I trust anything you say anymore?"

"Give me time to prove it to you," he murmured, moving closer to press a kiss to her forehead. "Please, Julianna, let me make it up to you."

He hadn't used her full name in the longest time, and the way he spoke it now, it sounded like an endearment.

If his words were poisoned again, they were sweetly lethal, she thought, surprised at this display of tenderness from one she'd no longer believed had the capability for it.

Even so, his last words triggered a different memory.

Dominick.

He'd used similar words in last night's dream, hadn't he? Yet that argument had stemmed from a misunderstanding. He'd acted from what he thought to be a betrayal, while in Roger's case, he'd ***caused*** the betrayal himself. Two different situations entirely.

Dominick... her mind repeated. Would he vanish from her dreams forever if she accepted Roger's invitation to try again? In fact, would he vanish anyway in days to come?

Turning back to face Roger, she tried to look in control, but it was a hopeless gesture. Despite her best efforts, she was confused again. As if sensing this, Roger used her silence to advantage, pulling her close to hold her.

Somehow, she couldn't find the will to break free.

"Julianna, how I've missed you," he whispered. "It's going to be different this time, I promise you."

Promises in words but not actions! her angry thoughts reminded her. Yet logic wasn't always as easy to accept as some seemed to think, warring with her former feelings. Instead of pushing him away, she simply frowned and said nothing.

"Why don't we spend the day together to do some catching up?" he suggested. "We can go for a drive, and find a restaurant where we can get lunch and talk."

For long moments, Julianna considered the offer.

Until logic finally took full rein, prompting her to shake her head. "I'm afraid I can't," she said. "I have some work due tomorrow that can't wait, and I want to get it done before I'm too tired later. You'd better go."

Roger pulled back to stare into her eyes as if about to rebel, but then to her surprise, he accepted her words with a calm smile.

"All right," he agreed. "But I'll be back later to rescue you from that workload. Maybe over dinner?"

"Roger…"

"Shhh… just think about it."

Not certain how to reply—admittedly, only half listening now—Julianna could only give a slight nod. Before she even realized it, he started to leave, stepping back to pull the door shut behind him. Just before it shut completely, he added with a smile, "It's good to see you again, Julie. I can't tell you how much just now, but I will."

The door's closing hammered against her ears, but even when Sammy's abrupt pleading for another cookie began, Julianna was too at a loss for words to pay any attention to either. After all this time, why on Earth had Roger suddenly rendered her speechless?

It wasn't as if she'd completely forgiven him for what he'd done, so it made no sense. So much different from last night when she'd wholeheartedly forgiven Dominick for his actions without reservation. Dear heaven, she wished he was here right now to hold her and to kiss her concerns away as he did so well. If he'd been here beside her, she wouldn't have hesitated to send Roger walking without a second glance. And she'd certainly have told him ***where*** he could go tonight!

But that wasn't what had happened at all.

Instead, she'd been caught off-guard by a weak moment.

"Oh, Dominick..." she whispered brokenly, clutching her arms tightly. "I wish you were here."

*****

Buddy and Inferno stared at Dominick with confusion as he sauntered into Lost Limbo with the unmistakable air of better spirits. The girls at their table were equally puzzled over the grin on his face, but Kiri assured them with a conspiratorial smile that her psychic ability would pick up any conversation the guys might have.

"Your best, Zantarl!" Dominick called out cheerfully.

The near middle-aged bartender, who instantly returned a smile as the dreamphaser approached, wondered what had changed since his argument with Buddy yesterday. His curiosity showed through his amber eyes, although they were only good at seeing through material substances—not reading minds, like Kiri could.

As the proprietor of Lost Limbo for many years, despite his fairly youthful appearance, Zantarl had become well acquainted with Dominick and the group he associated with. He related to Dominick the most though, since the lad was alone more than the others—except for his dealings with various women, here and there—and had such a distant relationship from his parents.

In fact, since Zantarl had all but been there when Dominick was born, he came to regard him as the son he never had—having five daughters from his current marriage. Fortunately, his wife Dreeana had been even more attached to the boy, always being available with a brownie and a warm hug over the years. Yes, while they loved their own children dearly, no mistake about that, Zantarl and his wife both looked at Dominick with the fondness of family.

As for their daughters' reaction to Dominick, they rarely protested his visiting, particularly since a few had cases of 'puppy love' since he'd transformed from a cute boy to a handsome man. But despite his charm with the ladies, Zantarl never worried that Dominick would turn his amorous attentions on his own girls, since he stated quite clearly one time that he loved them all as the sisters he never had. No, Dominick regarded them as his foster family, and he was a good lad. A bit rough around the edges sometimes, but good deep down.

"Well, it would seem you've gotten the brawling out of your system for one day," Zantarl said finally, placing the newly concocted drink on the counter, before leaning on one arm. "Care to let me in on the secret behind this?"

"No secret, Zan," he replied lightly.

To the careful observer, his words sounded more like 'No secret, Dad', but Dominick took this in stride since it seemed true most of the time. Stirring his drink absently, he gave Zantarl his usual enigmatic look, yet for once it seemed a bit more serious.

"Right," the clever bartender murmured, not masking his disbelief. "And you're a guardian angel with a shining gold halo to match. The truth now, son." Dominick gave a short laugh, explaining the past three days he'd spent with Julianna, not to mention their first meeting two months ago. Zantarl listened quietly, mixed emotions flashing across his face, until he finished. "Ah, I see now. Your latest love for the time being. No, hear me out. Now Chaos knows there's no stopping you when you've set your sights on a pretty female, but don't you think it's about time you let this one go, for her sake if not your own?"

The younger man's face sobered somewhat, but he shook his head. "You don't understand, Zan. I can't just let her go. Maybe at the very start I could have, but not now."

"Dominick, for once try to see reason."

"Reason?" he sneered, staring up at the ceiling with a

weak smile. “No, I’m afraid reason doesn’t stand a chance anymore. And you have no idea what Julianna’s like.”

“I can guess. Flawlessly beautiful and passionate like the rest.”

“No,” Dominick protested. “I mean... yes, she’s beautiful, and surely passionate too, but she is ***not*** like the rest. She’s beautiful on the inside too, Zan. As sweet as honey, with a fiery spirit to match.”

“Really now?” laughed Zantarl. “How could that be favorable?”

“Maybe for someone who’d like a woman with a little fire within, rather than some of your guardian angel types who are so sweet you’re afraid of their dissolving into fairy dust in your hands. I’d prefer my spirited Julianna to them any day of the millennium. Because even with those moments, she’s also very loving and considerate, and most of all, understanding.”

“It would seem so after your rushed-to conclusions last night,” Zantarl agreed sternly. “You know you should have asked her who those people were, before you assumed the worst.”

“Believe me, I won’t make that mistake again.”

Zantarl nodded, his expression softening. “It’s nice that you took her out to dance afterwards to make up for it.” He leaned closer. “I would assume, in spite of omitting further details, more may have happened at this dream castle you created for her?” The younger man remained silent. “I see.”

“No, you don’t see,” Dominick protested, earning a curious stare from Zantarl. “There’s nothing wrong with what we choose to do together, and that is ***not*** my sole reason for wanting to see her again. Zan, if it was purely physical, I could have searched for someone else before. And I’m not going to deny that I didn’t enjoy our time together last night. But there ***is*** more to it than that. She has caring, intelligence, a good sense of humor, and a strong-willed spirit despite her underlying innocence. In a way, I feel like she's what's been missing from my life all these years."

Zantarl's curiosity became surprise. "I don't believe I've ever heard you speak so of any of your nocturnal liaisons before, let alone women here. Truthfully, what are your feelings towards this Julianna if it's not a temporary attraction?"

A question Dominick still wasn't completely certain about himself. Having never been in love before, his feelings for Julianna were stronger than any he'd ever known. But he needed to be sure that it was really love, the kind that Julianna would be happy with. Desire might burn itself out in time, but if it was love... time would reveal it.

After some deliberation, he replied quietly, "I'd rather not answer that just now, Zantarl. I can only say that my feelings for Julianna run deeper than any I've ever felt towards other women, and that I'll do my damnedest to make sure she isn't hurt, one way or the other. If that means staying with her until she says otherwise, then I'm willing to do just that. Fair enough?"

"I suppose it'll have to be," sighed Zantarl, patting his arm quickly. "You'd best see to your friends at their table now. We can talk more on this later."

"Thanks, Zan. I'm glad I can trust you."

As Dominick walked away, Zantarl smiled after him with new understanding. So the lad might finally have found love after all, and apparently someone who might very well feel the same about him. If that was true, Zantarl would certainly be happy for him, and yet he was forced to wonder...

What kind of love could exist between two people from such distant worlds, who could only see each other for a few hours a night in their dreams?

Thinking of his own dear wife, Zantarl could see how love might make those brief moments bearable, but he was infinitely glad that Dreeana wasn't separated from him in the same way. It was too bad really. He might have liked to have been introduced to this young lady of Dominick's. If his words were to be believed, she was special indeed.

"Zantarl, what's the hold up on our drinks!" came a shout from one table.

"Hold onto your shorts, Izzy, or you'll be dealing with a much longer dry spell!"

With that, the further details to the saga of Dominick and Julianna would have to wait until later.

In the meantime, Dominick sat with his friends while they amiably chatted, not noticing the attentive looks Kiri gave him. In fact, he seemed somewhat oblivious to the conversations altogether, although he smiled now and then. Kiri's eyes were seeking during his distraction, although with her mind reading ability it wasn't hard to read the very clear images in his mind.

One other watching at a table nearby looked equally interested in his distraction, listening in secretly.

Dominick smiled as he continued to toy with his drink, never actually drinking it, but staring ahead blankly while thinking of Julianna. Tonight perhaps she'd tell him more of her nephew that she adored so. With her liking for children, he supposed she might like one of her own someday.

If it was possible, he would have gladly obliged her there, but alas, the dream-state only provided so much reality. *A matter of no consequence right now*, he decided finally, turning his thoughts to brighter things.

Maybe this evening, they could have a romantic dinner beside the silvery ocean. The dream's night sky could be filled with bright rainbows—reminding him of her blissful words comparing them to their time together last night—and likewise, accompanying soft music could be made to fill the air. After dining, he had the perfect place to show her afterwards... but that would have to wait for now.

Glancing up at the clock on Lost Limbo's wall, a frown

replaced his brightness. There were still many hours to go before he could see her. Damn, but time could go so slow when one anticipated a rendezvous with a loved companion.

He stopped himself abruptly. There it was again. ***Love***?

But was it really love or just something that resembled it to the point of maddening illusion? Maybe tonight he could ascertain the truth once and for all, and perhaps also find out her feelings on the matter. He was a bit afraid that she'd proclaim last night to have been wonderful, but that a continued relationship could never be between them—and surely she was justified in believing so—although he planned on taking steps to investigate the real truth to that. For he certainly didn't want to lose her now, since he so valued their time together.

"Dom!" yelled Buddy, snapping his attention back again. "It'd be nice if you paid attention to us for a few minutes. Where ***is*** your mind anyway? Off daydreaming with that ability of yours?"

A smile of consideration crossed Dominick's face in silent response. Daydreaming, he mused... a possibility he hadn't considered. It would certainly be nice to see Julianna right now, and although he didn't make a habit of it, he knew it was possible.

But not an option he'd use, since to be honest, he didn't want to interfere with her daytime life. After all, he couldn't keep her mind suspended in a perpetual dream, now could he? A person had to eat, and while one could do so in the dream-state, it wouldn't be of any use to the person's physical body which would remain unnourished. Besides that, she'd briefly mentioned having a job too, which he wasn't about to risk jeopardizing.

No, he'd see her in a few hours, and that was that.

A sudden searing pain in his arm jolted him back to reality again. "Ow!" he exclaimed, glaring at Inferno. "What was that for?"

"Ah, the dreamer boy returns," sneered Buddy. "How honored we are."

Ignoring his remarks, Inferno shook his head apologetically. "I didn't use enough heat to burn you, Dominick," he said quietly. "It's just that when you're off in dreamland, it's very hard to pull you back."

Dominick was silent for a moment before smiling. "Okay, I'll buy that," he laughed. "Just make sure you don't try the same stunt at night, or I won't be responsible for my less tolerant reaction."

Inferno's eyebrows quirked up curiously. "Question. Are you still seeing that girl you were chasing?"

"Yes, I'm definitely still seeing her," he replied happily. "Although last night I'd say the chasing most certainly ended."

Buddy gaped at the implication. "Dom, you didn't..." Silence. "Oh, Chaos, you did," he sighed. "Well, maybe it's for the best. Now you can leave that poor girl alone, and..."

Dominick's expression was stern. "You know, it would be wonderful if my closest friends would start remembering for the umpteenth time that I'm not my brother. When I said the chasing ended last night, I meant as in we've found that we're mutually happy together."

"You're not going back to see her again, are you?"

"Yes, I am," he said evenly. "I promised her I would."

"I shouldn't be surprised! Far be it from you to... you did what?"

"She asked me to meet her again tonight, and I promised I would." He couldn't help giving a wearied sigh to his gaping friend. "You're reading something negative into something that is completely the opposite. The entire time I spent with Julianna last night brought me more happiness since I can't remember when."

The piercing sound of breaking glass abruptly jarred him into turning, along with the other occupants of Lost Limbo, to face an angry Sionne who now stood. "Well, well, well... so your new harlot has a name," she hissed softly. "Julianna, is it? From which corner did you dredge ***this*** one up, Dominick?"

He smiled darkly. "Sionne, if you were a man, you'd be missing several teeth right now for your insults. As it is, it's none of your business." He tried to turn away again, but she grabbed his arm.

"Your grandfather will no doubt see differently, since he's already decided we're to be betrothed."

"Really?" he chuckled, becoming serious. "Then I'm happy to hear it, and I accept completely." Sionne began to smile triumphantly, while his friends could only gasp. "Though you're a bit younger than I'd have expected for a new step-grandmother, I'm sure you'll be very happy together."

Moments later, the whole place erupted into laughter, including Buddy and Inferno, with the exception of Jarissa. Dominick maintained his composure with an icy smile, while Sionne's hands curled into fists, her face red.

"I'm sure your grandfather won't be quite so pleased by your amused mockery!" she yelled above the laughter, storming out angrily.

"Good one, Dom," chuckled Buddy, slapping his shoulder good-naturedly. "She certainly had that coming."

"Oh, really?" snapped Jarissa, her devil horns blazing red as he abruptly quieted. Turning to Dominick, she met his nonchalant look with ire. "You have a hell of a nerve, treating poor Sionne like that. She's done nothing but strive for a bit of kindness from you, yet all you can do is flaunt your illicit liaisons in her face and humiliate her."

"***Poor*** Sionne brought it on herself," he replied evenly. "Although leave it to a guardian devil to defend those with questionable motives." Even as Jarissa silently fumed, he continued, "Sionne knows we've never been a couple, I never agreed to a betrothal with her, and certainly have no ties to keep me from seeking out someone else if I choose."

"We ***all*** know that," Inferno said meaningfully. Even Psych nodded.

"Maybe. But speaking of liaisons, Kiri overheard that you managed to seduce that innocent girl in her dreams."

Dominick's expression darkened again as he turned to Kiri, who now stood beside her friend. "Next time, you'd best eavesdrop a bit more carefully," he hissed. "I didn't seduce Julianna. What we shared last night was completely mutual."

"For one night," she sneered. This time it was Dominick's gaze—not Inferno's—which seemed to shoot real fire at her.

"As I just told Buddy, we happen to be meeting again tonight," he retorted.

"Yes, and perhaps for a few days more, if she's intrigued you that much." Her eyes became accusing. "But beyond that, we all know it's a matter of time before you tire of her. The only difference is, when your days of meaningless loveplay with her are over, you'll leave without consequence, while she's left alone with yet another rejection."

This time, Inferno and Psych both stood up.

"Kiri, that's out of line," he protested. "Aren't you judging a bit prematurely?"

"Yes," agreed Psych, "Dominick would never treat a woman that callously."

"I ***know*** what I saw!" Kiri exclaimed.

Dominick had been silent for long moments, all too conscious of Buddy's questioning eyes upon him, but before Kiri could retort further, he broke in, silencing all.

"Your words twist things," he said finally, barely controlling his anger, "so allow me to clear up what you ***think*** you saw. As to our meaningless loveplay as you call it, I can assure you that you're ***completely*** wrong on that count, and you have no right to insult us like that. I already said it was mutual, and it has more meaning to us than you'll ever understand."

Pushing his chair in angrily, he stood to face her, continuing, "And before you proclaim yourself judge and jury over us, Kiri, I think we both know where your venom is ***really*** coming from. It's not ***me*** who would do something like that, but your on-and-off paramour Riff. Instead of railing at me, maybe you should aim your anger where it really belongs!"

Turning to Buddy and Jarissa directly, he added, "If the rest of you choose to think the worst of me, I can't stop you. Until this point, I'd credited you as being more understanding of me than that, so that really saddens me. But if all this means you're forcing me to choose between you and Julianna… then I'm afraid we have nothing more to say to each other."

He bit out the last as he slammed his chair against the table and stormed from Lost Limbo, leaving behind the gaping guardian pair, while Inferno and Psych unsuccessfully entreated him not to leave. Even Kiri looked apologetic at his departure. Zantarl shook his head and sighed upon witnessing this. He could only hope that this Julianna was worth as much as he claimed. If not, he feared that Dominick would lose a lot more than just his heart.

*****

Thank heaven for helpful siblings to solve a dilemma!

Julianna heard the door shut downstairs, following Roger's fairly loud disagreement over Crystal's explanation that her sister had suddenly developed a migraine that she needed to rest out. He protested that she was fine earlier when he'd spoken with her, but Crystal was soon backed up by her concerned husband. Jerry wasn't a fond admirer of Roger's either, and he wasn't about to let his younger sister-in-law see the man when she said she didn't want to.

Quietly peering out the corner of her window, Julianna saw Roger slam his car door and speed off. Sighing in relief that he was gone, she reclined on her bed and shut her eyes against the darkness. After completing her aforementioned work early in the day, and later receiving some helpful advice from Marybeth over the phone, she decided to put off meeting with Roger until she had more time to think things through.

*That is, **if** I decide to see him again*, her mind amended.

A knock on her door stirred a glance from her. "Come in," she said tiredly. As Crystal and Jerry's smiling faces appeared, Julianna echoed the gesture.

"It took a bit of convincing," sighed Crystal, "but he's gone."

"So I heard," Julianna agreed nodding. "Thank you both for being so helpful and understanding."

"Hey, it's the least a couple of old folks can do," laughed Jerry, earning a rap on the shoulder from his wife.

"Speak for yourself, mister," she admonished. "Just because you think ***you're*** over the hill, doesn't mean that ***I*** have to take part in that title."

Her husband kissed her cheek lovingly. "You never seemed to mind the title of being Mrs. Old Timer before," he whispered. Before she could reply, he slipped his arms about her waist to hug her close. "Maybe I can remind you of that later," he added suggestively.

At Crystal's quiet protests about discussing such things now, Julianna's bright laughter eased any tension. "Neither one of you are over the hill, and you're certainly younger than any old timers I've ever seen," she commented. "Now why don't you go work this out amongst yourselves, while I prepare to get some sleep?"

Jerry flashed his sister-in-law a quick smile, but aimed his words at Crystal. "I'm glad we kept this tactful sibling of yours with us," he chuckled. "Now all that needs to be settled is our earlier discussion on a sibling for Sammy..."

"Good night, Julianna!" interrupted Crystal, passing her husband without a backwards glance.

"Maybe you should settle your present discussion first," Julianna told her brother-in-law knowingly. "Otherwise, Sammy's liable to remain an only child."

"Ah, good point. I suppose I'd best switch to my alter ego of Humble Husband," Jerry replied, his eyes twinkling. "Good night, kiddo," he added, just before slipping out the door to follow his wife.

As Julianna heard him calling out to Crystal in a sugary voice, followed by her sister's sarcastic reply not to use such a tone with her now, she couldn't help but laugh quietly. She was glad her sister had found someone like Jerry. Despite their occasional bickering, they really loved each other, and she knew Crystal would be the first to agree.

Likewise, Vicki had been equally fortunate in finding her fiancé Luke. From the several times they'd chatted across the dinner table, Julianna could see that while Luke had an often reckless lifestyle, he certainly wasn't reckless over his love for Vicki. Constantly, flowers would arrive at the door for her older sister, along with notes of love and adoration from her most un-secretive admirer.

Up until a week ago, seeing her sisters so happy would cause mixed emotions. She was certainly happy for them, yet saddened over not having a companion of her own.

But now that Dominick had come into her life, suddenly she didn't feel so alone anymore. True, she could only see him in her dreams, but he still felt more real and wonderful to her than any man she'd ever known—including Roger.

To pass the time, she watched television until it was nearly ten, glancing at the clock repeatedly. Being a night person, she usually went to bed later, but tonight she didn't want to prolong being away from her dreams. In fact, she practically willed sleep to come for her, since she knew Dominick would be there for her.

At least she certainly hoped he would.

After today, inwardly she really needed his strength to lean on, since Roger had shaken things up earlier. If only Dominick was truly here, so he himself could tell Roger to leave forever. It would serve him right to be fed the same harsh medicine she'd forcibly swallowed over his affair with Marilyn.

The only difference was, she wanted more than just a temporary affair with Dominick, for she was more convinced than ever that she was falling in love with him—if she wasn't completely so already.

When caught absently sketching little drawings of him at work, a few of Julianna's co-workers had inquired with interest about her mystery man. She mentioned him in passing, but declined their suggestions to introduce him to them in person. They seemed to take her dismissal as amused jealousy, but Julianna knew better. *If only I **could** introduce him to you!* she'd wanted to shout, but sadly couldn't.

The night hours now erased her earlier sadness totally.

Against her shut eyes, Julianna smiled at the airy feelings sweeping across her mind. Her thoughts drifted away from Roger, her questioning co-workers, and all other problems currently in her life.

Soon she'd be with Dominick again, and all would be well.

*****

All was ***not*** well for one man.

Puffing for breath, Alarius Zaxelby was navigating the dark twisting corridor without much success. How he'd even ended up in this unforeseen mazelike territory, he had no idea, but there was no mistaking the loud growls of a distant creature heading towards him. Being half-elven, his ears could distinguish fairly well what it must be.

It was the sound of an angry dragon.

"***Give yourself up, Zaxelby!***" came a rumbling voice, no doubt from the dragon itself. A voice that was sickeningly familiar to the half-elf, who knew its owner well. "***Relinquish the map now, and I might spare your life!***"

"You'll get ***neither*** from me this day, foul beast!" Alarius yelled back, losing sight of where he was going.

Tripping over a hidden stone to crash to the ground, the fairly young man let out a sharp gasp, turning in anticipation of seeing the creature right behind him.

Not yet. There was still a chance he could escape.

*But where **is** the way out?* his thoughts demanded as he scrambled to his feet, running down another passageway. Reaching into his jacket, he pulled free the map in question. Given to him as a gift a few weeks ago by a generous friend who also lived on the island of Barokka—who discovered the map during his many nightly travels—the map's information granted its owner the whereabouts to a hidden portal.

Just within the doorway to this portal was a perpetual flowing waterfall, looking like a liquid rainbow. In actuality, this 'rainbow' of sorts constantly rained forth a cascade of colorful valuable jewels interspersed with its water, giving it its rainbow-like appearance. At the bottom of this waterfall—or perhaps more accurately, a 'jewel-fall'—several useful magical items had also once been left there. A veritable treasure trove!

While planning to follow his friend's advice to leave the magical items, Alarius planned to sell some of the endless jewels in order to give his poor family the life they deserved. Perhaps sparing a few colorful trinkets for his three children, soon to be four, and using some of the gems to create a beautiful necklace for his dear wife and now mother-to-be again.

He'd decided to seek this treasure after their fourth child was born in a few months, not wanting to be absent when his wife might need him sooner than expected.

But then a sudden twist had altered his plans.

Their youngest son Daric had become deathly ill.

An immediate cure was needed for the boy, whose

swiftly ebbing life required the services of an efficient but expensive healer in outer Chavernos. Since the healer demanded full payment up front, Alarius needed to seek out the treasure immediately. Leaving Daric in the capable hands of his wife and the local doctor—a wise elder man who promised to do his best to keep the boy alive until his return—it was with a heavy heart that the half-elf began his quest.

Under normal circumstances, Alarius should have had no trouble succeeding in his mission. The silvery-blond-haired half-elf appeared in his late twenties and as strong, although countless years older in actuality—due to his youthful long-lived elven blood. The same was true of his half-elven wife, who was equally capable, and might have accompanied him on the journey if she'd been able.

Thankfully, the portal's location wasn't very far away.

Unfortunately, neither were the two men who followed him, who'd learned of the map and sought to steal it.

If they were reasonable men, perhaps Alarius could have seen negotiating with them. But knowing many from Barokka, he remembered well who these dark followers were.

Their kind ***never*** bargained.

And Daric's life depended on him now.

The exit, blast it! he nearly yelled. *Where is it?*

As if in answer, a light began to brighten up ahead. Sighing thankfully, Alarius found an extra rush of adrenaline which helped carry him towards his destination. And then he saw it... the blessed exit!

Reaching his hands towards the sunlight just a few feet away, abruptly darkness fell upon the doorway leading out.

Replaced instead by the black scales of the dragon.

"***Thought you could escape, did you?***" it hissed.

Letting out a shocked yell, Alarius dropped to his knees, as the dragon loomed closer, its bloodstained talons outstretched. There was no need to ask whose blood would be added next to that already there, the half-elf considered dismally, feeling his heart race still faster.

"Please, let me go," he pleaded in a whisper. "My son... he needs help."

The dragon emitted a harsh laugh. "***Right now, you're the one who needs help, in case you're blind, man.***"

"You don't understand..."

"***No,* you *don't understand!***"

Hissing violet flames, the dragon slithered forward to grasp the collar of Alarius's shirt, dragging him from the ground to hold him suspended in mid-air. While the half-elf struggled to free himself, he found himself shaken roughly.

"***I'm not a patient man, Zaxelby,***" snarled the dragon, baring its sharp teeth of several inches long each. "***That map should never have fallen into your hands. It rightfully belongs to me and my associate Quell. Either give it to us willingly, or you'll find the rest of your family dead along with your son!***"

"You'd kill them anyway, you black-hearted demon," rasped Alarius.

The dragon broke into a fiendish grin, before tossing him to the ground. As the half-elf rubbed his shaken head, the scaly beast transformed itself into human form.

A human dreamphaser to be precise.

"I could indeed," the dark-haired man murmured through a malicious chortle, his voice sounding normally human now. "Especially the brats. Chavernos, how I do detest those little scavengers." *If not for their kind, you'd still be alive, Caralei.*

Waving his hand, he conjured up a regal-looking chair. Judging by his almost amiable smile now, one might easily neglect seeing past the coolly handsome features to find what really lurked within. Many had been fooled thus over the years by his seemingly dual nature.

Something which accounted perfectly for his known name... Dual.

Reclining lazily, he rubbed his chin knowingly. "But before killing all of them," he drawled, "I might spare your fair wife for a while, just so I could... sample her charms once or twice."

Alarius's eyes lit up like bright flames. "I'll see you rot in the demonworlds below before you set a finger on Laelea!" he hissed.

Dual quirked one eyebrow up. "Admirable, Zaxelby," he laughed. "I'd imagined you hadn't the spirit to threaten a dreamphaser. To find otherwise, I salute you." Stretching out his legs, he shook his head. "No, my dear Alarius, I have no wish to set my sights upon your wife presently. After all, she last appeared quite heavy with your latest offspring. I'm merely reminding you that I can make your life quite miserable, or end it as well, unless you cooperate."

The half-elf gave a forced laugh. "Cooperate! You mean for me to trade my son's life for my own!"

"Did I leave you with that impression?" Dual asked in mock surprise. "Surely, you simply misunderstood. You see, you're trading that map for ***all*** of your lives. Refuse to surrender it, and we'll kill your ailing son, followed by the rest of your limitless brood."

Seeing his hesitation, Dual waved a hand to reveal a floating image of Alarius's family waiting for him. The half-elf silently cursed the dreamphaser for his most effective cruelty. Just seeing Laelea again as she smiled upon the children, so far away, was a bitter torment to him now. As if she knew he was watching from afar, his wife looked up with a sad smile, one hand resting against their unborn child.

Alarius could also see the too small house they lived in, which would be even less suitable for yet another child. And his gaze fell upon little Daric, his pale form resting beside his attentive mother. The boy's eyes were closed from the fever, which held him in its deathlike grip, yet neither Laelea nor the doctor were willing to let him slip away... not while the hope of Alarius still remained.

A hope slowly dying like a candle flame being snuffed out.

"Think about it, Zaxelby," whispered Dual, his voice snakelike. "As you can quite clearly see, you'll soon have another brat if you lose this one, and you might even get back in time to see its arrival in person. One life for all... ***if*** you agree to the terms."

The vision faded instantly as Alarius glanced up in alarm. "Terms?" he repeated. "If I give you the map, you'll have what you seek, and I shall lose my son! What higher price must you ask, you cursed bastard?"

"A simple favor. The necessity of one word or two really." Spreading his hands amiably, he continued, "I just wish to know the party responsible for giving this map to you when it was meant to be ours alone."

Alarius's mouth drew into a tight line. "I found it myself," he said quietly. "No secret as to how. People often find things when they least expect to."

Dual's ill laughter cut him off. "Am I to believe that you merely ***stumbled*** across it, when the map was hidden in the deepest stairwell of one of the multiple towers on the hills of ice beyond?" Alarius wouldn't reply. "No, Zaxelby, don't debase yourself as a liar as well. We both know that only a few unique magic abilities would know exactly where to seek it, and both you and your wife have minor ones that wouldn't aid in such a search."

"Maybe you underestimate us," Alarius suggested lightly.

"Don't try my limited patience," hissed Dual, transforming into the dragon again. "***Since you reside in***

***Barokka, it's likely someone there gave you this rather valuable item. Either you give me the name of the culprit who did this, or I'll send Quell out to use his powers of silencing to finish off your family before you see them alive again. Now, Alarius...* choose *whom you wish to protect. Your traitorous friend who got you into this to begin with, or the family you cherish so much. Choose!*"**

Traitorous... The word echoed in Alarius's mind, but it could bear no truth to him. His friend of many years had given him the map in good faith to help him and his family to have a better life, knowing he wouldn't need the treasures himself. And despite Dual's words, he knew that the map did not rightfully belong to him or Quell.

His friend had merely found it first.

"He's no traitor," hissed Alarius. "Nor am I!"

"***You'd best learn differently then,***" sneered Dual, "***or* this *will be the next sight you see!***"

A new vision appeared, this one distorted and twisted. His house was engulfed in flames, the children screaming as they ran from it. Quell's image stood close by, using his malevolent powers to only partially 'silence' each one with paralysis as they passed through the flaming doorway, dropping them instantly to remain in the fire's path. All remained conscious, their agonized screams filling Alarius's ears, as the vision allowed no mercy. If not horror enough, he witnessed his beloved Laelea struggling weakly from the house, carrying the lifeless Daric, until Quell paralyzed them too...

"*No!*" yelled the half-elf, drowning out Laelea's screams with his own anguished cry. Dropping to the ground as the vision persisted to taunt him, Alarius's eyes shot fire. "Damn you, Dual! I won't let you harm them!"

The dragon's eyes softened knowingly. "***Of course you won't,***" he purred, finally allowing the horrific vision to fade out. "***Just give me the name, Alarius.***"

Alarius bit his lip, shutting his eyes painfully. "Damn you, Dual," he said once more, brokenly. In an equally shattered whisper, he added, "Forgive me, my friend... and my poor little Daric too. I had no choice..."

Dual leaned forward, his eyes glittering. "***The* name, *Alarius!***"

The half-elf wouldn't face him as the name slipped from his tongue. "Dominick…" he sighed. "Dominick Westbrooke."

The dragon remained motionless for what seemed like forever.

"***Dominick,***" he hissed finally, with no absence of venom. "***So... once more, the familiar sword in my side has struck again.***" Glancing up to face the bemused Alarius, his expression retained its anger, but his words were calm. "***You've done well, Alarius. You and your family are free from harm, and you may return to them as soon as this dream ends and you relinquish the map. We'll arrive to retrieve it shortly.***" The half-elf stared at the ground, unanswering. "***You should feel proud, my friend. You've saved many lives this day, your own included.***"

While feeling unable to speak, lest he bring renewed threats of destruction upon his family, Alarius continued to keep his gaze lowered, remorse filling his mind.

I shall never be proud of betraying a loyal friend, he thought silently, *and what life shall I have knowing I've forfeited my son's? None I can bear...*

"Damn you," he whispered, feeling the chilling winds tugging at him to announce the ending of the nightmare.

As he vanished, so did Dual.

*****

Reappearing in a place not far from the dreaming Alarius's actual slumbering form, the dark dreamphaser was once more in his human body. The dragon form was merely an illusion that solely existed in the dream-state, albeit it was certainly effective enough there.

Ignoring his ally Quell's enthusiasm regarding the map, Dual's thoughts traveled instead to the revelation he'd learned. Until tonight, he wasn't certain who had cheated the valuable map from him. And from Quell too, of course, although that was a more minor consideration. But now he knew the thief, and the name brought no surprise.

"Dominick, my old enemy," he hissed softly, "ever you plague me. And once more, you've earned another dose of retribution for your interference." His eyes narrowed with malice. "You'd best be on guard, my persistent foe. For when next we meet, you'll wish the day had never come!"

Chapter Eight

"I must be dreaming," whispered Julianna.

A moment later, she remembered how true this was.

Smiling as she glanced down at her attire, she found herself standing in a gown of aquamarine, made of a material that felt softer than silk. No doubt a complimentary gift from her nightly—or rather 'knightly'—companion.

She was a short distance from the castle they'd shared, located beside a beach of golden sand and a sparkling ocean that looked to be made of silver. Just in front of her stood a fountain that brought forth a similar translucent liquid through a shining marble statue. Glancing wide-eyed at the shimmering pool, she leaned against the edge and stared within. Through the countless ripples, she could see hundreds of rainbow stones twinkling up at her from the bottom of the fountain, like diamonds, winking back at the stars up above.

"Care to make a wish, my lady?" asked a familiar voice, causing her to turn. In formal white-jacketed attire, he looked even more handsome than before if possible, and she felt her heart beat faster at the loving look in his eyes.

"I don't need to now," she replied. "You're already here."

Smiling warmly, Dominick's arms surrounded her, his tender yet impassioned kisses warming her like a hundred suns, stealing her breath away. Moments later, the sound of sweet music filled the air, and Julianna's eyes opened with renewed surprise. *What on Earth?* she wondered, noting her companion's look of amusement as he broke apart from her.

Just before she noticed illuminated rainbows cascading in

endless directions towards the starry night sky. Something only a dream could create… or a dream companion.

"It's all your doing, Julianna," he said, smiling with mock innocence. "You said so yourself that there are rainbows and music when we're together."

"Yes, but I didn't mean literally," she laughed. "Thank you for remembering, my dear dream knight." Leaning forward, she emphasized this with a deeper kiss.

"Be careful with your kisses, my lady," Dominick replied smiling, breaking away long moments later, though not releasing her. "I had other plans for us this evening, but I'm only human when it comes to the charms of a most enchanting sorceress."

"Ah, I see," she replied with feigned seriousness. "Then you want me to be on my best undesirable behavior."

"Minx!" he laughed deep in his throat, brushing a few kisses across her neck. "You can't help but be desirable to me, Julianna," he whispered. "Even if you tied back your hair, wore the drabbest clothes, and painted your face green, I'd still want you."

She gave a slight pout at that. "Well, I certainly won't agree to try out the last part of that theory. Knowing you, you'd trick me into using indelible paint."

"And purposely hide such beauty from these eyes?" He thought for a moment, before adding, "Still, it might be useful to detract the attention of other admirers you might have." She swatted his shoulder at the last, but he simply clasped her wrist and kissed her hand. "Really, Julianna, we must have a talk about this aggressive tendency of yours. It's fine for passionate moments, but surely not all the time."

"You won't be so smug when I display no passion at all, Sir Dominick," she retorted.

"None at all?" he asked doubtfully, his kisses traveling down her neck while he hugged her close. A gasp escaped her lips and her eyes drifted shut, earning a soft laugh from him.

"The hell with smugness then," he whispered. "It's definitely not worth the sacrifice." Julianna smiled at his touch, even as he pulled away with a groan. "No, no, my temptress. There'll be plenty of time for this later. Right now, I wish to follow through on my request last night that I learn more of your life. Come."

Taking her hand, he led her up a few steps to where a decorated table with two soft chairs awaited, overlooking the ocean. Over a white tablecloth, two candles burned brightly beside each other. Like her and Dominick, she thought with a smile. If nothing else, he surely sensed her emotions, squeezing her hand once before stepping back to hold the chair for her.

The gentle echoes of the music flowed through Julianna like the sweetest melody she'd ever heard, complemented even more when Dominick leaned over her shoulder to kiss her cheek. As he took the seat adjacent to her, he reached out to hold her hand again, gently caressing her smooth fingers.

"I don't remember when I've ever been treated so wonderfully," she said softly. "And while I don't know how or why you've suddenly become a part of my life, I certainly wouldn't trade these past few days together with you for all the world."

Raising her hand to his lips, Dominick brushed a whisper of a kiss against it. "How... would take a long time to explain," he replied. "Though I will admit that Fate must certainly have had a hand in things. As to why, that reason should be more than obvious."

"Tell me," she coaxed.

For a moment, he looked about to reply, but then shook his head with a smile. "If we don't get started on our dinner now, this dream will be over before we get to dessert. And I certainly wouldn't want that to happen."

"You're putting cake before me?"

Dominick gave a short laugh. "I wasn't referring to ***that*** kind of dessert," he replied, with a mischievous glint in his eyes.

"Personally, I prefer something far sweeter than cake." Deciphering his words instantly, Julianna blushed. Flashing her a quick smile, he commented lightly, "Now to see about that dinner."

*****

An hour later, Julianna found herself wishing she could live forever in the dream-state. Not only was the food catered perfectly to her liking, but Dominick assured her that she wouldn't get sick from anything, either here or when she awoke, which only made sense since it ***was*** a dream.

Dominick merely asked what she'd like, and the food had materialized on silver trays, floating across the table, beside the neatly arranged china and silverware. He had good taste in everything she'd seen so far, this romantic dinner being no exception.

During dinner, Julianna told him of her family and life on Earth, hesitantly at first mentioning her brother-in-law and nephew. His warm responding smile soon eased any doubts from her mind, and she went on to assure him that her sister Crystal and Jerry shared a solid, happy marriage. At her continual references to Sammy, it was easy to see that she adored her nephew. Dominick's expression became curious.

"Would you like to have a child of your own someday?" he asked.

Caught off-guard, Julianna froze. "I used to once." Taking a sip of water to consider, she added, "But I could never see having a child if it wasn't with someone I loved."

He leaned closer, his eyes holding hers. "And if that was possible?"

Blushing, she forced a smile. "I've been monopolizing the conversation long enough. You promised to tell me more about you tonight."

Sitting back in his chair, his eyes twinkled. "Fair enough," he agreed. "Outside of the dream-state, I live with my brother on an island." Julianna's own eyes widened.

"You're ***real?***"

"Well, of course I'm real!" he laughed. "Hasn't this past week made that clear?"

She shook her head. "That's not what I meant. I mean, you said you exist ***outside*** the dream-state?"

Dominick took a sip from his wine glass. "Yes, as a matter of fact I do. You may have a creative imagination, Julianna, but you didn't conjure me up." At her surprised expression, he reached forward to squeeze her hand. "I'm as real as you are in the waking reality."

She reciprocated the gesture. "How is that possible?"

"I'm known as a dreamphaser," he replied, a smile forming. "As to the details, that might take awhile. You'd best keep eating while I explain."

Still reeling from the knowledge that he existed in reality, Julianna barely noticed the taste of the food as he explained his dreamphasing ability.

Once he did, it made sense why she dreamed of him so frequently, as well as retained vivid memories of him when awake. It did add new questions though. In all her life, she'd never heard of dreamphasing before.

"You said earlier you live on an island?"

"Very astute," he replied, raising his glass towards her. "I live on the island of Barokka, which is well separated from the distant shores of the outer regions. It's not the easiest place to reach if you don't know what you're looking for, and there's a protective mist farther out along the perimeter which obscures us from the outer area."

Julianna thought quickly. "I've never heard of Barokka before. Is it outside of Europe?"

Dominick gave a short laugh. "I'd have to say, 'Yes.' It's nowhere near that. More accurately, it's not going to be found on any map of ***Earth***."

As he emphasized the last, she dropped her fork. "You're from another ***world***?" He nodded, allowing her to process this newest revelation. "That's amazing!" she said finally.

Gladdened by her enthusiastic reaction, Dominick smiled. "Would you like to hear more about it?'

Eyes bright, she nodded. He told her of his home on the island, as well as some of outer Chavernos. Much as she had earlier, he spoke of his own family and friends there, of his grandfather Chaos and the palace. The more he shared, the more she wanted to know, and he was clearly pleased by her interest.

"This planet Chavernos of yours sounds far away," she told him, earning a nod. "So tell me, what galaxy are you from?"

"Oh... this one," Dominick replied lightly.

"***This*** one?" she said incredulously. "But that's impossible."

"Not impossible. Just well hidden." At her surprised gape, he started reciting the planets she knew of. "…and of course, there's Mars, Venus, Earth, Jupiter, and Chavernos." He nodded at the lack of recognition in her eyes. "I know. Your world doesn't know of us. But then, it is a large solar system."

"Even so, how can you miss a whole planet?"

"I'll try to explain, but you'll likely find it hard to believe. There's a mist obscuring our world. But not just an ordinary mist. It's a field of magic, which both conceals and protects it. Our oldest scientists have speculated it's always been there, although their own magic has enhanced it, and since all dreamphasers who have visited Earth have never heard mention of our world, apparently the mist is strong enough to conceal itself from even the strongest telescopes."

"You know of telescopes?"

"Of course. We have our own variant here, propelled by

magic which can see through the field, but still a means of viewing what's out there."

"Just how far away is your world?"

"Not as far as you might think. Most times we're opposite your own planet in relation to the sun."

"A hidden planet," she murmured. "Now I ***know*** I'm dreaming."

He laughed good-naturedly, continuing to tell her more about his world. Like a child enraptured by a storyteller, Julianna couldn't hear enough about it. Both on and outside the island, Chavernos harbored many unusual and wonderful beings, some of which she'd only read about in books.

Dominick mentioned having traveled in outer Chavernos quite often in the past, telling her of the very real elves, dwarves, sprites, trolls, and dragons, along with countless other unknown races and creatures.

"Then of course there are half-elves, half-dragons..."

"Half-***dragons***? Now you ***are*** kidding."

"No, really. They're not generally found in one specific place, but they do exist throughout the planet. You see, even most pure-blood dragons have the ability to take on alternate forms, such as human or elven, via a special magic. This magic is strong enough that it actually makes it possible for them to function completely in their alternate forms, so if a dragon should fall in love with a human or elf in that form, it is possible they can marry and have children.

"It is the children of such unions that have become known as half-dragons, who receive the traits of both parents. Of course, they can morph into dragon form at will when they learn how. However, while they usually maintain their human or elven form for outward appearances, they also have the inborn traits of: extended lifelines that rival the long-lived pure-blood dragons, resistance to fire and ice, and sometimes unique added magical powers."

"What's it like living on a world where magic truly exists?"

He shrugged with a knowing smile. "It has its advantages and drawbacks, the same as one might regard your world's technological advances."

"But magic, Dominick... ***real*** magic!" Julianna's eyes shone with wonder. "It sounds like such a wonderful place. I wish I could see it someday."

"Hmmm, maybe you can," he mused, halting her instantly before she could reply. "Wait, love, don't let me lead you falsely. I don't mean in the real sense, of course. But instead to draw from my memories to show you a sample of Chavernos in the dream-state."

Julianna nodded, a bit disappointed—partially because she would have liked to be with Dominick in reality—but still accepted his proposition for the future.

"Your world has its advantages too," he continued. "I'm glad I have the ability to reach it, even though it's only as one looks through a window, or I wouldn't have met you. In which case, I wouldn't have had the pleasure of masquerading as a mysterious rogue that second night in order to pursue a most tempting Earth damsel who ended up chasing me instead."

"I don't think I'll ever live that down," she admitted. "I must have appeared so desperate."

"Not to me," said Dominick, shaking his head. "What I saw that night was a beautiful, unhappy woman that looked like she could use a shoulder to lean on."

"And you most certainly provided ***that***." He gave a mischievous shrug, but didn't discount it, allowing a brief smile to cross his expression.

"To be honest, I don't think I've ever been more touched than to find you remembered my name, when I returned two months after our first meeting." He leaned closer to stroke her cheek. "Ever notice how a name can sound a thousand times more endearing when spoken by the one you care for?"

"Yes," she agreed softly.

As he brushed his lips against her cheek, her eyes shut blissfully.

"My Dominick..." she whispered.

"Always to you," he said, cupping her chin in his hand. "And you, my sweet lady, will always be my Julianna. A beautiful name that expresses the beautiful woman you are." He drew nearer to kiss her lips sweetly, lingeringly, earning a soft sound of agreement from her as he began stroking her waist.

She felt pleasantly lightheaded even as he gently disengaged from her to sit back in his own chair. In moments, he had the empty dishes and trays on the table vanish.

Despite his earlier words—although Julianna suspected his spoken motives would resurface soon enough—Dominick did bring out a few edible desserts for them. One of them was her favorite—and his, coincidentally enough—devil's food cake. Dominick told Julianna of the never-ending joke among his guardian friends Buddy and Jarissa that although Buddy's kind was supposed to appreciate angel food cake, he didn't, preferring the 'devil-cake' version instead.

"Another good thing about the dream-state is that eating this cake won't add a pound to your real body," he told her, noting her appreciative expression.

"Mmmm, I'm definitely moving into the dream-state permanently then," she decided, earning a laugh from him. Once they finished eating, Dominick zapped away the rest of the dishes and silverware, leaving only the candles upon the table. "This was nice. You really surprised me tonight."

"I'm glad," he replied smiling, "but it shouldn't surprise you that I'd desire something more between us than just the physical aspects of a relationship."

Julianna felt her heart skip a beat. "What do you mean?" she asked.

He was silent for long moments.

"Julianna…"

"Yes?"

"Have you ever stood at the top of a rainbow before?"

Despite her inner frustration at his evading her question, Julianna's curiosity was piqued, and she admitted having no knowledge of such. Dominick took her hand and led her along the beach to where one section of a rainbow seemed almost tangible, despite its colorful misty appearance. When he started to walk directly towards it, she pulled back apprehensively.

"If we walk straight through that, we'll head right into the ocean," she protested.

"Have faith in me, Julianna," he replied, gently coaxing her to follow him.

To her surprise, as soon as they stood directly in the rainbow mists, an invisible ground began to rise beneath their feet. Rather like walking up an invisible ramp. Sensing her slight apprehension due to the height looming before them, Dominick moved to her side, placing his arm comfortingly about her waist as he beckoned her onward. Whether due to its being a dream, or Dominick himself, Julianna felt her reservations ease, replaced by marvel at their present location.

"How is this possible?" she asked.

"A good imagination, the appropriate dreamphasing conventions, and a most pleasant companion to be with." Julianna somehow felt he'd evaded another of her questions, but said nothing. "You have to let go of your conventional knowledge, love. Being in a dream is like taking a trip in your mind, and there's no limit to the possibilities."

She was about to agree, but instead nearly lost her footing, prompting her to clutch Dominick while his hold on her strengthened protectively. "I think I'd rather not just let go as you say."

Not minding their current embrace, Dominick merely

smiled as they walked on. As the top drew nearer, the lights became brighter. He mentioned this being since the tail ends of a rainbow usually seemed to disappear first, so the colors were more vivid higher up. Julianna wondered if he wasn't simply teasing her, but it seemed an amusing—if not completely logical—explanation. When they reached the top, he stopped them to gesture towards the view below.

Julianna knew she shouldn't look, but of course curiosity got the better of her. One glance, and the overwhelming reality of the dizzying height took hold, her hands tightening around Dominick like a vise, earning a chuckle from him.

"Remember, love, it's only a dream," he told her comfortingly. "And even if heaven forbid you fell from here, I'd keep you safe."

"Right," she whispered, slowly calming down as he began to gently massage her tense shoulders. In no time at all, she'd forgotten just where they were standing, shutting her eyes and smiling.

"Feel better?" he asked, continuing his ministrations.

"Mmmm, I like what you're doing."

"Really?" he murmured against her cheek. "Then I suppose I shouldn't stop now, should I?"

She turned about to face him, so he could bring his mouth to hers, making no protest as his arms surrounded her. Nor when he reached down long moments later to place his arm beneath her knees, lifting her up before he gently lowered her amidst the dazzling colors of the rainbow's surface, sliding down beside her so as not to break their kiss.

"Dominick," she breathed, "we can't do this here. The rainbow..."

"Is the perfect place," he finished, gazing into her eyes. "Don't worry, love. The span of this rainbow is broader than it seems, and there are invisible borders along the edge to keep us safe." Sensing her relax, a mischievous smile stole across his face, as he ran his fingers lightly along her arm. "So, my lady, I take it you've never done ***this*** at the top of a rainbow before."

"Before last night, I've never done ***this*** at all."

"I know. I was there."

His mouth descended on hers again, expertly parting her lips to reach the softness within. Between his deep kisses and his strong hands sliding down to caress her, Julianna nearly forgot where they were, except for occasional glimpses of the soft colors that played around them. Although the ground had seemed highly solid on the trek up here, the surface they were lying on now seemed endlessly softer, no doubt thanks to her companion's forethought.

"Julianna… I want this time to last forever," he murmured, holding her easily with one arm, while his other hand reached within the top folds of her gown. At his warming touch there, Julianna found herself gasping, one bare knee revealing itself when it raised up, her gown falling back enticingly.

In response, while continuing his kisses, his hand retreated to move lower, skimming down along her waist to her bare thigh, stirring a tremor from her. Deftly stealing under the gown, he began to stroke upward, causing her to stir restlessly, breathing his name.

Smiling knowingly, Dominick withdrew to embrace her again, brushing soft kisses across her mouth. She returned them eagerly, reaching towards his chest to tug at the fabric she encountered. Gently assisting her in removing both his jacket and shirt, he then guided her hands back to his bared skin.

Her fingers ran across his strong muscles, marveling at this. "You must take good care of yourself to be this fit," she whispered in admiration. "Do you lift weights?"

He shrugged slightly. "Some of the time, but I get more exercise just from attending to the many matters regarding the island. Always places to go, people to see."

"Women to see?" she queried, glancing up at him.

"Now look," he laughed, brushing a hand across her hair, while leaning on one arm. "I'd think it's perfectly clear which ***woman*** I desire to see around here. Any others I meet are strictly business, Julianna. You have no need to feel jealous of them."

She looked skeptical. "Except for this Sionne you mentioned, who seems to want you served up on a silver platter and bound to her by a wedding ring."

"I don't look at Sionne in that way and never will," he said seriously, continuing to stroke her hair as it fanned out about her, shining and fiery against the rainbow's glow. "If I ever do choose to get married, it'll be for love. Not an arranged marriage by my persistent family."

"Well, at least one of us can still keep an open mind about marriage," Julianna sighed, shaking her head. At his apparent confusion, she explained, "Although knowing men's egos, I suppose I shouldn't say this... but I find it highly unlikely a man like you exists on Earth, and I could never settle for a lesser marriage."

Dominick's eyes held hers as they glittered. "Maybe you were never destined to marry a man from Earth," he said softly, brushing the top of her gown aside to kiss along her neck. "A woman who looks to the stars long enough might one day find her heart's desire among them instead."

"Maybe…" she agreed breathlessly, arching back as his kisses went lower.

Raising up slightly, Dominick's hands moved to her shoulders, sliding down the length of her. As they did, the gown melted away beneath them. Mildly surprised by this, she glanced up at him with glazed eyes, but unabashed this time as his gaze roamed over her.

He gave a low murmur of appreciation, pressing heated kisses against her neck again, and then traveling lower to do the same with her sensitive breasts, spurred on by her responding sounds of yearning.

Feeling her skin turn as hot as flames beneath his touch, his hands began to explore her body anew. It was when his kisses went lower to trace the same path as his hands that Julianna's soft cries of pleasure suddenly heightened, this intimacy so provocative to her reawakened senses.

"Dominick..." she pleaded.

"Shhh, I'm right here, love," he murmured gently, moving back to kiss her mouth again. Smiling seductively at her unbridled response, he discarded the last of his clothing and pulled her close.

Cradling her face in his hands, his kisses became feverish. The same fever caught hold of Julianna, her hands tangling in his hair to make sure he didn't leave her. A possibility that Dominick knew was impossible, fighting his impatient body to lengthen their loving as much as possible.

It proved to be a losing battle.

Soon possessed by desire so overwhelming, there was only one way to quench it, his eyes sought hers questioningly, expecting hesitation but receiving none. Instead, Julianna's fingers slid across his back to encircle his neck eagerly, murmuring his name as her eyes filled with unspoken adoration.

Mesmerized by her response with a tenderness even stronger than the night before, Dominick lowered his mouth to hers again with gentle reassurance, enfolding her in his embrace, long moments before he carefully eased within her. His prolonging this only heightened their senses, both shutting their eyes with soft cries of passion, their expressions sharing the same look of ecstatic joy.

This time there was nothing but mutual pleasure in their loving, as their bodies already knew each other, communicating this knowledge most sweetly. They slowly moved together as one, kissing each other leisurely, teasingly, sharing everything.

Their desire gradually built, until Julianna's hands ran

along Dominick's back, hugging him closer, silently expressing what she couldn't in words.

He understood all too well what she was feeling, and how new these feelings were to her, clasping her hand. Kissing her passionately again, she sweetly responded, as his free hand slid beneath her leg to pull her still closer. They ascended new heights together, while the softly continuing music blended in harmony with the sounds of their yearning.

"Dear heaven, Dominick," she breathed. "Is it always this wonderful?"

Reveling in her response as he rained kisses upon her, Dominick's glazed eyes slowly lifted and held hers, even as a new wave of pleasure softened both of their expressions. "Yes, love," he replied. "Always with us." Touching her cheek with a smile, he gazed at her lovingly. "Now, dearest..." he murmured encouragingly, "let me show you the stars."

His mouth closed over hers, swallowing her sounds of wondrous joy as he drove deep within her.

Julianna held fast to him, feeling as though she was melting, arching up against Dominick as he brought them to an intensely powerful release. Their hands still clasped, they soared through the shimmering heaven they'd shared, and then... gradually, drifted back against the surface of the rainbow, their fingers still intertwined loosely.

For several minutes neither even thought of moving, remaining entwined together in their intimate embrace, even as the music about them faded. Dominick stirred first, kissing Julianna as her eyes fluttered open to stare at him.

"A bit tired, sweetheart?" he whispered knowingly.

Julianna nodded with a languid smile, unable to speak. He smiled back in understanding as he shifted to move beside her instead, gently pulling her halfway across his chest, one leg protectively surrounding hers, while covering them with a swiftly conjured blanket. Murmuring soft acknowledgment, she snuggled closer.

Dominick stroked her shoulder possessively, thinking that she seemed more beautiful than ever, her passion-weary expression looking so innocent and content as she curled up against him. He was amazed at how she still exuded such an aura of innocence, after they'd certainly gone far beyond that tonight. Never before had he felt so soul satisfied, for Julianna was not only highly passionate, but he loved her for her mind and personality as well.

He loved her. This time he didn't shrug it off with hesitation, but smiled in acceptance. After tonight, he was certain it was the truth. He'd enjoyed their conversation over dinner, and she'd displayed a gift for imagination that rivaled his own. Not to mention, they were compatible in many other ways.

"Will it always be like this between us?" he heard her ask softly.

"I wouldn't object if it was," he murmured, turning to lean on one arm to gaze into her wakened eyes. He began to sense uncertainty behind her expression. *Does she still doubt my feelings for her?* he wondered. "Sweet Julianna," he whispered, caressing her back. "Intelligence, beauty, humor, and passion. What more could any man ask for in a companion?"

A companion, her mind repeated, feeling a twinge of pain.

She'd too often been regarded as that, but never found someone who loved her as well. And while she certainly enjoyed spending time with Dominick, and felt him to be a wonderful lover, Julianna felt a still deeper hurt. Despite his simple surface attraction to her, she knew that she loved him. He was undeniably handsome, intelligent, and she loved his sense of humor and personality, even when they disagreed on matters. And he was so romantic. Surely a woman couldn't ask for more either.

But she still desired one thing... a mutual love.

Yet could she leave what she had now with Dominick, simply because that emotion didn't exist for him towards her? Glancing up at him, nearly with tears, Julianna shook her head. *Better a short time of happiness with him now than nothing at all*, she decided, leaning her head against his chest again.

"I'm glad for the times we've had," she said quietly.

Dominick nearly flinched at her words, sounding disturbingly as if she'd determined their relationship would soon be over. Had he said something to make her believe that? If so, he wasn't about to let it remain that way. Kissing her forehead quickly, he moved from beneath the blanket to walk over to the rainbow's edge, rubbing his chin thoughtfully as he contemplated what exactly to say.

In response, Julianna looked up with sudden concern. Had she done something wrong? *Oh, great!* He must have sensed that she wanted more of a commitment from him, chasing him off as she'd originally lost Roger. Clasping the blanket to her chest, she got up to stand beside him, leaning against his shoulder. He glanced down at her with a brief smile, but then returned his gaze to the ocean.

"What are you thinking?" she asked, genuinely curious.

"Various things," he replied softly, evading a direct answer as he seemed to do quite often.

She bit her lip, but murmured, "Anything involving us?"

"As a matter of fact, yes. This relationship of ours isn't at all what I expected it to be."

The pain nearly choked her heart. As she'd suspected from the beginning, he only regarded her as a temporary paramour. And now he was no doubt trying to find the right words to break things off between them, perhaps trying to minimize her pain.

"Maybe I should leave then," she whispered, the words catching in her throat.

Dominick's gaze whipped to face her. She was heading

into that infuriating despondency again! It wasn't that he couldn't deal with it, but he hated seeing her in pain of any kind. She needed to understand how he felt.

"Julianna..." he began.

"Yes?" she asked hopefully.

"Care for a swim?"

Care for a what? her mind echoed blankly. "I... I don't know."

"Oh, don't worry. We're the only ones here. No one else is present to notice or object to two skinny-dippers enjoying a leisurely swim." At her blush, he took her hand and added, "It's all right, love. Although admittedly, I'm a fairly uninhibited individual myself, I understand your feeling differently." Before she could blink an eye, she found herself wearing a two-piece bathing suit beneath the blanket. Dominick wore a suit of his own now too, gently taking the blanket from her to send it back into the unknown. "Is this more to your liking?"

Admittedly, Julianna had always worn one-piece suits in the past, but seeing as they were alone and Dominick seemed to approve, it seemed silly to mention. Especially since her companion had already seen her several times now. Still, she did find comfort in the suits, smiling up at him.

"Yes, this is fine, thank you," she replied. Squeezing her hand once, Dominick brought her nearer to the edge of the rainbow, but she pulled free of him when they reached it. "What are you doing?" she asked in sudden alarm. "Aren't we going to walk down again?"

"Julianna," he laughed, "remember where we are. A dream. Now, let me show you what's possible." As he held out his hand, she hesitantly stepped forward to accept it, earning another reassuring squeeze from him. "You never have to fear anything with me, love. Now come with me to the edge." Once they stood against the invisible border of the color array, he continued. "On the count of three, we're going to jump."

"Jump?" she exclaimed loudly.

"One…"

"No, wait, I'm not sure about this."

"Trust me, love. Two..."

"Dominick, you can't be serious."

"Sure I can. Three."

"I don't want to..."

Julianna screamed as she was pulled along with Dominick when he jumped. She knew she should shut her eyes, but couldn't, even as it sank in that they weren't plummeting towards the sand below at a hundred miles an hour. Instead, they were gliding slowly downward, arcing back towards the beach.

"How?" she gasped, suddenly clutching him fiercely.

He didn't seem to mind.

"Dreams are capable of many things, flight being just one possible aspect." As their feet touched the sand gently, Dominick placed his hands on her shoulders and smiled at her. "You see? We survived. That's one less fear you'll have in the future of your dreams, love."

"I guess so," she murmured, half in amazement as she glanced back at the distant rainbow's peak. His hands fell away from her, but she was too surprised at the revelation of safe flight to notice. Before she could ponder it long, she heard the sound of splashing water. "Dominick?" she asked, whipping around. He was wading into the ocean, but at the mention of his name, he turned to her with a grin.

"Come on in, Julianna!" he called out. "These waters will be perfectly attuned to your comfort, so you can't give me that excuse, and if you can't swim, I'll teach you!"

"I can swim!" she called back.

"Then what's the delay?"

Not one to ignore a challenge, Julianna strode forward, yet stopped at the water's edge to tentatively dip her foot within.

Dominick's words were true. The waters were like those in a heated swimming pool. And despite the silvery appearance, the water droplets were crystal clear against her foot as she looked down upon it... just before a large splash of water soaked her, bringing a startled scream from her.

"This year, Julianna," laughed Dominick.

"Oh, you'll pay for that, dreamphaser!" she replied with a smirk, splashing him back and drenching him completely. As he brushed his eyes clear, Dominick strode forward with a grin, picking her up while she was lost to her own laughter.

"You're all washed up, my dear lady. Or soon will be," he chuckled, carrying her towards the deeper water.

She gave a mock display of protest, while he asked her what she'd be willing to do in exchange for his placing her back on the dry sand again. Some of her suggestions certainly seemed tempting enough! he thought, just before he tripped—truly by accident—dumping them headfirst into the waters.

They both reemerged laughing, just before they continued a playful contest of splashes. One that was abruptly dismissed shortly afterwards when Dominick picked up his opponent and began kissing her. Fortunately, she could stand here, although only her head and shoulders were visible, unlike Dominick who was taller.

Despite the aspect of water, it didn't deter certain desires in the dream-state, so in no time, the pair ended up skinny-dipping after all. Inwardly, Julianna had doubts about his intentions. After all, weren't they running the risk of drowning?

As usual, Dominick's persuasive confidence won out as he pulled her close, caressing her thoroughly beneath the waters, while kissing her thoroughly above them. Not certain what to expect, she let him take the lead, putting her arms about his neck to kiss him back.

"My sweet Julianna..." he murmured, smoothing her wet hair back against her forehead as he continued to kiss her hungrily.

She responded eagerly, even as he abruptly lifted her from the ocean floor, so he could reach her neck and the softness of her breasts without being hindered by the water. Helpless in his arms, she arched back and gasped, hearing as well as feeling him laugh in a seductively knowing voice against her bare skin. She decided it was a good thing it was dark out, so her newly flushed face wasn't so apparent.

He lowered her to kiss her mouth again, erasing any discomforting thoughts she might have felt. Even with the water all around them, Julianna was very conscious of the sensations her body felt as it slid down along his.

Apparently, he felt it too.

"By Chavernos," he groaned against her mouth. "I can see how mermaids like you might entice a man to risk drowning for them."

"I'd rather have the enticement without the drowning, thank you very much," she laughed.

"Even if it's merely a drowning in passion rather than water?"

"Mmmm, now ***that*** sounds tempting."

He gave a low chuckle against her cheek. "Then allow me to show you, my beautiful mermaid."

After a few more kisses, such playful teasing became more serious, as he lifted her again to follow through on his words. She caught on instantly, keeping her arms about his neck as her legs hugged him most affectionately. Even more when Dominick's hands supported her as he skillfully joined them underwater, earning a gasp of delight from her, and warm agreement from him.

They moved together as smoothly as the ocean waves, their voices blending softly as they did.

Spurred on by their passion, the pair allowed their desire to carry them through a whirlwind sea of emotions. When they soared over the final crest, she murmured Dominick's name, complementing his ecstatic reply.

Still clasping him to her, Julianna's head fell forward against his shoulder, tired again but blissful as she felt him kiss her neck and whisper endearments that she couldn't quite hear. The tenderness there was enough, she decided, still feeling a bit dazed as he shifted her in his arms slightly to carry her from the waters.

To her surprise, she glanced down to see them garbed in their swimsuits again. *How on Earth does he keep doing that?* she wondered.

As he knelt to place her gently on the sand, settling down beside her, while continuing to hold her close, Julianna felt such a wave of contentment and happiness flood through her, she decided to finally tell him of her feelings. Regardless of the outcome, at least she'd always have tonight to hold onto with fond remembrance.

"Dominick..."

"Shhh," he interrupted, placing a finger against her lips. "Before you say a word, I wish to continue our earlier conversation regarding what I said about being unsure of our relationship as it stands now. Julianna, after tonight, I'm even more convinced of this, since it seems to have gotten so... well, out-of-control very quickly and unexpectedly."

Her love-filled heart now felt close to shattering, and she could only pray he wouldn't notice the shudder that tore through her. He was about to sunder their relationship, and here she'd been about to tell him that she loved him.

Again, I'm a fool! her mind mocked her.

"I understand," she told him softly.

Dominick stared at her in surprise. "You do?"

"Yes," she whispered. "Will you leave now, or wait until this dream ends?" As his eyes widened silently, she bit her lip and continued. "I'd prefer it if you wouldn't mind waiting, since

I'll certainly miss you in the future. Unless... maybe it would be better for you to just leave now, and break things off quickly."

"No," he interrupted.

"No, meaning you'll stay until I wake up?" she asked hopefully.

He shook his head. "I meant no, as in I don't want to lose you at all," he said seriously. "Julianna, I don't know where you got the idea that I wanted to leave you after tonight, but I can assure you I don't. I happen to love you, my little temptress, and if you think I'm just going to sit back and let you share our intimacies with some other oaf like Roger Collins, then you're out of your pretty little mind!"

"You what?" she gasped, her heart nearly stopping in anxious anticipation.

"You heard me, Julianna. I won't allow another to..."

"No," she interrupted. "Before that. When you called me a temptress, you said that you..."

"That I love you?" he asked gently, earning a silent nod. His expression softened with a smile. "Yes. I love you, Julianna Sherborne," he murmured, kissing her tenderly. "And of course I want to keep seeing you, whether for long chats, candle lit dinners, or anything else."

"For how long?" she ventured.

Dominick's eyes held hers. "Indefinitely," he whispered. "I wish to see you night after night." His elation was soon dampened upon seeing tears in his companion's eyes. "Julianna? What have I said to upset you now? I thought..."

"No, no," she laughed, brushing her eyes clear. "I'm not upset; it's just the opposite. You see, that's what I wanted to tell you before. I love you too."

After a brief pause, Dominick echoed her laughter, pulling her close to kiss her cheek. "I think it's safe to say we deserve each other," he told her, noting thankfully that her shining eyes were happy again. He reached forward to clasp her hands, kissing them quickly. "My lady, this night is only the beginning. I promise I'm going to make all our future evenings as wonderful as this one."

Tears blurred her vision again, although her smile shone through them. "How could any evening be other than wonderful as long as you're with me?" she whispered.

In response, he embraced her again, rocking her gently in his arms as he gestured for the music to play again, both content with the revelation of their shared love. Dominick knew it would surely cause its own problems, and his grandfather would never understand. But despite his daytime separations from Julianna that loomed before him, he could only see that a few hours with her each night would be more precious to him than all the fulltime availability of any woman Chaos might prefer for him, including Sionne.

When daybreak prepared to separate the lovers again with its disturbing inevitability, it no longer mattered to the pair. Even as they kissed with a familiar desperate longing, feeling themselves gradually losing touch with each other, they knew it would only be a brief separation until the morrow would reunite them. The truth of their love remained strength enough until then.

Gone were any other worries.

Chapter Nine

"Gone?" Dual snarled, the next morning. "What do you mean he's ***gone***?" The man beside him fumbled at an attempt to reply, and the angry dreamphaser gave him a quick shake. "You were told to keep him here!"

"I-I didn't know he'd sneak out in the middle of the night," stammered the innkeeper. "I posted a man at the door."

"But not the window," drawled Quell, gesturing towards the telltale breeze whooshing through a pair of swinging shutters. "I'll say this for Alarius; he's certainly got more guts than I pegged him for."

"And more stupidity," hissed Dual, tossing the innkeeper to the floor roughly. Glaring at the cowering man, he added maliciously, "You're lucky I'm not in the mood to kill ***you*** for that same offense, you spineless idiot. Now get out of my sight before I change my mind!" The innkeeper gave a quick nod and vanished, leaving Quell chuckling in his absence. Dual wasn't pleased. "Listen to your name and ***quell*** your amusement, so we can deal with the matter at hand."

"Alarius? Be serious, Dual. He's a desperate man, but he can't have gotten far."

The dreamphaser sneered. "You're as foolish as he is if you believe that. An elf in hiding could take days or even weeks to uncover."

"Foolish is the way you decided to handle this whole affair," replied Quell. "By the netherworld, we should have just reasoned with Alarius and paid what he needs in exchange for that damned map. He's no doubt gone to find the treasure immediately, and after that, he'll probably have words with

Dominick, and..."

"Quiet!" thundered Dual, his gray eyes nearly glowing red. "It seems to matter little to you that the map was ***mine***, before that accursed dreamphaser stole it out from under me to give to his simpleminded friend who's just escaped with it. Alarius has no ***right*** to those treasures!"

As expected, Quell deemed it best not to comment further, knowing the dark dreamphaser's mind was closed once more to the merits of reasoning.

Reasoning! Dual sneered, as he often did with this subject. When had that approach ever proved useful? Ever since he was a child, Dual had developed a dislike against such foolishness, remembering how the tactic hadn't helped his prematurely deceased mother.

She'd been killed by his father's hand.

Not too surprising, since the man that sired him had been part demon himself, not to mention a corrupt and well-known assassin among the darker inhabitants of Chavernos. His mother, while by no means a saint, hadn't deserved what transpired over the years any more than her son did. Formerly a chorus girl in a tavern, she became enamored of the handsome dark-eyed assassin who frequented the place due to an admiration of her equally appealing form.

To the surprise of everyone, he married her.

To no one's surprise, six months later, Dual was born.

Over the next several years, constant fights escalated within that stormy household. Dual's father made no secret of his many affairs with other women during missions to rid clients of 'unwanted' disturbances. To this end, his wife made frequent attempts to reason with him, asking him to refrain from all of this, meeting with no long-term success.

Finally, her anger boiled over one night, threatening her husband that she'd have an affair herself, since ***he*** wasn't being faithful. Shouting that he'd kill her if she did, his father nearly beat her senseless that night.

Dual had been four years old when he accidentally witnessed the whole scene from the nearby staircase.

And then his father noticed him.

The boy, young as he was, could only see his mother curled up in pain, crying out as he ran towards her. When his father attempted to grab his arm, Dual began to beat his little fists against him angrily, not seeing the anger forming in the elder one's eyes. His mother did see it, and out of maternal instinct, tried to hold back her violent husband from venting his anger on the child. She failed, as with one blow, he rendered her unconscious.

Dual never forgot the beating he'd received from the man's hands that night, nor the many that followed over the next several years. After that night, his mother lived in fear, her husband threatening each night to come after them should they attempt to leave. Despite the weakened spirit his mother had been beaten into, the boy still loved her, promising to find a way to free them both one day.

A way which seemed to appear, when Dual turned eight.

A stranger came to them seeking food and shelter for the night, and since Dual's father was off on another of his assassination missions, his mother welcomed what could only be more pleasant company. The stranger proved to be a far kinder man, meeting quick approval by both mother and son. He visited them whenever Dual's father was absent, which was often.

Six months later, Dual's mother planned their escape to hopefully have a chance at a better life elsewhere.

That chance never came.

Having just been informed by a close ally of his wife's affair, Dual's father returned unexpectedly in the middle of the night to find the pair asleep together in a most compromising manner. Slamming the door, he awakened them instantly, wasting no time before beating his wife's lover nearly unconscious. Running to his side, she covered his battered body with her own, crying so much that she never saw her son peek through the door.

Having been frightened awake by the noise, Dual watched silently as his mother pleaded with his father to release her from their farce of a marriage, begging him to let them all leave in peace. Once again, an attempt at reasoning. For a brief moment, the boy thought that surely his father would agree, since it would benefit everyone—including his father, who could be free with his many other women again.

Dual's innocent mind never expected—or could ever erase—what ***did*** follow.

Swearing to see them damned in the netherworld first, and ignoring his wife's screams, Dual's father ran his razor-sharp sword through both, slaying them instantly.

The boy screamed as his father wrenched the sword free, only to stab them again for reassurance.

Afterwards, the man turned to Dual with a malicious smile, using gentle words to coax the scared boy closer. Despite his young age, the boy was no fool. He ran from the room and the house, escaping in spite of his father's attempts to catch him. Only his father's loud curses met his ears as Dual swore that night to return one day to kill the man who'd murdered his mother and the man who had been like a father to him.

More than twelve years passed, while Dual remained hidden in the home of a gruff but brilliant assassin sorcerer, before his day for vengeance arrived. Not trusting to magic completely, Dual learned the talents of assassins instead, doing mercenary missions of his choosing, while also honing his dreamphasing powers—a gift inherited from his mother—in order to locate his father.

In spite of his desire for vengeance, during the latter of these years, his travels took him through a small village, where he met a beautiful young girl named Caralei. Her golden hair shone as brightly as her smile and her eyes. Eyes that followed him long after he left, which prompted his return.

Since she was drawn to him as well, he befriended her, although using his alternate name, lest she accidentally be placed in danger. Also, for this reason, he generally visited her in secret. It helped when he became friends with her brother Quell, who would sometimes relay messages.

For a time, in spite of Dual's chosen profession, Caralei provided a bright shard of sunlight in his life, and over time, they fell in love.

In the meantime, Dual located his father, biding his time until the moment was right. With the sorcerer's help, he obtained a slow poison to drug the remorseless man, allowing him to remain alive just long enough for him to witness his vengeful son run him through with his sword.

For several months, Dual thought he could finally pick up his life and go on now that he'd avenged his mother's death. Having put the matter at rest, Dual's whole manner improved. He became betrothed to Caralei, keeping it secret between them for now, while planning to put his assassin days behind him and reside in peace.

This wasn't to be.

With his guard lowered, dark allies of his late father found revenge of their own, slaying the sorcerer, as well as his few friends from a nearby village.

But it was what followed that shattered whatever good remained in his soul.

In spite of his secrecy, it seemed someone betrayed him. On the eve of his wedding, the same vengeful assassins discovered Caralei's village, setting it aflame. Turning to a trusted friend from Barokka to see her safely away, Dual saw to killing the assassins and took out the majority of them.

His victory was short-lived when he saw the assassin

leader holding a knife to Caralei's throat, his friend nowhere in sight. If that wasn't enough, the leader took great pleasure in giving the credit for the attack to the missing man. Even when his friend appeared soon after, Dual knew that he was the only one who'd known where Caralei was, their secret wedding plans, and Dual's alternate identity.

Dual tried to bargain for Caralei's life, saying that they'd taken enough lives in exchange for his father's most miserable one, and that he'd rather give his own life than see an innocent girl die.

The assassin leader killed her anyway.

His heart shattered as it had when he'd seen his mother killed years ago.

Caralei's brother Quell, who had been out of town, arrived at the last minute and was a more difficult adversary to contend with. His ability to paralyze people instantly downed the few remaining assassins, and since he'd loved his sister too, he and Dual took great pleasure in killing them.

However, no vengeance could bring back the lost soul they'd both held dear.

Nor would Dual ever forgive the man who he knew had betrayed them, whom from that day forth he regarded as an enemy.

That night left scars upon both Dual and Quell that they would share forever.

Followed by endless years of corruption.

They became well-known assassins, assisting those of evil more and more. In time, their names became feared among all law-abiding citizens of Chavernos, so it was with no great loss to most when they departed to reside on the island of Barokka. There, they still caused havoc, but it was more contained, since the multi-abilitied supernatural ruler's nearly unlimited powers could banish both permanently if he chose to.

If that happened, no reasoning would change ***his*** mind.

Reasoning! Dual thought again, as his thoughts returned to the present. Forever a meaningless, useless ploy. After his sister Caralei's murder, Dual was increasingly surprised that Quell still considered it.

After all, hadn't he tried reasoning last night? Dual questioned, remembering how Alarius had supposedly 'agreed' to give up the map peacefully.

"Reasoning is for fools," he said curtly. "Remember your sister, if you believe otherwise, Quell." His words brought pained remembrance to his ally's face. "And if we're to find that map before that fool Alarius gets any farther, we'd best find him now." A bitter smile twisted his expression. "And when we do, maybe we should teach him the price of betrayal." Nodding once in dark resolve, he leaned against the wall. "Yes, it would seem, Quell, that poor Alarius's family might just miss him in the future after all."

*****

Darkness was the farthest thing from Dominick's mind, if one discounted the times he traveled through the strands of space to reach his Earthly companion. On the contrary, in the evenings that followed, he made good on his promise to keep their evenings interesting.

One night, Dominick took her ice skating, although she was a novice. He proved to be a good teacher, soon having her soaring across the ice as he held her, and she even managed to skate on her own for a bit. Not that she didn't prefer being held in the warm embrace of her tutor, whom she gladly went back to.

Afterwards, they toasted marshmallows over a campfire, which in reality would have melted the ice, but in this case, just provided pleasant warmth.

As Julianna leaned against her companion's shoulder, eyes closed happily, she started when her back was nudged. "Dominick, cut that out," she told him.

"Cut what out?" he laughed. "I thought you wanted another marshmallow."

"I mean…" Opening her eyes to realize he wasn't responsible, she turned slowly, her eyes widening. "Polar bear!" she screamed, while Dominick bolted around to face the creature staring at them with a muffled roar.

"By Chaos, where did ***he*** come from?" he gasped, as Julianna shot behind him to clutch him fearfully.

"You mean this wasn't ***your*** idea?"

"Julianna, why would I conjure up a polar bear while we're spending time together?"

"I don't know, but you do go for the unusual stuff."

"Not ***that*** unusual," he sneered, gesturing to the bear. As if being beckoned, the creature began padding closer to the couple, causing them to edge backwards.

"I don't think ***he*** knows that."

"Go back to your igloo!" Dominick called out, clasping her against him. The bear didn't seem to care for heeding dreamphasers, moving forward anyway. "That's it. We're heading back to the castle. Hold tight, love."

"Like I'm not already?" she whimpered, even as the bear raised a paw towards her. She shut her eyes with a scream, a moment before hearing Dominick laugh jovially.

Her eyes flew open with shocked amazement, finding Dominick petting the creature!

"He was just playing," he told her, earning a contented sound from the bear.

"Dreams!" she sighed. "I'll never get used to them." Upon seeing her frown, the bear padded over to lick her cheek. With cautious reluctance, she petted it too. "You're just a big teddy bear, aren't you?" Upon hearing five or six similar bearlike roars, both she and Dominick glanced up swiftly. "What is this, a bear convention?"

"Let's not stick around to find out," replied Dominick,

quickly teleporting them away. "Home at last," he said warmly.

He surprised her, bringing them back comfortably in front of a roaring fireplace, wearing their casual clothes again without the heavy furs. Placing his arms around her to hug her close, she snuggled back against him, glad that he'd read her mind for a much nicer alternative to continue the evening.

"Better?" he asked.

She smiled, entwining her hand with his. "Much."

Another night had them sailing on a raft in the ocean. For a while, they shared the equivalent of a picnic lunch, although Dominick had mischievously set them up in formal evening attire.

"Methinks thou hast gotten a bit too much sea air in thy brain, my lord," she laughed. "Have a good explanation as to why you've set us up in the middle of nowhere?"

"My dear lady," he replied with mock seriousness, "just because we're playing the part of a shipwrecked duo doesn't mean we have to look it." Handing her a sparkling glass of champagne, she took it graciously, clinking glasses afterwards as was customary. "And we're not going to be nowhere forever. I assure you there's a deserted island out there just waiting to be found."

"Ah... and if the sharks get us first?"

"Don't be silly; there aren't any sharks out here." A triangular black fin passing by seemed to indicate otherwise, earning an 'I told you so' look from Julianna. "It would seem I stand corrected, love," he amended. Gesturing towards the disappearing shark fin, he called out, "I'm sorry I didn't recognize you sooner, Roger! She never told me you were a dreamphaser too!" Julianna broke into laughter, giving Dominick a hug while he smirked knowingly.

"What if there's ***no*** island out there?"

He shrugged, taking another sip of champagne, and put his arm around her shoulders. "Considering this is a dream, does it really matter?"

Looking up at the peaceful sky which was now yielding a beautiful sunset, along with the unusually perfect calm of the ocean, she finally shook her head with a smile, leaning against him contentedly. "I'm exactly where I want to be."

"As am I," he whispered, smiling back as he kissed her.

Last night they'd been walking in a park beneath a starry sky, leading to an area filled with bubbles, many that were regular small bubbles and yet some that were quite large. Dominick transported them into one that was incredibly gigantic, able to hold them both. To Julianna's surprise, he assured her the bubble had an endless air supply, even though the walls were solid as well as transparent.

Slowly, the bubble lifted into the sky, and Julianna fell back into Dominick's arms, clutching him tightly as the ground got further away. "What are you doing?" she asked with concern. "You know I'm not good with heights."

"Don't be afraid, love," he replied, "I've planned something which will get your mind off that."

She started to question this, even as the velvety darkness of the sky intensified, whereas she could no longer see the ground, but only a translucent glow surrounding the bubble. "Dominick, what have you done?" she gasped. "Where are we?"

He merely smiled, gesturing towards the darkness.

As Julianna stared out, a brilliant green light—like a miniature comet—shot past. Shortly afterwards, a swirling magenta light trailed back in yet another direction. As her eyes widened, more and more lights filled the air around them, shooting about in random directions, and emitting pleasant humming sounds like an astral chorus. All the while, the diamond-like stars winked back playfully.

"Oh, Dominick..." she breathed, glancing at him with wonder.

Holding her close, he gestured again towards the array with a smile. "On some nights above the island of Barokka, the inhabitants are greeted with a display similar to this one. The shooting beams are as harmless on Chavernos as they are here in the dream-state, but they present their own magic in their sparkle, and in the musical harmony created about them."

"They're beautiful," sighed Julianna, watching in awe for long moments before giving a short laugh. "Since you're so good at conjuring this, maybe they should change your middle name to ***Laser*** instead of Phaser."

He gave her a wry smile. "If they do, I'll see to it they change your name to Bubbles."

"Hmmm," she murmured in consideration. Dominick interrupted her with a lengthy kiss, slowly breaking away. "On the other hand," she purred in response, "maybe I do prefer you simply as Dominick, my dream knight." He brushed his hand against her cheek.

"'Dream knight' is a title I can live with," he said, kissing her again.

They continued to hold each other, leaning back to watch as the mesmerizing lights cascaded about them, illuminating them with bright colors. She smiled at him, watching as he was haloed in a sudden flicker of bright blue. Looking back, he watched as a rose pink crown of lights spun about Julianna's auburn hair, making it seem more fiery. It was as if they'd become one with the lights themselves.

As he kissed her again, the sound of thunderous fireworks filled the air about them.

When she opened her eyes, a myriad of new colors greeted her.

"Did you just do that?" she asked breathlessly.

"We both did," he whispered, cradling her head against his chest. "Any time with you is pure magic."

Pleased tears in her eyes, Julianna couldn't find her

voice, hugging him instead with clearer meaning than any honeyed words.

Yet some time later that evening, as had often been the case during the past few nights, Dominick began to sense more beyond her silence. Usually, he'd simply made efforts to distract her mind, but now, his puzzlement became concern.

"A starbeam for your thoughts?" he inquired softly.

Slowly, Julianna shut her eyes and shook her head. "I'm a bit too tired to think right now," she whispered. "Please... just hold me."

Hugging her tighter as he stroked her shoulder, Dominick slowly gained a better understanding of what was really troubling her, vowing silently to do something to remedy this.

Now back on Chavernos, as his mind returned to the present, Dominick stared at the sky reflectively. Julianna's thoughts all seemed centered on two things: the wonder of when their current relationship would come to an end, and self-reproach for what their relationship had become.

If only he could bring Julianna here to Chavernos. Then he could give her more than just pleasant illusions, and perhaps ease her mind by granting her a more permanent future between them.

More accurately, a future marriage.

He'd never considered marriage very seriously before, having been content enough with his bachelor state. But regarding Julianna, the thought of a lifetime with his auburn-haired temptress appealed to him with an intensity he couldn't deny.

There was no question that he loved her, nor that he could give her a wonderful life here. And he was certain her feisty nature would always keep a marriage between them interesting. Not to mention the nights of infinite dreams they could share, let alone the joy of being together in reality.

But more than that, it occurred to him that a woman like Julianna would desire marriage, at least someday in the future. If he didn't ask her, eventually someone else would. Just the thought of her giving herself to another man angered him no end, leaving him with a steadfast resolve to make sure that never happened by marrying her himself.

Unfortunately though, no legal marriage could exist while their long-distance separation remained.

Blazes, there has to be ***some*** *way!*

Maybe there was...

The more he thought about it, the better the idea seemed. Maybe he couldn't bind her to him by a legal marriage while they were on separate worlds, but with all the magic Chavernos had to offer, perhaps that fact didn't have to remain the truth after all.

And in the meantime, why ***couldn't*** he see to enhancing his commitment to Julianna? Rubbing his chin with a smile, he nodded with growing conviction. Yes, maybe it would work.

There was only one way to find out.

Tonight.

*****

"Oh, not another one," groaned Julianna.

When the work phone rang for the hundredth time, she answered it with a detached attitude. Fortunately for her, it wasn't one of the latest inventions of visual telephones, or the company's clients might have seen a most dreamy look on this particular executive secretary's face, whose mind was elsewhere.

Not the look of a serious working woman at all.

Or so Marybeth thought, standing close by without her noticing.

When the customer seemed to be becoming irate, in spite of Julianna's politeness, she finally rolled her eyes. "I ***promise*** you," she sighed dramatically, "Miss Thompson will be most pleased to speak with you, as soon as she returns from beyond."

Gaping, Marybeth quickly grabbed the phone. "Please don't mind her. She's had a long night. Yes, we've got your name and number, and we'll make sure Miss Thompson gets back to you." Hanging up the receiver, she gave a stern look to her confused friend. "Now then, young lady, care to come back to Earth?"

Julianna rubbed her eyes tiredly. "No," she murmured. "I'd rather be on Chavernos." Abruptly realizing what she said, she glanced up quickly. "I mean..."

"Don't," interrupted Marybeth, sitting beside her. "You've been acting strange for the past few weeks, so I guess another day of it won't matter. But between you and me, if you want to keep your job here, you'd best pull your head out of that dream world you've been living in. Good ol' Almira may not be in the best of moods when she gets back from her flight this afternoon." Julianna nodded once, earning a smile from her friend. "You met someone, haven't you?"

"You're too smart for me," she laughed, turning back to her computer screen.

On it was the long letter she'd been attempting to copy from a handwritten version for the past half-hour, which was unusual since she was normally a very fast typist. Glancing at the monitor, Marybeth was forced to take a closer look, a smirk forming as she pointed to the bottom of the screen.

"'And in conclusion'," she recited, "'There is no proof that our sales figures are falling or that Chavernos doesn't exist.'"

"What?" gasped Julianna, blushing upon the realization that the words ***were*** staring back at her from the screen. "Good Lord, where did that come from?"

"That's the second time you've mentioned this caverns business," informed Marybeth. "What ***have*** you been thinking of lately?"

"I'm thinking, I'd better fix this letter before Almira

comes back. I'll talk to you later, all right?"

"You'd better believe you will," said Marybeth, striding away with a disappointed and perplexed expression.

After fixing the document, Julianna saved it, printed it, and exited the program, leaning back in her chair. Inwardly, she knew she ***really*** needed to get her mind focused on her work, but it was difficult, given the one man who'd captured her thoughts, both at night when they were together... and during the day, when she remembered the nights.

Strong and handsome of body, clever of mind, understanding of heart, and with a sense of humor that topped the men she'd met in the 'real world', he eclipsed Roger from day one.

And he was ***absolutely*** the ideal romantic, she thought happily with a smile. Not just in the physical sense—though he was indeed that—but because he'd also literally swept her off her feet, bestowing kisses and holding her lovingly at every opportunity, filling their dream castle room with flowers, and always greeting her immediately upon arriving.

Most importantly, Dominick made her ***feel*** loved as she'd never known before, and she certainly loved him in return. Now, she could admit this truth even when awake.

Funny how different this was from a few weeks ago.

After their second meeting, she'd worried that her dream man might lead her beyond friendship, and was hesitant at the prospect. True, part of her craved to understand the mystery of romance, but she wasn't too anxious to enter into a temporary affair just to satisfy her curiosity.

Two nights later, she'd forgotten all of this in Dominick's arms.

And now, two weeks later, she still didn't regret it.

Her only true regret was the distance keeping them apart. If only he could reach her somehow.

"***Miss Sherborne!***" bellowed a shrill voice.

Emitting a shocked gasp, Julianna looked up to find Almira Thompson glaring at her. *Of all the luck for her to be back early.* "Have a nice trip?" she managed.

"***You'll*** be on a trip to the unemployment line if you don't finish that correspondence I sent you yesterday!" Giving a low grunt, she stormed off, allowing Julianna to glare at her silently.

"I'd like to trip ***you*** up... over some hot coals," she murmured.

Marybeth, having overheard, seemed to think this to be a minor form of revenge against their rather cranky boss, thinking a pit of electric eels might be more fitting.

*****

At Lost Limbo, today Dominick finally made an appearance again. Inferno gestured to Buddy, who looked up hopefully, but their friend went straight to the bar to exchange greetings with Zantarl. The discouraged guardian angel shook his head and sighed, wondering if he'd lost his friend permanently over their recent disagreement. Even Kiri and the others looked a bit subdued from where they sat across the room, since they all missed Dominick's good-humored nature.

"If you had a guardian angel's wings, I'm sure you'd fly," chuckled Zantarl. "I'm glad to see you in better spirits, son. Correct me if I'm heading down the wrong direction, but does this have to do with a certain young lady you met a short time ago?"

"It does," he agreed, grinning. "Zantarl, I really love her. And what's more, she loves me too. Why, these past weeks with her have been no less than phenomenal."

"Ah, that explains your absence. No doubt she's turned your brain to mush every night, leaving you to make up for it by sleeping through the daylight hours as well."

"I might consider that if she was an avid daydreamer," he replied, with a mischievous glint in his eye.

"'She' meaning Julianna?" Buddy asked softly from behind, Inferno beside him. Dominick turned slowly to face them, his expression becoming unreadable. "I guess she means more to you than I thought," his friend continued. "In any case, it's your life, and if you choose to spend time with her, that's up to you two."

"Right," agreed Inferno. "We've put up with more girl-chasing stories from Riff than we can count, but we know your situation is entirely different."

"So..." sighed Buddy, "if you aren't really dozing away the daylight hours, can we go back to being friends again, Dom?"

Dominick took only a moment before grinning, clasping his shoulder. "I never stopped being that," he said amiably, turning to shake hands with a relieved Inferno too. Glancing once towards the three watchful females, he laughed. "And you can tell your curious gals over there the same thing later, although Kiri's probably already overheard." At the other table, Kiri blushed, folding her arms in a huff, while her friends tried to get her to explain. Seeing this, the men echoed Dominick's laughter. "Now stop looking so somber and tell me how you've been," he continued.

"We will, but first tell us more about this Julianna," Buddy said eagerly. "Is she short? Tall? Blue-eyed? Brown-eyed? Our curious minds want to know."

Laughing as they sat beside him at the bar counter, Dominick filled them in on the past few weeks, but of course omitted more private details. Zantarl gave the trio a look of glad appreciation that they'd finally sealed the rift between them. He spoke so highly of Julianna that both Buddy and Inferno asked if she might have a sister or two for them.

"She does have two," Dominick admitted, "but one's married, and the other's engaged." The pair groaned. "Don't voice your disappointment too loudly or Kiri's liable to tell your girlfriends back there." They didn't need to turn to feel the icy stares of Jarissa and Psych upon their backs, nodding to their friend's advice. "Seriously, guys, Julianna's sisters aren't like her anyway. She's one-of-a-kind, just like your present companions are to you."

"Maybe," sighed Buddy, "but not all of us can take our girlfriends for walks on rainbows."

"Or toast marshmallows with them on frozen lakes, while friendly polar bears watch."

"Or float in large sky bubbles with them, while lights, music, and fireworks are everywhere."

"***Excuse*** me?" Zantarl interrupted loudly in disbelief.

Dominick shrugged nonchalantly. "I'm a dreamphaser. When I want to share magical evenings with the woman I love, you'd better believe they're going to be amazing."

"I can see you like to impress her with your creativity. But, son, are you sure this is really love you feel for her, or just a means to show off?"

Dominick shook his head. "No, Zan, it's definitely nothing like that," he said seriously. "My feelings for Julianna and hers for me are very real, all dreams aside. The dreams just enable us to have dates that go beyond the ordinary. Besides, we do regular things too, like going skating, and going to a carnival on another occasion. She especially liked it when I brought her to a Renaissance Faire, Chavernos style. Not to mention, she's a fairly good card player. And from our conversations, I've probably learned more about her in these weeks than those who've known her for a lifetime. We just wish we could be together in reality, instead of just dreams."

Zantarl smiled. "Well then, I stand corrected. When you put it that way, it does sound like you really love her. She sounds like quite an enchantress."

Dominick's features softened. "Chavernos knows she does enchant me," he murmured, conjuring up her smiling image in his mind's eyes. "But in reality, she's still an innocent of her world. I could sense that from the beginning. She was hurt emotionally by a former boyfriend called Roger Collins. After he betrayed her with another woman, she was left alone and lonely."

"Until you came along to ***rescue*** her," declared Buddy.

Inferno shouldered him so sharply, he was nearly knocked from his chair.

"Don't make it sound like that," warned Dominick. "I love Julianna very much, and I won't tolerate any insults about her or us. She has a good heart, which is as loving, loyal, and giving as any man could hope for in a woman. Circumstance just left her an unhappy soul craving to feel loved by someone, and to give her love freely without fear of rejection. It's by the luck of the stars that we found one another."

"Just like a fairy tale," chuckled Riff, causing all to turn towards his table, unaware he'd been listening in. Fortunately, he was on his own tonight.

Dominick's expression darkened slightly with apprehension. Over the past weeks, his brother had traveled to the other side of Chavernos, and obviously returned without notice. Knowing how dubious Riff's reputation had been in the past regarding women in the dream-state—including some of Dominick's own liaisons—the others could fully understand his wariness.

"Leave it alone, Riff," he replied, turning away.

His brother shrugged indifferently, gesturing for Zantarl to get him a drink. "You ought to stop wasting all your time on dream women, and try the ones of reality for a change. There's a world of difference when you're not worried your companion's going to disappear by waking up."

"I'll keep that in mind," Dominick replied dryly.

Unfortunately, his determined silence only piqued Riff's curiosity over Julianna. Knowing how close-mouthed his brother could be prompted him to rub his chin thoughtfully. There were of course... other ways to find things out.

"Well, I'll leave you to your ***important*** chats," Riff told the group, picking up his prepared drink. "As for me, I'd best go talk to Kiri, lest she brain me for not greeting her properly upon returning. See you guys later, I hope."

"'Bye, Riff," Inferno spoke for the rest.

Dominick looked after his brother worriedly. "I don't trust him," he whispered. "Riff never leaves so amiably without a reason."

"Don't be paranoid," laughed Buddy. "After all, he ***is*** still your brother, remember?"

"Not to mention, the son of Discord, ***remember***?" Dominick mocked. "Don't get me wrong, my father has his good points too, but there are times when I think I'm not related to them at all."

Zantarl and the others silently agreed on this point.

*****

Thank heaven she could leave Almira and work behind after five!

To curb Julianna's daydreaming thoughts, Almira had dumped a heap of correspondence on her desk to be typed up. Add that to making ten copies of each, followed by mailing them to every address from here to Osh Kosh, while juggling the nonstop phone calls and clients who walked in...

It added up to one tired worker, thankful to be home.

One who was even more grateful that night had finally arrived.

Julianna stretched languorously in bed as the stars came out to shine through her window, wondering what whirlwind encounter Dominick would show her this night.

The memories of the past weeks always made her smile.

Life with Dominick had certainly been ***anything*** but dull. Thanks to him, she'd gained both happiness and confidence in how she viewed life and love now. She believed in love again, and wasn't afraid of it this time, and the mixture of romance and companionship was wonderful. Something only he inspired in her.

She'd equally enjoyed his teachings of things such as dancing, skating, card playing, horseback riding, sailing, and even a bit of fencing. He was all she'd ever wanted in a friend, a companion, a lover... and whatever else might be stronger.

Leaning back against the pillows, Julianna shut her eyes, content with the knowledge that Dominick would soon be with her. He might even be here now in his astral form, awaiting her secretly. Sighing with a blissful smile, she had no idea that the presence in her room now wasn't Dominick, but his curious and grinning brother instead.

How fortunate that Dominick had mentioned where she lived to the others, which he'd managed to overhear when he returned to his table, seemingly distracted by other people. To find the precise location of her home, however, he'd had to wait until his brother dreamphased. Once he did, Riff simply followed him secretly in his astral form to learn how to get there. From that point, he'd arranged in advance for a suitable distraction to prompt Dominick's return to Chavernos, in order to delay his brother's arrival tonight. After all, how else could he learn more of Julianna?

Was she thinking of meeting her familiar lover? he wondered, gazing at her peaceful smile. No, more likely, she was just looking forward to a night of romance in general. But no matter, by the end of this night, he'd find out just what had attracted his brother to this innocently slumbering woman.

And then, he'd find out just how 'innocent' and 'in love' this Julianna really was.

Chapter Ten

Julianna surveyed the scene about her with curiosity and confusion. Admittedly, Dominick had taken them to some unusual places before, but this one really puzzled her. She seemed to be in an office building, dressed in a gray business suit, in the middle of a hallway where several people quickly brushed past her.

He must be here somewhere, she decided, walking down the corridor to glance at each door's nameplate, searching for his own. She found one plaque that read 'Mr. Westbrooke'. A wry smile curled across her mouth, as she hoped he wasn't going to demand she call him ***that*** tonight after all their time together.

Mr. Westbrooke indeed!

Knocking on the closed door, she wasn't too surprised when it opened of its own accord, revealing someone's arm resting on a large chair that had its back turned to her. So Dominick was going to play the corporate executive type tonight, she thought in amusement. Well, maybe she could erase any thoughts of business he might have.

Using a quick concentration technique that Dominick had shown her one night, she altered her outfit to transform it into a sexy dress of a pretty, shimmering scarlet. Her shoes were now a matching red with reasonable heels.

Walking quietly towards the desk before her, she sat upon it, leaning forward provocatively with a smile. "Your secretarial 'lady in red' is here to assist you, sir," she said seductively.

The chair swiveled around, revealing not Dominick, but a man who resembled him, except for being a bit older and having green eyes. The man gave her a lazy smile, steepling his hands as he appraised her, lingering on the added view the scoop-necked dress allowed.

Only a glimpse, since she blushed more crimson than her attire and stood instantly. "You're not Dominick!" she protested, backing up.

"Really?" chuckled Riff, rubbing his chin thoughtfully. "Hmmm, I wonder what gave me away this time."

"Where is Mr. Westbrooke?" Julianna persisted.

Riff gestured with open arms, never once losing his expression of amusement. "Right here, darlin'," he told her smiling. "I'm Mr. Westbrooke."

"Liar," she spat, turning to leave. The door shut unceremoniously in her face, causing her to whip about. "How dare you!" she exclaimed. "You have no right to keep me here, when I'm expecting someone else!"

"All you asked for was Mr. Westbrooke," he retorted, walking over to her. As he advanced, she retreated, until her back was to the door and his arms were on either side of her against the wall. "You've found me," he said in a low voice. "And may I say, I most certainly approve of my new secretary and her present state of attire."

Ducking down as he leaned forward, Julianna deftly stepped away from him again, wondering what had happened to Dominick, but more conscious of the need to stay away from this stranger. Turning about to face him so he couldn't surprise her, she eyed him shakily.

"I'm not your secretary, and you're not Dominick Westbrooke," she said flatly. "So just who the hell are you?"

"Someone who's heard some interesting stories about you," replied Riff, backing her against the desk. As she remained frozen, his hand lightly brushed her arm. "Very interesting in fact." She shied away from his touch, but his arms surrounded her on both sides of the desk, leaning forward so she couldn't move away. "Since we're to be working so closely together, why don't you show me a sample of your... skills?"

As he smiled seductively, Julianna slapped him soundly in the face. "I don't know who you are," she hissed, "but I'm ***not*** that kind of woman, and certainly not with you!"

"But you are for Dominick?" he asked, clasping her wrist to pull her closer. At her surprised gasp, his gaze softened slightly. "Romancing on rainbows, flying in starlit bubbles, and no doubt much more." He stopped upon seeing her face drain of color. "Oh, come now, we're both adults here. And I have to say, as a fellow dreamphaser, I admire both of your creativity. But even Dominick's imagination has limits, whereas I could show you things he's never even thought of before."

He tried to lean closer, but she held him back at arm's length. "Where is Dominick?" she demanded, disturbed by this stranger's knowledge of their time together. Receiving only silence, she continued, "Look, Mr. ***Imposter*** Westbrooke, either you tell me where the ***real*** Dominick Westbrooke is, or I'll search for him myself."

At her words, Riff's eyes hardened with contempt. Never before had a female spurned him so backhandedly.

"You're an infuriating woman," he said in a low voice. "And if this venom is common for your attitude, it only makes me wonder why Dominick keeps coming back to you. Are you so good in the damned bedroom?"

Blushing furiously, Julianna slapped him again, sliding away from him while he was distracted to run towards the door. As she turned the handle to open it, Riff reached out to slam it shut again, grabbing her by the arm and spinning her about to embrace her.

"I'm warning you, if you don't let me go right now, Dominick will make you suffer for it," she hissed, choking down her fear to let anger rise to the surface, struggling futilely against the tight hold of his arms. "Get your hands off of me!" she yelled finally.

Riff appeared to consider this for a brief moment, but then shook his head. "No, I don't think I want to just yet," he replied, backing her against the door again. "After all, in spite of your attitude, you are most fetching."

"Not for you, I'm not," she replied.

"So you say now," he said, kissing her hand. "But I believe I could convince you otherwise." At her gasp, a devious smile crept across his face. "You know, I'm beginning to see how beautiful you are when you're speechless." His green eyes quickly glanced over her, as his free hand ran along her arm. "And most desirable." She opened her mouth to scream, but his hand prevented this. "No, don't waste your sweet voice. I've already taken the liberty of sending away the others in this building. I assure you, we're all alone."

Her head shook his hand away angrily, glaring at him coldly. "Why are you doing this?" she asked. "I've never even met you before."

"Ah, but that didn't stop you from throwing yourself at Dominick when you first met. Why should I consider now to be any different?"

"Because Dominick and I are in love with each other!"

"Love!" he sneered in disgust. "The only so-called ***love*** between you two is your shared fire in the heat of passion. Take it from me, I've seen enough to know that love itself is a myth. The bards just like to pretty up the reality of things."

"That's not true. Love may not always be easy, but it is real. Until I met Dominick, I had my doubts about love too. But the right person makes all the difference."

The sincerity in her voice and her eyes softened his heart, causing his irritation to fade, and making him regret his initial impressions of her.

"And if there isn't such a person?"

"Then either you haven't met them yet, or you aren't

seeing someone that's already there. Either way, chiding love as a myth won't help you to find it. And only someone who's been hurt reaching for love would have reason to shun it, wouldn't they?"

Have I been wrong? he thought privately.

Leaning his forehead against hers, he sighed heavily. "Oh, lady…"

Still not knowing who he was, Julianna was frozen in place, silently praying Dominick would show up to rescue her from this situation, before this man might suddenly become unstable once more.

*****

"You just woke me up from a sound sleep, and I still don't see why this can't wait until tomorrow," said Dominick, nearly hissing the words. Having just reached Julianna's home in astral form, the last thing he expected was for someone to jar him back to Chavernos by pounding his door off its hinges until he awoke. Being wrenched back abruptly was never pleasant to a dreamphaser, and certainly added to his foul mood when he discovered it was someone he didn't even know. The time he'd spent listening to the stranger's reason for being here didn't help. "Riff might not be back until much later, and I don't have time to entertain you while he's gone."

The stocky man before him shook his head. "Your brother owes me a considerable sum of money, and I'm not leaving until he shows up or you help me locate him."

Damn Riff! Dominick thought. He was used to hearing of his brother's spending binges, which usually resulted in bringing the people that he owed money to here. But never had they shown up at night like this, demanding payment immediately, while Riff was heaven only knew where!

His eyes turned to the clock and he growled quietly. No doubt Julianna was waiting for him, and this trivial matter was bound to detain him until he could either find Riff or calm this person into waiting until the morrow.

"Look," he said, forcing his voice to stay controlled, "just what's so urgent that you need this money tonight?"

The man looked flustered for a minute, but then said a bit uneasily, "That's none of your business. I deal with your brother alone."

So much for attempts at control, Dominick's thoughts mocked.

"Well, I'm ***not*** my brother, so you may as well face facts. He's not here tonight! Now I have other things to see to, so if you'll just be on your way..."

"No!" the man said emphatically.

Dominick growled in frustration.

"Did Riff give you any indication of where he was going tonight?" he asked finally. The man's long pause before shaking his head, led new suspicion into Dominick's eyes. "You're sure now." The man shook his head again, just before he nodded frantically.

"I was supposed to find out from you where he was."

"I see... who sent you?"

The man fumbled for a moment before answering, "Just someone I know. He doesn't concern you either."

Something was definitely amiss here. An instinct Dominick had developed after years of his brother's deceitful pranks. For some reason—call it a resemblance to Kiri's psychic instincts—he had the uncanny notion that he was being set up.

"You're lying," he said quietly, hoping the man would give something away.

"What?" the man stammered.

"Don't give me that. It's obvious by your actions that you're hiding something, and I'd bet Riff's behind this. Now why don't you save us both a headache and come clean. What's this all about?"

"I told you, I don't have to tell you."

Dominick's banked anger flared up instantly. Grabbing the man's shoulders, he slammed him back against the wall. "I've had just about enough of this ***game*** of yours, and now you're going to give me some answers! Unless you want to find out what painful tortures an angry dreamphaser can conjure up when you're next asleep."

The look of worry on the man's face was almost laughable. Dominick had never used his abilities in that way, although he knew others who had—and of course he was bluffing here—but it was a threat that most who knew dreamphasers' abilities wouldn't ignore. Having control over the dream-state could be a powerful weapon to wield, when necessary.

"I don't have to..." the man began shakily.

"Don't push me," warned Dominick. "Do you know what I'll do to you in your sleep if you still refuse to answer me?" The man froze, shaking his head slightly in negation. "Well, let me paint you a for instance. How would you like to have every limb torn from your body—slowly and most excruciatingly—and then to see those same appendages tossed to a pack of hungry wolves?"

That sounded convincing, he thought with amusement.

It was apparently working.

As the man visibly cringed, Dominick continued deviously, "Or how would you like having a dark dragon skin you alive, until there's nothing left of you but the skeleton beneath, and to have an army of ogres and trolls sent in to break what bones are left of you? Not a pretty sight, and also very painful. I'd say you'll be screaming for about a week afterwards, even while awake..."

"It was Riff's idea!" the man blurted out. "He just told me to keep you busy while he's gone, so you wouldn't enter the dream-state!"

Dominick's eyes lost their look of mischief, newfound

anger lighting them. "Why?" he hissed, earning silence. Slamming the man back against the wall again, he snarled, "Tell me why, dammit!"

"I'm not sure!" he protested. "Something about seeing a Julianna woman!"

His words sank deep.

"Julianna," breathed Dominick, his face draining of color. By Chavernos, Riff wouldn't... Memories of former incidents flashed through his mind. *Like hell he wouldn't!* his thoughts concluded, turning his gaze sharp again. "Why is he going to see her? Tell me now, or by Chavernos, I swear you'll regret it!"

"He didn't tell me!" exclaimed the man, shaking violently now. "I swear he didn't! Please don't skin me to bones in my sleep."

Dominick's expression remained hardened for a moment, but then he relented, sensing the man's last protest to be the truth. Pulling open the door, he roughly pushed him outside. "You're reprieved for now," he hissed, glaring at the cowering man. "But mark my words, if anything should happen to Julianna because of your trickery, there won't be anywhere in the dream-state or reality where you'll be able to hide from my wrath!"

Slamming the door, Dominick strode towards his room, cursing the man, cursing his brother, and cursing himself for falling for the simple dupe. Now it made sense why Riff wasn't home, obviously so he couldn't be stopped from sending out to the dream-state. And to make matters worse, Dominick had made the mistake of mentioning to his friends today where Julianna lived. Obviously, Riff had overheard. He could only hope that his brother hadn't located her yet, shutting his eyes to send out to the dream-state again to go to her.

*****

Long moments passed before Julianna could even find

her voice to speak. "Please… let me go find Dominick."

"He won't be here," Riff replied quietly.

"Why?" she demanded, fear giving way to a different, stronger fear. "Is he hurt?"

He paused, but had no chance to reply, as an invisible force suddenly grabbed hold of him, slamming him into the opposite wall. Riff's head smacked against the bricks that materialized there, sliding down to the floor with pained surprise as Dominick moved forward slowly to stand just before him.

He'd sensed Julianna's fear even before he entered the room, and when he saw his brother having cornered her, any need for an explanation vanished.

"Get up," he hissed in a deadly voice. Riff made no move to do so, even as Julianna ran over to stand behind her companion, clasping his arm shakily. Sensing her trembling, he turned to her worriedly, placing his hands on her shoulders. "Are you all right, love?" he asked softly. She nodded quickly, but upon seeing the shock still apparent in her eyes, he hugged her against his side protectively.

"Well, I guess you two don't need me anymore," Riff murmured, slowly backing up as he stood.

"Hold it right there!" snapped Dominick, his eyes shooting fire. Releasing Julianna, he stormed over to face his brother. "You know, I was a bit late getting here because I was temporarily ***detained*** by one of your buddies. He said you owed him money."

Riff's expression showed obvious relief. "Oh, well you know how I am sometimes, Phase. It's a weakness."

"Yes, I know how you are all too well," Dominick retorted, slamming his fist into Riff's jaw, knocking him backwards into the brick wall again. While he was disoriented, Dominick dragged him to his feet, no longer seeming the younger brother and certainly no less apt in strength. "You bastard," he hissed in a low voice. "You thought to seduce the woman I love, no doubt as another of your stupid games against me. But Julianna is the one woman I won't allow you to work your machinations on."

"Oh, listen to you!" Riff laughed in derision, turning to her. "I hope you realize, dear lady, that your precious lover isn't as chaste as you may have been originally. He's had scores of women in the dream-state dating back to his sixteenth birthday, if he didn't start earlier."

"I know that," she whispered.

"You what?" he gasped, shaking his head with unexpected surprise. "And it doesn't bother you?"

She shook her head. "I'm not happy about it, no. But they were in the past." Her thoughts turned to Roger momentarily. "Just like anyone I used to know."

Riff's eyes widened as he turned to face his brother incredulously. "I don't believe I just heard her correctly. You told her about your former affairs? Are you insane?"

"Yes, I told her," hissed Dominick. "And no, I'm not crazy. I happen to love her enough to be honest regarding the past, since it won't have any effect on our future. She knows I'd simply been searching for love without finding it, but that I do love her."

Riff turned back to Julianna. "And you believed all this?" he laughed.

Dominick's hands gripping his throat choked off any further words. "She believes it, because it's the truth! And you, my ***dear*** brother, should know better by now than to try seducing someone I'm involved with, let alone to try starting trouble between us. You're not going to get away with it this time, Riff!"

"***Riff?***" gasped Julianna. "You're Dominick's ***brother***?" He'd barely gotten out a nod before she lunged forward, her hands clawing at him, even as Dominick reached out to hold her back. "You rotten bastard! You knew I was involved with your brother, yet you put the moves on me anyway! How could you be such an insensitive jerk?"

Slowly, Dominick managed to calm her down, holding her comfortingly while his gaze never strayed from his devious brother. "I'll take care of this, love," he said softly, kissing her forehead once. "Why don't you go back to our castle to wait for me?"

"I'm not going anywhere without you now," she said, eyeing Riff with open distrust.

Understanding, he nodded once, gesturing her to one side. His silent look afterwards told her that there was still a matter to be settled, and she wasn't about to interfere.

"You never learn, Riff," Dominick said quietly, giving a forced laugh. "But fortunately for me, I have. I suspected this, even when you said nothing at Lost Limbo earlier."

"Look, I was curious, because you wouldn't tell me anything. I just came here to see what this Julianna of yours was like, that's all."

"Really?" sneered Dominick. "Well, let's just say I don't like your ***methods*** of introduction. And if you weren't my brother..." Stopping himself, he drew a breath. "But seeing as you are, however unfortunate that is, I'm above killing family."

"Gee, Phase, thanks a lot!" Riff replied sarcastically.

Ignoring him, Dominick continued, "Meaning I'll just have to settle for this retribution instead."

Punching his unsuspecting brother again, he knocked him to the floor just before delivering more blows.

Having similar strength, Riff used this to advantage, tripping his brother to fall to his level, before taking the initiative to strike back this time. Julianna gasped with each blow that contacted against Dominick, feeling as if she was being similarly struck, yet helpless to interrupt the struggle between the arguing pair.

"You and your petty women," sneered Riff, pinning

Dominick to the floor. "How long are you going to fool this one into believing you know the meaning of the word love? Another week? Two maybe?"

Rage contorted Dominick's features as he gave a low growl, punching Riff in the stomach and rolling away from him. As his brother clutched his stomach in pain, Dominick looked to him with loathing. "I'm not letting Julianna go, you idiot! Whether you believe it or not, I do love her, and not for some damned temporary affair!"

"Sure," scoffed Riff. "And what happens when the passion fades and the bed sheets turn cold?"

Dominick mumbled a low curse before attacking him anew, the pair wrestling amidst their punches and jabs. Julianna stood back from the fray, unable to hear everything said, but unwilling to leave Dominick, no matter what the outcome.

After a time, the fighting pair finally broke apart to steal some much-needed breaths. "Geez, Phase, why didn't you just tell me you were so possessive of this one?"

"You have the gall to ask me that after what you pulled tonight?" sneered Dominick. "You may have tricked some other women I've known, Riff, but Julianna's different. She's not going to be yours in any way whatsoever. And if I have to beat this knowledge into your thick skull all night, I will!"

Seeing Dominick looking all too anxious to do just that, Riff held up a hand in protest.

"Okay, okay!" he yelled. "You've proven your point. You said you were above killing family, remember?" Dominick's jaw flexed tightly, but he said nothing, while Riff rubbed the back of his head. "You sure are one hell of a headache when you're angry. And a backache... and a stomachache."

Eyeing his brother warily, but finally satisfied, Dominick walked over to Julianna. Longing to hold her, yet worried over her seeing his anger so blatantly demonstrated, he ran a hand through his hair instead and sighed.

She merely stared at him, remaining silent.

"I'm sorry you were here to witness this," he said quietly. "It's not the first time Riff and I have tangled over something. And when I got here to find him holding you trapped... Julianna, I swear I'd never hurt you. At the most, my anger might surface verbally, but that's the extent of it, so don't ever think..."

Her arms encircling his neck interrupted him, hugging him close. "I love you," she whispered simply. "And I know you'd never hurt me. I'm just glad you showed up when you did, and that you don't seem too badly hurt."

Not one to question this, Dominick welcomed her embrace, fully intending to hold her that way forever. For long moments, he savored the feeling that she was safe in his arms again, until he gradually remembered his brother. Still holding Julianna, he turned to Riff warily.

"Are ***you*** in one piece?" he asked evenly.

"Not by much, thank you," Riff replied sardonically, cursing his sore body as he tried to stand with difficulty. *Damn dreams can be too real for one's own good*, he mused, surprised when Julianna slowly broke away from her companion to stand before him, giving him her hand in assistance.

He turned a worried look to his brother, but Dominick merely watched him coolly, his gaze speaking both acceptance and warning at the same time. When Riff was fully standing and Julianna tried to move away, he wouldn't relinquish her hand. Sensing his brother's eyes darkening upon him, he persisted nonetheless.

"For whatever it's worth, I'm sorry," he said quietly. "I guess part of me is sorry that my brother found you first. You do seem different from the rest."

"And you're certainly… unique yourself, Riff," she replied, earning an amused laugh from him.

"Tactfully put, lady."

"But although you may own this company of sorts..." Her gaze turned to meet Dominick's with a smile. "My heart belongs to the other Mr. Westbrooke."

"Right," sighed Riff, recapturing her attention. He flashed her a brief smile. "Friends then?" he asked. She hesitated, but then shook his hand with agreement, even as his smile became a grin. "So, what are we all doing tonight?" he asked cheerfully.

"***We*** are going elsewhere," Dominick said decisively, stepping forward to place a protective arm about Julianna's shoulders. "***You***, my dear brother, are going back home, or at least somewhere far away from us tonight. If there's anything else, it can wait until tomorrow. Understood?"

"Does my battered body have a choice?" Riff asked, tossing a mischievous look over his shoulder as he turned to leave. "But if I may make a suggestion, skip the frozen lake idea next time. It would have been even worse if you decided to..."

"Good night, Riff!" he replied emphatically.

Riff's amused laughter echoed as he vanished in a brief flash of light.

Always a comedian! thought Dominick, turning upon hearing Julianna laugh softly.

"A bit too incorrigible for his own good, isn't he?" she told her curious companion.

"Mildly put," he agreed, smiling slowly as he reached forward to lift her off the ground. "Now then, my lady, I believe I suggested earlier for us to return to our dream castle."

"Ready to leave when you are," she replied, hugging him closer as the scenery about them vanished, soon replaced by the walls of their castle room.

Julianna expected him to place her on the bed, as he often did when they arrived here, but instead, he set her down in one of the chairs by the window. Before she could say a word, he knelt beside her, gently holding her hand.

"Julianna, are you sure you're all right?" he asked. "Riff didn't... hurt you in any way?" Knowing instantly what he referred to, she shook her head. "Thank Chavernos," he sighed. "Even so, you must be shaken up."

"I was afraid," she admitted. "I didn't know it was your brother, and even if I had, I would have been frightened by his earlier actions. Even though he did stop trying to seduce me to listen to reason at one point, I'm afraid I wasn't too sorry when you gave him a few good punches, after the way he treated me initially."

Dominick smirked slightly. "Well, he asked for it." Brushing a curl from her cheek, he added, "But I promise I'd never vent my anger on you like that. I'd only do what's necessary to protect you from any who might hurt you, and especially other men. There are things about you that I refuse to share with them."

"I'd never want to share what we have with anyone else," she agreed. "I love you, Dominick, and you're the only one I can ever see in that way."

"How fortunate the feeling is mutual, my lady," he whispered with a smile, leaning forward to kiss her. Shutting her eyes, she welcomed his gentle touch to wipe away the recent events.

Not breaking the kiss, he stood up to draw her from the chair, sweeping her into his arms again, and carrying her to the bed. As he placed her atop the covers before sitting alongside of her, she couldn't help noticing the interest in his eyes.

"I conjured this dress up earlier, thinking it was you in that room with me," she explained. "That was before I realized it was a stranger, of course, and then..." Her voice trailed off, as he reached forward to clasp her hands.

"What did happen?" he asked quietly.

Julianna told him all, but stressed that Riff had started to back down just before he'd arrived. His earlier behavior at their initial meeting was still enough to magnify his anger against his brother. Just the thought of Riff trying to put his hands on her made Dominick want to go after his departed sibling. But for now, he knew that any dealings with him would have to wait.

"Come here, love," he said gently, holding his arms out to her, which she accepted gladly. Clasping her tightly in his protective embrace, Dominick stroked the long hair streaming down her back, kissing her cheek as she held him tightly.

"I know nothing happened," she stammered, "but at first, it reminded me of that incident with Daffordshire, and I didn't know who he was. I was afraid you wouldn't come for me, and that he might..."

"Shhh, it's all right, love," he whispered. "You're safe with me now, and no one can hurt you."

He kissed her eyes, while smoothing back the curls from her forehead. Slowly, she began to respond, moving her head to welcome his kiss. His lips brushed hers tenderly, as light as the wind. While she understood his extra attentiveness to her earlier fears, another part of her craved more.

"Dominick, I'm not afraid with you," she whispered against him. His eyes met hers, questioning them as her trembling hand reached up to touch his cheek. "Please... love me like you always do."

Sensing an unspoken need for comfort within her words, a tender smile crossed his expression. "If you're certain, let it be as my lady wishes," he replied, pulling her close to kiss her more passionately. The flames of their ever-present desire for each other kindled anew, burning away the bad memories.

Cradling her face gently, Dominick caressed her as his kisses deepened, his mouth teasing hers open. A soft moan escaped her, spurring him to pull her closer, his hands stroking upwards. With the low-cut back of the dress, his hands instantly came in contact with her bared skin, even before they slid within to reach what was still hidden.

Julianna gave a short gasp against his kisses as the dress fell away, feeling his hands cover the softness of her breasts, warming and awakening them as his kisses traveled along her neck to earn a greater response.

"So beautiful," he murmured, still caressing her as he held her. Raising her chin for a moment, Dominick caught her gaze, allowing her to see the protective gleam in his own eyes. "I promise, my love, I'll let no other touch you again as my foolish brother did tonight. This which is between us is ours alone... forever."

Kissing her passionately to emphasize his words, she responded sweetly in kind, feeling that the bond between them had only grown stronger.

As if having read her thoughts, which of course she knew he could, he flashed her a smile, kissing her deeply once more before his kisses traveled lower.

She arched back in pleasure as his mouth warmly fell to her breasts that he'd just inflamed with his touch, her hands clutching his shoulders while he stroked her bare back. All memories of Riff's actions were erased, replaced by Dominick's loving caresses, as his mouth gradually sought hers again.

Impishly, she began tugging at his shirt, sliding it off his shoulders, to feel his skin grow heated beneath her touch. As her hands drew along his chest and lower, his breathing became ragged, while his eyes blazed fire.

His kisses held the same fire, consuming her as she entwined her arms about his neck. Easing the dress from her completely, Dominick's kisses trailed down the length of her, casting the thin fabric aside. Julianna felt rapture from his ardent kisses, feeling an intensity of possession from him that surely stemmed from what happened earlier.

Her last clothing melted away as Dominick kissed her deeply, just before he pulled away to take care of his own.

Nearly breathless, she smiled at the sight of him, watching the muscles flex in his bare back.

Casting patience aside, she reached out to put her arms around him, giving a laugh when he started at her touch.

He turned to her with a mischievous smile. "Can't wait half a moment?" he chuckled.

Julianna shook her head. "Not when it's you," she replied, kissing his shoulder before resting her head upon it, her arms reaching about to hug his waist. "Wake me when you're done," she murmured teasingly.

Dominick turned to face her, shaking his head with a laugh. "Oh no, my lady. You're not going to sleep on me yet."

"And how am I supposed to stay awake while you make me wait forever?" she asked in mock protest.

"Because, my love, your waiting is over," he said huskily, swiftly lowering her back against the pillows while looming above her with a most roguish smile. "And as to your staying awake, I assure you, I'll help you manage that now, my impatient little temptress."

To prove his words, Dominick proceeded to do just that, pressing searing kisses down her neck, as her hands reached up to hold him there possessively. He merely chuckled at the attempt, his mouth moving downward to kiss her breasts again while his hands traveled lower.

She nearly jumped at his touch, her fingers clutching at his hair. "Oh, what are you doing, Dominick," she breathed. "You're making me feel so..."

"Restless?" he murmured. "Lost to desire..."

Her attempt at a reply trailed off with glazed eyes.

He chuckled again quietly when Julianna began to tug at his hair, softly pleading for him to return beside her, and he acquiesced, his mouth capturing hers once more.

She decided to see about teasing him back. Her mouth escaped his to press heated kisses to his chest, distracting him as her hands slid past his waist. Her light caresses had full effect on him, as his eyes flew open to stare into her own devious ones, his hands grasping her shoulders tightly.

"You seem a bit restless yourself," she whispered, her hands still teasing him where they remained. He tried to protest, but the words didn't have a chance as her caresses became more intense.

"Julianna, you'll drive me mad," he groaned against her mouth, swiftly clasping her hands to draw them away as he shifted to cover her body completely with his.

Their senses were so heightened, it was the most natural thing in the world when he slid the warmth of his desire deep within the hot depths of her own yearning body, stealing exhilarated cries of pleasure from both. In moments, the undeniable heat of passion caught them. Julianna's hands clutched Dominick's back as he slowly stroked deeper within her, crying out softly as her legs tightened about him.

Their sounds of desire mingled as they kissed each other fiercely, while they sought sweet heaven. They glided on a wave of bliss, while the world disappeared around them, their passion building ever higher.

"Dear heaven, love," he breathed as her arms tightened about him. "Julianna... you feel so wonderful."

"So do you," she whispered. "Oh, Dominick, please..."

"Yes… Come with me... now, sweetheart."

His soft words inspired her to pull him closer, yielding sweetly as his deep thrusts sent them over the edge. Both cried out, their bodies exploding together as they soared through the warm mists of mindless ecstasy. Shuddering with pleasure, they kissed passionately anew, sharing the encompassing warmth of a most heavenly afterglow.

When Dominick finally relaxed against his companion, he brushed a hand across her passion-dampened forehead, kissing her tenderly once before cuddling her close in their desire's sweet aftermath.

"Did I mention before how much I liked your choice of a new dress?" he murmured, stroking her back.

A mischievous smile curled across her mouth in remembrance of how said dress had ended up on the floor. "You mean my 'lady in red' look?" she asked. He nodded with a seductive growl. "I thought it might keep you from thinking me too businesslike."

He gave a low laugh. "As long as all our business is conducted here, I don't mind," he informed her, twining a finger around her curls before kissing the reddish strands. "You realize that even if you wore nothing, you'd still be a lady in red, thanks to your hair," he added roguishly.

"And I have a temper to match the color," she said in mock warning. "You'd best remember that, my dream knight."

"How could I forget?" he murmured against her cheek. "I find it to be one of your most endearing traits."

"Really?" she laughed. "I do believe that's one of the best compliments I've ever received. Probably since you're the only one praising that particular trait of mine."

"I love all your others as well," he decided, a devious smile crossing his face as his arms encircled her waist beneath the covers. "Although I must admit to finding this passionate nature of yours most intriguing." Julianna smiled knowingly as he leaned forward to kiss her again. "Dear heaven, woman, it seems I'll never be able to get this desire for you out of my system."

The brightness of her eyes dimmed slightly. "And would you leave if that ever happened?" she whispered.

"Oh no, love," Dominick replied seriously. "You're not getting rid of me that easily. I love you for every moment we share, no matter what we do. I wouldn't leave you now, even if you imposed celibacy on me."

"Hmmm..." she murmured in consideration.

"But I hope you wouldn't be that cruel to this poor man who adores you so much," he continued, his eyes taking on an exaggerated look of melancholy.

"I'd be punishing myself equally as much if I did," she laughed. "Now please get that silly look off your face, before you complain of my laughing all night."

Resting his cheek against hers, he embraced her tightly. "Ah, Julianna, I love to hear your laughter, and you're certainly the last woman I'd ever complain about. Just to hold you like this is like holding the sun, and I've always been most fond of sunny days."

"Mmmm, me too," she murmured, apparently pleased, snuggling against him as she shut her eyes happily.

The perfect time, Dominick thought.

"Julianna?" he whispered, earning another quiet murmur from her. "We've been together for a while now, haven't we?"

Her eyes opened with puzzlement. "If you don't know the answer, then I'd say you've been out in your sunny days too often," she replied.

"No, that's not what I meant," Dominick laughed. "I mean, we've been happy together, in all ways. And after giving our relationship serious thought, I was hoping we might make it permanent."

Julianna moved back to sit up, pulling the blanket up to her neck. "Permanent, how?"

"Well… let me think," he replied, shrugging once with a boyish grin. While she sat confused, Dominick reached back to withdraw something from the night table drawer behind him, keeping his hand tightly closed around the object. "Now, I know this might sound strange at first, but hear me out."

She nodded for him to continue, and he opened his hand, holding out a small velvet box to her. Julianna gasped as the implication sank in, even as he lifted the lid to reveal a beautiful gold ring with a brilliant emerald in the center, a circle of diamonds surrounding the sparkling gem protectively. Before she could blink, he took her hand in his, placing the ring upon it gently.

"Dominick, it's beautiful," she whispered, touching the precious ring with shaking fingers.

"I remember how you once said how much you love both diamonds and emeralds," he said. "And since you're most beautiful to me in many ways, I thought it right to grant you a ring that has the same added beauty. A ring to symbolize how much I love you, Julianna." She smiled up at him with tear-filled eyes.

"You've been so good to me. How can I ever thank you enough?"

He took her hand in his, kissing it softly before caressing her fingers as he looked deeply into her eyes. "Would you do me the honor of marrying me?" he asked.

Julianna's eyes brimmed with new tears as she squeezed his hand. "Oh, yes..." she whispered. "Yes, I'll marry you, Dominick."

Giving a short laugh of happiness as he embraced her, her heart raced with joy. So much that she nearly forgot the all-too-real distance and circumstances separating them.

Almost.

Upon remembering, she slowly stiffened and pulled back, earning a look of concern from him.

"What's wrong, love? Is it the ring?"

"No," Julianna replied quickly. "It's wonderful. And I love you so much, Dominick. But for once, we have to face reality. How can I marry you? We can only be together when I'm asleep."

"So it seems," he agreed. "But I've given it some thought, and since our two worlds are both undeniably real, there may be a solution to our dilemma. I've decided to see my grandfather about trying to find a way to bring us together in reality as well."

Hope surged through her. "Is that possible?"

"I'm not sure, but if it is, I'm damn well going to find out. I'll do everything in my power to find a way. Until which time, at the very least we'll be engaged in reality, even though we can only share our dreams together at the moment."

Julianna shook her head in confusion. "I understand what you're saying," she replied, "but I don't see how this is going to work. After all, even if your world's dreamphasers can accept the truth to an engagement like this, ***I*** can't prove your existence on Chavernos to those of Earth. They'd think I'd lost my mind."

"That would be a problem," he agreed on a sigh. "In which case, I'm afraid the only thing you can do to prevent this, is to keep it a secret between us for now."

"But that's just the point," she argued regretfully. "Since there's no proof so far that we can ***ever*** reach one another to be married, why pretend otherwise with an engagement?" At his silence, she stared down at her ring sadly. "Everything's all been just a dream between us anyway. One that's merely taken us awhile longer to wake up from. Why bother with mention of an engagement at all, when it's only another illusion?"

As her words trailed off, she saw Dominick clasp her hand, lifting her head to face him again. The warmth of his smile affected her so much that she nearly forgot her question. Fortunately, he didn't.

"What we have between us is certainly no illusion, love," he whispered, kissing her palm. At her slight smile, he added gently, "Let me try to explain my reasons for wanting this engagement. In past times, I'd briefly thought I knew what love was, but always ended up confusing that emotion with something else. Yet with you, the feelings of love only grew stronger and clearer to me. Knowing you weren't one to give your heart lightly, and still innocent to the ways of love, you can't know what it meant to me for you to trust me that first night in our dream castle."

She blushed, as he continued on a sigh. "When you granted me the blessing of your love that night, it was more than magic between us. You touched the depths of my soul."

His smile dimmed slightly as a wave of regret filled his eyes. "And yet... ever since that night, although our evenings together have been more than wonderful, there are times when I've felt sadness from you. As if you've felt guilty regarding the passion we've shared, and that ours was only a temporary affair."

Clasping her hands tighter, he shook his head. "It could never be that now, love. You're the other half of my soul, and I need you with me always. That's why I want us to be engaged now, even if we can't be married immediately. I want you to know that my commitment to you is real, to ease your mind and heart, even though both our worlds can't recognize it yet."

Seeing tears in her eyes, he brushed them away lightly. "Sweetheart, I wish I could marry you right now in reality, and carry you off to my homeworld this night. But for now, I can only promise that we will be married in truth one day as soon as possible. Can you understand, and would you accept this, until we can be together at last?"

"I do understand, Dominick," she whispered, loving him all the more, despite the sharp cut of reality raking across her heart. "And I'm not questioning your devotion, which you've proven time and again. But you're overlooking something. What if there's ***no*** way to bring us together in reality. Then what will we do? Keep pretending otherwise?"

Dominick's gaze lowered, and he sighed heavily.

"I don't know," he said finally. "It's certainly not my choice that our two worlds separate us, but it's where our lives dictated us to be. I suppose if we can't be together in the waking world, we'll either have to settle for our time in the dream-state... or I'm not sure what."

*That **would** put a snag in things*, Julianna considered, biting her lip as another problem occurred to her.

"What about children?" she asked. "Is it possible to create them in the dream-state?" It seemed a moot question, but due to their unconventional meetings, Julianna wouldn't assume anything, until Dominick shook his head sadly.

"No, it's not," he whispered, meeting her gaze again. "Even powerful magic has its limits. We can't have children together unless we're both on the same world in reality." She looked away to consider this, as he expected her to, squeezing her hand once. "I know I'm asking a lot, with the future so uncertain." He shut his eyes painfully. "But if we can't reach each other... I'll release you from our engagement, and sunder all ties between us, if that's what you wish."

Julianna could hear the pain in his statement, but still had too many doubts which needed to be settled, even if they never affected them.

"What if..." she began uneasily, "before we can find a way to each other, one of us found someone else while in either of our real worlds?" His eyes darkened slightly. "I'm not saying it ***would*** happen," she continued quickly. "But if a great deal time of elapsed, and it did..."

"Our souls are connected, so it wouldn't," he interrupted, but as her questioning gaze remained, Dominick relented with a sigh. "***If*** that happened, which it won't, I would think it only fair for the person in question to be honest with the other, and break off our engagement first. In regard to the honesty and fidelity that go with commitment, I think that's only to be expected, don't you?"

"Yes," she agreed, more worried that he'd be the one to break this commitment if too much time passed.

He must have sensed her thoughts, for he suddenly gripped her shoulders tightly, locking eyes with her.

"Julianna, there's been no other woman in my life—either in reality or the dream-state—since the day I met you. I swear there never will be again. And in case you're curious, you're the only woman I've ever proposed to. After a decade of searching, I've finally found you, and I'm not about to let you go without a fight."

"Oh, Dominick, I'd never leave you either," she replied, leaning forward to hug him again. Tears stung her eyes as she continued. "Even if we can only be together at night, I'll settle for anything we can have, children or no, and not let the shadows of reality come between us. And I promise, I'll certainly never have an affair with anyone else. I love you too much for that."

"By Chavernos, Julianna, I love you too," he murmured, with a smile. "And all that you've said holds true for me as well, since no other woman holds a candle to you."

Kissing her quickly, Dominick added, "Now, as far as this engagement of ours goes, maybe your world can't recognize it yet, but I do know some people of my world who will. If it's all right with you, I'd like to arrange for some of my dreamphasing friends to be present tomorrow night, so I can introduce you to them, as well as to announce our engagement. At least it'll bring us one step closer towards our hopefully future marriage."

Julianna's eyes shone at the determination she found in his. How could she have any doubts with a man like this in her life? she wondered, touching his cheek. "I'll look forward to it," she whispered, kissing him deeply.

He responded in kind, rekindling their former desire. Gently easing her back against the pillows, his gaze met hers. "Since I know how you've felt lately regarding our nights together, if it makes any difference, we can wait on more of this until our engagement's official tomorrow."

"Hmmm, give me a chance to think about it." About five seconds passed before Julianna shook her head. "No, that's all right," she said finally. "With you, I don't mind this wild abandon anymore." She smiled knowingly. "Of course, if it's all right with you."

Dominick laughed quietly. "Sweetheart, I do believe you're gaining your own capability for reading minds." His mischievous smile matched hers, as they embraced each other again passionately.

Feeling the comfort of his arms around her, Julianna felt so much joy. Yet her unyielding thoughts couldn't help wondering.

"Dominick, do you really think it's possible?" she murmured.

He pulled back, never losing his smile as he gazed into her eyes with conviction.

"I promise, love… We'll find a way."

Chapter Eleven

There was no denying it. His grandson was crazy.

As Chaos paced about the large room, silently contemplating Dominick's words, the younger man stood calmly awaiting his response. The older man's piercing green eyes were calculating while his gaze appraised his grandson as if seeing him for the first time.

So the boy had finally fallen in love, as incredible as it seemed.

Despite his detached attitude towards most others, Chaos knew the feeling well, as it had never left him, even after his own beloved wife's death many years ago. If half the things Dominick said about this Julianna were true, then perhaps he'd made a good choice indeed, except...

In reality, they were literally light years apart!

Inescapable truth was never easily accepted by youth.

Running his hands through his pure white hair, his powers sometimes exuding a soft glowing aura about him when agitated, Chaos felt half tempted to pull out some strands in frustration. Clapping his hands together in silent decision, he spoke.

"Dominick," he began quietly, "I've always seen to it that you had everything you've ever wanted. Obviously too much. Even when I helped hone those dreamphasing skills of yours, knowing what you've used them for since you were a hotheaded teenager. Now before you say a word, I'll admit to your credit that your reputation with women in the dream realm is somewhat better than your brother's, although I still happen to disapprove of it, as you well know."

Dominick nodded, and the subject was dropped for once.

"However," Chaos continued sternly, his eyes deadly serious, "this latest stunt tops any of your former teenage escapades. Proposing marriage to a woman in the dream-state, not to mention one who's from another world! Have you lost your mind, boy? Do you honestly believe an engagement of this type holds any chance of withstanding the test of time?"

"Ours will," Dominick stated, his gaze never wavering. "We've had a minor disagreement or two, but we still love each other, and now wish to share our lives together."

Chaos was silent for a moment, just before a grin formed, throwing back his head with hearty laughter.

"Oh, Dominick, for all your years, you're still little more than that selfsame reckless boy of your youth." As Dominick stiffened in silent irritation, Chaos grew serious once more. "You've known the girl all of a few weeks or a bit more, and yet you profess to be in love with her. Dominick, even if love can happen that quickly, any marriage will only last so long without a solid foundation, and you may never even be able to get past the engagement itself. You haven't dealt with any world-shattering problems yet, and that's fine, but should this occur eventually, will your love sustain you through the hard times, including this long distance separation you're dealing with now?"

"Yes," Dominick replied firmly, fairly hissing the word. "Have I just been telling you all to have it cast back in my face? Grandfather, I love Julianna more than any woman I've ever known. We belong together, and it's only through a quirk of Fate that we're kept apart."

"Exactly!" said Chaos, slamming his fist on a table. "You ***aren't*** together in reality. Wake up from the dream-state, Dominick, and listen to me! You say you love each other ***now***, but what happens when the months and years roll by, and you're ***still*** separated? And also, what if one of you comes to need more than what you have in the dream-state, and seeks it with someone else in reality? While it might not be considered adultery, I guarantee it would still have the same bitter taste."

"That won't happen. I'd never cheat on Julianna, and I know she feels the same way."

"You ***know***," hissed Chaos. "You barely know the girl! Besides that, you've told me she wishes to have children of her own. Bear in mind, my dear naïve grandson, that for all the endless attempts you might make in the dream-state, you will ***never*** be able to father any children of hers there."

"She knows that, and she accepts it," Dominick replied quietly.

"Does she?" he sneered. "Yes, I suppose for now, she might be temporarily dissuaded from the notion. And for all that, she's no doubt as young and innocent—and foolish—as you are. But mark my words, Dominick, sooner or later, most women come to a point in their lives when the maternal instinct strikes them. When that time comes, this Julianna is bound to change her mind about how tolerant she can be to this aspect of your engagement. What will you do if she not only has an affair with another, but has a child by someone else as well? Will you condemn her for it later, or will you still ***love*** her as you claim?"

Dominick's jaw tightened angrily. "I told you, Grandfather, we've discussed this. And she knows I won't hold her to this engagement if such problems should become more than she can bear."

Chaos laughed again. "You should listen to yourself. You make it sound like the girl will suffer because of your relationship, and you're already planning out what to do ***when*** it ends. Why bother to announce an engagement at all? It sounds like she's been a willing enough partner to warm your nights so far without a ring on her finger."

His eyes flew open as Dominick abruptly turned, striding from the room. Chaos hadn't expected ***that*** response. But despite being many years older, he didn't need to rely on physical stamina to overtake the younger man. With a swift incantation, Chaos vanished to reappear just before him, gripping his shoulders tightly.

"Let go," hissed Dominick.

"Not until you've calmed down, boy. You look madder than a guardian devil who's had his horns removed."

Dominick shrugged his hands away, his eyes blazing. "What did you expect, Grandfather? That I'd either cast Julianna aside, or ask her to be my permanent mistress?" At Chaos's silence, a grim smile stole across his face. "Oh, yes, that's exactly what you thought, isn't it?" he snarled. "Well, you can forget that idea entirely!"

"Dominick, listen to reason."

"Your ***reasoning*** is nothing but a route to unhappiness, and I won't subscribe to it." He gave a short forced laugh. "You know what really bothers me? I actually came here to ask you to help us find a way to reach one another in reality, and I foolishly assumed you would. I suppose I should have known better, since you're so much like Riff!"

"***Cease!***" Chaos's tone had its desired impact, as the room fairly shook, silencing Dominick instantly. "Now if you can manage to keep your tone civil, what nonsensical help are you referring to?"

"It's not nonsense," Dominick said slowly, fighting to keep his anger down. "You're the most powerful multi-abilitied supernatural in Barokka. You've used those powers to make this island what it is today, a haven from those of outer Chavernos who've looked down upon us for our extraordinary abilities. Now if you can create an island paradise such as Barokka now knows, surely a means of teleportation is possible."

"As strong as my powers are, there are limits, Dominick. And while teleportation might not be the most difficult thing here on Barokka, or even the outer regions of Chavernos, teleportation to another world—one at least twice as far as the sun—would be much more complicated."

"Complicated... but possible?" Dominick interjected.

Chaos sighed heavily. "Many years back, there actually ***was*** a time when teleportation to Earth was possible," he replied, holding his hand up before Dominick could respond. "But that was ***many*** years ago, before you or your father were even born. The knowledge of that teleportation ability was lost after the Mage War."

"I've heard mention of the Mage War once but very little spoken of it."

"With good reason. It was a sad time for Chavernos that most would care to forget. Many good people and gifted sorcerers died for their beliefs."

"What happened?"

"Before I explain this properly, we'd best sit down." Chaos gestured to the chairs nearest them. Once they were seated, he steepled his hands. "To this day, I believe the reason for the Mage War was a foolish one. Regardless, to understand both sides of the argument, you need to know that long before I was born, the races and creatures of Chavernos had initially migrated from a world outside of this solar system."

Dominick nodded. "Yes, the schools do speak of this. They say our ancestors came here via crafts of purple light that were destroyed upon arrival."

"With what they felt to be good reason. All we know has been passed down from generation to generation, although it's said that some of the elder dragons, and possibly elves, may remember more than we know. What we've been given is that our origin world was once a thriving world where both magic and technology existed in harmony. They say there were many wise leaders to guide it.

"However, there were others of power that regarded the

peaceful world as weak, who were determined to take control to provide a stronger influence and shape the world as ***they*** saw fit. Several of the most powerful beings who desired this were dark sorcerers. In many ways, they saw humanity as especially weak, and sought either to control or destroy them, leaning strongly towards the latter. Wars were fought against them, but only keeping them at bay. The culmination was their use of technology that began to threaten habitability on the planet, but the dark sorcerers cared only for domination, ignorant to the needs of the world.

"Some of our prophetic Seers knew time was short, which is when our planet's ancestors, from all the races of Chavernos, fled via the crafts of purple light. The heavens were kind in helping them find what is now our world. At the time they fled, there was little habitability left, yet the dark sorcerers were determined to claim it regardless. What became of the planet and those dark sorcerers is unknown to us, although it is possible the elder dragons and elves may know more.

"When our ancestors discovered Chavernos, they were determined to prevent technology from destroying their new world similarly, destroying the crafts of purple light and knowledge of how to create them. Many years passed, and this world was cultivated into what we now know."

Listening patiently to this point, Dominick raised one hand. "All of this is certainly a fascinating history lesson, Grandfather, but how does this have anything to do with teleportation to Earth?"

"I'm getting to that," Chaos assured him. "When our dreamphaser ancestors ventured out in our new solar system, it wasn't long before they discovered Earth, including the human populace. Since this was many, many years ago, it was initially thought to be a world relatively devoid of magic without the kind of technology our world eventually progressed to. Many dreamphasers would astral travel to Earth, largely out of curiosity, never contacting the inhabitants physically but merely seeking information. There's speculation that our language was initially modified to be closer to theirs, in the event our planets would one day communicate openly, which is why we can generally communicate with them easily in the dream realm.

"However, it didn't take long for our Seers to discover that Earth was leaning towards technology, and that one day they would progress towards the route our world once had. The elders then deemed it best for us to leave Earth well enough alone, and even dreamphasing to Earth was discouraged for a long time. It's further speculated that the mists that surround Chavernos may have been enhanced by our own ancient sorcerers to make certain our world was kept hidden.

"This doesn't mean that dreamphasers wouldn't travel to Earth occasionally in the dream realm. They just had no desire to find a means to actually travel to Earth. More years went by, and many people—including dreamphasers—forgot about Earth altogether. Likely because of this, it was almost in blissful ignorance that the Mage War ultimately happened.

"Many years later, a fairly large family of sorcerers, the Magus Clan, came into being. They were a peaceful people that worshipped learning magic, residing in a once-beautiful territory of green fields that seemed to go on forever. Next to their love of family, their foremost goal always was to discover and harness magic wherever possible to improve the quality of life for themselves, their families, and especially others. Some of the magical devices we have today were created by them, although little is mentioned of this.

"It will come as no surprise that some of the Magus Clan were supernaturals, including dreamphasers. Some of the more adventurous dreamphasers astral traveled out in the solar system, once again locating Earth. The same curiosity for knowledge was there, so they traveled there frequently to learn more of it. Unlike the ancestors; however, they saw no reason not to attempt to reach Earth in reality, as brave explorers would. It took years, but one of their greatest discoveries was a means of learned magic by which teleportation to another world was possible. Finally, they could physically travel to Earth. Unlike their other discoveries, the Magus Clan kept this knowledge strictly to themselves, using it to explore the other world and learn more about it for several years.

"When dealing with those of Earth, they were discreet, never mentioning our world to them, for they did believe that the exploration for knowledge should still be tempered with caution where appropriate. However, there were cases where some of the sorcerers spent just as much time on Earth, and even established homes there when they wished to reside there longer. Overall, their motives always stemmed from the noble quest for knowledge, and since they were suitably discreet, they saw no wrong in this. Something I happen to agree with."

Dominick nodded. "Obviously, the ancestors concerned about Earth wouldn't agree."

"Exactly. That's when the trouble began. Somehow it slipped out that the Magus Clan had not only discovered a means of teleportation to Earth, but that they'd traveled there for years, which brought immediate dissent from many of the powerful mages. Even though most were descendants of the founding ancestors, they felt it their responsibility to see to it that Chavernos remained protected from the outside influence of Earth. The last thing they wanted was to see a repetition of another heart wrenching evacuation. The mages went to speak with the Magus Clan to forbid them from continuing their explorations to Earth, adding that they needed to destroy the records of teleportation magic they'd created.

"The Magus Clan refused, protesting that those they met of Earth knew nothing of Chavernos, and they never had any intention of revealing our world to them. They saw even less need to destroy knowledge, which was kept solely on our world.

The arguments persisted until finally violence broke out, and there were killings on both sides, becoming a full-fledged war. The Clan fortified their holds with magic in defense—joined by outside allies who agreed with their viewpoint—but even though they were among the most gifted sorcerers of our world, there were still more mages opposed.

"When I was a younger man, I myself was called in from Barokka to mediate between the leaders of both sides, hoping to find a peaceful resolution to stop the War. Unfortunately, the meeting was sabotaged, and the leader of the Magus Clan was killed." His expression was regretful. "They were good people, and they didn't deserve their Fate, but the mages wouldn't be stopped. Those of the Clan who evaded the sword, fled to the forest, and in desperation they jumped within the Black Pool." At Dominick's horrified look, he nodded. "Yes. The legendary Pool of No Return."

"A terrible time in our history," Dominick agreed. "And certainly no good excuse for harming innocent people. They could have found another way."

"I agree completely, but… that time is done. After the Magus Clan was wiped out, the mages set fire to the green fields of their homes, destroying everything there, including all documentation of the teleportation magic. After this desecration, the loyal allies of the Magus Clan rose up to avenge their deaths by annihilating a great many of the warring mages. Those mages that survived became pariahs, having been said to have unjustly preyed on our own people because of their delusional fear of the unknown future.

"If any good came out of the Mage War at all, the Magus Clan were exonerated as fallen heroes who fought to protect freedom among their people. Unfortunately, that's of no consolation to the fact that their entire Clan was lost—including some of the most brilliant sorcerers of Chavernos—with only their allies to carry on their memory. In addition, of course, to the loss of their library of knowledge."

"And there's no one living that knows their secret of teleportation magic?"

"None that I know of," he replied quietly. "So you see, I can't say it's still possible. Even if it were, the risks are far greater that you'd never even reach her world, and instead die instantly from the sudden exposure to airless space. Despite your special abilities, you're still human enough to die out there, and I won't be a party to such madness regarding one of my only two grandsons."

Dominick's expression darkened. "Then you won't help us."

"It's not that I won't by choice. The truth is, I can't." Chaos gave a forced laugh. "Dominick, no matter how powerful you think I am, my powers ***are*** limited to the regions of Barokka and Chavernos. I don't have the ability to send you to Earth, nor to bring this Julianna here if you wished it. If I knew a way, which guaranteed your safety, maybe I'd see what I could do. But I'm afraid I don't."

There was a long silence before Dominick bit his lip with a nod. "Then I suppose there's nothing more to be said, is there?" Another silence. "I'd best get home now. Julianna will be expecting me in a few hours, and I have to get in touch with some friends of mine so she can meet them tonight when I announce our engagement."

Chaos reached out to clutch his arm sharply. "I don't believe I'm hearing this. You're still going to persist in this fool's notion to remain engaged to that girl in reality, despite everything I've told you?"

"Of course I will," he retorted. "Just because you may not have the necessary magic to bring us together, doesn't mean I'm going to stop searching for another means. And let me assure you, I won't rest until I ***do*** find one. If the Magus Clan could find a way, then so can I." Seeing the chagrined look on his grandfather's face, he continued solemnly, "As for tonight, I assume you won't wish to be present, since you disapprove so strongly."

Once more, an air of frustration creased Chaos's features. "Dammit, boy, I'd move Chavernos itself if I could guarantee your happiness! Do you think I'm such a stern leader to Barokka that I don't care about my grandchildren? Despite your rebellious attitude, and Riff's as well, I love the both of you dearly as if you were my own sons."

He took a deep breath. "And regardless of what I think, if you still mean to announce your engagement to this Julianna Sherborne in the dream-state—foolish as it stands—then of course I wish to be there when you do."

A smile tugged across Dominick's expression as the pair hugged one another. "I'm glad, Grandfather. I wouldn't have been completely happy without your blessing."

"Yes, you'll have that," sighed Chaos, patting his back once. Almost immediately, his expression changed. Stepping away, he rubbed his chin thoughtfully. Dominick stared at him curiously, just before his grandfather glanced up to the ceiling with a growing smile. "And maybe... if you and your future bride can be patient, I might be able to give you more than that."

"What do you mean?"

"Lendric," replied Chaos. At his grandson's look of confusion, he snapped his fingers in a prompting manner. "Think, boy, you remember who Lendric is. The dragon sorcerer in outer Chavernos that visits on occasion?"

Lendric? Dominick mused for a moment, just before recognition lit his features. Yes, now he remembered. Although he usually saw Lendric in his elven form, the powerful sorcerer was a gold dragon, who bore a pair of emerald green eyes in either dragon or elven form.

While the dragon could alter his immense size to human/elven height when necessary—especially to fit in an average room—Dominick had seen a few occasions of Lendric at his full formidable dragon height which was even taller.

Thankfully, he was a friend!

Dominick had first seen the dragon in full-scale form when he'd been a child of seven, at the time never having seen a dragon close-up. Lendric had a soft spot for children, and although his true form tended to frighten most youngsters initially, Dominick hadn't been frightened... merely awed. He'd even boldly asked Lendric if he could go flying with him. The dragon laughed, pleased at his early signs of fearlessness, and afterwards, he demonstrated that he could alter his form to that of an elf, surprising the boy anew.

It had been several years since Dominick had last seen Lendric in person—close to a decade in fact—but dragons with their infallible memories always maintained respect towards their friendships with humans, as Chaolyn, Roderlin, and Alysadaria had. Since like all dragons, Lendric was relatively ageless in either dragon or elven form, he might look to be Dominick's age or a few years older; however, in reality he was many actual years older and still far from his prime.

Dragons held the record for life spans.

"I remember him," Dominick said finally, "but what does he have to do with my situation with Julianna?"

Silently mumbling about the need to explain ***everything*** in detail to youngsters, Chaos replied slowly and simply, "Lendric has demonstrated the power to travel between worlds."

Moments later, Dominick's energetic grin could have electrified the whole room with its enthusiasm. "By Chavernos, of course! Didn't he once mention many years ago that he'd made a trip to another solar system in the past?"

Chaos nodded once with a knowing smile. "That's what I seem to recall."

"Then Earth can't be impossible to reach after all. Grandfather, this is just the news I've prayed for! Wait until

Julianna hears."

"Hold on, boy, before you rush off to celebrate this news with your betrothed, I'd advise you not to get your hopes too high. For while Lendric might be able to travel between worlds himself, there's no guarantee that he can teleport someone with him. Only he has the answer to that, and you'd better discuss the matter with him first."

Dominick considered this, and then nodded. "Good point," he whispered, eyeing his grandfather seriously. "All right, I'll just share with her what you've told me regarding the Mage War, since at least it proves there has been teleportation between our worlds before."

"True enough," said Chaos.

"I'll just tell her I'm researching it further, but as soon as I talk with Lendric..."

"By all means, if all signs are positive, tell her then. But for now, maintain a little caution, Dominick, even in regard to your own optimism. I don't want to be faced with a sudden terminal depression from you should Lendric negate the possibility."

"I'll keep that in mind as well," he agreed. "Now, how do I get in touch with Lendric?"

"That... is why I asked if you wouldn't mind being patient," sighed Chaos. "You see, when I last contacted him six months ago, he said he had pressing business elsewhere on Chavernos, and since he practically lives for traveling, he might not have returned yet."

"But if it's been that long, he should be back."

Chaos shrugged once. "Maybe, but I know him too well to count on it." Upon seeing the sudden disappointment on his grandson's face, Chaos gripped his shoulder tightly. "Now don't lose heart, boy. If he isn't there, he'll return sooner or later. I'll send word for your mother, so she can take you there. It's too bad her teleportation magic only has limited range, or maybe she could have solved this problem for you."

"I considered that, which is why I didn't ask," replied Dominick. "But if she can get us to Lendric's, that will be help enough."

"Agreed. Just tell him all you've told me."

"I will," sighed Dominick. "I just hope he can help us."

"Since he is one of Chavernos's greatest sorcerers, he presents as good a chance as anyone else," Chaos suggested chipperly. "In the meantime, you may as well take advantage of your time together, since it could still be awhile before you can be brought to the same world." For a moment, his smile lingered, before abruptly dimming with new realization. "Which brings up an interesting point. Just which world ***will*** you both live on if you're brought together successfully?"

Dominick paused, unsure of the answer himself. "I'd have to discuss the matter with Julianna," he said. "If it was up to me, I'd like to bring her to Chavernos to live on the island, since I could certainly give her a beautiful home here. She's often mentioned her love of the ocean, so I know she'd be happy with a house overlooking it."

"Excellent," Chaos replied quickly. "I'll see to it that you have the best. Perhaps a small castle reminiscent of the one you share in the dream-state."

"But..." Dominick interrupted, "Julianna may not want to be so uprooted from her homeworld. And if that's the case, I'm just as willing to remain with her on Earth, to try to adjust to life there instead."

"***What?***" exclaimed Chaos, sudden anger nearly choking out his words. "And leave Chavernos forever?" This was one aspect he hadn't considered—before mentioning Lendric—and it pained him to realize that if his grandson left, it was partially his fault, though done with the best of intentions. "Dominick, you're one of my succeeding heirs. I can't simply condone your leaving forever."

"Riff's still here. He'll do well enough without me, if need be."

Chaos counted to ten to keep calm, and then decided a hundred might be necessary instead.

Inwardly, he knew Dominick's words were true. Riff was a highly strong-willed and confident man who would certainly handle Barokka with all the authority Chaos had. In many ways, Chaos always felt that Riff was more like him than his father, and it both pleased him... and annoyed him sometimes. But Dominick...

Dominick was different. He had the strong will and the confidence, but even more, he had a strong sense of integrity and a compassionate nature, as well as a most loving heart. No doubt a trait he'd picked up from his late grandmother whom Chaos missed so much.

His dear Ylana... he reflected, who had often been regarded as a soft-spoken, clever and understanding mediator in troubled times. If for no other reason, it was because Dominick seemed so much like Ylana sometimes that Chaos had taken such a liking to the boy. Although he was surely fond of Riff too, that fondness was different. Only his innermost thoughts knew this, for over the years, he'd made sure to give both boys an equal share of his attention, so neither felt slighted.

It was Dominick he tended to worry about the most, when all was said and done. Loving hearts could so easily be crushed by the cruelly thoughtless individuals who thought they controlled the others who revolved about them, and his grandson's own heart was no exception.

Upon hearing of Riff's occasional pranks in hurting his younger brother via his shenanigans in the dream-state, especially in regard to seducing the women Dominick knew, Chaos couldn't help but feel some distaste for his elder grandson. Although Chaos knew his own reputation hadn't been spotless over the years, Dominick shouldn't be made to suffer for Riff's antics.

It was due to Julianna's adamant refusals to Riff's persistent attitude that Chaos found himself both glad that Riff had been taken down a peg, and even more pleased that the girl had her own strong share of morals. If she was to be as loyal to Dominick as she'd been recently, then Chaos had no qualms about welcoming the girl into the family as his new granddaughter. And reading between the lines, if Dominick and Julianna got along as well in reality as they did in the dream-state, he might just see several great-grandchildren over the next several years.

That is, unless those great-grandchildren were to be kept from him, along with their parents, due to the painfully real light-years of separation.

"Even with your brother to take over one day, since your father has adamantly refused," he began, "I think it's in Barokka's best interests if you take your place beside Riff."

That much was certainly true, Chaos thought inwardly. Especially since Riff would need Dominick's more levelheaded nature, if Barokka was to continue to run smoothly, he mused to himself. Granted, Dominick sometimes had one hell of a temper, but his heart usually ruled well above it, and Chaos knew he'd treat Barokka and its inhabitants with fairness and devotion.

"As I've said, I'm hoping she'll agree to live here, but that's premature to worry about until I can get in touch with Lendric," replied Dominick. "Then, we'll see what happens." At his grandfather's silence, a brief worry sobered his expression. "In any case, you wouldn't try anything underhanded to keep me here, would you?"

"I'd do anything I could to keep ***both*** of my grandsons here," he said firmly. Upon catching sight of the suspicion in Dominick's eyes, he quickly amended, "But... if your happiness is only to be found with this girl, and if you insist on living out your lives on her world, I suppose I have little chance of standing in your way, do I?"

Dominick smiled gratefully, earning a sudden gruffness from the elder man. *Blazes!* Chaos thought inwardly. There were times when children—or grandchildren—could be so stubborn in facing facts! A truth which he'd need to remedy sooner than later, before he ended up losing one grandson to another world forever.

A fact that he wasn't going to give into lightly, although he knew better than to tell Dominick this.

"Now then," he said solemnly, "before I'll be willing to even ***consider*** sending my grandson off—Chavernos knows where—in the solar system, I'd appreciate meeting my future granddaughter tonight, when you announce your engagement." A sly smile stole across his face. "That is, if you can spare some time away from your dream castle."

"Of course we can," Dominick laughed. "Tonight seems as good a time as any to introduce you both, and I'm sure you'll like her."

"Yes," Chaos agreed softly. "If you truly love one another, and she's responsible for the happiness in your eyes, then I'm certain I will too."

Even though your relationship will have to end, if Barokka's to guarantee holding onto one of its two future leaders, his silent thoughts added grimly.

Inescapable truth came no easier to elders sometimes.

*****

As Zantarl tabulated the check for the young woman who stood at the counter, she eyed him with a catlike smile. She knew without looking behind her that the outfit she'd chosen, combined with her body's perfect curves, had the attention of every male—human or otherwise—in Lost Limbo.

Brushing back a long strand of her golden blonde hair, she placed her braceleted hand on her hip, leaning her other arm on the counter. Her violet-blue eyes, sometimes mistaken for those of certain dragons—although she definitely wasn't one herself—were as apt at charming men as her hauntingly melodic voice. A voice which granted her the powerful ability of enchantment, and whose siren-like call had dubbed her the name of Sireni.

"The next time you come to Lost Limbo," growled Zantarl, "try wearing a skirt with actual material, lest you leave the male customers here nearly catatonic again!"

"Zantarl," she purred, "would I do that purposefully?"

The older man smiled at her brightly, just before it dimmed to an icy glare. "You always do."

Sireni laughed off his words, waltzing out of Lost Limbo, humming as she went. A most clever tune, thought Zantarl, as three good-looking men went trailing after her. It was a good thing he was strong-willed and immune to her ability. Elsewise, if he'd been a bit younger... the thought nearly made him pour a drink of his own.

Strange, since Zantarl couldn't stand alcohol himself.

Upon reaching her home, Sireni turned an innocent expression on the sole remaining man standing beside her, having already sent the others away by releasing her charm on them. "Don't you think you should be off with your friends?" she inquired.

The man merely grinned, placing his hands possessively about her waist. "They can find their own way home," he murmured, bending his face closer to hers.

She blushed becomingly, although by no means innocent anymore—having mastered the fine art of bewitching men with her ability—touching a finger gently upon his neck to feel his pulse quicken. She could sense through her powers that this one would be a more than willing temporary companion for the day, and since she was equally willing, at least it would ease the boredom until tomorrow.

"Yes," she laughed merrily, brushing her lips against his.

"I suppose they can."

Intoxicated by her magic and her undeniable physical appeal, his hold strengthened on her until she was pressed tightly against him, not caring who might be walking by to notice. Nor did Sireni have any discretion either, which was why neither noticed a certain dark-haired man approach them, clapping slowly.

"A stunning performance, Sireni," remarked Dual, prompting her to whip her gaze towards him with surprise. The surprise soon faded into her familiar catlike smile though, ignoring the bewildered man who still held her. Dual grinned knowingly, gesturing his arms wide. "Did you miss me, my jewel?" he asked.

"Always," she replied, pushing free of the other man to rush into his arms. Not that the chagrined man was willing to leave so easily.

"Hey!" he snarled, striding over to break her apart from Dual again. Gripping her shoulders so she faced him, his eyes were dark. "Who ***is*** this guy you apparently know so well?" he demanded.

A sharp lancing pain in his wrist, caused by pressure from Dual, freed his hold on her. "Someone who's known her for a lot longer than you, and ***won't*** allow your kind to interfere. Now be on your way, or you'll find your worst nightmares become so unsettling, you'll have white hair when you awake." His hold on the man's wrist tightened much more painfully. "Unless you wish a sample now of what I can do to distractions such as you."

Boring his murderous gaze into the other man's eyes threateningly, Dual's words hit home, effectively breaking the charm and sending him off without a backwards glance at Sireni. Looking after him with a shrug, she turned back to Dual, wrapping her arms about his neck.

"That one wasn't as strong as some of the rest," she

sighed, smiling up at him seductively. "But then, you always were a tough man to find an equal to." She kissed him quickly, but as she tried to pull away, he refused to release her, his kisses bruising as he backed her against her door.

As his hands roamed lower, she moaned against him, moments before he tore his mouth away, glaring at her. Breathing heavily, Sireni eyed him with slight confusion. "When are you going to get it through your head that you're ***mine***," he hissed, gripping her shoulders. "Must I kill these unfortunate suitors of yours whom you insist on luring into your spider's web, before you stop your endless games?"

Her eyes narrowed. "If you wouldn't leave so often, no doubt to find your ***own*** endless rank of paramours, maybe I wouldn't need these mindless fools!" she replied in kind. "Why I bother with you at all, I have no idea, since all you ever do is..."

Dual cut off her words with another forceful kiss, breaking down her attempted resistance to his advances. Pulling her leg around his, his hand skimmed upward, a deviant knowing look in his eyes at her responding shiver.

"Because, my jewel, you know I'm the only one who can give you what you want, both in reality and the dream-state," he whispered against her ear, lifting her into his arms before she could protest. "Maybe you need a reminder of this," he added, kissing her again as he brought her inside the house. For her part, Sireni needed no further convincing, kicking the door shut lightly with her foot.

*****

An hour later, Sireni stretched contentedly beneath her bed covers, eyeing Dual as he stood gazing out her window, leaning one arm against the wall.

They were a well-matched pair, she knew, neither one seeking marriage or commitment, but holding a bond between them that no outside paramours could sever. Both shared the same dreamphasing ability, often meeting in the dream-state, even when they were separated by distance across Chavernos. Not to mention, both reveled in creating havoc wherever they went.

Running one finger lightly atop the blanket as she shifted to one side, Sireni leaned on her elbow and smiled knowingly. Despite Dual's constant arguments over what she did in his absence, it was never enough for him to deny the passion they could only find with each other. She might not be using her magic on him, but he was as caught as the others were—perhaps even more—nonetheless.

Just the way she liked things.

"Still so angry, you don't want to come back to bed?" she asked.

He turned to her with a knowing smile. "You know anger's never a deterrent between us where ***that's*** concerned," he replied softly. "No, I was merely thinking how to handle another current problem, regarding a certain old adversary of mine."

Sireni gave a bored sigh, leaning back against the pillows again. "I won't ask which one ***that*** is. Dual, you really should end this vendetta of yours against Dominick. You always end up at an impasse, and if the pendulum swings any one way, it's on his side."

"Ah," he laughed, waving one finger at her. "But not this time. Not when I have his friend Alarius held hostage." Sireni bolted upright, knowing instantly where this was coming from.

"Since you mention Alarius, did you get the treasures?" she asked breathlessly.

"As monetary as ever," he replied with a low laugh, walking over to stroke her cheek. As she shrugged his hand aside, impatient for him to continue, he quickly obliged. "Unfortunately, Alarius attempted to find the treasures first, and disappeared with the map."

Sireni's eyes darkened as she hit him once on the chest. "You idiot!" she yelled. "How could you let that inferior half-elf get the upper hand over us?"

Grabbing her wrist, Dual tightened his grip to silence her. "You didn't let me finish, my clever viper," he hissed, immediately regaining his earlier nonchalance. "Quell and I prevented his complete escape, obtaining both the map ***and*** the treasures from him. Half of which we've brought back with us already." He gave a short laugh. "Ironically enough, we're storing them in the same place that we're keeping poor Alarius, fool that he was to interfere."

She sighed at the last. "Why bother with him?" she asked with annoyance. "If you have the treasures, let him return to his family and be done with it. After all, if Chaos finds out he's missing, you'll be at the top of his list of suspects."

"I know," he replied offishly. "I adore living on the edge, despite that pitiful excuse for a ruler."

"A ruler who could use his powers to destroy you, if he chose," she reminded him. "You certainly didn't choose very wisely to become an enemy of his grandson."

"Ah," he said, touching her chin lightly. "But then one cannot choose whom one hates... or loves, now can one?"

Sireni cast her head back with a forced laugh. "Love!" she replied derisively. "I know better than to believe ***that*** emotion exists between us, so don't hint otherwise. But do tell me what Dominick's done this time to incur your wrath."

"He was the one who gave the map to that simpleton," hissed Dual, "and the one who stole it from the castle ruins to begin with." Sireni groaned in frustration. "Before you consider the matter so trivial, remember that the self-same map was responsible for bringing in ***your*** portion of the treasures."

That ***did*** put things in a different light, she thought.

"So what do you intend to do with Dominick this time? Send another death battalion after him in his dreams?"

"Interesting notion, but no. Not this time." Dual's smile became a dark grin. "He's gotten off too easy in the past. This time, I intend to seek out a vulnerable weakness in him, and then strike hard where it hurts him most. After that, I imagine he'll think twice before interfering with my plans anymore." Reclining leisurely against the headboard, he reached out one hand to cup Sireni's cheek. "Tell me, my fair-haired vixen, do you know of anything I might be able to use against this eternal enemy of mine?"

"Funny you should mention that," she said, smoothing her hair back. "When I was over at Lost Limbo today, I learned that there are rumors among the dreamphasers that Dominick's sending out invitations to his friends to appear for a gathering tonight for some reason."

Dual warded this off with one hand. "I'm sure it's nothing important," he replied. "That bunch always seem to pack together like drow-beasts."

"Hmmm, maybe, but let me tell you the rest. Since further rumors have declared Dominick absent in meetings with his friends over the past few weeks, it's been assumed that there's something going on, leaving everyone curious to find out what. Naturally, those who've overheard the communicated invitations have told others, so nearly ***all*** the other dreamphasers ***also*** plan to appear at the scheduled location in the dream-state."

His easy smile faded into a dark expression. "That ***does*** sound a bit peculiar," he decided in a low voice. "And perhaps worth looking into."

"Does that mean you're intending to be there without his knowing?" she inquired.

"Perhaps. At least until I find out what's going on." Twining a strand of her blonde hair about his fingers, he pulled her closer with a suggestive grin. "But that won't be until later," he whispered, kissing her quickly. "Until then, let me demonstrate my appreciation for your helpful information."

Sireni merely smiled in pleased responsiveness.

*****

Julianna hadn't been able to concentrate on anything today, so it was only by some miracle that her work got accomplished, partially due to some helpful assistance by her concerned friend. When Marybeth asked if she was well, she'd said she was. Yet inwardly, she couldn't deny the mixed emotions plaguing her.

She was engaged to marry the man she loved, who treated her with more love, respect, understanding, and devoted affection than she'd known with anyone else.

An engagement to be announced solely in a dream tonight.

And alas, the possible prospect of only being allowed a few hours a night with Dominick for the rest of her life couldn't help but sadden her. Rather like Cupid and Psyche, except those two both existed on the same world, and at least they could ultimately be married.

Although she wouldn't burden Dominick with her other concern, she was also truly saddened by the knowledge that they couldn't have children unless they reached each other. Watching Sammy playing now, she sighed with regret. She would have loved to have a child with Dominick someday.

But who knew? Maybe one day it would be possible.

She'd already decided that she'd rather be happy with Dominick for the allotted time they had, than be subjected to a life of unhappiness without him. For she knew that she could never love another similarly, nor could she see sacrificing so much as she was willing to for Dominick.

Right now, what bothered her most was that she couldn't tell anyone of her engagement, lest they think she'd lost her mind entirely. Hell, it wouldn't be hard for her to believe so either, if not for Dominick's recurring appearances every night... and if of course, she didn't love him so much.

Now home, sitting on the sofa, she carefully touched up the sketch she'd been drawing of him, which she'd been working on for an hour. She hoped her minor art talent combined with her vivid memories could do her future husband justice. It would seem so, because once she held back the picture to appraise it, she felt a wave of immediate longing. This might well be the only way she'd ever see him in reality, and it pained her terribly.

She wasn't even aware of the tears in her eyes, until she felt Sammy's little hand patting hers gently. "Aunt Julie, why are you crying?" he asked, his eyes filled with curiosity. She had to smile in spite of herself. Young as he was, there was little her precious five-year-old nephew missed.

"I'm all right, sweetheart," she told him, brushing the tears away. "Just a bit of dust, that's all."

"You look sad," the boy persisted.

Maintaining her smile, she brushed a loose strand back from the boy's forehead and nodded. "Yes, I am a bit sad, Sammy," she replied softly. That was all her adoring nephew needed to hear. He instantly jumped on the sofa, hugging his arms around her and gazing up expectantly for a reason, just before he noticed her drawing of Dominick.

"Who's that, Aunt Julie?" he asked.

Julianna was about to disclaim its being anyone in particular, but just the notion renewed tears in her eyes. Without much thought, she whispered, "Someone I care about very much."

"But who ***is*** he?" She looked down at her nephew with fond sadness, knowing she couldn't tell him the truth either.

But then again, she also knew that children often had an odd capacity for understanding and believing in what adults didn't. Surely it wouldn't be wrong to mention Dominick lightly, as he himself had inquired about Sammy.

"He's a dear friend of mine," she began. "His name is

Dominick, and he lives far away from here."

"In another state?"

If only it was that simple.

"Well... not exactly." With a smile of conspiracy, she lowered her voice. "If I tell you where he's really from, you'd have to promise to keep it to ourselves."

"You mean, like a secret?"

"Exactly. Promise you won't tell anyone else?" He nodded vigorously, a smile lighting his features too, as it seemed like a fun game, and he sensed one of Julianna's creative stories about to begin. "Dominick comes from..." She cast a furtive glance in both directions to seem more dramatic, and lowered her voice. "Another world, Sammy!" At his intake of breath, she had to stifle a laugh as she nodded.

"You mean like Mars?"

"Well, not Mars. He comes from a hidden planet on the other side of the sun known as Chavernos."

"Ka-ven-us," he replied, testing the syllables.

"More like Kah-vern-ohs," she corrected gently. The next time he said it, he'd recited it properly, earning a grin of admiration from his aunt at his quick learning ability.

"If he's so far away, how'd you meet him?"

"Ah..." Julianna said dramatically. "Through a special magic power he has."

The boy's eyes brightened like stars as she told him how Dominick had appeared to her in her dreams every night—carefully omitting, of course, the romantic aspects of their nightly meetings, since those things certainly weren't meant for a child's ears!

Sammy didn't seem to mind, fascinated by Dominick's rescuing his aunt from some bad guys, involving their daring escape from the space ship. Julianna altered its ending slightly, since it hadn't been very pleasant at the time.

From her words, Sammy mentioned wishing that he

could have been there to see a real spaceship, and that he would have helped Dominick protect her. She nearly laughed, but instead told him quite solemnly that she knew the bad guys wouldn't have stood a chance against the two bravest men in her life, earning a smile of pride from her nephew.

Unknown to both, Vicki was standing just outside the doorway, listening in to this rather strange tale of Julianna's. If nothing else, she'd admit her sister certainly had one hell of an imagination! Having arrived in time to overhear most of the tale, she'd carefully avoided the pair's notice, but had to force down laughter several times. It was after secretly eavesdropping for nearly ten minutes that Crystal came up behind her, startling her slightly.

"What are you doing?" she asked, earning a quick shushing from Vicki. "Why are we whispering?" she continued in a softer voice.

"Julianna's regaling Sammy with another story," replied Vicki, giving a short laugh. "This one's about her meeting a man in her dreams every night, who's supposedly from another world. Really, Crystal, I don't know where she comes up with her far-fetched stories. The way she's talking now, I'd think she's beginning to believe her own words."

Crystal gave an indulgent smile of amusement at that. Knowing she had other things to attend to, she was about to walk away. But... since Julianna's story seemed to have piqued even Vicki's curiosity, she couldn't resist listening in for a few moments herself. Without another word, both pressed closer, although still undetected by the pair in the room.

By the time Julianna had finished, Sammy asked when he could see Dominick in person, wanting to meet this man who sounded like a hero from the adventure movies he'd seen.

"I'm afraid that's why I'm unhappy, Sammy," she confided. "You see, last night Dominick asked me to marry him, and I said yes, but..."

"Really?" the boy interrupted eagerly. Outside the door, Crystal and Vicki exchanged worried glances. Julianna was carrying this fictitious story a bit far, wasn't she? "Will he come live with us too, and be my uncle like Aunt Vicki's friend Luke?"

"I suppose he will be your uncle someday," she agreed. "But I'm afraid Dominick and I can't be married—at least not yet—until he can find a way to travel from his world to ours."

"Not ***yet***?" gasped Vicki. "What's she talking...?"

Quickly clapping a hand across her mouth to silence her, Crystal pulled her aside and then called out loudly, "Julie, are you home?"

Flustered, Julianna held a finger up to shush Sammy, reiterating the need for secrecy. The boy promised to keep quiet about all she'd told him, and then innocently went back to his earlier game.

"Sammy and I are in here," she replied finally.

Moments later, Crystal and Vicki strode in, the former giving her younger sister a bright smile.

"Hello, you two," she said cheerfully. "Been keeping busy I see." Casting a shrewd eye to the sketch in Julianna's hands, Crystal gave it an approving nod, even as she silently tried to identify the man in the drawing. No, he didn't look familiar, and he certainly wasn't Roger. Was it someone she'd just met, perhaps at work, that she simply didn't want to mention yet?

Before she could comment, Vicki jumped in. "Cute guy," she said, trying to hide her amusement with minimal success. "Who is he?"

"You mean from this?" murmured Julianna, touching the sketch lightly. "Oh, it's just a drawing."

"Hmmm. Anyone you've ***met*** recently?" she drawled.

Julianna shook her head, unsure where this was heading. "I told you..."

"It's a picture of Uncle Dominick," Sammy supplied with a grin. At Julianna's sudden look of dismay, he clasped his hands over his mouth, his eyes apologetically wide.

"***Uncle*** Dominick?" Vicki asked with deliberate slowness, a laugh breaking through. "What happened, Julie? Anything we should ***know*** about? Did you get married behind our backs without telling us?"

Instantly, Julianna felt her face color—Vicki's questions adding to her curious suspicions as to what she and Crystal might have overheard—but she was unable to say anything on the matter as Jerry appeared in the hallway.

"What is this?" he chuckled. "A family meeting?"

"You might say that," laughed Vicki. "Or better make that a soon-to-be-family meeting." A piercing shush from Crystal cut her off, just before she turned to smile at her husband.

"I think it's about time for you to put a certain young man to bed," she decided, gesturing towards Sammy. Sighing once, but compliant under the circumstances, the boy gave his mother a quick hug, and then Vicki. When he reached Julianna, he still seemed to feel a bit guilty, shifting his feet and at a loss for words.

Seeing this, Julianna brightened reassuringly and patted his shoulder. The last thing she'd do was to let her caring nephew blame himself for something that she'd indirectly brought on herself.

"Don't worry about it, Sammy," she whispered. "We're all human, and everyone has a slip of the tongue now and then. Now wipe that frown off your face and come here." As she opened her arms to him, Sammy gave her a tight hug and she reciprocated, smiling against him warmly.

"I hope Uncle Dominick comes here soon," he said quietly, so as not to be heard by the rest.

"So do I, Sammy," she replied, patting his back and allowing Jerry to scoop him up for a piggy-back ride out of the room. As the pair retreated upstairs, Julianna noticed the equally puzzled stares of her sisters and grimaced. "Shall the inquisition begin?"

"Inquisition?" asked Crystal. "My, what you must think of us. We're just curious what Sammy meant when he called the man in your drawing 'Uncle'. After all, he doesn't usually drop such titles accidentally."

"Yes, well... there's always a first time."

At the evidently flustered way she'd spoken, Crystal sat down beside her sister and rested a gentle hand on her shoulder. "Julie, I'm not going to lie to you. We overheard your story, and we're worried about you."

"Worried that you're losing your mind is more like it," laughed Vicki. "When you throw yourself into that wild imagination of yours, you don't miss a trick. A future husband from another planet? Julie, if you're that desperate for a man, you really should try to find someone real, rather than a fictitious dream guy."

During her short speech, she completely missed the way Julianna's face drained of color while her hands clenched tightly, but Crystal didn't, her eyes narrowing. "All right, Vicki!" she snapped, quieting her again. "You've made your point. Now why don't you head back to the kitchen and find something to stuff in that big mouth of yours?"

"As you wish, your highness," sneered Vicki, casting a last glance to Julianna before exiting amidst more laughter.

Sighing once, Crystal turned back to her. "She didn't mean anything by that," she said quietly. "But to be honest, Julie, that story wasn't your typical bedtime tale."

It isn't a tale at all! Julianna nearly shouted, feeling even more miserable at the incredible joke that Fate had played upon her. She'd finally found the man of her dreams—literally—and he existed a million miles away. Much more, in fact, since it was nearly a hundred million miles to the sun alone, and his world was twice as far. So even if he was truly in this solar system, she still had no proof to offer anyone.

"I assure you I'm fine," she replied finally. "I was daydreaming, and it just came out as a story."

"Is that really all there is to it?" asked Crystal.

Forcing a smile, Julianna gave her exactly the response she wanted. "Of course that's all," she replied, through an equally forced laugh. "The next thing you'll be asking is whether or not dragons are real." Maybe so in actuality, if Dominick's words about them were true. "Dominick's just a man from my dreams, that's all," she continued, feeling tears well up in her eyes. Before Crystal could notice them, Julianna stood quickly to head for the staircase. "Look, if you'll excuse me, all this amusement has tired me out for one evening."

As she turned to leave, she was halted by Crystal's hand clasping her arm. "Despite what you say, I know something more is bothering you about all this. And while I can't force you to tell me what, just remember I'm ready to listen if you change your mind."

For a moment, Julianna just stared at her eldest sister. She always ***was*** the open-minded one in the family. Maybe if... "Crystal, I..." *No*, she decided. Not even Crystal could be ***that*** open-minded.

Sensing her closing herself off, Crystal pressed coaxingly, "What is it, Julie? You can tell me."

Julianna shook her head abruptly. "It's nothing," she insisted. "I just wanted to say good night, that's all." Quickly ascending the stairs, she was unaware of her sister staring after her skeptically.

As unusual as her story was, one underlying truth remained in Crystal's mind. There was something her younger sister wasn't telling her, and sooner or later, she intended to find out what it was.

Chapter Twelve

Julianna wasn't surprised to find herself outside the dream castle, although she felt a bit awkward since everyone was no doubt already inside. A new shot of nerves grabbed hold of her, as she didn't really know anyone in this realm except Dominick, and she hoped that the others wouldn't disapprove of her because she wasn't a dreamphaser too.

"Not everyone on Chavernos is, and they'll love you," said Dominick, his arms encircling her from behind. At her smile, he kissed her cheek, still holding her and smiled back. "They're not here anyway. I just decided it would be easier for us to meet here first. However, since the rest are at the second location, we probably should go now."

"Fine by me," she agreed. She wasn't surprised by the short ensuing silence confirming his reluctance to relinquish their time alone. Smiling as he leaned forward to kiss her neck, she spoke again amidst a soft laugh. "I don't know where we're going, hon. I'm afraid you'll have to do the teleporting there."

"I know," he whispered. "By Chavernos, love, I want you so much," he breathed against her cheek. "There's only one place I feel like teleporting us to, which certainly isn't among a bunch of people, and a hell of a lot closer than they are."

She glanced thoughtfully at the dream castle. "We could meet your friends a few minutes later," she suggested quietly.

Without a word, he swept her into his arms, prompting her to wrap her own about his neck. He kissed her then, deeply, his desire for her sending its signals to her own yearning body and back. His grip tightened as he pulled her closer, he murmured her name... and then suddenly expelled a sharp breath.

"Chaos, there are times when I wish I'd been a loner," he groaned, meeting her gaze with an impish grin. "As long as I had you with me for my sole company."

"You seem to do well enough there," she laughed, her mind flashing through their numerous romantic meetings. "If we were any more alone than we've been lately, we'd never have the strength to leave our castle room."

"Mmmm, which one?" he teased.

"If you don't know that, then you must be an imposter to my future husband," she said knowingly. "In which case, I'd better warn you, he totes a mean dream gun."

"Does he now?" he chuckled, sending kisses down her neck and lower. At her soft gasp, he looked up to grin at her again. "No, my memory's better than that, and I know exactly which room you were thinking of—which I'll gladly take you to later. No imposter here, sweetheart."

"Ah well, I don't mind being wrong on occasion," she decided, tousling his hair affectionately. "Still, maybe another kiss would convince me beyond any doubt."

"No doubt a man who always accepts a challenge," he agreed, his mouth capturing hers again.

When he finally broke apart a minute later, she smiled into his deep blue eyes—now laced with desire—and caressed his neck with her gentle hand. Those selfsame eyes seemed to be wrestling with more than passion, confirmed when he gave another low groan.

"I think we'd better postpone anymore such kisses for a while, love," he told her gently. "Otherwise the only destination we'll get to will be our dream castle bedroom, and my friends will wonder what's become of us."

"Can't we just let them wonder?"

"A tempting thought," he laughed, gently running his hands along her back while his arms remained about her. "But seriously, there's someone in particular who I'd like to introduce you to, so I'm afraid we'll have to take a raincheck on this for now. All right by you, love?"

"From you, a raincheck is always acceptable," she replied cheerfully, hugging him tighter as she felt the winds of teleportation sweep them away.

*****

To greet their arrival, an array of colored lights and the sounds of dancing music filled Julianna's senses as she glanced about an enormous room. This room was more modern than the former ballroom location. Half of it catered to dancers, while other people were seated at tables or leaning against them, chattering away. Several seemed to be around her age, while many others were a few years older like Dominick. But even so, the thought of getting lost among so many unfamiliar people gave Julianna pause, and she instinctively clutched Dominick's arm tighter.

Smiling down at her, he patted her hand reassuringly, even as he called out to a small group of people seated at a nearby table. They all looked up, beckoning the pair to join them. Julianna smiled back shyly and felt herself led over by Dominick's comforting arm around her waist. There were six people seated, three men and three women, sitting alternately. One of whom she recognized.

"Here's the happy couple," laughed Riff, standing to slap his brother's shoulder good-naturedly. Quieter, he added, "What took you so long anyway? We were starting to think you might have gotten sidetracked or something."

Julianna blushed, knowing he wasn't far off.

"Never mind that," snapped Dominick. "What are ***you*** doing here after what you pulled last night?"

"Now, Dom," he replied, "I know I made a slight error in judgment…"

"***Slight?***"

"Okay, maybe a bit more than that. But how could I not

be here when you invited the others to a gathering for something you said was important?" He gestured towards Buddy and Jarissa. "Besides, those two aren't dreamphasers, and needed an escort to be here."

Dominick took a deep, calming breath. "You're not off the hook. We'll discuss this later."

"Great!" Riff replied jovially, turning an appreciative glance at his companion. "And, Julianna, you're looking most enchanting tonight," he said, giving a wolf-whistle.

Dominick gripped his shoulder meaningfully. "That's enough out of you, brother," he said, forcing a smile which had an edge to it. "Or there will be more than ***words*** when we get home."

"Fair enough," sighed Riff, sitting beside Kiri who was shaking her head. "What?" he remarked quietly. "I was just being a gentleman." The others laughed audibly. "Hey, hey… that's enough out of you. We're not ***all*** guardian angels at this table!"

Turning to the three women beside their respective companions, Dominick smiled cordially to each. "Ladies, might I say you all look ravishing tonight, as you always do." The trio beamed, leaving Julianna curious, even as another woman walked up to them.

"Always a charmer, Dominick," said the woman with flaming red hair.

"I have to be so around such lovely women, Capricia," he told her, flashing her a wink. "Although I must admit being partial to one certain redhead here."

Julianna missed the knowing look exchanged between the pair, seeing only Dominick's intense stare upon the flawless beauty Capricia. No doubt appropriately named! The woman's eyes danced as she tossed back the long, fiery red hair that cascaded past her shoulders. No doubt a natural red, Julianna thought enviously, wishing her own hair was truly that, as it used to be in her childhood.

Having realized from the start that she wasn't truly a redhead, Dominick had once told her that brown hair or red, she'd be beautiful either way, boosting her self-esteem several points. But now, noticing his lingering gaze that seemed so drawn to this redheaded woman—while remembering his last comment to her—she wondered with hurt just what the look of interest in his eyes meant.

Oblivious to her expression as Capricia walked away, the other women at the table laughed merrily, causing Julianna's cheeks to flush. It wasn't just the redhead. The way they all eyed him, she couldn't help but wonder how well he knew them. Were these some of the girlfriends he'd once sought out, and was he now missing their company, even as he resigned himself to spend his life with her? she wondered sadly.

Just noticing this, Dominick eyed her gently and hugged her close. "Capricia came with her boyfriend, who happens to be a friend of mine as well. We've always been strictly friends, love, as is true of all those here," he murmured, feeling her relax as he clasped her hand tightly. "And I assure you," he added with a knowing smile, "there won't be anymore women in my life other than my beautiful bride-to-be, who coincidentally happens to be the same redhead I referred to."

At the look of understanding that brightened her eyes, he emphasized his words with a long kiss, even as one of the other men coughed to break them apart again.

"Is there something you're not telling us here?" he inquired, his eyes mischievously questioning. "Come on, come on, we need more details."

"All in due time, Inferno," laughed Dominick. "Julianna, this is one of my most trusted friends."

Julianna smiled and reached out her hand towards him. "I'm glad to meet someone Dominick thinks so highly of," she said, surprised when Inferno took her hand—not to shake it—

but to kiss it gently.

"And it's most certainly a pleasure to meet a very beautiful lady that my friend apparently thinks equally highly of," he said. "By that glow in your eyes, I can tell that you must be as fond of Dominick as he is of you."

She blushed with a nod, taking a moment to appraise him. He had neatly trimmed sandy blond hair, with warm amber-brown eyes that seemed to emanate a welcome. From his strong set chin, the wisdom in his expression, and his amiable smile, it spoke volumes of trust and confidence.

"His name was aptly chosen for his ability to both conjure flame or extinguish it," Dominick continued. "As is the case with many dreamphasers, it's a second inborn ability."

She cast another look at the man and found herself agreeing that the name indeed suited him. It was in the man's eyes, she decided, which almost seemed to hold the flicker of flames themselves.

"As you can see, Dominick isn't the only charmer at this table," laughed the woman beside him.

Julianna noticed that like the redhead, this woman also had a striking beauty. Her fair blonde hair was long and shimmered, a striking contrast to her sun-tanned skin and dark emerald green eyes. Eyes that now looked adoringly at Inferno, easing any worries Julianna had about her wanting Dominick.

"That's Psych," he told her, earning her attention again. "Our resident songbird. She can hit notes that register outside normal hearing, although still in pitch."

She nodded appreciatively at the comment. "That, plus if you ever need to get attention, I can let out a sound that will overwhelm any other. Great for quieting a crowd in a hurry."

"Which might be useful later," Dominick agreed, turning towards his brother. "You've already met Riff, obviously," he murmured, clearing his throat.

Riff took on a look of hurt. "Dom, you wound me," he

said with mock seriousness, turning to Julianna. "You don't have to worry, dear lady. I assure you, I'm a most trustworthy soul when you get to know me."

Dominick glared at him. "She knows enough, and if you want that 'trustworthy' ***body*** of yours intact, just mind yourself."

"He'd better," sing-songed the woman beside him.

As Julianna met her gaze with a short laugh, they exchanged friendly knowing smiles that indicated an instant camaraderie. The woman had upward brushed shoulder-length, wavy copper hair with gold highlights, and bright brown eyes that glittered with intelligence and fun, not to mention a look of mischief that Julianna knew quite well herself. Dominick smiled at the pair, not surprised that their similar attitudes would make them fast friends.

"Julianna, this is Kiri. A lady who has more than just a quick mind. She has the ability to read the thoughts of others, when it comes to surface thoughts, in addition to occasionally being able to get impressions from objects about events occurring around them."

Kiri reached out to shake Julianna's hand. "That last part helps when you use healing magic on someone unconscious, to find out what may be the source of the problem when they can't communicate it."

Julianna's eyes grew curious. "But if you're already also a dreamphaser, wouldn't healing be a third ability? Dominick mentioned that supernaturals only have one or two."

"My healing powers are learned magic, not inborn. Many of Chavernos are scholars of learned magic, who never had inborn abilities."

"Could I learn, even though I'm from Earth?"

"It's certainly possible, though some take to it easier than others. If you were on our world, I'd be happy to help with what I know. Mind you, there are others more versed in learned magic here tonight, including one you know quite well." She smiled at her silent friend. "Dominick, don't tell me you haven't mentioned your own abilities outside of being a dreamphaser."

He shook his head. "It's hardly worth mentioning."

Riff snorted. "That's right, ***don't*** tell your girlfriend you're working towards being a high-ranking mage. Who'll notice when furniture rearranges itself, or dinner is served from a floating tray?"

Julianna's eyes widened. "Is that true? Can you really do magic outside of the dream-state?"

"Yes, it's true, although I still have much to learn."

"That's amazing!"

Visibly pleased, he shrugged. "It helps when your dragon companion knows a thing or two. But before Kiri gives away all of my secrets, it might interest you to know that she's an avid reader of romance novels too."

Kiri leaned forward conspiratorially. "It helps to pass the time while you're waiting for Mr. Right."

"Hey!" protested Riff.

"What, 'hey'?"

"Your Mr.'s ***right here***, in case you've forgotten."

"Please! You wouldn't know the meaning of romance if it bit you on the…"

His mouth effectively silenced hers with such conviction, the others were taken aback. Just when she visibly softened, he pulled away, his eyes defiantly looking into hers.

"Tell yourself that," he whispered, abruptly getting up from the table.

Although the others didn't stop him, Kiri still looked a bit dazed.

The third woman at the table, with long, curly brown hair, leaned forward in her chair. "Okay, then," she said, smiling playfully at Julianna. "And I didn't even have a hand in that one. Though very often, guardian devils like to stir up mischief between two lovers."

Kiri's eyes lost their glazed look. "We're ***not*** lovers!" she protested.

The guardian devil sighed. "Not everyone needs to be a mind reader to figure ***some*** things out." Ignoring her friend's angry blush, she refocused on her audience. "I'm Jarissa. Half guardian devil, half guardian angel, which means…"

"Chaos," mumbled the remaining man at the table.

She smirked at him. "Leave the dreamphaser out of this, halo-boy. Now, if you'll be your good, half-angel self and stop interrupting…" He growled, while she turned back again. "It means, although I may cause minor mischief, I do try to watch out for my fellow sisters on this world. When Dominick first mentioned you, it took a little convincing to realize his intentions with you were honorable." The guardian angel coughed loudly. "All right, a ***lot*** of convincing. But I'm glad he proved my concerns wrong, for both your sakes."

Julianna smiled as Dominick hugged her close meaningfully.

"Which brings us to this last gentleman," he said, gesturing. "This is Buddy, who is a primary guardian angel, but with a half-devil side as well. Not surprisingly, he shared similar concern, though I think we all understand one another now."

"Very true," agreed Buddy, kissing her hand cordially as Inferno had. "Welcome to our humble group, dear lady."

"Did you just say 'humble'?" exclaimed Riff, rejoining them with a drink. The others echoed his curious look.

"Hey, it's an expression!" Buddy protested. As the others slowly laughed at his seriousness, he sighed. "They're a tough crowd sometimes, but they're still fun on occasion."

"So it would seem," laughed Julianna. "I'm honored to meet all of you." A few raised their glasses politely. "So, do you all get together here frequently in the dream-state?'

Kiri shrugged her shoulders. "Now and then," she agreed, a smirk forming. "Except recently without Dominick for some reason. You wouldn't happen to know where he's been for the past few weeks, would you?" As a few of the others laughed, Julianna found herself blushing, but tried her best to maintain a confident air.

"Could be," she said cryptically, eyeing Dominick knowingly while sharing a mischievous smile with him that two errant teenagers might wear.

Squeezing her hand, Dominick spoke quickly. "Not to interrupt, but dreams only last so long," he stated simply, his smile becoming serious. "Thank you all for coming, my friends. I wanted all of you to be the first to hear the news."

"Finally!" Riff whispered noticeably, earning a rap on the shoulder from Kiri.

While the others looked on curiously, Dominick clasped Julianna's hand, gazing at her warmly just before he continued. "As you all know, I haven't been easy to reach lately, but I had good reason. You see, several weeks ago, I met this special lady, whom I'd first met months before, and when we least expected it, love crept up on us both. So to cut to the chase, my bachelor days will soon be over, since Julianna and I are engaged to be married."

The group's loud and simultaneous, "***What?***" echoed through the whole room, successfully halting conversations and prompting a lowering of the music's volume. A wave of curious silence remained, except for a few quiet murmurs, causing Dominick to sigh and Julianna to blush again.

Riff gave the couple a smile. "I'll handle this," he assured them, turning to the crowd. "Sorry, folks, didn't mean to disturb you!" he proclaimed. Seeing as they were reluctant to let it go at that, he stood up to add louder, "I said, go back to your entertainment! My brother's just getting married, that's all!"

Even days later, Julianna would never forget the wave of literal chaos that swept about her and Dominick like an opened floodgate, as countless people rushed up to surround them. Suddenly feeling like a famous star facing a persistent mob, she hastily clung to Dominick, burying her head against his chest while her wide-eyed gaze viewed the spectacle, a bit afraid that he too would be overwhelmed by this unusual reaction.

To her continued surprise though, Dominick took it all in stride, shaking hands among well-wishers while confirming the news with several sad-eyed females. Too many females for her own liking, Julianna thought privately, holding her fiancé tighter, but for a different reason this time.

She'd had absolutely no idea that Dominick was so popular with so many people. But then again, of course he was surely well known for his status on the island, she reminded herself. Not that the crowd was willing to let her get off easily either, upon finding out she was Dominick's intended bride. They swiftly bombarded her with endless questions, the leading one being when the marriage was to take place.

"We haven't been able to set a date just yet," she replied, earning more questions as to what the story was behind this. "We are engaged in the meantime. We're just... separated by a long distance." *Too long!* she thought inwardly. "It has yet to be resolved, but as soon as we can reach each other, we'll be married then."

Several of the older women congratulated her like mother figures, wishing both her and Dominick a wonderful future. However, some of the younger ones—obviously jealous—began sharpening their claws. One of whom inquired how she planned to grant Dominick an heir or two via long distance. This truth was pounced on by several others, proclaiming her an unsuitable bride, and leaving Julianna at a loss.

Feeling her tense, having overheard enough of their venom to know why, Dominick shot the pack of females a meaningful glare as he held her closer.

"Just so we're clear," he shouted to them, "we've also decided that my brother can provide those future heirs just as easily if we choose not to!" This quieted the lot. "So if you're so interested in casting out your cat claws," he continued evenly, "you'll have to go elsewhere. I have no intention of marrying anyone except Julianna, children or no children. Clear enough, ladies?"

Several of the men, as well as the mother figures, cheered him on this, while his words brought grateful tears from Julianna's eyes as he kissed her forehead lovingly.

Immediately after though, the swarm of endless questions continued.

Julianna became so overwhelmed by it all that her vision became bleary towards the endless faces, feeling her strength drain away with the non-stop noise. Throughout the tumult, she vaguely felt Dominick's arm lock firmly about her waist, as if he was afraid she should be lost to him amidst the seemingly endless crowd.

Moments later, a loud booming voice suddenly rang out, "In the name of Chaos, will you all please shut-up?"

Julianna didn't know the one who'd spoken, but to her disbelief, his authoritative words silenced everyone.

Looking towards the stares of the rest, but not releasing her hold on Dominick, Julianna saw the speaker. A well-dressed man in a formal suit gradually approached them. She softly asked Dominick who he was, but her future husband merely shushed her gently.

Turning to face the stranger again, Julianna noted that despite his white hair, this man definitely exuded an air of strength, power, and authority. No feeble elderly man, this one! Her mind raced back to her earlier brief conversation with Dominick before they came here. Was this the person he wished to introduce her to? she wondered.

Her question was soon answered as Dominick gestured

to him. "Julianna, this is my grandfather Chaos," he said, smiling at the surprise he saw on her face, just before he turned back to Chaos. "Grandfather, this is the woman I wish to marry."

Chaos's green eyes, more similar to Riff's, were now unreadable as Julianna slowly disengaged from Dominick to step forward. His expression unnerved her, but after swallowing once, she managed shakily, "I-I'm happy to meet you, sir. I'm..."

"My grandson has already introduced us, remember?" he said, almost gruffly. Before she could reply, he turned to the waiting crowd with a glare. "Back to your own lives!" he growled, immediately sparking their former chattering state, along with louder music again. "Eavesdropping puppies," he murmured, "can't keep their minds on their own business."

"I'm sure they're just curious," Julianna said tentatively.

"Curious!" Chaos sneered loudly, causing her to retreat a step as he eyed her sternly. "They're trying to get on my good side through my family. A side—I might add—that doesn't exist, although those idiots don't know it." Upon seeing the hint of a smile from her, Chaos raised one eyebrow and folded his arms, standing taller to appear more formidable. "What?" he barked. "Don't believe me, girl?"

After a slight pause, Julianna's smile grew and she shook her head. "No," she said. "But I believe that you want everyone else to think that's true."

His eyes boring into hers, he growled once, and moved to sit at an empty table nearby, slamming his fist upon it. "Can't the tired head of an island get any service in this infernal dream-state?" he demanded, his iron gaze drawing several nervous waiters and waitresses to him. "That's better," he replied, fairly pulling a menu from one before flinging it back moments later. "A moon tonic, no ice, and I want it within five seconds or there'll be chaos to pay."

"Five seconds?" murmured Julianna. "How do you

expect..."

Chaos's steel eyes met hers again, like an angry parent might regard an outspoken child, silencing her just as one waiter materialized a drink on the table. Glancing up at the nervous man, he said evenly, "That was six."

The man bit his lip. "I'm sorry, sir. I..."

"But considering I'm in a slightly less than abominable mood, I'll let it go this time," he replied, warding him away with his hand. The waiter and his companions nodded and then hurried off, apparently hasty to depart before Chaos could order anything else, leaving Julianna gaping in their wake. Dominick's grandfather certainly wasn't at all what she'd expected, she thought inwardly.

"And just what ***did*** you expect?" demanded Chaos.

Julianna gasped sharply upon facing him again, having forgotten Dominick's mention of his grandfather's multiple supernatural abilities, not the least of which included a dreamphaser's extra perception in the dream-state.

However, she didn't have to turn to feel Dominick stiffen beside her. Apparently, he wasn't too thrilled at the way this meeting was going either, thus far remaining a silent observer. He wouldn't have remained so, but when she squeezed his hand, he realized that she wanted to try and work this out herself and thus let her continue.

"I guess I was thinking of what my own grandfathers were like when they were still alive and I knew them as a child," she replied softly. "They were very..."

"Different?" he broke in, giving a sarcastic laugh that soon changed to a tight-lipped frown. "No doubt they would be," he said disdainfully. "But then again, I'd wager they weren't in charge of governing a whole island as I do."

Her chin set proudly. "Maybe not, but at least they could provide a civil conversation."

"Ah, and no doubt you're about to add that you're as

perfect as your illustrious ancestors."

Julianna bit her lip and forced her next words to remain quiet. "I am ***not*** perfect, have no wish to be, and never claimed I was," she replied.

"That's just as well, for I wouldn't have believed otherwise," Chaos stated curtly, folding his arms.

"Dominick never told me you believed ***yourself*** perfect," she retorted.

Several sharp gasps from the group indicated a sign of warning, causing her to bite her lip again at the words which had tumbled forth. But before she could attempt to retract them, his eyes darkened noticeably.

"So, Miss Sherborne, it would seem that Dominick's cast aside his former wifely candidate out of his so-called ***love*** for you." His mouth curled into a sneer over the word, continuing nonchalantly. "She is of course a woman on our world in reality, unlike yourself. Tell me, if things remain as they stand, just how do you propose to provide him a son one day. Through another lover, perhaps?"

Julianna's mouth fell open, but Dominick wasn't about to let her answer this comment. "Chaos, that was totally uncalled for," he retorted. "It's by my own choice that I wish to marry Julianna rather than Sionne. As to children, I've made it perfectly clear that even without them, I won't marry anyone else." His eyes narrowed. "And as to the notion of her taking on another lover, I'm quite confident she won't find the need for one while she's engaged to me, nor after we're married. If you want to discuss this further, you'll speak with me of it, not her."

Chaos gave a low grunt, but didn't press the issue, shifting his sharp gaze to Julianna again. "You've certainly blinded my grandson," he hissed. "But what deep, dark secrets are ***you*** hiding from him? For you're certainly no model of a guardian angel."

"No, of course not."

"***Absolutely*** not," he nearly growled, his eyebrows lowering even more. "You know, Miss Sherborne, I think I'm beginning to see what attracted Dominick to you. I suppose in all fairness, one might easily be fooled by your surface appearance and your simple-seeming innocent attitude." His expression hardened, his voice becoming a sharp whisper, "But if we're to believe that, it should be further remembered that a slight shadow mars your pristine soul... a matter involving your fine morals which placed you in his bed after only a handful of days." At her shock, he sneered again. "And if not for the timing of dreams, you might have joined him there sooner. Surely not the attitude of a fine, honorable woman, as you'd have us believe."

Julianna's face flushed of embarrassment, since his words weren't really lies, and to an outside observer, it might indeed seem that way.

"I've never been given to those impulses before," she said, struggling to keep her voice calm. "If things have happened rather quickly in our relationship," she added, shooting Dominick a quick glance, "I'm afraid you'll have to chalk it up to the fact that your grandson is a bit more... persistent and persuasive than others I've met."

Dominick's eyes glittered knowingly while he flashed her a quick smile, but he still said nothing, only catching a glimpse of Chaos's mouth tightening after hearing her last words. A growing suspicion formed in his mind—since he hadn't expected this backlash from Chaos—where he couldn't help but wonder just how ***accepting*** his grandfather would be if he and Julianna decided to live out their lives on her world.

Before he could question this, Chaos interrupted in a low-toned voice. "Forgive me, Miss Sherborne, if I don't buy your story that you two are in love as you claim to be, because several weeks of physical attraction hardly condones a rushed engagement, let alone a future marriage."

Julianna set her chin sharply. "Others have gotten married after knowing each other for less time than we have, so ***that's*** a moot argument. As far as our relationship is concerned, it happens to be based on more than just physical attraction, and I fully intend to keep true to our commitment to each other."

"So you say ***now***," said Chaos, "but it will remain a case where we have to trust to your... already questionable honor. I'm not as willing as my grandson to blind myself to that."

Sighing once, Julianna nearly folded against the man's stubbornness, but ultimately her love for Dominick won out, and she decided to try once more to reason with him.

"Mr. Westbrooke..." she began.

"There's no need for such formality. I'm simply Chaos."

"All right, Chaos then," she whispered, her calm attitude gradually receding. "Look, I don't know what I've done to make you dislike me, since I've never even met you before now, so I'd appreciate it if you'd..."

"Reserve judgment on you?" he finished cynically. "I don't think so, Miss Sherborne. I believe the facts speak for themselves already."

Before he could continue further, Julianna's eyes narrowed in sudden anger, her spine stiffening. "You know, sir, for someone who frowns on eavesdropping, ***you*** certainly do it often enough."

Once again, this earned surprised disquiet from the group, and others nearby who began to listen, leading her to believe that they weren't used to seeing people stand up to the man. Her ears burned from the renewed whisperings of some of the crowd, yet she still managed to interrupt Chaos before he could reply.

"No, I'll save you the trouble of speaking my thoughts again. You've already made it quite clear that you insist on being a grim, inflexible, disagreeable man, and that I'm a no-good trollop that isn't worthy of your grandson, so I guess there's no hope of convincing you otherwise."

She stole a quick glance up at Dominick, before stepping back. "I'm only glad that your grandson doesn't seem to share those traits." Her initial confidence spent, Julianna quickly strode from the group, disappearing into the crowd despite Dominick's protests.

Through the ensuing chatter that spread like wildfire through the crowd, Chaos's steel-handed grip prevented him from going after her, prompting him to turn to his grandfather angrily. "Satisfied?" he hissed.

"What?" Chaos asked, with an air of feigned innocence. "That I've proven the girl has an attitude problem that you knew nothing of? Or that she's admitted herself that you're not meant for one another?" Chaos hadn't counted on Dominick's friends loudly protesting against his accusations, their discordant arguments causing him to cover his ears with his hands. "Quiet, all of you!" Slowly, they complied, but Riff stood up to face him.

"Chaos, I'm sure I speak for all of us in that you didn't have to grill the girl as you did, subjecting her to that humiliating display in front of everyone. Now why don't you tell us just where your anger against her is ***really*** coming from?"

"I'm a bit curious to that one myself," said Dominick, eyeing his grandfather suspiciously. "Just what ***is*** the problem between now and our discussion earlier? Is it that Julianna hinted that you have more than a gruff attitude? Is it that you wanted to see if you could control her with your indomitable nature like so many others?" He folded his arms knowingly when his earlier suspicions returned, his tone becoming harshly accusing. "Or is it that you want to make absolutely certain that I remain here on Chavernos, even if that means my losing Julianna altogether?"

Chaos's silence was answer enough, as the group loyally continued to protest that surely his grandson was old enough to dictate his own life and that maybe the situation could be further negotiated as to where the couple might choose to live.

Again, Chaos raised his hands to silence them, but this time there was weariness in his voice as he spoke. "I've heard this argument before from Dominick," he told them, turning to his grandson. "Yes, the aspect that you might leave Chavernos for a girl you just met a few weeks ago bothers me. But if she can't handle the concerned opinions of a future family member, then best to find out now."

Dominick shook his head with a dark expression. "You still don't understand, do you?" he hissed through clenched teeth. "What Julianna and I decide to do about our future is ***our*** decision, not yours! And incidentally, your plan backfired. After tonight, I'm even more convinced that I should live on ***her*** world instead. Good night, Grandfather!"

Before Chaos could reply, he stormed off into the crowd. "Dominick, come back here!" he shouted, gaining no response. Swearing under his breath, he glanced once at the six pairs of angry eyes silently challenging him, deciding that he'd rather deal with his grandson's anger instead, purposefully going after him.

*****

During this time, Julianna had hastily found the building's exit and left, the tears finally falling now that she could give vent to her churned up emotions. How could she ever marry Dominick while that infuriating grandfather of his plastered ill notions about her at every turn? she thought miserably.

At first, she found a bench to sit down and think, but as a small group of people noticed her alone and came over to pester her with more inquiries about her engagement to Dominick, she quickly fled, running around the other side of the building to lean against it. Sliding down the brick wall to sit, she curled her knees up to her chest and wished that her fiancé was here to hold her with the strength of his protective embrace, because she certainly needed him now.

A hand on her shoulder abruptly startled her from her musings, causing her to jerk her head upward. "Dominick?" she asked softly, just before her tear-filled eyes cleared to reveal a stranger she'd never seen before. "Oh, I'm sorry," she whispered. "I thought you were my fiancé."

The man smiled down at her. "And I thought I noticed a damsel in apparent distress running this way," he replied, moving to kneel beside her. Julianna sniffed as she brushed a hand across her eyes to clear them further, getting a better look at the stranger.

He was good-looking, probably around Dominick's age or a bit older, with an air of confidence. His dark hair framed his marble-like face, with a pair of cool gray eyes. In a way, he resembled one of Dominick's friends she'd just met, although she knew it wasn't him. Even kneeling, the man was noticeably taller than she was, apparently well-muscled, and bearing a genial expression.

"I had to leave in a hurry," she told him, gesturing her head towards the building. "Those pestersome people will question me all night if I let them."

"Hmmm," he said, rubbing his chin as if considering something. Then abruptly, he snapped his fingers with sudden realization. "***That*** explains why you looked familiar. You must be the future bride of Dominick Westbrooke."

Hesitantly she nodded, just before suspicion lit her eyes. "Are you some kind of dream-state reporter?" she accused. "Because if you are..."

"Perish the thought, my dear woman," the man laughed. "I happen to have my own aversion towards those nosy people. I merely recognized you from the sudden crowd disruption earlier."

She gave a slight groan. "Don't remind me."

The stranger turned his head to one side curiously as he continued to stare at her appraisingly. "Since you're to be Dominick's wife, shouldn't you be back inside with him?"

"I ***would*** be," she agreed, her lips forming a sneer. "That is, if his royal highness King Chaos would stop shooting his poisonous insults at me." After she sniffed once more, the stranger materialized a handkerchief for her, which she gratefully accepted.

"Ah yes, Chaos," he said softly, sounding as if he'd dealt with the man before. Julianna was too busy drying her eyes to notice all he said, nor the hint of biting sarcasm in his tone. "Dominick's grandfather is indeed a piece of work. Not surprisingly, it seems to run in the family with his ***dear*** grandson..."

"I'm sorry, what did you say?" she murmured absently as she looked up from the white cloth.

His smile renewed, the stranger removed the handkerchief from her grasp and questioned her further. "Not to sound like those wretched nuisances within, but just when are you and Dominick getting married?"

"The way you're speaking, you sound like you know him personally."

The stranger's mouth twitched once, but he maintained his air of calm composure. "Yes, we do know each other. If I may say so though," he added, extending his hand amiably, "this humble dream traveler is glad to make the acquaintance of his most beautiful bride-to-be."

She took his hand with a smile, nodding once. "Pleased to meet you too, I'm sure." The man's eyes glittered in response as he kissed her hand. A bit flustered by this, she managed to free her hand to continue quickly. "In answer to your earlier question, Dominick and I are planning on being married as soon as we can."

Sensing her sudden concern over his attention, the

stranger's eyes twinkled, but before he could say anything, she sighed distractedly. "Although now, I'm beginning to wonder if it will ever happen at all with Chaos around."

"Don't worry, my dear. I'm sure everything will go according to plan," he assured her, secretly masking a different smile from her. Suddenly, Dominick's voice was heard, calling out Julianna's name.

"That's my fiancé," she explained. "I'd better go to him. If you'll excuse me."

The man stood with her, taking hold of her arm. When her eyes questioned this, he smiled lazily. "Julianna," he whispered. "A beautiful name for a fair damsel."

"Thank you," she replied, blushing this time. "Now please, I have to go."

"Of course," he agreed, nodding once before releasing her. "But rest assured, my dear Julianna... we will meet again in the future. After all, I happen to know your future husband quite well, though it's been awhile since we last talked."

She smiled at the sound of camaraderie in his tone, but couldn't comment before Dominick's voice shouted out her name again, this time more loudly. Waving once to the man, she ran back around the building, completely missing the look of amused resentment that flashed across his face.

"Oh yes, my dear woman," Dual hissed quietly to himself, "I know your future husband ***quite*** well indeed. As I'll one day know you." Nodding once with a devious grin as he dropped the handkerchief to the ground, he vanished just as the white cloth burst into flames behind him.

*****

"Julianna!" Dominick shouted again, by this time genuinely worried over his betrothed's mysterious absence. Could the crowd have mobbed her again, cornering her for details? he wondered, silently cursing the lot of them for interfering with his personal life.

Not that it was anything less than he expected, since being the grandson of the ruler of Barokka, he'd assisted in helping keep the island the paradisiacal place it was, no less so among the numerous dreamphasers residing there.

Quite often, he traveled throughout the island to keep tabs on things, and saw to improving conditions where necessary and possible, so he'd met a great deal of Barokka's inhabitants personally. Some of the women in past years, he thought ruefully now, he'd known more than just casually. But since Chaos had often warned him to be careful of the gold-digging type, he'd always been careful to steer clear of any deep emotional involvements.

Since he'd also been careful to avoid women who were currently involved with other men—especially the married kind—he'd also avoided the wrath of the male population, and thus was well liked by most everyone on the island. Of course, a few men still couldn't hide their pleased reaction that one of the most eligible bachelors was leaving the female chase. So it wasn't really a shock that so many were congratulating him on his engagement.

He'd only displayed a slight grimace towards the several people he'd conferred with who asked what his plans were in regard to future heirs. Sticking to what he'd told the women speaking with Julianna, he murmured that it wasn't a concern or a necessity. Yet inwardly, he supposed it could be one day, if Riff decided against fatherhood himself.

To be truthful, Dominick had been especially fond of the many children of Barokka he'd met along the way, which was why Chaos suggested he see to settling down and having a few of his own. Up until now, Dominick had merely laughed at the suggestion, saying he doubted he'd ever find a woman he wished to devote his whole life to.

That was before Julianna had unexpectedly come into his life to change all that.

Another biting irony. He'd found an ideal companion—who would probably like to have children with him someday—but the children Chaos wished for him to have were an impossibility. *At least for now*, his thoughts amended. This disturbance was still present as he prepared to shout for Julianna again, just before he heard her respond.

Turning, a thankful smile crossed his expression as she reappeared. He held out his arms to embrace her as she ran to him. Just holding her close again erased his former dark thoughts completely, as if she'd suddenly become the sun to brightly burn them away.

"Darling..." he murmured against her ear as he kissed her cheek, "please don't run off like that again. I was beginning to worry that you'd left me for good after hearing what my grandfather was spouting on about."

That was a thought that had indeed distressed him upon his first exiting the building and finding no trace of her. Heirs or not, he decided firmly as he held her now, he wasn't willing to abandon this woman he loved so much, no matter how strongly the others might argue. They'd find some way to work it out.

She shook her head tearfully. "Oh, Dominick, you must know I'd never leave you," she told him, her voice breaking. "I love you more than I can ever express."

"I remember, love," he whispered, breathing in her sweetness. "Dear heaven, I could never forget, since I love you the same way as well." His expression became serious. "This wasn't at all the way I planned this evening," he told her honestly. "I was sure my grandfather would accept you after telling him about you earlier this day. I guess I should have known better with Chaos, who's more than earned that title."

"It wasn't your fault, Dominick," she replied, shaking her head. "I just wish your grandfather wasn't so close-minded."

"No matter," he said, pulling her back to meet his gaze. "I intend to marry you in the near future, Miss Sherborne, as long as I still have your consent to proceed."

Smiling happily, she clasped her arms around his neck, with a mock sense of airs. "By all means, Mr. Westbrooke, I'll gladly accept the role as your dutiful wife."

He was only silent for a moment before laughter overcame him. "Since being dutiful indicates obedience, I'm afraid that's one role you'd never qualify for, love."

"You never argue when we're alone together," she retorted with a slight pout.

Pulling her closer until his mouth was mere inches from hers, he smiled upon her. "Maybe because I much prefer you just the way you are, feisty and unpredictable." Brushing a light kiss across her lips, he felt her soften again. "You know, love, your earlier suggestion comes to mind. Would you be terribly disappointed if we left early to salvage something pleasant from this night?"

"Hmmm," she murmured, even as she smiled against his ever-persuasive kisses on her neck. "If this has anything to do with a certain raincheck, I guess I'm willing to make the sacrifice," she decided through a soft laugh, just before Dominick swept her up in his arms with a grin, his laughter echoing hers.

"Wait!" interrupted a loud voice.

Startled, the pair looked up to find Chaos striding towards them, holding up a hand as if he could hold them there by sheer will.

Julianna's smile faded instantly, while Dominick's expression turned cold, gently setting her on her feet again while still holding her possessively. As Chaos drew nearer, she noticed a faint softening of his features, and wondered at the oddness of it.

"I see you wish to leave, but if I could have a moment of your time before you go, I'd appreciate it," said Chaos, his tone surprisingly quiet. "Please," he added, giving a meaningful look to both.

"You have your moment," Dominick replied evenly.

Chaos smiled at the embraced pair before he began. "I couldn't help witnessing the two of you together just now. You remind me of happier times, when I still had my precious wife Ylana beside me, watching our son and grandsons growing up peacefully."

He sighed heavily in remembrance. "Ylana and I had our own share of hardships to overcome. Perhaps not as great as this distance separating you, but they existed. In any event, we never would have let anything or anyone keep us apart either. And bearing this in mind, I suppose I shouldn't have allowed my own feelings to condemn what you've already chosen to do with your lives. After tonight, seeing how happy you are with each other, I know your future marriage will happen someday. And this being the case, I'd rather be a part of your lives than an outsider."

Chaos turned to Julianna with the hint of a regretful smile. "If I may be allowed to retract my words to you earlier, I do believe that you genuinely love my grandson, and I suppose I can understand full well how impulses can take hold of one. After all, I've been no stranger to them myself over the years."

As she gave a silent nod of acceptance, Chaos stole a quick knowing glance at Dominick. "And there's no arguing your words that my grandson is a rather persistent and persuasive lad for all that, so I can further understand what steered you towards a serious relationship so soon." At the warning look in Dominick's eyes, Chaos warded it off lightly, turning back to Julianna. "As to what you said earlier, about my being a grim, inflexible, disagreeable man..."

She blushed at the memory. "Sir, I didn't mean..."

"Contrary to my earlier words, you don't strike me as being a woman without honor, so don't pretend to feel differently," he interrupted, but without any sternness this time.

"After all, your instincts are quite correct. I am all those, and have damn well learned to build a reputation around it."

A warmer smile lit his face as he reached forward to take her hand gently. She gave no resistance, since she was still caught by surprise from his speech.

"Your instincts were also correct on the count that I do have a different side that isn't so gruff, although I can't allow most to know this. You're one of the few to see it, to your credit, only reassuring me that you're every bit as intelligent and warmhearted as you are a beauty. Most certainly a fit match for my grandson, and you'll both have my blessing at the time of your future wedding, along with my sincerest congratulations over your engagement now."

Julianna gaped for a moment, her eyes shining, and on impulse she reached out to hug the older man. "Thank you, sir," she whispered.

He patted her back, breaking apart from her to emit a gruff excuse for a smile. "That's Grandfather to you, so don't forget it in the future."

"Of course," she agreed, feeling a surge of happiness as she felt Dominick's arm tightly clasp her waist with pride.

"One last thing before I leave you both to... your other plans?" He smiled knowingly at the sheepish looks on the pair's faces. "I would hope Dominick has mentioned that if you were to choose to live your lives on Barokka one day, you'd want for nothing."

Julianna gave him her warmest smile. "Oh, sir..." At the sudden quirk of Chaos's eyebrows, she caught herself. "I mean, Grandfather… as long as I have Dominick, I wouldn't want anything else. But as to living together on Barokka, I'd be thrilled to live there, not to mention to meet you and his friends in reality. That is, as long as you wouldn't mind my visiting Earth on occasion, if possible."

"If the means are available, you'll have your visits,"

Chaos agreed heartily. "And as an added wedding present, as I suggested to Dominick, I'll see to it that you have your own castle on the island. After all, I wish for you and all my future great-grandchildren to have the very best of everything." He shot Dominick a glance. "You will be sure to use that persistent and persuasive attitude towards arranging for those great-grandchildren, won't you?"

"As many as Julianna wishes," he agreed, turning to her. "What do you think, darling?"

"Hmmm, I suppose two or three kids might be nice," she agreed, smiling blissfully at the thought.

"Good!" Chaos said brightly, just before he caught himself with a serious harumph, returning to his former reserved attitude, though his green eyes twinkled. "And on that note, I must be off. I'll see to it that your friends and the crowd know that your engagement is official. In the meantime... carry on, you two."

Julianna would have sworn he'd hidden a smile as he walked away, leaving her to turn to her grinning fiancé. She reached forward to hug him, laughing as he lifted her off the ground to spin her about once.

"I can't believe it's all going to work out," she said honestly.

"Ah, for the millionth time, love," he chuckled, "never underestimate the powers of a dream knight."

"Nor the power of the love of one's dreams," she added.

"Nor that," he agreed with a serious smile, kissing her with desire, just before picking up his joyful betrothed to teleport them back to the familiar warmth of their beloved dream castle.

Chapter Thirteen

As the Westbrooke brothers sat side-by-side at the bar counter, Zantarl eyed them both with what looked like parental disapproval. Now several days since their dispute regarding Julianna, the bartender had agreed to mediate a civil meeting between the pair. Barely civil so far, since neither spoke, only shooting constant glares at one another.

After a long pause, Riff spoke. "For the millionth time, Phase, I said I was sorry for the other night. How was I supposed to know that you were so in love with the girl that you'd planned on proposing to her that evening?"

Dominick continued to glare at him. "Even if I hadn't, it doesn't excuse your trying to force your attentions on her."

"I would have let her go in another minute," he sneered. "Hellions are more interesting when they're willing, not when they'll claw you otherwise."

"That hasn't always stopped you from persisting," Dominick replied acidly. "Especially when you've derived extra pleasure from seducing the women I've known."

Riff's eyes narrowed, and he replied quietly, "For your information, regardless of what stories you've heard, I may be persistent, but I have ***never*** ever been intimate with a woman that didn't wish it. And although I don't want this getting about, there are those women who refused whom I did walk away from honorably." His brother looked genuinely surprised. "And as far as my seducing some of your former paramours, maybe I shouldn't have, but the fact is I wouldn't have been able to if they'd really loved you as Julianna does. You should be glad, in that I indirectly did you a favor."

Dominick's surprised look turned to irritation. "You ***would*** see it that way," he retorted. "Not that you'd ever understand the meaning of the word ***love***, since you only regard the bedroom aspects of a relationship."

As Riff loudly protested, Dominick countered back, their voices raising to a din. Zantarl, however, wasn't about to put up with another verbal escalation. Slamming a bottle on the counter, he distracted the brothers, earning their undivided attention.

"That's better," he growled. "Now look, you two. Either settle this problem of yours, or I'll ban you both from Lost Limbo until further notice." Turning to Dominick, he began, "Riff's apologized several times, of which even once is a rare feat, as we all know." Hearing the stirrings of protest from the other man, he flashed his angry eyes upon him. "And as for you, Riff, I'm sure that you'll think twice before interfering with your brother's fiancée anymore, let alone question the validity of their relationship. So if we're all in agreement, why don't you settle this with a handshake?"

The pair eyed each other with scowls, but gradually, they reached forward to clasp hands, their features softening. Riff spoke first. "I'm sorry I doubted your feelings for Julianna, and for the incident the other night. It won't happen again."

Dominick nodded once. "All right then, I accept your apology," he said quietly. "And for what it's worth, I'm sure you'll find love someday."

"Julianna indicated as much when things calmed down," sighed Riff, "though I find it hard to believe that day will ever come."

Dominick smiled slightly. "I once thought the same thing, remember?"

Riff nodded slowly.

"And…" Dominick continued, brightening, "if you can stick to your words, maybe you'd consider being my best man at our future wedding."

Riff's face lit up considerably. "Are you sure about that, Phase?" he asked, half expecting a hidden jest.

"Very sure, unless you go to great lengths to change my mind."

"Then I accept," Riff replied with a grin, exchanging a rare hug with him. "It ought to be the wedding of the decade, since Chaos will no doubt have a hand in it. Which reminds me, where did I put that number for the dancing girls...?"

As he started rummaging around a small book, Dominick gave a low groan. Leave it to Riff to cast aside any semblance of a serious subject, let alone to send the wheels of chaos turning. Reading his thoughts, Zantarl chuckled quietly, whispering to him, "Maybe you and Julianna would be better off eloping instead."

"Believe me, it's tempting," Dominick whispered back, even as Riff's expression suddenly darkened.

"Look what the guardian devil dragged in," he said in a low voice, gesturing towards the door. All three men focused on the new arrival, and all shared looks of unmasked loathing.

Grinning as if he owned the world, a confident Dual strode into Lost Limbo, waving boisterous greetings to his friends, while remaining impervious to many cold stares. But then, nothing seemed to bother him on this world or in the dream-state.

Ever a renegade, the dark-haired man bore a most striking resemblance to Buddy. Thanks to his shared looks to the guardian angel, Dual often took great amusement in attempting to fool Jarissa into mistaking one for the other. Not to mention the fact that he'd made many attempts to seduce her away from Buddy, although she'd once claimed she'd rather return to the guardian realm permanently than do that.

Not very flattering to say the least!

One of the most apt and notorious dreamphasers on

Chavernos, Dual easily used his powers to gain access to the party the night before. His trait for granting nightmares to his enemies, his persuasive ability for corrupting innocents, not to mention his assassin missions, had earned him a dark reputation among all but the baser inhabitants of Barokka. So it wasn't surprising why his presence affected many in Lost Limbo quite negatively.

Not only in Buddy's case, but especially Dominick's. Many times, the latter had avenged those that Dual had wronged, usually amongst the females, also disrupting many of his other dark plans over the years. One time, he'd even rescued Jarissa from Dual's dark intentions, his constant opposition only fueling their bitter enmity.

And now there was the added incident of the map.

Just thinking of the truth he'd learned from Alarius, Dual was determined to get back at his longstanding enemy yet again, but only when ***he*** deemed it a suitable time.

Turning to catch sight of the trio at the bar, a slow smile spread across his face. Sitting down at an adjacent table, he then turned his back to them in order to converse with his own friends. Dominick and the others realized full well that he could easily eavesdrop, but all silently recognized that Dual was a difficult slime to get rid of.

"It's been months since he last came here," Zantarl quietly told the pair. "I wonder why he's decided to foist his presence upon us this time."

"Let's hope it's a very short visit," murmured Dominick. "Of all the times when I don't want to deal with him, it's now, with word of my engagement circulating about."

"I wish I could have been there last night to hear it firsthand, son," Zantarl replied with a sad smile. "But alas, a dreamphaser I'm not. The best I can hope for is that one day you'll find a way to bring your bride here, so I can meet her at your wedding."

"A hope we share, believe me."

"Any word from the folks yet?" asked Riff.

"No," sighed Dominick. "But unfortunately, there ***has*** been word from Julianna's ex-boyfriend. His name's Roger Collins, and she used to have strong feelings for him since they met as teenagers."

"Really? Well then, are you sure she wouldn't go back to…"

"No," Dominick interrupted adamantly. "He's hurt her badly emotionally, fooling around with another woman as retaliation when she didn't want to sleep with him, and she wants nothing more to do with him. The problem is, now that Julianna and I are happy together, that bastard's decided that he's ***sorry*** for the way he treated her and wants another chance. She doesn't want to give him one, but it seems he refuses to leave her alone. He keeps calling her."

"And you're sure she harbors no old feelings for him?"

Dominick considered this silently, his mind playing back the memories of their time together. Over the past few weeks, Julianna had only mentioned Roger in passing, regarding his bothering her. Dominick had asked her how she felt about this, and she firmly stated that she'd sooner become a nun than have Roger so much as touch her now. The conjured image had been so amusing to both, considering their nightly encounters lately, that they were soon overcome with mutual laughter. After that, they'd used the remaining hours of the night to remove any notions of her setting down the celibate road.

"After all the time we've spent together, I'd swear that she doesn't." The unfocused, distant look in Dominick's eyes confirmed that he was once more lost to those memories, earning a knowing smirk from Riff.

"Considering your probable notions of a never-ending honeymoon with Julianna, if you bring her to our world, Chaos should have no problem getting those great-grandkids he wants so badly. If not for the impossibility of having kids in the dream-state, I'm sure I and everyone else would wonder if you didn't ***have*** to marry her by now..."

Dominick elbowed him sharply in the ribs, only bringing forth soft laughter from his endlessly joking brother. Inwardly he knew that this side of Riff's humor was harmless, and that he only did it to annoy him, but it was often difficult to remember this all the time.

From where he sat, Dual grinned at what he'd just overheard. So that tempting morsel Julianna had another admirer on her homeworld, did she? And someone she'd known for years. *Dominick must surely be* ***thrilled*** *by that knowledge!* he thought. It certainly brought him no little amusement to hear of his enemy's problems, to provide for what might otherwise be a rather uneventful visit.

Come to think of it, why not add to the amusement? he decided, getting up to walk over to the bar counter. The three men looked up at him suspiciously, but said nothing.

"Zantarl, get me something with a little kick in it," he said nonchalantly.

"I'd like to give him a kick..." murmured Dominick, quickly calmed by his attentive brother.

Feigning surprise, Dual turned to his frowning adversary and grinned again. "Ah, by the dreams of night, if it isn't Dominick of the Westbrooke brothers. It would seem those nightmare beasts I sent after you a few months ago haven't roughed you up any worse for the wear."

"Nor has one managed to rearrange your sick attitude," hissed Riff, locking angry gazes with him for a moment before Dual gave his annoying smile again. If nothing else, both brothers shared the same hatred of him.

As if he'd disappeared, Dual returned his attention to Dominick, who was doing his best to ignore him. "So how has your sweet betrothed Julianna been lately? Still as lovely as she was at the announcement of your engagement the other night?" As expected, Dominick's head spun around to face him.

"Keep your filthy thoughts from my fiancée," he growled in warning. "She's done nothing to you, so leave her alone."

"And why would I wish to harm her?" he laughed. "I found her to be a most enjoyable companion that evening."

Dominick nearly jumped out of his chair, stopped only by Riff and Zantarl on either side of him. "Liar. She was with ***me*** that night!"

"Not when she ran away from you, remember? A most remarkably beautiful woman when one sees her in the proper light. Long auburn hair that curls most enticingly around her, brown eyes that sparkle in the light, soft skin just made to be touched..."

Not a dreamphaser to be held back when provoked, Dominick pulled free of the rest to connect a direct hit on Dual's jaw, knocking him into another table. Giving a lopsided malicious grin, Dual was up in moments, scoring a few punches against his enemy. About evenly matched, Dominick's anger gave him a slight edge though, and with a sharp jab to the stomach, Dual was finally downed.

Glancing up with a bleeding mouth, his eyes shot fire as he pointed a menacing finger towards Dominick. "You've just made a big mistake, Westbrooke," he hissed. "Up until now, I only chatted with your precious Julianna. But no more... because now I finally know how to strike where you'll feel it in your guts forever. You'd just better watch your back, my not-so-wise enemy... and ***hers***!"

Dominick's own expression darkened warningly. "If you touch her, Dual, there won't be a grave deep enough to hold all the pieces I'll break you into!"

Before he could step forward again, Zantarl gripped his shoulders, turning an ominous look to Dual. "You've been warned. Now you'd better leave, lest I decide to press charges for your brawling in here like a madman."

Dual was about to protest, but then thought better of it. "Clever, Zantarl, considering he was the instigator. But I have other sport to plan, so I'll let it go this time." Shooting a last meaningful glance at his enemy, Dual added, "By demon's teeth, it's not over yet between us, Westbrooke. Not to mention, your supposed bride-to-be. Enjoy having her all to yourself while you can, because it won't be for long." In moments, he'd departed.

"I should kill him," hissed Dominick.

"And be forced behind iron bars where you'll have even less chance of spending your life with Julianna?" Zantarl asked firmly. "No, son, I think not. Better you forget this meeting with that black-tongued demon and simply look forward to your wedding. His barbs will probably lose their poison by the end of this day."

Slowly, Dominick shook his head. "I'm afraid Dual doesn't operate that way, Zan," he said knowingly. "But so help me, he'd better think twice about bothering Julianna. Because if he ever touches her, then threats of jail will be a minor penalty for bringing his miserable life to an end."

He never noticed the pair who appeared behind him, their faces grim.

*****

Last night's bridal shower in the dream-state—due to Dominick's thoughtful friends—had been quite a surprise to Julianna. Having expected to be with her fiancé, she'd instead found herself in another location with Kiri and the gals, who quickly explained that although they couldn't give her the typical bridal shower presents until she came to Chavernos, they could certainly get a head-start on the party itself. In the meantime, they mentioned that Dominick was being similarly thrown a bachelor party by the guys.

That last met with some concern from her, knowing all too well what could go on at those parties on Earth, and what was no doubt the same regarding dreamphasers in the dream-state!

"You're absolutely right," agreed Kiri, folding her arms. "Men and their bachelor parties... why, if I ever decided to get married—especially if it was to Riff—I'd show up as a dancing girl at his bachelor party and ***really*** give him something to stare at!"

"No doubt wielding an axe," murmured Psych.

"Or a spiked mace," added Jarissa.

"Gals, gals, hold on," interrupted Kiri, resting a sisterly arm around Julianna's shoulder. "Now I think we're all unanimous on our opinions about the men and their bachelor party, but we're not going to let our little bride-to-be spend the night worrying about it, are we?" There was a chorus of negation from the pair, earning a broad smile from Kiri. "Good!" she said, turning to Julianna cheerfully. "We'll show those men that they don't bother us with their shenanigans."

"Fine by me," she decided with a smile. Inwardly, their soothing words were nothing less than Julianna expected from her newfound friends.

What she ***hadn't*** expected was their plans for her bridal shower.

Moments later, the lights dimmed around them, earning her curiosity. No doubt a show of some sort, she thought, just before realizing what ***kind*** it was. As stage lights came on, several very handsome—very stripping—men appeared who won the cheers and applause of the many other observing women.

Julianna could only gape, eyes wide, until she suddenly heard Jarissa shout, "Over here, honey! This one's planning on getting married soon!"

Whirling to face her, she said in a piercing whisper, "Jarissa, what are you doing?"

The latter merely grinned conspiratorially as one of the

men jumped from the newly lit stage to stride over to their table. Julianna turned towards him slowly, feeling her face blush crimson. He looked very much like any other handsome brown-haired, blue-eyed muscle man, differing only by the aspect of his being garbed in minimal attire.

"So you're the gal Westbrooke's marrying, are you?" he said jovially, earning a silent nod from her. "He chose well, ma'am. You're a beauty indeed."

"Th-thank you," she gasped out, trying hard to keep her eyes strictly on his face.

"And since the groom seems to be elsewhere at the moment, I guess it wouldn't hurt to get in a little dance time with the bride." Before she could say a word in negation, he swept her up in his arms as lightly as a feather, carrying her towards the stage. "Come on, sweetie, smile," he encouraged. "This is your night."

"N-no, really," she protested futilely. "I-I'm not used to this sort of thing. One of the others..."

He shushed her quickly, whispering in her ear, "Don't worry, my lady. Your future husband understands the gals you're with, and being a good friend of his, I'll make sure these guys stay in line." At her hesitancy, he added, "If it'll cheer your mood any, he's sent a message that he loves you alone, and that he has no desire to seek the company of the females brought to his bachelor party."

Julianna glanced up at his eyes. "You wouldn't deceive a bride-to-be, would you?" she whispered back.

The man laughed with a shake of his head. "No, fair maiden, and certainly not in your case. In fact, I wouldn't be at all surprised if you're removed from this party a few hours early, if your future husband has any say in the matter." That did brighten her mood, and she smiled warmly. "Feel like dancing now?"

"With stars at my feet," she replied, earning the pleased

cheers of her friends.

All in all, it proved to be a most enjoyable evening. The men, while boisterous, turned out to be much like the first man, making her laugh as they danced. Jarissa and the girls—not to be left out, of course—fairly leaped from their table to join her at the invitation of one of the men, and thus, Julianna learned a whole new definition of what bridal showers could be like.

Not that Dominick didn't indeed show up to rescue her halfway through it, cleverly sneaking them both out to find time alone...

Unknown to her, this action—when realized by the guys and the gals—incited a major ruckus among the separate groups who then sought each other out, arguing that the groom and bride-to-be weren't supposed to ***disappear*** from their own celebration parties.

It was a pointless argument though, since the groom and bride-to-be had cleverly gone to a place other than their dream castle, and were nowhere to be found.

As to what they'd done in their seclusion...

Julianna smiled at the memory as she went about her work, feeling that nothing could remove her from the wave of happiness she was floating on.

At first she thought she was imagining Roger's voice behind her, now talking with Almira, but as the voices grew louder, her face drained of color and she stopped typing.

"Our company has always admired the way you do business," he said. "Which is why they've sent me as a representative to settle the details of the account you're proposing. I hope we can come to a mutual compromise."

"Oh, I'm sure we will," Almira replied with enthusiasm. "Mr. Collins... or may I call you Roger?"

"Roger would be fine," he agreed, folding his arms with a smile.

"You're kidding me…" whispered Julianna, shutting her

eyes in frustration as her suspicions were confirmed. Roger had business ties ***here*** now? Maybe she could arrange for a transfer.

Wait a second! her angry thoughts interrupted. *If Roger is working with this company, he'll be dealing with Almira alone. I have nothing to worry about, so what do I care what he does?*

Not one damn bit, she decided, typing more briskly.

As if sensing her agitation, Roger glanced in Julianna's direction, a smile curling across his mouth. Ah, so she knew he was here, he surmised. Good. Then maybe she wasn't as immune to him as she seemed to think.

He strode towards her, while Almira kept pace with him, looking ahead curiously to follow his stare. Miss Sherborne? she thought, surprised. What would he want with the likes of ***her***? Now if he wanted a ***real*** businesswoman... she herself was more than available.

"And who is this enterprising lady?" he asked, surprised when Julianna refused to turn towards him.

"That's Miss Sherborne," Almira fairly hissed.

"Rather efficient I see," said Roger, rubbing his chin thoughtfully. "Are all your workers too busy to speak for a brief moment?"

"Busy doesn't describe this one most of the time," murmured Almira. *Too busy daydreaming, if anything!* she thought. "Miss Sherborne, if you can interrupt what you're doing, we have a visitor from..." Noting the girl's ignorance as she continued typing, seeming unusually preoccupied, Almira's eyebrows sharpened. In a much louder tone, she continued, "Miss Sherborne, would you mind paying attention to a prospective client of our firm?"

Julianna sighed once, ceasing her typing, and prayed for inner strength. Replacing her dismayed look with a plastic smile, she lifted her head to turn towards the pair. "I'm listening," she said quietly.

Clearly forcing a smile, Almira gestured towards Roger, who was now grinning knowingly. "This is Mr. Collins, who's going to be working with us for the next several months, as soon as a contract can be worked out and signed..."

"Ah," interrupted Roger, raising one finger. "That's only ***if*** we can come to a final agreement on terms," he reminded her. Julianna was surprised to see Almira displaying a cowed look. ***No*** one ever cowed that woman! Either she ***really*** wanted this deal... or perhaps Roger?

That thought almost had her laughing. Roger and Almira? In some ways, it certainly seemed fitting.

Somehow though, she doubted that match was on Roger's agenda.

"Yes, of course," murmured Almira. "If we could return to my office, perhaps we can work out the details."

Ignoring her, Roger turned towards Julianna again with a broad smile. Extending his hand, he said gently, "It's a pleasure to meet you, Miss Sherborne." Unable to refuse in front of Almira, she shook his hand, finding it difficult to get him to release hers afterward.

"And most ***interesting*** to meet you here too, Mr. Collins," she replied, aiming thinly veiled sarcasm at him. "Now if you'll excuse me, this is an office, and I have work to finish."

Before she could turn again, he moved to stand in front of her. "You seem quite efficient already, Miss Sherborne. Perhaps a little change of scenery over lunch could provide a break from this workload you seem to have."

"Knowing Miss Sherborne, she'll be too busy spending lunch with her co-worker Ms. O'Neill," protested Almira. "You see, she always meets with her, and I'm sure they wouldn't like a sudden change from the norm."

"Well then, in this case they can make an exception," replied Roger, almost icily. Almira nodded mutely, catching sight of an odd pleading look in Julianna's eyes. It seemed almost as if she didn't want to go to lunch with Roger any more than Almira wanted her to.

A moment of rare agreement between the pair.

"Mr. Collins, we've made it a policy that our workers don't associate in the dealings with our clients."

"Not even when some constructive feedback would be appreciated from the secretaries in this division?" he asked. Before she could reply, he continued, "After all, Almira... I can call you Almira, can't I?" She nodded. "If we're to be doing business, it would be in the interest of my company to know whom we'll be working with. Less than that, and I'd think we should be looking elsewhere, and advise our other business clients similarly."

Almira's eyes widened at the negative possibility, while knowing where this was leading, Julianna instantly spoke up. "***Mr.*** Collins, my job description doesn't say anything about owing my lunch hour to the company. What I do with that time is of my own choosing. If you need assistance, one of the other secretaries can help you."

Roger smiled at her, but she didn't miss the underlying challenge in it. Turning from her, he started to walk away, nodding once to Almira. "It's been a pleasure meeting with you. Perhaps some other time our two companies can be more agreeable with each other."

Going beyond the niceties, Almira grabbed his arm, flashing an angry look at Julianna. "Miss Sherborne, considering your questionable job performance lately, I'd say this business lunch would only begin to make up for it. If you value your job, you'd best reconsider your decision."

Julianna frowned silently at the implication.

*There's **no** justice in the work world these days.*

*****

Still less justice existed in Dark Haven, a bar on the opposite coast of Barokka, equally known, but more often avoided. While Lost Limbo had scattered patrons from the whole spectrum, Dark Haven catered to the darker and shadier inhabitants of the island. If an innocent unfortunate wanderer came here—not knowing its reputation—that wanderer could find himself subject to much more than trouble, and might never be able to leave.

Dual merely smiled when he entered the building. Ah yes, Dark Haven was just like a second home to him.

In moments, he'd found the one he sought, beckoning to a cloaked man across the room. Like the shadows he was named for, the man Shade slithered towards him, his black cape swishing along his equally black boots. Somewhat older and rail thin, though strong, Shade had the highest agility and dexterity, and the special boots and cape he wore masked all sound of his movement. While one might first cast him off as insignificant, in truth, he was one of the most deadly assassins in Barokka, although he often roamed in outer Chavernos as well.

An assassin who used his knife to pry secrets from people's minds.

Not that he always did the actual killing. More often, he waited amidst the shadows to collect information that his clients would need to finish the job themselves. His most deadly ability was akin to Kiri's ability to mind read. Except, he could also delve beyond a person's mere surface thoughts to pick out a person's fears, or seek out information that was thought to be carefully hidden from all others.

Under different circumstances, this ability could have brought him great renown and done great services for the wronged individuals of the world to see justice done, but Shade chose to serve darker purposes instead, as mercenary as anything else.

"Dual," his sharp voice hissed, reaching out a slender hand to clasp the other's. "Been awhile since you've graced us with your presence. How did your search for the map go?"

"We recovered it, of course," Dual replied offhandedly, toying with his dagger, "and I was hoping I could pay you a small sum of the treasures to carry out a favor for me."

Shade smiled eerily. "For an ally, a small sum is all I'd require. What information do you seek?"

"Something simple really," he replied, leaning forward. "I need for you to search Dominick Westbrooke's thoughts for the location of a certain woman's residence. You see, due to the dreamphasing bond we all share, I was able to meet this woman in the dream-state the same as everyone else the other night, when he used the bond to draw his friends together. But unfortunately, in order to find her myself, I need to know exactly where she resides."

"I see," agreed Shade, with a nod. "Give me the woman's name, and I'll get the information before nightfall."

"Her name is Julianna Sherborne, and she's currently Dominick's betrothed. Is this enough to go on?"

"I would imagine so, since his thoughts must be with her often." Leaning back in his chair, he smiled thoughtfully. "So tell me, what do you have planned for this woman when you find her, as if I need to ask?"

Dual laughed slightly. "Very astute. Tonight, I have a plan to separate them, since a threesome is out of the question. After that, I intend to use this Julianna to prove to that idiot Westbrooke once and for all just what I'll do in reality if he keeps meddling in my affairs. I imagine afterwards, he'll steer clear of me for her sake... if, of course, he still wants her after I'm through with her." Taking a deep draught of ale, he slammed it to the table. "It's about time he feels the same pain of love shattered with the woman ***he's*** betrothed to."

Shade's eyes glittered, remembering the incident with Dual's late fiancée Caralei well. Nothing could fuel an assassin's wrath more than to lose what was most important to him, and Dual's dark future was solidified that evening.

"Ah, yes," Shade said knowingly through a short laugh, raising his drinking glass. "To the sweet taste of revenge."

"Something my former, trusted ***friend*** earned years ago," hissed Dual, staring ahead blankly while taking another long drink. Shade stared at him coolly, keeping his glass where it was until Dual finally noticed. "To ***revenge***," he agreed, lifting his own glass to clink against the other man's with finality.

*****

"Since when have you become a murderer?" barked a sharp voice, causing Dominick to whirl about in shocked surprise. "Dragons got your tongue, son, or would you care to answer me?"

"Dad... Mother... what are you doing here?" he asked.

The man known as Discord turned to his wife with a slight sneer. "He's been living with Riff too long obviously, since he can't seem to answer a question without silence or another question."

His wife Warp seemed to agree, casting a worried smile at their son. Some argued that she didn't look old enough to be Dominick's mother, since her fair hair was still gold with no hints of gray, and her striking deep blue eyes—similar to her son's—were still warm and youthful as ever.

Her light appearance was almost a total contrast to her husband's dark hair and features—which both their sons possessed—and his often grim expression that followed him everywhere. Discord bore no gray hairs yet either, the trace of a five-o'clock shadow grazing his chin, but since the mystical magic aura surrounding Chavernos aged all people somewhat slower than planets like Earth, this wasn't too surprising. His brown eyes fairly blazed as they gazed upon his youngest son now, and his eyebrows tightened.

"Chaos informed us that you've gotten yourself into another of your famous predicaments, and insisted we get the information from you," continued Discord. "I thought given your age, he must be exaggerating, but apparently if your words bear any truth regarding talk of murdering someone, it would seem he was absolutely right."

"I was speaking hypothetically, and I have no intention of killing anyone," Dominick replied finally, his eyes slowly narrowing. "But I'm sure I'm not the only one to hold the opinion that Chavernos wouldn't regard Dual Arrovill's death as a great loss."

His father sighed knowingly, as Dominick's enmity with Dual had gone on for many years. Not to mention, he'd heard plenty of stories regarding the assassin's other dark dealings as well. In this, he could understand his son's vehemence. "Fair enough," he agreed, resting one hand on his shoulder. "But the last place I want you is rotting away in some prison for the better years of your life. Now, you mentioned some woman before, which I can only assume is part of this new anger towards Dual. Care to explain?"

It took less than ten minutes for Dominick to apprise his parents of the situation.

And less than ten seconds for Discord's explosive response.

"Another dream-state woman?" he growled. "No, don't stop me. I want to make sure I'm hearing this right. You intend to ***marry*** a woman who exists millions of miles away on Earth?" Not letting Dominick reply, he continued, "How many times have I told you and Riff to stop abusing your powers this way... a million at least? Yet you just ***wouldn't*** listen, so now this impossible situation is the result!"

Warp touched his shoulder gently. "Dear, don't you think..."

He flashed an angry stare upon her. "Don't you ***dare*** tell me you're going to condone our son's recklessness in this supposed engagement of his!"

Not one to cower, and certainly not to her husband,

Warp set her chin to return his expression twofold. "Now see here, Discord," she said coldly, "Dominick is my son as well, and just because he doesn't have the ultimate role models for a father and grandfather doesn't mean I'm going to hold that against him now. Now pipe down and keep that angry lid on your head for five seconds!"

Folding his arms with another grumble, he turned away from both, and especially his wife's icy stare. Warp was never an easy woman to facedown when angry.

Softening her expression towards Dominick, she smiled slightly. "I agree with your father that I've never been too happy with what you've used your powers for in the dream-state either, but despite this, I hoped you might find a woman to love. Even if you met her in a dream, I assumed you'd then seek her out on Chavernos in reality. I suppose after all these years, I never gave much consideration to the notion that you might find her on Earth."

"The possibility wouldn't have seemed real to me once either," agreed Dominick. "But despite our challenging beginning, I can safely say that I love Julianna more than life itself, and I'd go through the demonworld and back to be with her always. I'm sure she means as much to me as Dad does to you."

Warp cast a quizzical eye at her husband, whose responding gaze challenged her to voice a sarcastic reply. Instead, she smiled understandingly. "Yes, then I imagine this love you feel is strong. And since even Chaos approves of her, I'm sure she's more than worthy." Gesturing her open hands toward him, she continued, "Now, how can we help?"

"Chaos seems to think that the dragon sorcerer Lendric might be able to bring us together. I need to get in touch with him immediately, if he can be reached."

"Lendric?" Discord jumped in. "Oh, Chavernos... Son, something tells me you might be better off remaining engaged to this Julianna across a distance, lest you accidentally end up in the real Limbo..." Warp's meaningful jab to his stomach winded him into silence. "Ever the violent type," he said with a grimace.

"Only when called for," she replied sweetly, turning back to Dominick. "That isn't a difficult request. I can use my powers to send us to his residence."

"That must have been Chaos's assumption," Dominick said through a smile. "I'm glad I can count on him now."

"Was there ever any doubt?" asked Discord. His son cleverly avoided mentioning the incident of the other night, not wanting to start further trouble, merely shaking his head once without answering. "I just hope Lendric can be counted on. After all, despite his best intentions, his magic doesn't always do what it's supposed to. I'll never forget the time he opened the annual Barokka Festival many years ago, planning on conjuring up rainbows in the background. Instead, he only delivered the rain part... complete with thunder, and lightning, and high winds, ***and*** a hurricane..."

"And stop calling for trouble!" snapped Warp.

"Hmmm... if I recall, Trouble's on your side of the family," he laughed, turning towards the sky innocently.

Unfortunately true, she thought sullenly, struggling to stick to the issue at hand. "You realize of course that my powers are limited, and I can only teleport us as far as the cavern's entrance to Lendric's domicile. To actually get to him, we'll have to ascend the pathway through the cave, dealing with whatever bars our way to the inner door."

"I understand," Dominick replied with determination. "If it comes down to fighting whatever creatures are in there, I'm willing to take them on alone."

"No," whispered Warp, shaking her head, resting her hand on his shoulder. "This time, you won't be alone." Giving him a quick smile, she added evenly, "Your father's going with you."

"***What?***" exclaimed Discord.

Warp gave a short laugh, before turning to him. "I'm just kidding, dear. You're not obligated to see Lendric as well. But as for me, I will go too, since I wish to see our son safely to his destination."

"The creatures in that place can't be ***that*** bad," he mumbled in reply.

"Why, Discord, do you mean to say you'd consider..."

"Oh, hell, stop making a fuss about it, and get us to outer Chavernos! At least Lendric might be able to stifle our son's headstrong nature and your sharp tongue for a while."

Clasping his mother's hand, as she likewise took hold of Discord's, Dominick whispered in her ear, "Thanks, Mom."

She merely squeezed his hand with a smile, as glittering lights surrounded them, moments before she sent them on their way.

*****

"Now then, Miss Sherborne," began Roger, lifting his menu, "the sky's the limit today. What would you like for lunch?"

Having said little while he'd driven them to this restaurant, Julianna glared at him now. He had an inflated ego if he believed an expensive meal would erase the anger she felt at his placing her job in jeopardy, let alone the past humiliations he'd subjected her to.

"I'm not hungry," she snapped, folding her arms and turning away. Less than an hour and she'd be free to return to the comfort of her desk.

"A pity," he sighed, clicking his tongue. "Almira will not be pleased, Miss Sherborne."

"Knock it off with the phony business act, Roger!" she exclaimed. "You had no right to interfere with my job today, so back off in the future."

Roger sighed once, resting his head on one arm as he

glanced at the menu. "You wouldn't meet with me otherwise, Julie. I felt I had little choice."

"You brought that on yourself," she said, pulling her chair back to stand. Roger grabbed her arm before she could do so, his eyes boring into hers.

"You know, you always were stubborn, even when we were teenagers," he said, shaking his head. "Whenever we had the slightest argument where you felt you were in the right, you made it practically impossible for me to get back in your life. Like that time when you put me on ice after hearing a rumor I'd kissed another girl during study hall."

Julianna shrugged once. "Why not? It was true."

"No it wasn't," he protested. "Which is exactly what I'm talking about. Even now, you're still holding grudges for ancient arguments that weren't even justified!"

"Justified?" she hissed. "Was it justified when I caught you with your precious Marilyn, and then she moved in with you afterwards? No, Roger. Maybe I made some errors in judgment when younger, but that's not why I don't want to see you now. It's your recent deceptions that locked you out of my life."

"I see," he said icily. "And are you saying you're so perfect, you've never made a mistake you wished to change?"

She sighed, feeling very much as she had around Chaos. "No, I'm not," she replied. "But that doesn't mean I should be subjected to forced meetings with you, when I happen to be seeing someone else. So why don't we forget all this, go back to the office, and…"

"Just a second!" he growled, his eyes dark. "Backtrack to this mention of someone else. Who is he?"

Julianna bit her lip. She hadn't meant for that to come out the way it did, since she had no proof to back up Dominick's existence. Still... maybe she could tell him part of the truth. It might get him to stop bothering her.

"I met him a few months ago, and we've been seeing

each other for a while now. His name is Dominick."

"Dominick... Dominick what?"

"Westbrooke," she supplied hesitantly. "Now do you see why I've been reluctant to get together with you again?"

"Hold it," he interrupted, raising one hand to silence her. "Westbrooke. That name doesn't ring a bell. Is he from this neighborhood?"

"Not exactly," Julianna said carefully. "Look, Roger, I don't see how this is any business of yours."

"If it concerns you, it is."

Great, she thought. *As if I want your concern anymore.* Spying a flash of movement, her eyes widened upon seeing Marybeth standing several feet away. Answering the silent question in her eyes, her friend gestured towards the back, earning a nod from Julianna before she disappeared.

"I find it very coincidental that you mention this new guy all of a sudden, when until today, you've made no mention of him," Roger told her. Wary of his new hostility, Julianna slowly began pushing her chair back again. "Where are you going now?" he demanded.

"To the ladies' room," she said through a forced smile. "Do I have his majesty's permission?"

Growling once more, he waved his hand in a dismissive gesture. "We'll continue this discussion when you get back," he decided.

*Sure... in your **dreams***, she thought, as she strode to the back. Shutting the bathroom door behind her, Julianna turned to Marybeth thankfully.

"I'm certainly glad you're here," she sighed. "Roger's beginning to get on my nerves with his third-degree questions. How did you find us here?"

"It wasn't difficult, since Almira began ranting about your leaving with her prospective client." She grinned slowly. "Or should I say, prospective male companion." Even Julianna couldn't withhold a smile at the thoughts conjured up by that again. "As soon as I overheard the name of the restaurant, I raced here on my lunch break to get you away from that egotistical excuse for a man."

"It's appreciated, but what about Almira? She won't like it if I stand up a business client."

"Roger's business has nothing do with ***actual*** business, and if Almira needs an excuse, just say you were food poisoned and had to leave without paying your respects."

"Food poisoned?" laughed Julianna. "I haven't even eaten yet."

"Then just tell her you started to feel sick."

"Well... Roger does tend to inspire that in me these days." She smiled conspiratorially. "All right, I'm convinced. Let's go."

Fortunately, at the time the pair decided to sneak out, Roger was busy discussing his order with the waiter, allowing them to escape his notice. When a more than reasonable time passed though, he suspiciously called the waiter back again.

"I was dining with a red-haired woman in a velour top, about five-foot-five, with a beige handbag." The waiter nodded in recognition. "Good, you remember. Did you happen to see where she went?"

He shook his head, just before another waiter walked up to the table. "I believe she and another woman left a short while ago, sir."

"Damn!" shouted Roger, slamming his hand against the table, causing several others to stare his way.

He ignored them, rubbing his chin angrily. With Julianna, he should have expected something like this, but she was living in a dreamworld if she believed he was simply going to accept her brush-off. No, right now he had only one goal on his mind. To find out just who this Dominick Westbrooke was, and to see just what competition he was dealing with.

Chapter Fourteen

"It's been months since I've wielded one of these," murmured Dominick, holding up the sword he held. The silver blade gleamed against the sunlight, its gold hilt carved with the runes of dreamphasers. A fitting gift for his eighteenth birthday from his father.

It had been Discord who suggested they return to Barokka to pick up a few weapons, since many of the caverns of Chavernos were far from secure as life on the island was, some being deadly. Fortunately though, Lendric's home didn't sport any demons guarding the entrance.

At least none that they'd seen when last here.

"Let's just hope you won't need it," replied Warp.

Like many of the caverns, this one sported the rough outlines of a trail, occasionally sprouting other passageways to tempt unknowing individuals with what was hidden beyond, issuing its own surprises in the dark.

The sound of Discord's boot hitting a squishy substance alerted their attention instantly. "What the hell is this?" he exclaimed.

"Look out! Acidic slime!" shouted a voice.

Knowing the deadly substance well, the other pair jumped back instantly with a gasp and a scream, while Discord tore his boot off, swearing. Dominick quickly cast an illumination spell, but as light was cast upon the boot, all could see it was dampened only by an ordinary puddle of water and a smidgen of mud.

"Just kidding!" snickered the same voice, soon echoed by the laughter of several others. Moments later, a barrage of multi-colored lights flooded the tunnel, causing the trio of humans to duck, while the lights flew over their heads to escape outside, vanishing towards the horizon.

Growling at their mocking laughter, Discord shook his fist after them. "Damnable fairies, if I ever get my hands on you, I'll tear your blasted wings off!"

"And another useless human threat comes into play!" chuckled the initial fairy, floating by the entrance with folded arms. Although only about a foot high, the reddish-haired little man clearly wasn't intimidated, grinning with amusement. "Been a long time, hasn't it, Discord?"

"Xavier!" Discord hissed.

"Ah, ye remember me. I'm touched."

"I'll do better than that, breaking every bone in your miserable hide, you pint-sized pixie!" he snarled, making a grab for him, though missing by inches.

The mischievous fairy laughed again. "Sorry, but I have better plans for the day. Maybe some other time… if ye can catch me."

Discord made a second lunge for him, but the fairy disappeared from his hands, fairy dust springing up in his wake. As the frustrated man sneezed several times, Xavier's echoing voice called out, "Better luck next time." His laughter trailed after him.

Sensing Dominick and Warp's amusement behind him, Discord whipped about to face them, but their smiles faded into nonchalant seriousness.

"Not one word," he warned quietly, glaring at them once before storming down the corridor, threatening dire vengeance against the tiny pranksters.

When he was out of hearing distance, both his wife and son muffled their pent-up laughter before following him.

*****

Dominick kept up an illumination spell to aid them

through the darkness.

With only minor creatures found within the caverns, which skittered away from them harmlessly, it was only the uphill incline of the long path that was tiring. When they finally reached the entrance to Lendric's home, there were no lanterns, but there was a wooden door which had a luminous glow.

"It's about bloody time," said Discord, breathing hard as he reached towards it. Sparks flew from his hand as he pulled it back with a yell. "Blazes, that thing's made of fire!"

A musical, condescending laugh echoed about them. "What did you expect of a dragon's domain? A snow-laden entrance?" mocked the same voice, just before a tall fair-haired man in dark blue robes materialized. Before any could speak, he continued more seriously, "Do you have an appointment with the great dragon sorcerer?"

Discord's eyes narrowed. "Great dragon sorcerer, hell! You tell Lendric, this is Discord Westbrooke, and I've brought my wife and son to meet with him."

"I'll let him know, and he'll get back to you by the end of the week."

"By the end of the ***week***?" snarled Discord, his face reddening as he took a threatening step towards the somewhat lanky man who then wobbled back slightly. Obviously due to the rough footing of the cavern, the man would have insisted.

Glaring at Discord, he snapped, "You can attempt to beat my brains in, Mr. Macho, but don't think you'll break this door quite so easily! Only the right spell can open it."

"Then you'd better use it ***now***, or by Chaos, I'll..."

Warp's gentle touch on his shoulder drew his attention slowly. "Dear," she whispered, "there are other ways to handle situations like this. Observe." Flashing a sweet smile to the man, she gave a brief laugh. "You'll have to pardon my husband," she said aloud, leaning forward slightly. "Terrible temper when he's angry, I'm afraid."

"Yes," said the man, casting a wary eye at Discord. "I can see that. But I have my orders, and the great dragon sorcerer doesn't speak to just any riff-raff."

"It's a good thing my brother stayed home then," Dominick laughed quietly, his pun lost on the bemused man.

"Fortunately," continued Warp, recapturing his attention, "I happen to be a bit more reasonable. If you won't open the door for us, then I'll simply have to use another method. But don't worry, I'll put in a good word for you as a security guard." Waving once, she vanished in a flash of lights.

"What?" sputtered the man. "B-but she can't do that!"

"Too late," Discord replied with a deep laugh, folding his arms. "Now that you have a spare moment, you might want to brush up your job resumé."

"Or you might open the door, so we can find my mother before Lendric does," suggested Dominick.

His blue eyes narrowing with irritated defeat, the man finally clenched his fists and growled. "Oh, very well! But he's not going to like being disturbed by your little troop!"

Waving his hand at the door, the man recited an incantation that caused the glow to fade. Pushing the heavy door open, the man strode inside, glancing about for the missing Warp.

"All right, Mrs. Westbrooke, you've had your little game of hide-and-seek!" he snarled. "Come out right now, you deceitful demoness or I'll..."

"You'll keep a civil tongue in your head," came a deeper voice, just before a curtain parted several feet away. "Please excuse him, my lady. He may spout venom like a viper, but he does have his good points." Warp reappeared, the arm of a blond-haired elf around her shoulders.

Smiling amiably as his emerald eyes twinkled, the dragon sorcerer known as Lendric led his companion back to the awaiting pair. Though even older than Discord and Warp, he didn't look it due to being a dragon, instead seeming to be a man in his prime. Upon reaching maturity, all dragons aged too slowly to be noticed for countless years, making five hundred years seem like five.

Dressed in a leather outfit considered a favorite among the elves, a forest green cape flowing behind him, one would hardly guess by his slender frame that a dragon's heart beat within.

Magic—even on a world filled with it—was still wondrous to behold when capable of transforming a majestic dragon into a human or an elf. They could transform into other forms just as easily, but those were the norm.

Discord stepped forward instantly, his expression grim. "I suppose we should be honored that his royal imperial majesty has a few moments to spare for the meek and humble," he murmured, with a feigned bow.

The gateway man jabbed his shoulder. "Show respect for his greatness, beast!"

Discord's eyes flashed warningly, just before he reached forward to pick the man up with one hand, his grip tightening about the man's throat.

"***Beast***, you were saying?" he hissed, his dark eyes beginning to swirl with the magic he was named for.

The man stared down at him with bulging eyes, only able to get out a soft rasp. Lendric sighed wearily. Discord's temper was well-known, often exceeding that of Chaos, and since he had the strength to match it, he was formidable when pushed too far.

"Now really, Discord," he interjected. "I don't take kindly to guests choking my assistants, so kindly release Normrynth." At his initial reluctance, Lendric's eyes flared red, and his voice deepened even more. "***Now***, my friend," he said with deceptive quiet.

Glaring once more at the assistant, Discord casually

relaxed his hand.

Normrynth dropped to the floor with a loud, "Ooof!" He then sat up with a murderous expression. "Next time, Westbrooke, I'll drop you like a pebble from the top of Chavernos's highest mountain!"

"In your case, that shouldn't be much of a threat," growled Discord, earning an angry mutter from him as he left the room. Folding his arms, he turned to face Lendric. "We meet again, o' dragon of ages."

"Yes," he replied with a smirk. "Glad to see you too, o' discordant son of my old friend. How is Chaos these days?"

"Chaotic as usual," drawled Discord. "You know, you really should put some lighting in this place. That outer tunnel is so dark, you'd have to be an elf with infra-red vision to manage without it."

"What would you have me do? Put up rows of lanterns for the 'tourists'?" he asked sarcastically. "Besides, that's what torches are for, and in my elven form I do have the required vision anyway."

Knowing better than to match wits with Lendric, Discord gestured to his side. "I take it you've become reacquainted with my wife Warp."

"And bewitched by her as ever," agreed Lendric, kissing her hand gently. At her uncharacteristic blush, Discord stepped forward to pull her back, clasping her hand meaningfully to entwine her fingers with his own. The silent gesture spoke volumes. Smiling slightly, the dragon elf shook his head knowingly. "The Westbrooke men are ever possessive about their women, are they not?"

"That's why they're ever in demand by the ladies," agreed Warp, squeezing her husband's hand reassuringly.

"Which brings us to the reason we're here," continued Discord. "But perhaps our son should be the one to explain this, since it involves him."

Lendric turned to the younger man, his smile becoming surprise as he appraised him. "Well I'll be a son of a wyvern, if it isn't... wait, don't tell me..." He rubbed his head thoughtfully while mentally searching for the name. Before anyone could interrupt, he brightened. "Ah, I remember. Demonic, right?"

A short laugh escaped Discord. "More usually his brother, but at times I'd agree with that," he murmured, just before Warp nudged him into silence.

"It's ***Dominick***," she corrected, glaring at her husband. "Our son's ***true*** name, despite Discord's efforts to make it seem otherwise.

Needing to cast his irritation somewhere, since her catlike grin was only making things worse, he turned to their son. "I still don't understand why you prefer that ordinary appellation your mother insisted on naming you," growled Discord. "Phaser holds more status to your ability."

"That's just it," argued Dominick. "I never wanted to be looked at solely for that. Besides, it's not my fault that Grandfather decided ***your*** real name should be..."

Discord swiftly covered his son's mouth before he could utter a syllable of the mysterious name. Some things he didn't need blabbed to the entire world, or in this case, Lendric.

"I get the idea," chuckled the dragon elf, smiling. "I'm sorry to have forgotten momentarily, Dominick, but it has been quite awhile since our last meeting. I still remember you as a boy when I was much taller than you, but now we stand as equals."

"Time changes all of us except you, Lendric," replied Dominick, his eyes twinkling as he shook his hand. "One of these days, you've got to show us where you hide your fountain of youth."

"Ah... all internal, dear boy. Can't be marketed." He winked conspiratorially. "But if you ever find a way around that, let me in on it. We'd make a fortune!"

"I'm sure we would," he agreed.

"A pleasant thought. But introductions aside, why don't we get down to business?" Gesturing towards a group of chairs, Lendric waited until they were all seated before continuing amiably. "So, what grand trouble brings you here, Dominick? The need for another potion to send Riff croaking?"

Dominick grinned, albeit a bit sheepishly when his parents turned to him questioningly. They'd never known about ***that*** incident! When he'd been twelve years old, a whopper of a fight with his brother had prompted him to venture forth to locate Lendric in the dream-state, asking the dragon sorcerer if he'd grant him a potion to turn his scheming older brother into a frog.

Lendric had been highly amused by the boy's request, but told him that he obviously couldn't just go turning ***anyone*** into frogs! Seeing his point, Dominick came up with an alternate... more ***subtle*** means to get even with his brother.

Placing a minor spell of illusion, which Lendric taught him, upon the fifteen-year-old Riff—who had lately become quite favored by female attention—he suddenly developed a slight crimp in his style. For the next time he tried to kiss one of his many girlfriends good night, the spell caused her to see herself kissing a frog. Riff nearly jumped five feet at the girl's scream, afterwards scratching her name out of his 'little black book'.

It was only after the same thing happened with several other girls that Riff finally cloistered himself in his room and bemoaned his fate to become a monk for life.

Unfortunately, overhearing this was Dominick's downfall.

Since he began rolling on the floor with laughter outside his brother's door, Riff put the pieces together and deduced that he had something to do with his sudden trouble with women. To find out for certain, he met his brother in the dream-state under another guise to trick the information out of him. After discovering the truth, he turned into a hideous beast and frightened the younger boy into waking up screaming.

From that day on, the pranks continued nonstop, some of them quite serious when they were older, such as with Riff's seducing Dominick's girlfriends behind his back, or in front of him. Followed by Dominick's spreading rumors to Riff's girlfriends about various illnesses and diseases he'd contracted.

In other words, it was war.

A constant war that Lendric occasionally tuned in on for amusement!

"Ah... no frog potions today," Dominick replied quickly, distracting his parents before they asked questions. Certain things were better left unsaid! "What I need now is a very powerful spell of teleportation."

Lendric's eyebrows raised in amazement. "A realm of teleportation beyond your mother's remarkable ability?" he queried. "I find that hard to believe."

"It involves teleportation to another planet."

The dragon elf clicked his tongue with a chuckle. "Now, Dominick... I'm sure your brother may seem to deserve banishment to Mars on occasion, but to actually teleport him there for good..."

"This has nothing to do with Riff," Dominick interrupted, a slow smirk forming. "Although I may note your suggestion for future reference. But seriously, I was thinking more along the lines of traveling to another world to be united with the woman I wish to marry."

Lendric's wide grin nearly rivaled that of his dragon form. "And I thought I'd seen everything in all my years as a dragon," he laughed, patting Dominick's shoulder companionably. "Congratulations, dear boy! What's the lucky girl's name?"

"Julianna. The problem is..."

The dragon laughed again. "It's about time you decided

to settle down and give that grandfather of yours a few great-grandkids. Now maybe he'll stop pestering me over it."

"He probably will, but first..."

"I'm sure you'll be very happy together. So tell me, when's the wedding? I wouldn't miss it for the universe." Seeing the younger man murmur in frustration, he stopped instantly. "You were saying something?"

"What I was saying was, the sentiment is appreciated," replied Dominick, "but you're missing the point. Julianna lives on another planet in the solar system, and I've only been able to spend time with her while in my astral form in the dream-state. So while we both love each other and want to get married, we can't in reality until we can be brought together on the same world."

"Hmmm... that would present a bit of a problem, wouldn't it?" murmured Lendric. "She's not from Mars, is she?" Dominick shook his head. "I'm glad to hear it. I doubt your grandfather would approve of you living there for the rest of your life. So, where is this girl from then?"

"The planet on the other side of the sun... Earth."

"Earth?" exclaimed Lendric, brightening slightly.

Dominick's eyes narrowed curiously. "You sound as if you know something of it."

"I should say so," he agreed. "I've been there."

Nothing could have pleased the younger man more, feeling as if he'd just been granted the key to the solar system, his thankful smile illuminating the room. "By Chaos, Lendric, you're a wonder. This means the problem's solved, and Julianna and I can have a future together in reality."

"Well… not exactly."

Dominick's enthusiasm died instantly. "Not exactly?" he murmured. "I don't understand. You just said you've been to Earth."

"In the past, yes I have," Lendric said uneasily, "but as of three months ago, this mode of teleportation has disappeared." Seeing the expected confusion on the younger man's face, he patted his shoulder once. "Half a moment, and I'll explain. You see, my brothers..." Abruptly, Normrynth ran in, immediately tugging at his shoulder.

"Your pardon, Master Lendric, but someone else..."

"Wyvern's wings, man, can't you see I'm busy?" he growled. "Tell whoever it is to come back later! As it is, this place is becoming more crowded than a medical waiting room."

"Yes, but she's being most stubborn."

Lendric blinked at that. ***"She?"***

In answer, a voice shouted out, "Lendric, you gold-scaled demon!" Leaning back, the dragon elf sighed wearily, just before a beautiful woman with bright red hair strode into the room. "Will you kindly tell this upstart of an apprentice just who I am, before I'm given cause to do so ***my*** way?"

Lendric gestured towards her. "Normrynth, this is my sister Carilya I once mentioned. Kindly don't bar her entrance the next time."

Normrynth blanched, stuttering nervously. "Oh, my word, I didn't know..."

"You do now, you arrogant toothpick!" snarled Carilya, hands on hips, rounding on her brother. "Lendric, I sent you word that I'd be arriving. Didn't you get my letter?"

"Yes, I got it," sighed Lendric. "Is ***he*** with you?"

Carilya's face turned as red as her hair. "His name is Devon, and you ***will*** treat him with respect." As her brother nodded once, she turned about. "Sweetheart, I told you he'd see us. Come and meet him."

A tall dark-haired man walked in, granting a respectful nod to Lendric. All the while, his eyes remained wary. "I presume you're my wife's brother?"

Lendric managed a crooked smile. "And I presume, you're my sister's ***human*** mate, Devon Williams."

"Aye," he declared. "As human as she's a dragon, but bearing her no less love than any man."

"So you say," he replied. "I would assume she's told you of the potential consequences to this marriage if you ever have any offspring." Devon remained silent. "They'll all be part dragon as she is: strong, resistant to the elements, and long-lived past you by countless years."

"Indeed," agreed Devon. "As they'll all be part human as well."

Eyes narrowing, Lendric added, "Due to that factor, you may end up condemning one or more to bear the onus of the violet eyes, attracting them dark enemies from birth!"

"Carilya told me of this," he replied. "But since I've had to survive by my wits since being orphaned at the age of ten, I think I'm more than capable of protecting any children we may have."

Lendric laughed without humor. "Clever fool!" he sneered. "Think your frail human skin will protect you against the demons and dragons of the night that would run you through or set you aflame in a heartbeat?"

"She's told me that children of the violet eyes develop a great power in time. That shall aid them protection."

"Carilya left out one point then. Those powers never develop before they reach maturity, and generally not until they reach the age of twenty-five." Devon's cheek twitched, but he remained silent. "In any event, it would seem I have no choice but to accept what is already true. Therefore, you are welcomed by our family. I just pray for both your sakes, and your possible future children, that no tragedy will result from this."

Smiling proudly, Devon stepped forward to shake the dragon elf's hand. "You have my word, I'll protect my family with my life."

Lendric's eyes remained somber. "Pray you never need to test that, Devon Williams."

Clapping her hands once, Carilya brightened. “Well, I’m glad that’s settled. Now, would you mind introducing your other guests?”

*****

“Now, back to the situation at hand,” Lendric sighed shortly afterwards, turning back to the awaiting Westbrooke trio. “It’s rather interesting you should mention the need to travel to Earth, Dominick. Only a few years ago, I went there myself, and I was planning to again in the near future.”

“You visit Earth regularly?”

“Well, from time to time,” said Lendric, spreading his hands. “It’s an unpredictable universe, and sometimes there are necessary reasons for doing the unusual.”

Discord coughed loudly, folding his arms while glaring at his son. “Yes, I believe Dominick and his brother are no strangers to the unusual so to speak. Especially this one. Falling in love with a woman from another world.”

His wife touched his arm gently to silence him. “You mentioned a method of teleportation earlier. What was it?”

Lendric nodded once, waving a hand in the air to cause a misty vision to appear. As the vision grew clearer, he gestured towards it. “This is the legendary Myzalik Teleportation Staff, and the device you require.” From the vision, it looked like an ordinary dark brown wooden staff, with the exception of a crystal orb—the size of a golf ball—positioned at the top, which emitted a glow of rainbow colors.

“It is to the best of my knowledge, the only teleportation device which survived the Mage War intact, and only a select few—yourselves included—know of its existence. Not something I would want known to the masses, so please keep it within your own family.” They all nodded.

“It was named for its creator, the human sorcerer Astorian Myzalik. He was a long-time ally of the late Magus Clan, who as you may know, discovered the means of teleportation to Earth."

"Yes," Dominick agreed somberly. "Chaos reviewed their history with me." At his parents' confused looks, he smiled. "I'll explain later. Lendric, please continue."

The dragon sorcerer nodded. "Astorian was old but survived the Mage War. Sometime before his death years later, he passed it on to his only son Cyrus, who was also a sorcerer, and who underwent a transformation to become a half-dragon to match the years of his dragon wife Melanthe." He smiled slightly. "Cyrus and Melanthe are my parents, and they passed the Staff on to me."

The younger man looked shocked. "Did they die too?"

Lendric laughed, shaking his head. "No, dear boy, they're very much alive and well. But my father knew of my curiosity for other worlds and decided I would appreciate it more, as well as be responsible with it."

Sighing heavily, he abruptly shook his head. "But I'm getting ahead of myself. The Myzalik Staff is undoubtedly one of the most powerful items on Chavernos due to its seemingly limitless range of operation."

"Can the Staff send more than one person there and back?" asked Dominick. Lendric nodded slowly, sparking a suspicion. "You mentioned your brothers earlier. Do they have it now?"

The dragon elf smiled. "Insightful as ever," he replied. "Which brings us to what happened several months ago. My elder brother Zaruldar, and my younger brother Pyrozill, wished to borrow it for the span of a few weeks. While I would be more hesitant to loan it to Pyro alone, with his often juvenile attitude despite his age, I presumed that Zaruldar's wise counsel would be sufficient to accompany him."

Carilya clicked her tongue as she reentered the room with her husband. "Apparently, you were wrong," she replied. "You should have known better with Pyro. By now, he's obviously gotten them lost elsewhere in the galaxy."

"Or worse still, the universe," sighed Lendric, rubbing his forehead. "When it had only been a month, at first I thought they'd simply gotten sidetracked. But even Zaruldar wouldn't disappear for longer than that. They were due back nearly three months ago, and there's been no word from either since."

"But surely there's some way to contact them," pressed Dominick. "A spell of communication?"

"It's been attempted, with no success. Even skilled dreamphasers were unable to find them. Seeing no other choice, I contacted some demons I know and sent them after my brothers a month ago, in the hope of locating and bringing them back."

"You sent ***demons*** after them?" asked Discord. "Aren't you concerned they might steal the Staff for themselves if they do find them?"

"This pair won't, since they already owe me for several debts, let alone I'm taking care of their infant son in the meantime."

Carilya's eyes widened. "You have a demon child ***here***? Do you have any idea what kind of trouble they cause?"

As if in answer, a loud wail erupted, followed by what sounded like a small explosion. Lendric glared at his sister. "Dammit, Carilya, you ***know*** that even from infancy, they're highly intelligent and temperamental when offended. Thank you for indirectly destroying my back room!"

Another explosion emphasized this.

Not wanting to deal with another tongue-lashing from her brother, Carilya went to see to the infant, along with Devon, both hoping the damage wasn't as bad as it sounded.

"As I was saying," continued Lendric, rolling his eyes at an angry screech from his sister, "those demons are my most reliable sources, as well as friends of my brothers, and they're equally concerned by their disappearance. If anyone can locate

Zaruldar and Pyrozill, they can. In which case, if the Staff is brought back safely as well, I can surely bring you and your Julianna together in reality. But until then, there's not much I can do to help you."

Dominick leaned forward in his chair, clasping his hands. "Then I suppose that'll have to be enough, unless an alternate means can be found," he sighed. "I only wish I'd met Julianna six months ago, when the means was still a certainty."

Lendric rested one hand against his shoulder. "Time and space cannot bar the path of destiny, Dominick," he said quietly. "If you and Julianna are truly meant to be together, a way will be found. And I swear I'll contact you as soon as I have more information."

The younger man glanced up at him with a somber nod, oblivious to when his parents stood. "We'd best get you back to the island now, sweetheart," Warp interceded. "Night falls quickly at this time of year, and I'd hate to push our luck with the creatures of this area."

Seeing their son's hesitancy to speak, Discord patted his back once. "Hey," he murmured, earning Dominick's attention. "It's not like all hope's been snatched forever here. The Teleportation Staff's still a viable possibility. It just may take some time to locate it and its two bearers, that's all. Look at the bright side. At least Chaos won't force you to wed Sionne in the meantime."

As if he could, Dominick thought, nodding silently with a grim smile.

"It's just as well," Warp added curtly. "There's something about that girl's nature that seems to be more of an illusion than that ability of hers. I'm sure your Julianna will be a much more suitable marriage partner."

"I doubt the boy would be putting himself through this ordeal if he thought otherwise," retorted Discord.

"Hmph!" sneered Warp. "He should only know the

ordeal I went through getting you to the altar, with us being on the ***same*** world."

As she swept past her husband, Discord gestured towards Lendric with a forced smile. "If you'll excuse me while I straighten out my wife's obviously confused memory on the subject, I'll wait with her by the exit."

Dominick stood quickly. "Actually, Dad, would you and Mom give me another few minutes with Lendric. I have something else I need to speak with him about, and it shouldn't take long."

"By all means," Discord replied. Smiling meaningfully for his benefit, he added, "And no need to rush, son."

Glancing after the departing couple, Lendric laughed quietly. "Some things never change," he remarked.

"Maybe not," agreed Dominick. "But there may be one other way you could help my situation with Julianna." Lendric nodded for him to continue. "Is there any way to prove to her beyond a doubt the truth of our existence and Chavernos?"

The dragon sorcerer rubbed his chin thoughtfully. "Hmmm, you don't ask easy requests, do you?"

"It would mean a great deal to me if she was granted the truth, so she needn't doubt the legitimacy of what we have." Sighing once, he stared at the ceiling. "I thought of two solutions myself, but even they can only prove so much."

"Which are?"

"The first is that I can appear to her in my astral form while she's completely awake," explained Dominick, "but it would still be difficult for her to see me then, and she might think it to be a hallucination.

"The second method involves her eldest sister Crystal. From what Julianna says, she seems fairly open-minded, so I've considered the notion of visiting her in the dream-state to try and convince her of the truth."

"Which might only result in having Crystal believe she's

conjured up images of you from Julianna's stories, proving little."

"Exactly," exclaimed Dominick, "but what else can I do? As things stand, I know part of Julianna wonders if ***any*** of this is real at all."

Lendric was silent for long moments before replying. "There may be one other way," he replied softly, "but if I tell it to you, you must swear it will never be revealed to anyone else on Chavernos, with the exception of Chaos. Since he's the one who sent you here, it's only fitting that you can share this information with him, and my old friend does well in keeping things confidential when needed, as do I."

"All right... go ahead."

"This is ***most*** serious," hissed the dragon, his eyes glowing red. "And I must ***insist*** you swear silence of it!"

Sobering completely, Dominick met his gaze. "On my honor, you have my word, I swear I'll tell no one on Chavernos besides Chaos," he replied.

His eyes returning to their normal shade, Lendric clasped Dominick's shoulder. "Please forgive my apparent harshness. It involves a boy I brought to Earth years ago, along with his parents."

Dominick's eyes widened. "Others from our world reside there?" he asked incredulously.

"A few, yes, but in secret, for reasons I'll explain." Steepling his hands, his expression became concerned. "The boy I speak of is a half-dragon, as my sister Carilya's children will be, and he bears the trait of the violet eyes. As you heard from my conversation with Devon, you know what this means. He was sent to Earth, with his parents, to protect him from the forces of darkness on Chavernos who would kill him before he reaches adulthood—when he'll gain his full powers, whatever they may be."

Neither noticed Devon's presence as he overheard

Lendric's last words, nor saw the somber look on his face as he returned to his wife in the back room.

"While it's imperative their whereabouts be kept secret from those of our world, I see no reason you can't share this with your fiancée."

Understanding dawned instantly with Dominick. "So if Julianna locates his family, they can provide proof that Chavernos exists, since they're from our world."

Lendric nodded slowly. "There is but one thing you must stress to her. She must speak ***only*** with his parents, for he isn't meant to know his true identity until his time comes to return to Chavernos. For now, he believes he's from Earth and is completely human as anyone else. We mutually agreed from the start that it would allow him to grow up normally on Earth."

"I'm sure she'll comply with that," he agreed.

"Good. You can explain this to Julianna and her sister, but don't tell anyone else, and tell them the same as well. Only they have reason to know the truth of our world for now, including the family they'll meet." Dominick nodded.

Another wail from the demon child rang out, sparking a series of curses from the pair in the back room. Sighing once, Lendric commented with a smirk, "You know, if you showed your grandfather that demon child, he might think twice about his request for great-grandchildren from you."

"That won't be necessary," laughed Dominick. "When Julianna and I are married, we'll be happy to grant him several."

"Be sure to have them visit their Uncle Lendric when you do," replied the dragon sorcerer, eyes twinkling, before he continued. "Now, let me give you the full details of how your future wife can locate the family of Oliver Dragend."

*****

Dual stood grinning as he eyed the captive man before him. Bound to a chair and gagged, Alarius glared back at him, his expression fierce. Without a doubt, if he could have, he'd have torn his captor to pieces in a heartbeat.

Or at least tried, Dual thought with amusement.

"You really should have made things easier on yourself to begin with," he told the half-elf. "By now, Quell and our assistants have gathered most of the jewels, and should complete their work this night. Did you really think you'd manage to escape without my tracking you down?" Seeing that Alarius was unable to speak through the gag, he deftly remedied this. "Well, ***did*** you?" he demanded.

"I had no choice but to try," hissed Alarius. "As it is, when word of my disappearance spreads, there will be allies of my own who'll catch onto your handiwork. And when they do, they'll see you banished from Barokka forever."

"Maybe," chortled Dual. "But that won't help you or your precious family, since I'll most certainly kill you first." The half-elf wouldn't reply, turning away. "Oh, by the way, it might interest you to hear the latest regarding your traitorous friend. It seems he's presently engaged to be married." Alarius blinked once, genuinely surprised. "Yes, I'm sure I was equally stunned to hear a woman had actually agreed to spend the rest of her life with that fool."

"Better him than an assassin derelict from the swamps."

Dual grinned menacingly, slamming his fist into the half-elf's jaw. His blow drew blood, but not a sound from Alarius, who merely continued to face him icily. Raising a finger in warning, Dual hissed, "Remember, that derelict you speak of ***is*** a professional assassin many times over. And one who won't hesitate to cut out your tongue if you don't curb it."

"Undoubtedly a specialty of yours," spat Alarius, a slight trickle of blood stemming from his mouth.

His captor laughed harshly. "You have no idea what other 'specialties' I've conjured up over the years. But as to your friend's engagement, you might wish to hear what I have planned as a... wedding present." Alarius's eyes narrowed as he continued. "It's a tricky preparation, since his precious bride-to-be Julianna resides on the planet Earth, but my trusty associate Shade has kindly lent his assistance in finding her location. Thus, I can freely visit her in the dream-state this night."

"By Chavernos, Dual, leave her be! She's an innocent in this endless war of yours with Dominick."

"She's no longer an innocent since accepting him into her life, thus I can feel no remorse for what retribution must befall her."

Alarius smiled bitterly. "I doubt your former innocent betrothed Caralei would condone your logic."

Dual's fist plowed into the side of his head, nearly rendering him unconscious this time. "***Never*** speak her name upon your filthy tongue again!" he hissed. "It's because I was once a fool to trust people like you that she died!"

"She died because of the allies of the evil demon who sired you," Alarius replied quietly. "A demon whom you killed, which started a chain reaction..."

"Enough!" snarled Dual, lifting Alarius's chin with the sharp edge of his sword. "Understand this, half-elf, if anyone is to suffer due to a chain reaction, it will most certainly be your trusted ***friend*** this time. In fact, you're to be a major key to this whole affair."

Alarius's expression became wary, but puzzled. "You see, I've sent a most alarming note to your dear wife, which should inspire her to beg Westbrooke to rescue you. And while all this is transpiring, he'll be too busy searching for you to notice my visiting his future wife in the meantime to pay her my own respects. And just think," he laughed, "if you'd acquiesced peacefully earlier, I wouldn't have this useful means to deter Dominick tonight."

Before the half-elf could protest, Dual quickly replaced the gag over his mouth. "Ah, no words are necessary, Alarius. I know just what you're thinking. And I assure you, not only will

I take great pleasure in keeping his betrothed occupied, but a suitable group of attackers will also be here to greet him should he find you. After that, your usefulness will end, along with your life."

Against Alarius's muffled curses, Dual rubbed his hands in gleeful musing. "Yes... all in all, I'd say this should be a most memorable evening for all of us."

*****

Julianna decided it was a good thing Roger had been forced to leave the office on another business matter by the time she returned from lunch with Marybeth. Surely he'd complain of her impromptu departure to Almira the next day, but for now she was reprieved. No doubt the whole event would earn Dominick's amusement later! she thought with a smirk.

Now much later that night, she tucked Sammy in for bed, since Crystal was busy putting away the dishes downstairs. "All set for dreamland?" she asked cheerfully. Sammy nodded once, just before his expression grew curious.

"Aunt Julie, how's Uncle Dominick doing?" he asked.

Frozen by surprise as she clasped the covers, she gradually resumed her task, smiling slightly. "He's fine," she whispered. "He even asks after you sometimes."

"Really?" Sammy replied with a grin.

She nodded once, handing him his toy dinosaur. "I told him how much you like dinosaurs, and while he says they don't have any on Chavernos, they do have dragons there."

"Dragons?" he breathed, suddenly frowning. "Bad ones?"

"Well… maybe a few," she agreed, "but he says there are many good ones too. One of the blue ones is a close friend of his, called Roderlin, whom he's known for many years."

"Will I get to meet a real dragon?" he asked with more enthusiasm.

Julianna laughed. "Maybe someday," she replied, "but

probably not for a while. In the meantime, you'd better get some sleep."

Nodding once, Sammy curled up with his toy and shut his eyes. Julianna smiled upon him, kissing his forehead before leaving the room. As she closed the door behind her, she turned to bump into Crystal. "Oh, I'm sorry," she said quietly. "I didn't see you standing there." Before she could pass, her sister prevented this.

"I think we need to talk," she said evenly.

"There's nothing to say."

"I heard you telling Sammy about Dominick again."

Julianna bit her lip and met her gaze. "What of it? It's just a game between us." At her sister's continued silence, her patience reached its end. "Don't believe me? Fine. Then what if I told you that my story to Sammy is true and that Dominick really exists out there?" As soon as the words were out—successfully leaving Crystal gaping—Julianna regretted them, pushing past her to head downstairs.

She wasn't surprised to hear her sister's footsteps trail after her. "Julianna Sherborne, you're not going anywhere!"

That's what she thinks, thought Julianna, heading for the front door. Crystal beat her to it, holding it shut. "Get out of my way," she murmured.

"You don't have to run this time, Julie," replied Crystal. "There's no one else in the house with us except for Sammy, and he's in bed. You've always been able to come to me with everything in the past, and I think it's time you leveled with me about this Dominick. Now... who is he really, and where did you meet him?"

Pausing a moment, Julianna locked eyes with Crystal. "He's as I've told Sammy, and as you've overheard."

Crystal groaned, rubbing her forehead. "I remember. A dream person who exists on another world, but meets you each night, that you're supposedly engaged to. Julie, if you don't want us to meet this man, just say so. You don't have to conjure up stories."

"I didn't conjure up anything," Julianna retorted brokenly. "Dominick ***does*** exist on another world, and we ***are*** engaged to be married. I just wish to heaven I could convince you how true this really is." Brushing a hand across her eyes, she wasn't surprised to feel dampness upon it.

"Julie, you're crying," whispered Crystal, prompting her sister to turn away. "I don't think I've ever seen you get so upset by a story before, whether it's one you've read or one you've come up with yourself."

"For the last time, it's ***not*** a story!" snapped Julianna. "It's the truth!"

Crystal shook her head, clasping her sister's hands tightly. "Julie, don't talk that way. I know you're lonely, and you sometimes wish you had someone in your life, as I have Jerry and Vicki has Luke. But we love you too much to lose you to a fantasy world you've conjured up. If you repeated this to an outsider, the results could be disastrous."

"Don't you think I ***know*** that?" Julianna laughed bitterly. "I wouldn't dare tell anyone, despite the fact this secret's nearly choking me to death. So rather than confide in you or Vicki, I told Sammy instead. At least he's an innocent child who won't condemn me for the truth." Her eyes dimmed to a withering look, while she shook her head. "What's true already doesn't need your belief."

Her sister's ensuing protest died, replaced by an odd expression. "All right, Julianna. For now, just between us, let's assume that your words are true. Going by that assumption, I want you to tell me everything from the very beginning. I promise not to laugh, and I'll hear you out before giving any more opinions."

Uncertainty in her eyes, Julianna glanced at her sister. "You really want to know?" she asked softly. Crystal squeezed her hands and nodded.

"I really do," she replied, smiling. "If your sketch the other day does him justice, he looks like a handsome man."

"In more than looks," she agreed.

Still hesitant, but too tired to argue anymore, Julianna gradually told her everything from the moment she'd first seen Dominick to the present. She went on to say that although it sounded impossible, her dreams of him were always vivid each night, and recollected every morning with undeniable clarity. A cycle that had gone on for several weeks now.

When Crystal read between the lines, she asked her sister just how far their relationship had gone. Even before Julianna said a word, her flushed face more than revealed the answer, earning a knowing smile from her sister. Yet it was Crystal who was left gaping when her 'innocent' younger sister lightly touched on the numerous romantic encounters she'd had with her otherworld companion.

As ironic as it was, it was those selfsame descriptions that convinced Crystal that there might be some truth to her sister's words. After all, as imaginative as Julianna was, she had limits to what subjects she would freely conjure up for stories... and romance wasn't one of them, until now.

The mention of Chavernos earned mixed feelings from Crystal. After having been brought up in a world believing the solar system to consist of the planets she'd known, it was hard to imagine there being a hidden one. Yet since it was more than unlikely that Earth harbored the only humans in the universe, perhaps it could be true.

"Dominick just found out from his grandfather that there was a time when Chavernians traveled to Earth," Julianna commented. "Unfortunately, a war broke out over this, and those who knew the means to travel between our worlds were killed or lost."

Crystal rubbed her chin. "If it was possible once, then

surely another means could be found."

"That's our hope, and he's looking into it now. Anyway, he says that according to the elders on his world, Chavernos has been in existence roughly as long as Earth, and that those of his world migrated there many years ago to live. Their dreamphasers—in their astral forms—discovered Earth soon after, and before they worried of Earth's potential technology, they adapted to our language, which is why the similarity exists."

"Since they're both in the same solar system, that makes sense," agreed Crystal. Even as she nodded, inside she thought, *I can't believe I'm considering this!*

Yet truth or not, she couldn't deny that her sister seemed to have an endless supply of details for Chavernos. Something that at least made it sound more believable.

"Once they realized ours was a world of technology," Julianna continued, "they shut down the possibility of communication between our worlds, magically enhancing the mist that hides Chavernos from view."

As she finished relating what she knew, tears blurred her eyes again, earning her sister's curious concern. "I'm crying because this should be the happiest time in my life, but I can't tell anyone. You're the only one whom I've told everything, and I can't even blame you for thinking me crazy too. It would sound crazy to anyone."

"Hold it right there," interrupted Crystal. "I already told you to let me reserve judgment, and I certainly don't think you're crazy. Okay?"

Julianna nodded slowly. "All right," she sighed, "but even if you do believe me, I can't prove Dominick's existence." As she shut her eyes, her hand rested against her forehead wearily. "Even though I want to be Dominick's wife more than anything else, and I won't let anything change that, I can't help but feel how difficult this uncertain waiting is going to be."

Crystal's hand on her shoulder made her look up.

"The proof of Dominick's existence is in your eyes," she said softly. "Along with your drawing, and the way you talk so lovingly of him. As to the restrictions of this rather unusual engagement of yours, remember this. To all intents and purposes, you're separated for roughly the same amount of hours that a daytime work schedule separates most couples. In a way, it's like you're living two different lives, although being married myself, I fully understand why you've chosen to remain faithful in both."

Her words caused Julianna to blink with surprise and building hope. "You believe me?" she whispered.

"As much as I'm able to... yes," Crystal sighed heavily. "After all, you haven't lied to me before, so I can't think why you'd start now. Especially not with a story like that."

A new joy lit Julianna's expression. "Oh, Crystal, you can't possibly know how much it means to hear you say that."

"I think I can guess," she replied with a smile. "While I'll be the first to admit that you still have an incredible imagination, Julie, your tears convinced me that your words might somehow be true. Not to mention," she added slyly, "I've never heard you make up romantic stories like those you just told me." Giving a short laugh at her sister's blush, she continued, "I'm just glad you're feeling better, because we all love you, and we want you to be happy."

A worried look crossed Julianna's face. "Crystal, even though you can accept what I've told you to some degree, I doubt Vicki and the rest..."

"Say no more," her sister interrupted. "To avoid any scrutiny from the others, it'll remain a secret just between the two of us." Before a correction could be spoken regarding a certain little boy, she added, "Or should I say, between the three of us?"

"Sammy doesn't seem to mind the notion of Dominick

for an uncle," said Julianna. "And from what my fiancé says, I think he'll be thrilled to have Sammy as a nephew too."

"Well, as long as he makes you happy, I'm sure we'll all like him when we meet him eventually."

Frowning slightly, Julianna shook her head. "I told you before... that might never become possible."

Crystal warded this away. "Maybe not. But let's try and keep open minds about it. After all, I've more than kept my part of that bargain, haven't I?"

"Much more," agreed Julianna, leaning forward to hug her sister. "Thank you so much for believing me."

"It's no more than I've always known from you," said Crystal, giving a slight shrug as they broke apart. "Yet even so, I must admit that it would be much easier to accept if you could somehow back up your words with proof. Have you given any thought to the matter?"

Julianna nodded. "Dominick and I both have, but it's not an easy task. Physical proof is as elusive as a way to bring us together on the same world." Sighing once, she eyed Crystal knowingly. "I suppose I can't have your complete belief until we come up with something."

"It is difficult, although I'm doing the best I can," she agreed. "But if you do think of a way, I'll be glad to see your story proven true beyond a doubt."

"That's good enough for me," said Julianna. "Crystal, I promise you, if Dominick ever does find a way here, I'll be more than happy to introduce him to you, Sammy, and the rest of the family as well."

"Yes, and that's not all you're going to do if he shows up here," Crystal replied firmly, piquing her sister's curiosity. "If your future husband intends to keep his two sisters-in-law from reprimanding him later, he'd best duly consider the notion of not only marrying you on ***his*** world, but on ***this*** one as well, so ***we*** can be present for it. And you can tell him I said that."

"Believe me, that's one request I'll gladly agree to, if we're brought together," Julianna said hopefully, staring out the window with a smile. "And if my fiancé was here right now to back me up, I'm sure he'd agree, even without your wrath or Vicki's to contend with."

"Smart man," Crystal said thoughtfully. "Best hold onto that one so we can someday meet him for real."

Julianna gave a short laugh. "Don't worry, Crystal," she replied knowingly. "I've finally found the man of my dreams... and damned if I'll let him get away from me now."

*****

Dominick and Julianna's story continues in
Dragons and Dreamphasers Book Two:
"From Dream to Reality"

*****